The Magical Mancer Novels
DON CALLANDER

The adventure... ...swers a
strange adverti... ...to learn
the MYSTERIES and SECRETS of WIZARDRY in the Discipline of FIRE . . .

PYROMANCER

"THE SORCERER'S ANIMATED KITCHEN IS A DELIGHT, AS IS HIS BRASSY BRONZE OWL . . . THERE ARE NICE ORIGINAL TOUCHES HERE." —PIERS ANTHONY

Then the young Pyromancer meets his match—a beautiful and beguiling apprentice learning the Mysteries of WATER . . .

AQUAMANCER

"GOOD SENSE OF HUMOR!" —Publishers Weekly

Finally, the Pyromancer and the Aquamancer try to free a tribe of men enslaved in stone by a treacherous Master of the EARTH . . .

GEOMANCER

THE MANCER NOVELS ARE "DELIGHTFUL . . . FUN TO READ!" —South Florida SF Society

Dragon Companion

Don Callander

ACE BOOKS, NEW YORK

This book is an Ace original edition,
and has never been previously published.

DRAGON COMPANION

An Ace Book / published by arrangement with
the author

PRINTING HISTORY
Ace edition / November 1994

ISBN: 0-441-00115-7

ACE®
Ace Books are published by The Berkley Publishing Group,
200 Madison Avenue, New York, NY 10016.
ACE and the "A" design are trademarks
belonging to Charter Communications, Inc.

PRINTED IN THE UNITED STATES OF AMERICA

10 9 8 7 6 5 4 3 2 1

This adventure is for my scholarly son, Neal Matthew Callander, a Master of Arts (History), employed at this writing by the University of Virginia. He would love the post as Librarian to the Historian of Carolna, Murdan of Overhall. He'd love being a Dragon Companion, too.

DON CALLANDER
Pineedle Point
Longwood, Florida
July 22, 1991

Dragon Companion

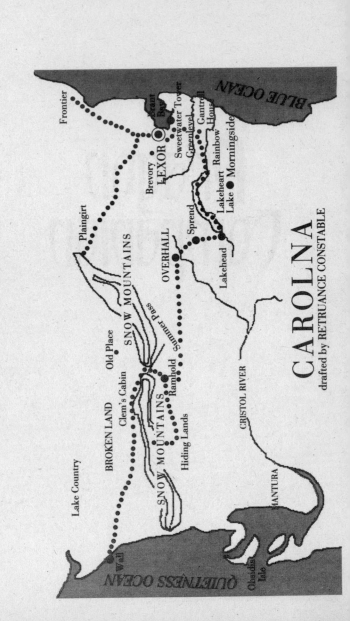

Knollwater

WATERFIELDS

GULF OF CAROLNA

Untracked Jungle

N

Map of Carolna

Scale — 1 inch = 50 miles

✦ 1 ✦
Displaced Librarian

WHEN he left this world, Tom Whitehead was daydreaming of a lady of his acquaintance and didn't even notice when he disappeared from the Capitol Hill Metro station.

He was fantasizing she'd be his very first grand passion. He was too proper, perhaps, to suggest anything more intimate than a drink at his place after their first date at the National Geographic lecture on—what was it?—the ancient Minoans.

Perhaps his doctoral research on late Medieval poetry was touching some latent romantic spot deep in his soul.

It's all fiction and never was like that at all, but that sort of life had a lot to recommend it. Damsels in distress. Sorcerers and . . .

His reverie was interrupted by a rush of warm, damp air. He was suddenly aware again of the world about him. It wasn't a Metro train at all.

It was a severe shock.

The stony brink of the low bluff on which he stood overlooked a wide river valley between rugged, wooded hills, and offered him a view of the valley treetops, green in the midday sun.

His first numbed dismay turned to a shaking surge of disorientation and disbelief, a crescendo of panic. This place! It wasn't Iowa or Missouri, and certainly not the gray-white Federal buildings and tree-lined streets of the District of Columbia.

My God, I've gone insane! he screamed silently, but then he shook his head angrily. *No! I've lost my memory! And wandered here in an amnesiac daze.*

Seeking desperately for something based in solid reality, he looked at his wristwatch: *5:25 P.M.–Mar 15–Fri.* No time had passed at all between the cool subway platform and this

1

sunny bluff's edge. . . . *Where in God's name am I?*

A flock of large, red-and-black birds shot close overhead, squawking happily, and dived into the stream valley. Even in his stark terror he saw they were ducks—but ducks that flew in shallow swoops with frantic beatings of short wings, like sparrows. They flew in a cloud, like crows, not in the neat chevron formations one would see over Iowa's fields or Maryland's wetlands.

The discontinuity brought him abruptly to his senses. He stepped carefully back from the brink and took inventory, like a man checking to see if anything was broken after a car accident.

What is real? He wore the familiar gray wool suit and vest he had put on that morning, and carried his suit coat and topcoat. He still wore the comfortable old black oxfords he'd bought years before, when he first came to the Capital from Missouri to take on his new, exciting post at the Library of Congress.

He folded his coat and topcoat slowly, neatly, laid them on a flat rock, then sat on them. His watch now said *5:27* P.M. but the sun was almost directly overhead—closer to noon than evening.

"I'm *not* insane! At least, I don't *think* I am," he insisted aloud, "and if I didn't have a loss of memory, how did I come to be here? And where is here, for Pete's sake?"

There were no sensible answers. There were dozens of nonsensical ones, of course. He knew the words—*teleportation, translation, enchantment*—but he just didn't believe in them. Not for twenty years, since his early Iowa childhood. Or . . . *had* he stopped believing?

He laughed unsteadily. If this wasn't insanity, it was awfully damn close.

Tom gazed distractedly at the sunlit landscape until its peace was shattered by a great crackling and thumping among the trees at the foot of the bluff, along the bank of the rushing river. Treetops were tossed like rows of wheat in a summer's gale, until he saw a terrible beast emerging from the trees. It was fully fifty feet, from twitching nose to sharp spear-pointed tail.

Dinosaur! was his first thought, but when the fierce-looking animal turned in his direction, he saw it bore only a superficial resemblance to the thunder lizards in books or reconstructed in the Smithsonian.

For it was scaled like a carp, light green-gold in color with touches of red at the neck and mouth. It had four sturdy legs, four wickedly clawed feet, and a pair of vast, leathery, batlike wings. It also had *four* pointed ears and a tapered, muscular tail as long as its body, ending in an arrowhead point, obviously a formidable weapon.

The beast left the edge of the stream where it had been walking on all fours, and raised its upper body until its wide-set, intelligent green eyes were at blufftop level. Noticing the young man for the first time, it snorted in surprise. A ten-foot yellow flame smelling of burning sulfur and hot asphalt shot out of its nostrils.

Tom jumped back and cried out in fear.

"Holy Cow! *A Dragon!*"

"Right the second guess. Not a cow at all. A Dragon!"

The all-too-real, by-your-leave Dragon coughed a cloud of yellowish green smoke behind a polite paw. Tom's wild disbelief was so top-heavy it broke down altogether. He spoke to the Dragon in an almost normal, if somewhat shaky, voice.

"I thought you were a dinosaur."

"Huh!" the Dragon snorted again. "A mythical being? Do I look like something from a human tale?"

It turned away in a huff and a puff, preparing to ford the stream.

"N-no, no, don't go!" called the Librarian. This talking Dragon, no matter how terrifying, was a source of information. Tom needed information.

"I'd like to ask you some questions, please," he shouted after it. The Dragon turned back.

"You didn't really mean to insult my Dragonhood, did you?" it said, the tone forgiving. "Some say I'm too touchy about that sort of thing, and I guess perhaps I am. I'm sorry!"

"No, no! Please forgive me and my ignorance. I'm a stranger here, you see."

"I do see. As I live and breathe! You're a *human*!"

The beast curled its tail under itself, snapping three good-sized trees as it did so and cocked its head to the left.

"Yes, I am a . . . a human."

"I was sure of it! One can't always be certain at first glimpse, of course. But there are little things that give you *humans* away. Nobody else dresses like that! And that haircut! Well! I'm amazed to see that your kind is really . . . *real*."

"At the moment," Tom admitted, uneasily resuming his seat on his coats, "I am not all that positive. Where am I?"

The Dragon looked long and closely at the human before it responded.

"This is the Kingdom of Carolna. We're about in the center of the country, for that matter. A few miles west from the seat of Murdan the Historian. He's lord of this Small Achievement."

The displaced Librarian thought this over while the Dragon idly splashed its tail in the river, much to the consternation of a school of purple-stippled fish, which swam off with a noisy splashing.

"Well, what's an 'achievement,' then?" Tom asked at last.

"You really *are* a stranger!" exclaimed the huge beast with some satisfaction. "Let me see! An 'Achievement' is a parcel of real estate and its inhabitants under the legal, social, economic, and political control or ownership of a ruler or group of rulers. A ruler 'achieves' power over the land and its people and it becomes his 'Achievement,' you see."

"Ah, I see. But why 'Small' Achievement?"

The Dragon shook the water from its tail.

"I suppose because there are other Achievements that are 'large,' " he said with a shrug.

This conversation has definitely taken an Alice in Wonderland turn, thought Tom. Before he could comment, the Dragon added, "I'd love to stay and chat all day but I must be on my way. I'm already late for an important meeting."

The young man looked so lost and frightened that the Dragon paused out of pity.

"Come along! I'll take you to Murdan. He's a Historian and it's his job to answer hard questions."

"Okay, but how?" asked Tom, spreading his hands to indicate his helplessness there in the wilderness.

Without further ado, the huge beast took the human in his gleaming foreclaws and set him on the flat top of his head, just behind his brow ridge and between the four pointed ears.

After a moment of breath-lost panic, Tom found the perch to be quite safe, although the Dragon's head-scales were hard, smooth, and slippery, like rounded tiles. He sat cross-legged upon them and leaned forward to steady himself by grasping the beast's front pair of ears.

The Dragon carefully handed up the human's coats and, before Tom could protest or question, launched itself into the air, beating its vast wings in a series of loud cracks to gain altitude, and circled smoothly up into the warm, still air.

His fear under control at last, Tom looked about curiously. They were moving away from the jumbled lands along the escarpment above the river, climbing at an ever-increasing speed over the tallest of the tors. Leveling out like a living airplane, his new friend glided high over a gently rolling plain that melted in the distance into a purple haze of hills. Far beyond were azure, mauve, and gray mountains, rank on rank, snowcaps gleaming like beacons in the midday sun.

The land immediately below them changed rapidly from open woodland to clear grassland dotted with blue lakes, then to neatly plowed fields separated by hedgerows. Here and there sturdy-looking farmhouses, barns, and sheds clustered under groves of shade trees.

Once, Tom thought he saw a small castle, surrounded by low stone walls and a water-filled ditch, but it rushed by beneath before he could study it further.

There were people working in the fields, and cattle and sheep grazing, but none of these paid the least attention as the Dragon flashed overhead.

After a time, Tom ventured to speak to his strange mount, "By the way, my name is Tom Whitehead."

Said the Dragon, "And my name is Retruance Constable. A very old, respectable name, Constable," it added.

Tom wondered dizzily if it would be proper to ask Retruance Constable's gender, but decided he didn't need to know.

"Charmed," he called above the wind, instead.

"I suspect that's true," rumbled Retruance with a nod that threatened to toss Tom high in the air. Only the Librarian's firm grip on the Dragon's forward ears saved him from a long tumble to the ground. "Charmed, maybe even enchanted or ensorceled. You, I mean. Murdan might know."

Their speed was difficult to judge. They were approaching the foothills when Tom glimpsed three tall, silvery towers against the darker background of a steeply rising ridge.

"Overhall Castle," Retruance Constable told him. "The seat of Murdan's Achievement. My honored ancestor, Altruance Constable, built it. That was in the days of Queen Alix Amanda Alone, when Murdan first came west."

The castle seemed small at a distance, but proved enormous when they neared it. It clung to a long, rocky spur of the foothills. Its three soaring towers were of different heights, all perfectly matched, like the masts of a graceful ship.

Red and gold pennants flew from each conical tower top. Splotches of color marked windows and balconies lower down, awnings spread against the bright upland sun. The whole great complex was surrounded by thick triple ring walls of dark red stone, twice as tall as a man on horseback. Each wall was pierced, in one place only, by a solid gate-fort so placed that no one gateway stood in line with the others.

Tom saw movement within and without the walls. An army of men was fighting on the grassy flat under the walls, near the fortified drawbridge and gate.

"Soldiers!" he cried, leaning forward over the Dragon's brow to see better. They carried long spears or lances. Others, on the fringes of the skirmish, bent short, recurved bows, letting fly whirring clouds of arrows.

Other bowmen stood on the ramparts and shot down at the warring parties from on high. The Dragon and its passenger heard a rumbling, roaring sound, occasionally a piercing scream or a mighty blare of signal horns.

"I fear so," said his companion. "Murdan's trying to regain his Overhall from a troop of Mercenary Knights who captured it while Murdan was away. The Historian has been besieging his own house since his return, I've been told."

The Dragon dropped like a stone toward the melee— much too swiftly for Tom's stomach—roaring at the top of its thunderous voice and spitting great gouts of orange flame. At the sight, sound, and scorch of his approach, the

black-clad soldiers ceased slashing at the men in orange and
retreated in orderly fashion, back through a sally port in the
outermost bailey wall.

Tom goggled in horror at a dozen bloody bodies littering
the grassy plain. Wounded blackcoats were being helped
into the castle while the orange soldiers dragged their own
casualties down to a camp under the edge of a wood.

A company of orange-clad archers sent flight after flight
of arrows after the retreating defenders, but most fell short
of the too-distant marks. Even before Retruance Constable
came gliding down in the midst of the tents, relative peace
returned to the scene. The soldiers of Murdan threw themselves to the ground to catch their breath well out of arrow
flight, among their tents.

Retruance Constable landed as lightly as milkweed down
before a gaily flagged and pennanted orange pavilion with a
commanding view of the stretch of greensward sloping from
the forest's edge up to the level ground before the castle
gatehouse. The Dragon lowered its head to the ground and
Tom gratefully slid from his seat between its ears just as
a huge man in tangerine-gold half armor burst from the
big tent.

"Retruance Constable, you insufferable gargoyle! Where
in the depths of hell have you been? Hey? Answer me that,
oversized salamander!"

The huge Dragon, to Tom's great surprise, actually looked
sheepishly down at the angry man of middle years, florid
face, and short gray locks who stood, fists on hips, scowling
at them.

"Now, now, now! Murdan!" Retruance sputtered. "We
have a guest . . ."

"Burn the blasted guest!" shouted the gray-headed Historian. At once five husky marshals rushed forward to grab
Tom's arms and began to drag him away.

"I want to know why, in the beloved name of Breedge,
you took seven staggering, stultifying weeks to get here,
you and your brother!"

Tom's escort paused, not wanting to miss the confrontation between the Dragon and the Historian.

"Now, now, now!" repeated the Dragon, waving his
foreclaws at Murdan placatingly. "I came as soon as I
got your message. Furbetrance will be close behind me,

if he's not yet here, I'm sure. There, now really . . ."

As suddenly as it flared, the Historian's temper cooled and he rushed forward to embrace the Dragon's scaly snout, deftly avoiding a flaming sigh of relief. It occurred to Tom that the two were really quite fond of each other but, at the same time, that the Historian had great power, even over his new friend.

"Am I glad to see you!" cried Murdan. "Now maybe we can get something done here. Come along! We'll have a long talk and look things over."

He turned to stalk away but Retruance called after him.

"Our guest," he hissed, smokily.

"Guest? What guest?" rumbled Murdan the Historian.

"The one you just ordered burned at the stake," Retruance pointed out. Indeed, now that the argument had waned, the soldiers were resolutely dragging Tom toward a large stack of firewood piled around a post to which were attached iron chains and manacles.

"Oh, for . . . Here! *Here* . . . stop that! Cancel that last order," Murdan shouted. "At ease, men! Halt! Bring the young man to me."

Once Tom stood before him, the Historian gestured for the soldiers to let him go.

The two men exchanged long, evaluating looks. Tom decided at once that a bold face was necessary, but he kept silent until the older man spoke.

"A youngblood, friend Dragon, somewhat scholarly for all that. But a few days and nights hacking and banging on the killing field will put him in fighting shape. I misdoubt but he'll make a good soldier, good as any here, if he manages to keep his head on his shoulders."

"Yes, sir," Retruance replied, meekly.

"Sirrah, you have the gift of a closed mouth, which I like, but tell me your name and from whence you hail."

Tom took a deep breath to still his racing heart and cleared his throat twice.

"I am Tom Whitehead. I'm from Iowa and Washington."

"Where are these places? I've never heard of them." asked the other.

"In the U.S.A.—er, that is, in America, sir."

"Ah!" Murdan said blankly to the Dragon. "An enchantment at work, I would guess?"

"I would so guess," replied Retruance.

"And a human, unless I miss my guess! They're so scarce, many disbelieve in them, I know," continued the Historian. "Tell me of your human self, sirrah, pray do!"

"I am twenty-six years of age, and a professional Librarian," Tom hurried on. Every time he felt he was gaining a grip on reality, it slipped away again. He'd never thought of humans as being scarce.

"A Librarian? Very good! That's most interesting," boomed the Historian. "If you're not bespoken, I can use a Librarian in my service, lad."

"Well . . . ," Tom hesitated.

"Now don't be slow to make up your mind. You'll spoil the impression I've gotten of you," chided Murdan.

Tom grasped at the chance for the stability of regular employment without thinking further about it. He would at least have some protection and a known place in this unknown land—which promised to be a highly dangerous place, as well. He remembered the bleeding bodies on the slopes before the castle gate.

"Er . . . providing the terms are fair," he said quickly, surprising himself with his boldness.

"Best in the kingdom!" promised Murdan with a laugh, obviously pleased. "A hundred vols, payable at the first of each month, and all you can eat if we have it to give you. A bed, dry most of the time, and two blankets if it's cold. Mounts, of course—"

"He'll ride me," interrupted Retruance suddenly. He gazed proudly at the Librarian he'd found. Tom blinked back his gratitude.

"Very lucky, too, my boy!" cried Murdan. "A Dragon Companion is to be envied."

"I am sure of it, s-s-sir," replied the Librarian, although he had yet some doubts about riding a Dragon. "Forgive me, but I don't know the value of a vol."

"A vol—well, it's a thick silver coin the size of your thumbnail. A vol is one-hundredth of a prone. A prone is enough for a man to live in comfort for a year," Murdan explained.

Turning to the Dragon, he said, "I do like a man who takes care of himself in money matters! Will he do as well in battle?"

"How could it be else?" asked Tom, made breathless by the speed of events but recalling how the black-clad soldiers had fled at the sight of the Dragon. "With such a steed as Retruance Constable? Who could best me?"

"None but another Dragon Companion," said Murdan, seriously. "And then it depends on your own abilities and resources, Companion!"

"Dragon Companion?" asked the Librarian, wonderingly.

"The title of such men as a Dragon chooses to carry, of course. Retruance Constable has given it to you," Murdan responded. "Come along, now that's settled, you two. There's revenge to plan."

The odd pair, Dragon and Librarian, followed the Historian to the great orange-and-white pavilion. It was pitched on the highest point in the camp, under the eaves of the forest. Before entering, the Historian spun about and gestured over his shoulder at the castle towering above them, even at this distance. Tom saw now that between the sloped field of battle and the gate tower was a broad, steep-banked moat, filled with swiftly rushing water. It was spanned in front of the fortified gate by a heavy timber drawbridge, now raised on enormous chains.

"It's been more than two months now," said Murdan to the Dragon. "That Basilicae, rascally bastard, sneaked right in when I was away to Spring Session. Killed three of my good soldiers out of hand! Chased my daughter and her family out in the cold! Scurvy-ridden, curly-bearded son of a—"

Retruance Constable said hastily, "How have you fared since?"

"Surrounded 'em, cut 'em off from resupply. They're hungry, I'm sure."

"They've got all the water they'll ever need, of course," mused Retruance, thoughtfully. "Great-Grandfather Altruance planned the castle too well for that! But he thought *you* would be on the inside."

"Unfortunately, they have Gugglerun, yes," agreed Tom's new master.

"Guggle . . . ?" asked Tom.

"Gugglerun," explained Retruance. "It's an underground stream that fills the castle cisterns and the castle moat.

Great-Grandfather rerouted an existing mountain freshet to supply all water needs. If this Basilicae didn't have it, he would flee or surrender much more quickly. But . . ."

"Can't you dam the stream above the castle, at least temporarily?" asked Tom. He knew the medieval mind. It seemed the sort of thing the heroes of his epic poems might have done in such a case.

His two companions stopped looking at the castle and turned together to look at the newcomer.

"Now," puffed the Historian, "now, I call that thinking on one's feet! Why didn't you think of that, Dragon?"

"Well, no one has ever done it," said Retruance doubtfully, returning the Historian's accusing glare.

"A good reason for trying it once," observed Tom, getting into the spirit of the discussion, despite himself.

"Good idea!" cried Murdan. "This human might earn his keep, after all. See to it, Dragon and Companion!"

And he went into the tent and flipped the flap shut.

"Now wait a moment!" cried Retruance after the Historian's retreating back. "What if we *do* stop up Gugglerun? What advantage to our people then?"

"You stop the stream and deny them water and they'll be out of there like an arrow from a bow, I guarantee," said the Historian, popping his head out of the tent. "Get busy!"

He raised one great arm and shook his fist at tiny figures visible on the battlements atop the castle wall. At once a shower of black arrows flew but fell just beyond the moat, far short of the edge of camp.

"We'll see to it," agreed Retruance. "Come, Companion! Let us explore Gugglerun in depth."

✦ 2 ✦
The Gugglerun Puzzle

TOM followed the huge beast out into the open square amid the tents.

"He seems to think I can . . . well, *solve* the Gugglerun thing," he complained to Retruance. "Am I supposed to be some sort of wizard, or something?"

"No, no, not a wizard. Wizards are a vol a dozen! Overhall is protected by powerful spells, so wizards are of no use. You can be sure Murdan would have called in a few by now, if they were.

"Now, practical things like how to build an arbalest, that's what Librarians are supposed to know. Or find out," Retruance Constable explained. It picked a mossy spot under a spreading oak to stretch out its fifty feet of scales, wings, and talons.

"Where I come from," said Tom thoughtfully, seating himself on a protruding root, "Librarians take care of storing and retrieving information, usually in books."

"Books? Oh, you mean those paper-and-leather things nobody ever looks at. Well, I suppose someone has to care for them."

"Books," said Tom firmly, "are storehouses of knowledge. Someone has to look after them, keep them in order. When people want to know something, they have a Librarian look in the books to find the information for them. It's . . . it's a sort of puzzle game, really. The challenge is to know exactly where to look for the answer."

"No different from the Gugglerun puzzle, then," said Retruance sleepily. "Your challenge is to find a place to stop up the stream. I suggest you start looking. Murdan seems a jolly old elf, but he can't stand slow or stupid retainers. Especially highly paid ones like you."

"I'm neither," bridled Tom. "But . . ." He leaned his elbows on his knees and shook his head to shake out the woolliness within.

But was it so different, this challenge? If he were in the Library of Congress now, he'd look up *Gugglerun* first, and then research *underwater streams, castle moats, castle water supplies, hydrological engineering, local geology,* and certainly *Overhall Castle history,* in particular, for clues to the basic problem—how to block the stream temporarily and force the invaders to face death by thirst, to run or surrender.

"Retruance?" he asked.

The Dragon was asleep in the late-afternoon sunshine, blowing out tiny blue puffs of smoke to the sound of gentle snores. At the Librarian's call, it popped open its near-side eye and grunted.

"A question," said Tom.

"Ask away."

"Are there any papers or records regarding the layout of Overhall? Your great-grandfather built the place. He must have kept records, accounts, plans, that sort of thing."

Retruance rolled over onto its stomach.

"Certainly! Stacks and crates of dusty old documents, notes, drawings. Altruance was a very careful, meticulous worker."

"Can I see them? Are they far away? If he diverted Gugglerun in the first place, perhaps there's a sketch or a plan, or even a memo to his construction foreman."

"I know exactly where they are. A whole room filled with 'em in trunks and crates."

"Let's go look at them, then!"

"There's a problem, you see," the Dragon said, sadly. "Great-Grandfather's storeroom is in Middletower, up there."

It pointed a long, sharp claw at the castle, now very beautifully catching the level rays of the setting sun, glowing golden, slashed with deep purple shadows—like something from a Maxfield Parrish painting, Tom thought.

"Damnation!" he said.

As twilight fell on the forest's edge, Tom returned to his seat on the root, resting his forehead on his hand to aid in thinking. After a long while the Dragon stirred and sniffed the air.

"Ah, supper's ready!" it cried. "Come along, Companion. Let's be at the head of the chow line!"

It led the way to a field kitchen, where several score soldiers in orange livery already stood in line, mess kits in hand, waiting impatiently for supper to begin. Under the canopy of the kitchen tent, cooks and servers bustled about importantly, putting all in order and waiting for the signal to begin.

Retruance inserted its great head at the front of the line. The men already there moved back respectfully to make space for it and Murdan's new Librarian.

"I don't like jumping to the head of a line," Tom objected.

"Nonsense. R.H.I.P.!" said Retruance, blinking in surprise.

"Huh?"

"Rank has its privileges," the Dragon quoted. It nodded toward a large tent across the open square. "If I weren't so bulky, we'd eat in the officers' mess over there, but it's much too small for me."

The soldiers took their intrusion with good grace. They called friendly insults to the Dragon and made room for the Librarian without demur.

"Corned beef and cabbage!" exclaimed the Dragon. "My favorite."

It didn't seem to be a favorite of Murdan's soldiers, judging from the uncomplimentary name they had for the dish, but once Retruance had collected its great bowl of the savory mixture and Tom had received his own portion, the line moved briskly along, with each man taking away to the tables generous helpings. They fell to eating with evident relish.

Tom found the corned beef and cabbage quite tasty. His lunch, eaten at his library desk, had been a bologna sandwich on white bread and an apple. It seemed at least a month had gone by since then.

He ate it all, topping it off with a sweet bread pudding after he decided the black specks weren't weevils, after all, but tart, dried currants.

"What will the boss do if we fail to find a way to stop Gugglerun?" he asked.

"Nobody ever fails when Murdan expects something done," said Retruance. It was much too large to take a seat at the mess table, but lay mostly outside with just his head and forelegs inside the tent. "I am not at all sure what would happen to *you*. At me, he'd scream a bit, I suppose, but no elf has the power to harm a Dragon."

"I suppose he'd fire me," guessed Tom. "I wouldn't like that."

"No, I suppose being burned at the stake is a most unpleasant way to perish," agreed Retruance.

"Burned . . . ? Just for failing an assignment!" cried the Librarian.

"It's often the prescribed punishment."

"Ugh!" It was all Tom could think of to say.

FILLED with good food, the Dragon showed signs of going back to sleep. While he felt he should get some rest, too, Tom found sleep difficult. Nobody offered him the dry bed promised by the Historian in his verbal contract. Tom thought it best not to be too visible, just then, so he gathered together a few armfuls of fallen leaves under their oak and made them up into a fairly comfortable bed. The temperature had fallen sharply since the sun had gone down, but lying close to the sleeping Dragon was quite warm. He covered himself with his topcoat.

I hope it isn't a restless sleeper, he thought. But Retruance slept like a stone, unmoving except for a slight rising and falling of its enormous chest and an occasional twitch of its leathery wings or tail.

Tom set his mind to the problem of Gugglerun but gave way at last to weariness well before the watch changed at midnight.

He was awakened at dawn, when someone prodded his ribs with the butt of a spear.

"Librarian, is it?" asked someone.

Tom rolled over. A scowling soldier stood over him in the gray light.

"Huh? What?"

"He's just a tough old sergeant," murmured Retruance without opening his eyes. "Curse him roundly and maybe he'll go away."

"You this Tom Librarian?" repeated the sergeant, paying no attention to the Dragon.

"Yes, I'm Tom . . ."

"Chief is asking for you over to the pavilion," grunted the noncom. He thought seriously of prodding the sleepy civilian again but, as the Dragon was now watching him through one slitted eye, he left, instead.

"Better see what our old Historian wants," sighed Retruance. "You won't need me. I'll wait here. Keep the spot warm, you know."

Tom paused at a community washstand to splash cold water on his face, trying to put his rumpled clothes into some order as he hastened to the Historian's tent.

He heard the voice of Murdan long before he reached the tent. He was admitted by heavily armed cavalrymen with long, curved swords drawn. The Master was in a foul mood, Tom realized, and he sought to slip into the back row, unnoticed.

Murdan spotted him at once.

"Here, Librarian! Have you stopped up Gugglerun yet?"

The officers around Murdan's chair parted quickly to allow Tom to move to the front, helped by a gentle shove disguised as an encouraging pat.

"Uh, no, sir," Tom stammered. "I find that there is little or no information on Gugglerun and the castle waterworks available here."

Murdan scowled angrily, grating out, "I depend on you, young Tom. My men are waiting for you to produce results. Many will die if you don't."

"Give me a break," Tom cried in exasperation. "I've been here only an evening and a night!"

His response rather startled the Historian, who was more used to obedience than objections.

Before he could comment, Tom plunged on.

"I'll need at least a day or two to solve your problem, sir. I have decided how I'll proceed but I haven't enough daylight to act."

"I like a man who speaks his mind, even if he hasn't yet proved he has one," Murdan told the assembled officers. "If he succeeds, all to the good. But if he fails . . ."

"Mere men fail at times," Tom interrupted. "Threats of punishment won't make the solution easier."

"Back off, then," the Historian said quickly. "What will you do?"

"I'm not prepared to say just yet. May I have today to work it out?"

Murdan turned to a senior officer standing to the left of his chair.

"Captain Graham, what do you expect the Mercenary Knights to do today, after the failed sortie of yesterday?"

"If the enemy runs true to form, sir, he'll rest today. Perhaps he'll sally again late this evening or tonight. He hasn't tried night operations, yet."

"A good thing," grunted Murdan. "Now, Librarian, I won't bluff you on this. I can't afford to carry on this siege longer than a few more days. I must recover Overhall and my assets within quickly. Another week and my men will have to eat promises and fight without pay. Soldiers who fight without food don't fight their best. You understand?"

"I will, of course, do all I can," replied the Librarian.

"That's all I ask, really." Murdan's tone had turned quite mild, rather worried and sad. "Come up with a way to stop Gugglerun by tomorrow night. Remember, it must be a temporary stoppage only. Without water, the castle will be useless to me afterward."

"I'll begin at once," promised Tom solemnly, and an idea at that very moment popped into his brain. "I may need some help."

"Come to me personally for anything within my powers," said the Historian. "At any time. Wake me, if necessary!"

"For the moment, all I need is the Dragon Retruance," Tom said.

"Get on with it, then, Librarian."

The Master of Overhall gestured dismissal.

TOM found the Dragon waiting at the head of the breakfast line exchanging small talk with the soldiers. These made way again for the Librarian to stand beside his mount's head.

"I've been thinking of your great-grandfather's storeroom filled with papers," he told Retruance as they ate. "I've got to see them, either that or crawl inside the mountain and look for Gugglerun, on site."

"Your first idea is the best," agreed Retruance. He downed six whole red-cheeked apples in quick succession, seeds, stems and all, chewing rapidly. "I take it you intend to sneak into the castle."

"The only way," said Tom with a shrug.

"It shouldn't be too difficult. A diversion seems required. I noticed when we arrived that everyone on the castle walls was watching the battle. We can slip in behind their backs if they have something outside to watch. Once inside, I can lead you to that storeroom."

"*I* might slip in through some crack or other," considered the Librarian, shaking his head, "but *you* are much too large to go anywhere unnoticed, Retruance. I'll have to go alone."

"Oh, nonsense!" Retruance Constable scoffed. "I can take care of that with a wave of a wing."

It did just that, snapping two six-inch claws on its right forepaw together. The sound made everyone in the mess tent jump and reach for swords and daggers. When they looked, the huge gold-green Dragon had disappeared!

Not exactly disappeared. Looking down, Tom discovered a half-foot-long version of the fifty-foot beast modestly refolding its wings on the edge of the table.

"Is that you, Retruance Constable?" he asked in surprise.

"None other!" said the other in a small voice. "Overdid it a bit. Out of practice at reducing, I guess. But maybe not. This size I could fit in your coat pocket if I curled my tail. From there I can tell you where to go."

"We'll talk to Murdan first, to arrange a convincing diversion," decided the Librarian. "Best get started."

Retruance hopped off the table and followed the Librarian to the Historian's pavilion.

✦ 3 ✦
Breaking and Entering

THREE companies of foot soldiers marched in good order up the grassy slope toward Overhall's main gate. As they marched they yelled out insults at the defenders and before they had moved halfway across the green, the battlements were black with Mercenary Knights, shouting back in derision.

Halting just within range of the gate towers, the soldiers of Murdan each crouched down on one knee. A double rank of archers hidden behind them rose on tiptoe, bent their bows, and sent a blizzard of orange-shafted arrows arching toward the battlements.

The black-clad soldiers quickly ducked back behind protective crenellations, but not before a half dozen screamed in pain and fear and, twisting about, fell from the walls into the rushing moat.

"Archers!" someone shouted in a commanding voice. "Take your stands! Shoot the bowmen!"

Easier ordered than done, for the orange soldiers made poor targets at that distance, half-hidden in the tall grass. Murdan's expert bowmen popped up to loose a second and a third flight, each time clearing the walls for several moments.

In the interval, ten pairs of soldiers in orange dashed forward. In each pair, one man carried a large, square shield over his head while the other carried a coil of rope in one hand and a three-pronged grappling hook in the other.

At the verge of Gugglerun moat, the grapplers crouched beneath their heavy wooden shields and waited while the sharp blows of the black-clad archers reduced their protection to pincushions, with an incessant rattle like hail on a shed roof.

Watching from the edge of the field below the forest,

Murdan saw that none of the grapplers fell in the first volley from the walls. Timing was everything here. If his archers did their work properly . . .

The orange bowmen leaped to their feet again, sending a fourth and fifth cloud of arrows at the defenders on the battlements. Four of the orange fell to the grass, joining several of the foot soldiers in death. But at least eight enemy archers fell, either back into their comrades' arms, or into the waiting moat.

Now the grapplers, as the defending archers drew back into cover, stepped from behind their shields, whirled the heavy hooks about their heads three or four times and let fly at the end of the drawbridge, fifteen feet over their heads and twenty feet across the moat.

Most of the hooks fell back into the water, to be reeled in by the throwers. Of the ten thrown, two caught!

"Now, get the hell out of there!" cried Murdan aloud, waving his arms frantically.

As if they had heard his order, the grapplers and their shield men waited for another volley from the field and then dashed out of range as fast as they could run. Only one stumbled and fell, a black shaft through his calf, but a running mate threw away his heavy shield and grabbed for his arm, helping him hobble out of range.

Enemy arrows fell on all sides of them but the pair reached safety at the bottom of the field without further harm. The soldiers and officers watching cheered lustily.

The two hooked lines that had caught on the end of the draw were carried back with the retreating throwers, all the way to waiting infantry. Everyone within reach grabbed onto the ropes and pulled as they fell back, just out of bowshot.

The drawbridge, almost vertical, was supported by heavy chains on each side, with links as large as a man's two hand spans. For a long moment, as the slack was taken up in the ropes, the chains resisted. The archers above showered the field with futile arrows, all falling short of the tugging orangemen.

A brave soul in the gate tower climbed to the top of the draw with a knife in his teeth, intending to slash the straining ropes. At a signal blast from a horn, a small party of mounted archers dashed across the field, shooting at the

climber as they rode. An arrow flying close caused him to
lose his grip and drop his knife. He slid, yelling, to the
bottom of the span.

Before the mounted archers could retreat beyond the
reach of the defenders' arrows, a ragged volley shot two
from their saddles. The fallen were expertly plucked from
the ground almost before they hit. The party rode back to
the forest edge.

By now, the hauling on ropes overbalanced the counter-
weights inside the gate tower. The bridge slowly came down
and crashed on the near edge.

A dozen black-clad men sped out onto the bridge, shooting as they came. Someone slashed the ropes. The soldiers
hauling on the ropes fell on their backs as the tension was
released.

Before the orange archers could dash forward to shoot
again, the drawbridge was rapidly cranked up.

MURDAN glanced up at the sun, took a moment to shake his
fist and bellow an obscenity at the battlements, then turned
back to camp.

"It almost worked!" said Graham, grinning broadly.
"Something to try again, I think. Only a couple of our
men dead to at least ten of theirs. That's remarkable in
siege warfare."

"And it should have given my new Librarian time to
cross the rear footbridge without being noticed," said the
Historian. "I hope, at least. Anybody see if they made it?"

But everyone had been watching the frontal attack on the
draw. They had forgotten to look for Tom and the shrunken
Dragon.

"LOCKED!" Tom gasped, out of breath from the dash across
the one-plank footbridge to the postern door of Overhall.
"Damn it to hell!"

"Take a breather," advised the tiny Dragon in his coat
pocket. "I'll take care of it."

Leaning far out of the pocket, Retruance blew a white-hot
jet of flame as thick as a pencil at the lockplate. The rusty
metal glowed red, then white. Then it cracked loudly and
crumbled to several pieces as the wood around it smoked
and flamed briefly. The castle's back door swung ajar.

"In! In!" urged the Dragon.

Tom stopped only to beat out the flames that licked at the wood around the lock, lest the smoke attract someone's attention.

"You and I should become burglars," chortled the Dragon.

"Later!" muttered the Librarian. "Which way now?"

They plunged along a bare stone corridor between the aftermost and the middle of the castle's three towers. Retruance had identified them by name—Foretower, Middletower, and Aftertower. Middletower was the tallest by thirty feet or more, and while the other two were of nearly equal height, Aftertower was set highest on the ridge and thus appeared the tallest.

On the west side, all three rose in a graceful, shallow curve from the ridge on which they were built, but were connected to each other on the east by a long, high-walled inner court. The court was lined with stables and barracks, the household kitchen, a bake house, workshops, and storerooms, both up against the bailey wall and beneath the towers themselves. The road between them was broad enough to drive a pair of wagons side by side, but the rise from front to back was quite steep. In places, steps had been carved in the stone for foot traffic.

Into the upper part of this court the burglars came from the rear sally port. Tom paused to look about. There was no one in sight. As they had hoped, everyone had rushed to the front of the complex to watch or participate in the defense.

"That door over there, under Middletower," whispered Retruance, pointing with his tail. "Hop it! Sounds like the diversion has about run its course."

Tom sprinted across the road and dodged between a deserted smithy and a holding pen for horses waiting to be shod.

"Watch yourself!" hissed the Dragon to the horses. "Keep quiet about us!"

The three horses obediently turned away and resumed munching contentedly on oats from a feedbox attached to the pen wall.

"Horses can talk?" said Tom, panting as they reached the small service door.

"Of course they can, and they'll oblige a Dragon over a spurred horseman, any day. Besides, nobody listens to horses, except maybe stable lads. They'll forget about us in a couple of minutes, anyway. Short memories."

Tom twisted the doorknob and pulled at it. It wouldn't budge.

"Damn!" he swore.

"It opens in!" Retruance prompted. "See, the jamb is on the *other* side."

"Oh!" Tom breathed in relief. He pushed the door so hard he almost fell through when it swung open.

"In! In!" repeated the pocket-size Dragon. "Get it shut! Someone is coming up the road!"

Inside it was as black as a coal mine, but once under cover Tom took time to catch his breath and let his eyes become accustomed to the gloom. Ahead of them a corridor led straight into the base of Middletower, and on either side there were narrow stairs, one winding down and the other up.

"We go up," Retruance directed. "Household offices are on the second and third floor and Great-Grandfather's rooms are on the fourth."

"And above them?" asked Tom, climbing the stair. A dim cresset burned fitfully, high overhead, making it somewhat easier to see.

"Lady's quarters. Mistress's quarters, but Murdan's wife is long dead, so they may be empty. Children's nursery. Lookout post. Belfry under the roof."

They passed the second floor, moving silently on the dusty, worn steps, and then the third. No sounds came through the thick stone walls.

"I've seen lots of pictures of castles. Never been in one," puffed Tom when he paused to catch his breath. "Your ancestor seems to have done a superb job on Overhall, from what I've seen. The floors even here are level, the stairs are evenly spaced, and the walls aren't damp at all."

"Thank you, Sir Librarian," said Retruance, a bit sarcastically. "My family thanks you, too."

"This is the fourth level," Tom declared when they resumed climbing. "But there's no door!"

"Trick of the trade," explained the Dragon. "Here. I'll find it."

It struggled free of Tom's pocket and flapped across the inner wall, examining it carefully.

"Ah, here 'tis!" it cried softly. "In Altruance's day it generally stood open for ventilation."

The Dragon triggered a hidden catch, and a door appeared in outline on the wall. The Librarian put his shoulder to it and swung it inward. Beyond was a vast cavern of a room, half-round in plan, big enough for a full-grown Dragon or two to move about and work in.

A vast, dust-covered drawing table stood under three filigreed windows on the south wall. Sunlight poured in, making sparkling diamonds in the dusty air.

On the west wall was an enormous, low bed with ornately carved posts and a sagging canopy of dull reddish material. The center of the room was devoted to an out-sized divan and normal-sized chairs, so that the Dragon and his guests could sit together in comfort, read from the scrolls and books piled on the floor everywhere, and talk.

The north wall was a partition of beams and plaster with several high archways cut through, leading to what seemed to be a kitchen, a bath, a smaller sitting room (if you could say anything made to Dragon scale was "small"). At the side opposite the service door was an open stone staircase leading up and down, common access for all the upper floors of the tower.

Next to the stairway, the western windows were set in wood, not stone. Double leaves could be swung inward, like huge doors. A Dragon could fly in and out this way, rather than squeeze up and down the stairs.

"You live here?" Tom asked as he looked about for a place to begin.

"Summers, once, when I was a kit. I was only seventy when Altruance burned out—"

"Burned out!"

"That's the way we Dragons go, you know, when we get very ancient," replied Retruance solemnly. "Quick and painless, I'm told. A good way to die after a long life."

"Dragons live a very long time, then?"

"It varies. Altruance lived to be five hundred and fifty-one. My father lives still, as far as I know, at three hundred and four years. He disappeared almost a decade ago and hasn't been heard from since. My brother Furbetrance and

I were off looking for some trace of him, in case he needed help, when Murdan's call came, a month back."

"And your mother?"

"Female Dragons live by themselves after their children grow to full size. Mama lives in the Far South. I visit her every year or two. She lives a very quiet, retired life, assisting the fisher folk from her island lair. In many ways I envy her."

"I've got to ask. I assume that you are a male Dragon, Retruance?"

"Oh, my, yes! Females are considerably smaller than we males, with much daintier scales and are usually pastel colored. I didn't realize you might be confused."

"I wasn't sure I should ask," Tom admitted. "Where is Great-Grandfather's storeroom?"

"There," said Retruance, pointing a claw at a heavy, iron-strapped door in the corner near the stairs. "It may take a while to open. Altruance used some strong locking spells on it. I think I can remember them, however."

"How long do you think we have? Will anyone come this way?"

"If the living quarters upstairs are being used, someone might come up or down at any moment. I don't think any-one's been here for years from the looks of it all, though. Certainly the Mercenary Knights haven't done any looting here, yet. However, someone has been using the stairs, I think, to judge by the lack of dust."

"I think we should go into the storeroom and close the door."

"Good idea!" agreed the Dragon. He went to the closed door and began to work what Tom realized were unlocking spells.

✶ 4 ✶
Middletower at Midnight

WHILE the Dragon chanted softly to unlock Altruance's storeroom, Tom went to the south-facing windows and peeped out, careful not to be seen accidentally by anyone looking up at the tower.

He watched the final minutes of the diversion at the foregate, or what he could see of it that wasn't blocked by the bulk of Foretower. At least he had a good view of most of the battlements and the crowd of black-clad defenders gathered there, shooting and shouting at the orange attackers. It sent a shiver through him to see men, pierced with orange-shafted arrows, fling up their arms and collapse screaming among their fellows.

He had never seen war and killing before except on a television or movie screen. The distance from the scene rendered it more bearable, however, until he remembered that these men had been hurt or had been killed just to get him into the castle unseen.

"There!" grunted Retruance triumphantly, after four long minutes of intense unspelling.

"Get inside! The battle's over and the Mercenary Knights are returning to their normal duties," said the Librarian. The two went quickly through the open storeroom door and Tom swung it shut behind them, cutting off all illumination.

"Need a light?" asked the Dragon. Not waiting for a reply, he released a thin jet of yellow flame into the dusty, musty air.

"Whew!" Tom exclaimed. The cry was brought on by the sight of a room larger than most gymnasiums, packed from floor to ceiling and wall to wall with cabinets, crates, bundles, sacks, and barrels, all filled to overflowing with books, scrolls, and papers, yellowed and fragile.

"Great-Grandfather saved every scrap, I'd say," said Retruance proudly.

"I'll say he did!" exclaimed Tom. He opened the first cabinet beside the door and peered at the top sheet of a stack on the highest shelf.

"Here's a lantern. I could keep my own light burning for hours, but it would cut down my usefulness," Retruance said, again suiting action to words.

He found a second lantern still half-filled with fragrant oil, and lighted it also. The light was clear and steady, making it easier to read the sprawling, decorative script of an elderly gentleman Dragon with no reason to think anyone other than himself would ever need to read it.

But such holographs were food and drink to a professional Librarian, and once he'd studied the hand (claw?) for a few minutes, Tom found he could decipher it fairly easily.

At least it's more or less in English, or whatever they call the language here, he thought. *Seem to be some French and German words here and there, but mostly it's good old English.*

With a faint clap of wings, Retruance made himself somewhat larger—not full-sized by any means, but large enough to reach the mountains of papers all about them.

"We're looking for anything about the building of Overhall," Tom reminded him. "Your ancestor seems to have been an orderly person. What is at the top of the stack is probably what was filed last, with older documents toward the bottom."

"Look at this!" exclaimed Retruance excitedly.

Tom dropped the document he was reading and went to stand beside the Dragon.

"His holiday shopping list!" exclaimed Retruance. "Here's my brother's name—and here's my name, too! Let's see, he scratched out the half ton of coal and overwrote 'a mere bootful will do for the lad.' Humph! Wonder what I did to make him cut my present to a bootful?"

Tom laughed despite himself.

"Not much to do with the building of Overhall," he reminded gently, seeing his friend was moved almost to tears by the intimate glimpse of the departed ancestor. "You can read them all to your heart's content, once we've run the knights out."

"Right you are," Retruance gulped. "Business before pleasure, Great-Grandfather would have said."

An hour passed and then a second while they read and read and read, beginning at the wall cabinets to the right of the door and proceeding systematically around the room. Occasionally they stopped to rest their eyes and move the lamps into better positions—and to listen carefully for any sounds of life outside the storeroom.

Sometimes they heard faint footsteps or the call of the sentries on the walls, but for the most part this tower seemed deserted. A child cried, far off, then stopped. Horses' hooves clopped on the cobbled courtyards. Dogs barked.

Hope they don't come up here, thought Retruance, who had great respect for dogs, and especially their abilities to observe and smell. He went on picking up papers, studying them briefly, and putting them back in another neat stack when he had decided they contained nothing about Gugglerun.

"We'd better speed this up," he said when they reached the first corner of the room. "At the rate we're going, we'll be in here a week."

"I do believe old Altruance was neatly efficient," Tom said, pausing also. "Made a good Librarian, he would have. That's a compliment, Retruance."

"I took it as such."

"If we read the top sheet of each stack and don't bother to look at all the pieces underneath, we'll perhaps come on his notes and papers on Gugglerun much faster. Unfortunately, he didn't seem to alphabetize his subjects. Probably arranged them in order of their importance to himself."

"In that case, the proper papers are probably buried at the bottom of the furthest pile," Retruance said grumpily.

"You're probably right! He'd have little cause to refer to them regularly, once construction was completed. Try those old crates at the far corner, then. I'll work my way down this wall, as I said, as rapidly as possible."

The wooden cases in question undoubtedly contained the oldest files in the lot. Someone had almost illegibly scrawled on one, "XVI yr Alix R."

"What do you think this means?" asked the Dragon.

Tom examined the inscription. "Clearly, the sixteenth year of your Queen Alix Amanda. You mentioned her name, yesterday."

"Yes, she was queen of Carolna when Altruance came to build Murdan's Overhall!"

He ripped the top off the crate but slowed his claws immediately when the top sheets inside crumbled to yellow scraps.

"Blast me!" he exclaimed. "Hope they weren't important . . ."

He read silently as Tom plowed through three more stacks, reading as rapidly as possible. *It must be past dusk outside, by now,* he thought.

"This is it!" hissed the Dragon. He carefully carried a sheaf of ancient papers, some sort of drawings, to the best light.

"Let me see," said the Librarian eagerly. "Careful, now!"

The first sheets were a description of the stone underlay beneath the triple ring walls of Overhall and the next bundles were detailed drawings of their construction: twenty feet high and fifteen feet thick at the bottom.

"By George, we're getting close!" Tom said. "Go to the next crate, now. If Great-Grandfather follows his usual pattern, the deeper the stack, the older the bottom papers are. To plan and build Gugglerun, he must have done it early in the job, don't you think?"

"That I would agree," replied the Dragon. "Say, you were right! This Librarian stuff can be exciting!"

They worked furiously but carefully for another two hours and stopped only when Retruance's stomach began to make protesting growls. They turned off one lamp to conserve the dwindling fuel and ate bread and sharp cheese they had brought along.

"If we don't get out of here tonight, we may have to wait until tomorrow night," observed Tom, dolefully. "Murdan will be beside himself when we don't show up in the morning."

"I have been thinking of our escape," Retruance said around the last mouthful of cheese and a gulp of warm apple cider. "I forgot Altruance's big flight door in the west wall. Did you notice it?"

"Yes, I saw it. He used it to get in and out without climbing the stairs?"

"Of course! He was wider by a half than I am, and it would be a tight fit around corners if I tried to climb the stairs. What we'll do when we're finished, daylight or nighttime, is throw open the doors, clap the old wings, and fly out to the forest camp in no time. So quietly, I would think, that the knights won't even know we've been here. Or if they do see us, they can't know what we're here to find."

Bolstered by this new plan for escape—neither cherished the idea of creeping out of the castle afoot—the two returned to the ancient documents.

It was midnight when Tom picked up a slim sheaf of papers tied together with a silken cord in the bottom of the fourth large crate.

"*Gugglerun!*" he read. "Hey! This should tell us something!"

"At last!" sighed Retruance. "Any more than that?"

"It was the last of the lot in this crate and the last of the same kind of crates, so I assume they go together, pretty much. Try the top stuff in the next cabinet over, just in case."

But the cabinet contained material regarding the construction of the great towers. Across the bottom of the last drawing, labeled "Elevator," Altruance in his flowing hand had written: "Power insufficient to lift useful weight beyond second level. Setting this aside, further study. XVIII yr. Ed IX."

"Too bad he didn't finish the project. Imagine living in a castle like this with a machine to lift you to the top of a tower without having to climb a stair!" said Tom.

"Doesn't bother me much," said Retruance. "Trouble with towers is they have such small windows."

"Bit short of time for looking at everything here. I think we should take a chance that we've got all we need and get out of here."

At Retruance's suggestion they searched the apartment until they found a large leather folder still intact enough to protect the fragile documents. Tom padded it generously with other papers, to keep them from flopping about, then stood by, ready to open the wide flight doors.

The Dragon gave himself plenty of wing room, so as not to crush the Librarian, knock over furniture, or make a lot of noise, and indicated his readiness.

Tom nodded, grasped the flight door handles, and pulled them inward. The ancient hinges shrieked in rusty protest.

The Dragon clapped his wings and expanded to full size with a loud pop!

A very pretty girl with piled-up blond hair, wearing a high-necked, floor-length nightgown of heavy blue-green silk and carrying a guttering candle, appeared on the wide stairs, staring in surprise at the intruders. When the Dragon suddenly became full-size, she had dropped her candle with a startled scream that seemed to echo all over sleeping Overhall.

"Who are you?" she cried into the sudden gloom. "How did you get here? Whatever are you doing?"

"Lady, you picked a very bad time to ask good questions," said Retruance.

He reached out his right forepaw, scooped up the girl, reached out his left paw and gathered in the stunned Librarian and flung all three of them through the open flight door into the black and empty air.

✦ 5 ✦
The Gugglerun Papers

THE cool night wind whipped past them as the Dragon plummeted unchecked toward the rocks below the castle walls. There was hardly time for his passengers to know fear, however, before his great leathery wings snapped open and Retruance fought to pull out of the nosedive.

The girl and the Librarian screamed together and clung to the Dragon's claws. With a terrible ripping sound the Dragon's trailing edges vibrated wildly with the force of the recovery. Gravity threatened to snatch the girl and Tom from the beast's strong but gentle grasp.

Retruance strained outward and then upward as he plunged past the base of Middletower, past the top of the ridge on which Overhall perched. He at last leveled out, shooting at tremendous speed out over the grassy lowlands west of the castle.

"We're okay now," Tom called to the girl. "He's really a very good flier."

The other passenger stared at him wordlessly, wide eyed and openmouthed. Even so, he was struck by her beauty and self-possession in a terrifying situation.

Retruance's speed took him miles out over the meadows, but he allowed himself to decelerate slowly until it was safe to make a wide, gently banked curve and head back toward the Historian's camp.

"Are you all right?" Tom asked the girl. She'd been staring at him with evident curiosity but now looked quickly away. "What's the matter, miss?"

The Dragon chuckled deep in his fiery chest, sending spheres of varicolored flame far ahead of them, like balls from a great Roman candle.

"She's a properly bred lady, is the matter. She hasn't been introduced to you yet, so cannot bespeak you. However, as I happen to be her godfather . . ."

"Retruance Constable!" cried the young lady. "You rescued me, Retruance Constable!"

"What are godfathers for, if not an occasional rescue? And introducing you to young gentlemen. The gentleman you share my paws with, my dear, is Tom the Librarian, surnamed Whitehead, an employee of your Uncle Murdan's. Now you can speak to him."

"Oh, thank goodness!" exclaimed the girl, smiling brilliantly at Tom. She nodded her head—curtseying being impossible—and said, "Pleased to make your acquaintance, Master Librarian."

"The pleasure is mine," replied Tom. It seemed perfectly normal to say the words, even here in midair.

"This girl-child is named Alix Amanda," continued Retruance, beginning his shallow glide down to the war camp. "Haven't seen her in some years and I'm pleased she's turned out as well as she has. I recall her as a smudged-faced urchin playing in a sand pile at Morningside, much to her foster-mother's dismay."

"It *has* been some years," Alix Amanda said to Tom. "I'm no longer a child, Godfather!" she added to Retruance.

"Well, there are certainly some questions to be asked and answered, but let's save them until we meet your uncle," suggested the Dragon, still chuckling. "Here we are!"

He made a last, smooth, dipping curve and a feather-light landing before the Historian's darkened pavilion. As he carefully placed his passengers on the turf before the tent, between four startled guards, a light was struck within and Murdan rushed forth, clad in nightdress and tasseled cap.

"Thank goodness you're back, although I could have waited until morning to hear your adventures," he called, but seeing Alix Amanda standing with Tom, he stopped short.

"Niece! How came you here? I thought you were with your cousin, my daughter!"

"No, Uncle Murdan. When the castle was taken I was captured and held prisoner in Middletower. I'm so glad to see you! Retruance and this nice Librarian came to my rescue, you see, and I'm most grateful to them and to you, dear sir!"

She flung herself into her uncle's arms and gave him a huge kiss, despite his scratchy half night's beard.

"Now, now, I wish I deserved your thanks for rescue," he said, honestly, "but I didn't even know you were here in Overhall. Did they harm you, child?"

"Oh, no! The Mercenary Knights were quite courteous, I assure you. They intended, they told me, to use me as a bargaining chip, if you should gain the upper hand."

"But they held you prisoner!" protested Tom.

"I had the run of Middletower, down to the housekeeping level," the Historian's niece explained. "I watched the awful sorties and battles from my bedroom window."

"They fed you well, and were . . . polite?" asked Retruance.

"Yes, both," responded Alix Amanda. She certainly looked none the worse for her captivity. "I passed the time in study and reading, playing Aunt's harp, drawing pictures, and exploring the upper reaches of Middletower. I probably know it better now than any living creature. Did you know," she turned back to Retruance, "that the belfry is home to a tribe of bats who claim common ancestry with Dragons?"

"They always do," snorted Retruance, "and we've always seen fit to disagree with them."

Alix Amanda rattled on and on, keyed to a high pitch of excitement by her rescue and the wild flight from Middletower, until Murdan sent for his physician-magician, a Northerner named Arcolas, who produced a soothing draft for her.

"Distilled from the nectar of sweet marjoram," he murmured. "You'll awake refreshed and ready to face the world and all its vicissitudes, Lady."

"Take my own bedchamber within," decided Murdan with a yawn. "There are no other ladies with my troop to play chaperon to you, so . . ."

"No need for nursemaids," cried the girl, but she drank the potion offered by Arcolas without objection and in a few moments excused herself to enter the tent and sleep.

"Now, as for you two," growled Murdan when she had gone, "what have you accomplished other than to foist another worry and responsibility on my overburdened shoulders?"

"Sorry about that!" said Tom, a shade sarcastically. "But we were successful in finding Altruance's plans for Gugglerun!"

"What's to be done next?" asked the Historian eagerly.

"Slowly, slowly, sir," cautioned Retruance. "We haven't even had a chance to study them yet. Return to your rest and we'll have some word for you in the morning—after breakfast."

Murdan yawned greatly and agreed it was wisest to tackle new plans by morning light with a good night's sleep behind them. He bid them goodnight and disappeared into his tent.

"I'm not the least bit tired," claimed Tom. "I think I'll start looking over Altruance's papers."

"Suit yourself," said Retruance. "I'll go with you and get a bite to eat before I take to my woodland bed. The mess tent is the only place you'll find light at this time of night."

Good as his word, the Dragon ate two dozen fresh doughnuts frosted with sugar icing and went off to his oak-leaf bed. Tom turned up a lamp and spread the contents of the leather case carefully on the table, wishing he had sheets of vinyl to laminate the fragile pages. *Must find some way to preserve them,* he thought.

It took less than an hour to find what he sought—a complete description, with maps and scale drawings of the course of the underground stream known as Gugglerun. By some means Tom didn't understand—magic, possibly—the Dragon constructor had diverted the stream from the mountains, under the solid rocky ridge, spilling it at last into a great basin between Aftertower and Middletower. The overflow was caught by a deep cistern.

From this, conduits led some of the water to various parts of the castle, to living quarters, kitchens, and workshops in need of running water. From the cistern a series of enclosed, sloping drains emptied at last into a very deep shaft driven straight into the rock with a huge storage tank at the bottom. Waste water from the castle was led by a separate system to another vast underground pond.

"Good old Altruance!" exclaimed Tom at this point. "Anyone else would have dumped the sewage into the valley and let it stink!"

Some of the fresh water entering the courtyard basin, however, was led into the moat around the outer walls, then run off over a pretty waterfall into the valley near the Historian's war camp.

The rest of the stream, by far the largest part, drained through another underground tunnel, into the Overhall river.

At first the Librarian considered blocking the inflow of the stream. However, Altruance had tunneled it from its source, high in the mountains where melting snows fed it the year around. Nowhere, Tom saw, was it aboveground anywhere closer than thirty miles away and several hundred feet higher than the castle. As this entrance to the underground portion was all but inaccessible, given the time and manpower available, he was forced to reject it as the site for his dam.

Digging down to the channel closer to the castle seemed possible, but the notes indicated that this part was buried under yards of hard granitic rock. How long would it take to cut a shaft to intercept the stream? With experienced well diggers, weeks at least. Even in Iowa, with a fairly shallow water table, wells took a long time to dig, and with modern drilling equipment at that. And there was the problem of hitting the narrow tunnel precisely from high above.

"Damnation!" he swore. Weariness was catching up with him. He decided to go to bed and tackle the problem fresh, in the morning.

As he lay on his bed of oak leaves against the warmth of the sleeping Dragon, the solution leaped into his mind, plain and simple and complete.

Before he could jot it down to remember, however, he fell asleep, and dreamed of artesian fountains and enormously high waterfalls—and a beautiful girl with high-piled blond hair and cornflower blue eyes in a sea green gown.

✦ 6 ✦
The Great Gugglerun Backwash

"YOU'VE decided what's to do?" asked Retruance over breakfast of sausages and eggs—two dozen of each for the Dragon.

"Once I knew the course of outflow, it was obvious," said Tom. With but four hours of sleep he was wide awake and eager to test his theory—or rather, his plan, for he was confident of its success.

"Let's go tell Murdan, then. Put his mind at ease," suggested Retruance, withdrawing his head from the mess tent. "Sooner we get him off our backs, the better."

Tom grinned at the Dragon's change of pronouns, from referring to the problem as "yours," to terming it "ours."

"We can handle this ourselves, I believe. Just you and me, and Altruance's papers."

"Fine with me, but I advise you to tell Murdan we're working on it. Give him something to look forward to. Historians don't like to be kept guessing."

"There's always an off chance our plan will fail because I missed some little point," Tom admitted. "Engineers have a saying: 'Damn that decimal!' "

"I heard Great-Grandfather Altruance say that a hundred times," agreed the winged beast. He then looked puzzled. "Never really understood what it meant, however."

"Come on! If you think we must, we'll see Murdan."

"We could say good morrow to Manda, too," added Retruance, offhandedly. "Let her thank us for rescuing her, once again."

Tom glanced obliquely at his companion to see if he was being teased, but there was no way to tell and he refused to ask.

Alix Amanda was the first person they met when they arrived at the Historian's pavilion. She was brushing her hair in a spot of bright sunshine, stooping a bit to see herself in a tiny camp mirror.

"We came by to say good morning," Tom said when she looked up to greet them with a smile.

"And to blush with you, too," said Retruance, straight faced.

"To what?" both young people asked.

"Oh, nothing. Never mind," said the Dragon. "Is Murdan around, missy?"

"I believe he's still asleep" said the girl, putting aside her brush and beginning to plait her long hair in a single, thick braid. Tom watched in absorbed fascination.

"Don't you think we should . . . er . . . get started on our Gugglerun project?" the saurian asked.

"Oh? Yes!" replied Tom. "Retruance calls you Manda for short. Is it right for me to call you that, or should I call you Alix Amanda for long?" he asked.

Retruance rolled his eyes up to the sky but held his tongue.

"My family calls me Manda. Alix Amanda is overly portentous among close friends, I think. . . ."

"Yes, I remember. Alix Amanda Alone was queen a while back."

"A very great queen, too," agreed Manda with a nod. "So Alix Amanda is much too formal. I use it only on party invitations and when signing things."

"You know, I do the same thing," Tom laughed, delighted to find something they had in common. "To my friends I'm just plain Tom—*never* Tommy!—but when I sign checks, I write Thomas Alva Edison Whitehead."

"Such an impressive name!" cried Manda. "I'll save that for formal occasions, shall I? I'll call you just plain Tom. It has a much more friendly sound. '*Tom, fetch me a sherbet!*' Or, '*Tom, I've lost my glove. Find it, be a dear!*' "

Even the Dragon had to laugh at her flibbertigibbety impression. Hearing their laughter, Murdan burst from the tent, lathered to the ears and carrying a wickedly gleaming razor.

"Are you done with my mirror, Manda? Return it to me before your uncle slices off an ear. Oh, hello, Dragon, Librarian! Gugglerun stopped up, yet?"

"Shortly, sir," Tom assured him. "We were just come to say you can expect results by the end of the day, if all goes well."

"See that it does!" growled the Historian, waving his razor. "What do you want *me* to do?"

"Be ready to strike, sir," said Tom, sounding more mysterious than he intended. "If our plan works, you'll know it, without a doubt. I think the Mercenary Knights will want to leave Overhall very quickly."

"Well, it's results I want, not details, just at the moment. Get you to work!"

Murdan nodded in curt dismissal, snatched the mirror, and stalked back into the tent, calling for Graham at the top of his considerable voice.

"Can I come along?" asked Manda, rather shyly. "Life in an armed camp is very boring when you're supposed to be a lady. It would be more fun if I were still a child."

"Don some suitable clothing, then," said Retruance. "You shouldn't be seen about the camp in that nightdress, I should say, although I'm no expert on etiquette."

"Something sturdy enough for riding Dragon-back and climbing about hillsides," suggested Tom. "A pair of sound boots, if you can find them. We'll fly a ways, but after that . . ."

Manda disappeared into the tent, calling her uncle's name.

"What a *splendid* young lady!" said Tom to himself, but aloud.

"Easy, Companion!" Retruance cautioned him.

"What?" the Librarian asked, somewhat dreamily.

"Ask yourself why she's named Alix Amanda," suggested the Dragon.

"Alix Amanda? Yes, I know. A beautiful name! Wait," said Tom. "Are you implying that she is . . ."

"Implying, hell! The present king of Carolna is Eduard Ten. He's Murdan's half-brother."

"And Manda is Murdan's niece! You mean Alix Amanda is the king's daughter, a princess?"

The Dragon grinned broadly as the princess reappeared from the tent dressed in a soldier's orange tunic and baggy black hose, cinched to fit her narrow waist with a wide belt.

"Let me pull on these boots," she said. "Fortunately, Uncle Murdan's valet has tiny feet!"

Retruance murmured to Tom, "Don't fret, however. Your rank is nearly that of a belted knight. You need not fear her family will refuse her company to you, as long as she wishes it. Especially not after you rescued her from Overhall."

"*You* rescued us both, Retruance Constable!" protested the Librarian.

"A matter of viewpoint, I'd say," chuckled his huge companion. "Now, are we ready to fly?"

They were and they did.

MANDA and Tom sat side by side between the Dragon's foremost ears, their legs dangling over his brow ridge. They had only to steady themselves with one hand on the nearest ear to keep their seats on his smooth, hard scales.

"Down lower," directed Tom, pointing. "There's the spot Gugglerun flows into the river, you see!"

"Ah, yes," called Retruance. "Set us down on that rocky ledge, shall I?"

"What a marvelous way to travel!" enthused Manda. "I could go on like this for days and days. Much smoother even than a palfrey mare."

"Later, perhaps, my dearest godchild," replied Retruance. "Right now, we've a dire task to perform. Plenty of rocks here, and if we run out, there are plenty more on yon hillside."

"I thought you could do the heavy moving better than a horde of soldiers," said Tom.

"Much better, because I understand what we're driving at."

"But not I," protested Manda. "Can you tell me? What does Gugglerun have to do with driving the Mercenary Knights from Overhall?"

"Come on," Tom said, jumping from the Dragon's forehead to the ground. "I'll explain as we work. Simple and elegant!"

NOON came.

Murdan saw nothing happening in or around his tall castle. Bees buzzed lazily between the meadow flowers and a hive hidden back in the trees. Soldiers drilled to a sergeant's shouted orders on the flat ground at the foot of the castle slope. The *thunk-thunk-thunka* of arrows into rolled-straw butts in the lacy shade of outlying trees was surprisingly soporific.

"Damnit all!" yelled the Historian. "What are you doing and when, dew-eyed Librarian! If I don't clear those bloody knights out of Overhall soon, I'll lose my whole Achievement! I'll have to start over again from scratch—at my age, too."

Graham, his captain of the guard, said nothing but shook his head. They were seated at a frugal lunch outside the pavilion, so placed to see the looming front of Overhall Castle without hindrance.

"Get me a horse! I'll just ride down to see what they're up to, that Librarian and that Dragon—and my niece in man's clothing!"

"I believe Retruance is a suitable chaperon," remarked the old soldier, purposely misunderstanding his chief's remark.

Murdan glared at him in exasperation, then laughed and shook his head.

"I'm not worried about the Princess Royal. If she could stand up to the Mercenary Knights as she did, she can handle a love-struck Librarian."

"This Librarian, however," said Graham, "strikes me as somewhat tougher and abler than your usual run of scholars—yourself excluded, of course. Didn't hesitate to go into Overhall to find the old Dragon's plans, did he?"

"I wonder if 'twas bravery—or fear of the stake?" wondered the Historian.

"One learns quickly to live with fear," observed the other, "but bravery either exists or does not in a man. I say it was bravery."

"You are overlooking another possibility. Insanity!"

Graham laughed. "Who isn't insane at times? I like the boy."

"Well, so do I, greatly," admitted Murdan calming again. "But if you ever tell him I said so, I'll bind you at the stake and set the faggots a-burning, single-handed."

MIDAFTERNOON brought a brief, warm rain shower and a bit of thunder and lightning up in the hills, but the orange-clad soldiers, resting after noon mess, didn't bother to move into shelter.

When the shower passed, Overhall gleamed like purest silver in the bright, newly washed sunlight, a most pleasant sight but for the black Mercenary Knights flags flying from the three towers' conical roofs.

Murdan scowled up at them. The sun would soon dry the walls, the steeply peaked roofs, the stone-paved pathway climbing the hill to the main gatehouse in sweeping switchbacks.

The pathway? He called for his most powerful spyglass and studied the facade of his castle.

"Here, old man! Take a look at this and tell me what's going on," he said to Graham. The soldier focused the glass, sweeping it back and forth in short arcs.

"Water! Running out the gate under the portcullis," he murmured. "Quite a bit of water, at that. I wonder where it's coming from? It didn't rain *that* hard, did it?"

"Not here, at least, but maybe up there . . ."

"The Dragon is flying in circles over the castle, I see. Looks like he has young Tom and Princess Manda aboard. They seem to be watching something within."

"Let me see," cried the Historian.

"Sallyport just burst open," exclaimed Graham, leaping to his feet and dropping the spyglass to the turf. "Sound the call to arms!"

Bugles blared and the well-rested troops dashed to fall in files and ranks on the near flats, craning over their shoulders to see what was happening above them in front of Overhall.

Murdan recovered the discarded glass, unbroken, from the ground. He eagerly studied the castle.

"I see clear water . . . gushing from the lowest arrowslits," he called. "Damned if it's not! How in the world . . . ?"

"He's dammed Gugglerun at the bottom end," cried Graham, "and the water is overflowing the great cistern, backing up into the castle. Instead of denying them water, he's given them far and away too much!"

"Yes! Yes! I see!" Murdan laughed in high glee. "Truly wonderful! That Librarian is more than I had hoped he'd be."

A minute later he called to Graham again.

"At the rate Gugglerun flows in at the top, the whole lower part up to the first story will be awash in no time. He'll have to open the main gate to let the water flow out. Quick, march the men up the hill. Quick, Graham! Someone or something is going to give, soon. I feel it!"

"Carefully but speedily," Graham ordered his sergeants. "If the forecourt fills with water to more than a story, you can be sure the great gates will give way. It'll wash the gate, the portcullis, and even the drawbridge entirely before it. Watch where you stand your men!"

"Aye, sir," chorused the sergeants, and the men in orange started to march, double time, up the hill. A few defenders fired hastily aimed black arrows over the battlements, but they all flew wide of the moving men.

Inside Overhall, Captain Basilicae strode along the rampart at the top of the outer wall, shouting encouragement to his hardened professionals.

"Stand your ground, archers! Your target is that blasted Dragon. Shoot at will!"

"Sir," called his second in command, "the water level has reached the six-foot mark at the gate and still rises!"

The knight captain made a furious gesture and swore mightily. "Open the main gates, at once! Let the water out. Maybe it'll wash the orange men back down the hill again."

"Sorry, sir!" called the senior noncom in charge of the great gate and its draw and portcullis mechanisms. "Sorry, sir, but the gate opens inward! The water won't let us open 'em!"

"Axes!" cried the chief, sloshing as close as he could to the gatehouse without having to swim. "Chop it lose."

But the water was already too high.

"Wait a minute," advised his second officer. "See? The gates are already leaning outward. Soon they'll open themselves!"

IT'S a great tribute to Altruance's construction standards that the gates are holding as long as they have, Tom thought as the Dragon circled Foretower once more. Now streams of water carrying floating debris, loose furniture, and trash were pouring between the dentals atop the battlements, squirting far out from the walls and thundering into the overflowing moat.

"There goes the gate!" shouted Manda, beside herself with excitement and pummeling Retruance's left ear with both fists. "Oh, Uncle, get your men to cover!"

"No, see?" said the Dragon, hovering for a moment like an enormous hummingbird, wings thundering. "The moat carries most of the water away. Our people may get wet but not swept away."

"I hope," he added.

The orange sergeants on the slope ordered their men to fall to the ground as a first, three-foot-high wave of water spouted from the shattered gate, flowing toward them faster than a man could run. His men grabbed handfuls of brush and grass and dug in their elbows, knees, and toes, fearing the worst, but by the time the wave reached them, halfway down the slope, it had flattened to only a few inches in depth.

"Up, up, and forward!" shouted Graham, who led them. "A little wetting won't hurt you, you stable sweeps. Archers! Keep them strings dry! Forward and guide on the drawspan."

His choice was apt. The great drawbridge chains had snapped like kite strings when the great valves had given away. It had fallen into place with no way left to drag it up again, if the defenders had so wished.

They, however, were having troubles of their own. The sudden surge of water when the gate blew swept at least half of the black-clad defenders, already standing waist-deep or more on the low, outer battlements, from their places and flung them cruelly through the open gate, into the moat and beyond.

Among them was Knight Captain Basilicae, weighed down by polished but businesslike body armor.

"ALL the inner courts funnel the flood into the outer bailey," Tom explained to the girl beside him. "The narrower the passage, the higher the water and the greater its pressure."

"I see! It's terrible, awful—but glorious!" Manda shouted back.

"Keep an eye on the survivors," warned Retruance. "Watch where they hole up. Our soldiers will have to root them out of the upper baileys and the towers."

"I think we can leave that work to them, though," decided Tom. "See, they've already come in through the sallyport! It's almost time to unstop Gugglerun, to make it easier for them to mop up."

Retruance and the princess laughed at his unintentional pun while the Dragon circled twice again, to make sure the orange men had things well in hand inside Overhall, where the enemy, realizing that they couldn't fight under such circumstances, were surrendering right and left.

Only then did the threesome return to where they had dumped tons of rocks into the Gugglerun tunnel mouth to back up the flow into the castle.

"I HAVE to say 'well done,' young Librarian!" cried Murdan expansively when they found him on the drawbridge, surveying the damage. "Good job! Excellent thinking! Minimum damage to the castle and a clean sweep of the baileys and lower tower floors, also, according to Graham. Greatest spring cleaning ever," he added his own unintentional pun and then laughed long and loud when he realized what he'd said.

"The most iffy part was whether the sewage drain would prove small enough to let the water build up," said Tom to Murdan, who was still pumping his hand joyfully. "I must admit, sir, that the water level was much higher than I thought it would be."

"Old Altruance would be proud of his work—and yours,

too, Librarian. My congratulations, also," said Graham, rescuing Tom's hand from the Historian's.

"I couldn't have done it without Retruance Constable," insisted Tom. "He did the greatest part of the work. You should have seen the size of some of the boulders he moved to plug the drain!"

Everyone was talking furiously at once. Orange bowmen who had waded against the current to be first through the burst gate now returned, shepherding a long double line of bedraggled black-clad mercenaries and their officers, confused and very damp.

The knight captain was found half-conscious and disarmed on the lower slope and brought to Murdan, his wrists bound before him.

"My congratulations, Lord Historian," said he, gravely. "The strategem of flooding us out was inspired."

"I thought so, also, sirrah," said Murdan. "I wish I could say as complimentary things about you. Your invasion of my Achievement, young man, was a black-handed thing to do . . . sneaking into a castle at night when the lord was away. Fortunately for us, most of my men at arms were with me, not sleeping in the castle barracks."

"Our client ordered the way it was to be done. Most of us thought it unseeming, to say the least, but the client said it was his way, or no way."

"Ah, yes, your mysterious client," muttered Murdan. "Well enough, and can you give us some help there, in exchange for your freedom and your cutlery? Whatever your name is."

"Basilicae, sir Historian, of Plaingirt."

"Never heard of it," responded Murdan, frowning.

"Little place at the eastern end of the Snow Mountains? Poor as mice?" asked Retruance.

"Yes, Sir Dragon. Most sons of Plaingirt leave home to make their living fighting in foreign armies. I was lucky to prove myself able enough for the Mercenary Knights."

"Well, you'd best go home now. There'll be no good tidings for your client, I fear."

"Yes, Historian. We lost more than a third of our best, almost all our Knights, for they were, to a man, overburdened with steel and iron."

"Will you tell me anything of this client who wanted Overhall so badly?"

The beaten knight had shook his head. "No, such information is our professional secret. The fee was high—"

"And is no doubt salted away somewhere safe," put in Graham, who made no secret of his contempt for freebooting mercenaries of any stripe, no matter how good they were.

"I will tender it in ransom for my surviving men and myself. To do less would ruin me in my profession. Who would fight for me again, or hire us, for that matter?"

"I have a better idea than that," said Murdan. "Damage was done to Overhall by your soldiers, I'm told, and then the water that drove you out did much more. We will put you on your professional honor to make full restitution for the repairs. I'll swear not to inflate the cost unreasonably."

Basilicae agreed immediately. A simple contract was drawn up and signed, witnessed by senior sergeants on both sides.

"I need no piece of parchment to remind me of my duty," objected Basilicae.

"Who knows what your next client will ask? You could easily be killed. Your successor conveniently might not remember our pact, when time came to pay," lectured the Historian. "Thus, it's better for your honor and our peace of mind to have it on parchment as well as in the memories of men."

They watched the mercenary soldiers skulk away, hurt in more than just their pride.

"Here, my boy," said Murdan. "Keep this contract among my papers up there in Middletower. It's your responsibility, you know."

"Gladly," responded the Librarian.

On his employer's other side, Princess Manda leaned forward as if better to watch the departing foe.

But she winked at Tom instead.

✴ 7 ✴
Life, Lessons, and a Loss

WHEN the dust settled—or rather, when the floodwaters had at last dried—Overhall became no longer the enormously strong fortress held by invading warriors, but a bright, sunny, pleasant, and fascinating place to live.

The orange levies enjoyed their victory banquet, at which almost every one of them got pleasantly sloshed on some very good beer from the vast, cool cellars under Foretower. The next morning they straggled off to their farm and village homes, nursing various hangovers.

They went, composing in their minds tall tales about the Gugglerun War to be told around Midsummer Bonfires and at Long Night's Eve skating parties for decades to come.

That left the large Overhall household and a troop of forty house guards, the permanent core of Murdan's levy, still in residence. The full-time soldiers lived in apartments within the castle walls or, if unmarried, in low wooden barracks set against the wall of Middle Bailey.

The Historian's household, which included the new Librarian, was quartered in roomy, wood-paneled or brightly muraled apartments in either Middletower or Foretower.

Aftertower, the shortest of the three, contained the castle armory, several prison cells, and storage for equipment and supplies. With the only ground floor in the castle to escape inundation, Aftertower's storerooms were quickly replenished with the vast amounts of foodstuffs needed to feed household and guards, and prepare for future emergencies.

Tom was assigned a small, bare suite of three rooms on the third level of Middletower, with Guard Captain Graham to one side and the physician, Arcolas, on the other, just beneath the rooms of the architect Dragon, Altruance, on the fourth level.

Tom's windows faced east and caught the rising sun every morning. His rooms were soon filled with sturdy but comfortable furniture, gifts from Murdan or from Princess Manda (who again occupied the children's level, two floors above), and other necessities requisitioned as needed from the Aftertower storerooms.

In this way he acquired a good bed, a dresser, an armoire big enough to hold his new wardrobe, several easy chairs and straight chairs, as well as a large table to use as a desk.

Shortly after the departure of the levies, Murdan called his Librarian to his own office in Foretower.

"Your service was outstanding, I need not tell you, young Librarian. If I've not said my thanks, it's not because I'm ungrateful."

"I'm very pleased that I helped," said Tom. Murdan waved him to a chair.

"We must discuss your duties and my obligations more in detail," said the Historian. "We must first inventory what the Mercenary Knights consumed and destroyed during their weeks in Overhall."

"I agree. Much of that, I should think, would be the work of your accountant," said Tom. "I am a Librarian. I care for, index, shelf, recover, bind and mend damaged books, and find needed information quickly."

"My definition of Librarian includes all that, plus helping preserve and, when needed, restore records. The king expects a strict accounting of my stewardship of my office, among other things. I'll introduce you to Master Plume, who is my comptroller and accountant. He'll exchange information with you, generate figures and reports for you to index and file. Check them, bind them, and store them in a safe place. You agree?"

"Of course! Again, I'll do what I am able. Sir . . . ?"

"Yes, Librarian?"

"When Retruance Constable found me I had just been somehow . . . er . . . transported is the word I must use . . . from my home world, which is—was—an entirely different sort of place from this. I was confused, frightened, and the Dragon assured me that if I talked to you, you would be able to help me understand what has happened to me. What brought me to Carolna? Am I to live in fear that I will be swept off somewhere else all of a sudden without warning?"

Murdan leaned back in his high-backed chair, rubbing his chin in thought.

"Yes, that's a concern. I am not a wizard myself, but I've enough experience to recognize very strong magic when I see it."

He fell into a deep study, gazing off across the room, almost as if he had forgotten the questions. At last he stirred and turned his look back upon the Librarian.

"I'll have to study this when I have time. Ask some trained people some questions, you see? Forgive me if I can't answer you right off the mark. If it's any help, I think your being brought to Carolna was no random accident. Someone decided you were needed here."

"I understand. As you're addressing my problem, I feel much better about it. I've learned, already, to admire and appreciate your land and people. Few beings have been as friendly as the Dragon Retruance, sir, and your own kindness in taking me in, on my word alone—"

"Leave that! I said I've experience. It includes making judgments about people and beings at first sight," said Murdan gruffly. "Don't prove me wrong, young man!"

"No, sir."

"In the meantime, you have your work. I expect you to pursue it diligently. And I'll seek consultation with some knowledgeable persons about your sudden appearance. It may take some time. You're welcome here in my service and you may be sure that I'll spare no trouble and expense to protect you from any ill. Beyond that, I can't offer you any reassurances at this time."

"I understand, sir. I'll get to work at once."

"I CAN'T say that I need much help," Accountant Plume said sourly. He was a wizened little man with a permanent worried frown. "I have been doing the Historian's books for years now. I just need some time to bring them up to date."

"As I understood Murdan's instructions, I was to help in any way I can. Also, I am to bind, index, and shelve in his library the records you compile."

"I'll comply with the Historian's demands on that, of course," said Plume, although he didn't seem too pleased with the idea. "I'll inform you when I have papers to be bound . . . after I have completed my work and Murdan has approved of them."

"I would like to take time to sort and index Altruance's archives, also," said Tom. "There is perhaps other useful data there."

"Ask the Master on that," snapped Plume, waving his hand in curt dismissal. "What you do is a matter of indifference to me."

"A man needs to know everything there is to know about his house," said the Librarian. He'd returned to Murdan and reported the conversation.

"Plume is a sour little dried-up apple," said the Historian, nodding. "Pay his attitude no heed, young sir. Collecting and cataloging a decent library for me is important, or I would not have hired you. Concentrate on historical matters. I've been remiss in my duties as Royal Historian. We're in danger of losing much of our past through neglect. That, now, includes Altruance's papers."

Murdan was quite serious about his Historian duties, Tom found. He carried a tremendous amount of information in his head. Surprisingly little of it was committed to parchment or print.

Tom suggested the castle hire its own printer. Murdan promised to look into it when next he went to Lexor, capital of the Kingdom of Carolna. Printing was still a young art and printers were scarce.

"Some months off yet," he explained. "I left the Spring Sessions with the king and his ministers to rush back here when I learned the castle was taken. The government will get along without me for a while."

The Historian wrote his own correspondence, which was quite large, much of it official. Tom suggested a secretary or scribe, to make things more efficient, but the Historian thought less of this idea.

"I can outwrite any quill pusher in the kingdom!" he snorted. "Why settle for less than the best?"

Tom let the matter drop, but soon found that he was often conscripted from his books and scrolls to assist his new employer when Murdan fell behind on letter writing.

The sour-visaged but meticulous Plume worked with the household accounts, carefully and slowly, much to Murdan's loud impatience.

"When he gives me the inventory and the budgets, I want you to check 'em over," he said to Tom. "How's your arithmetic?"

"Passable," said Tom, wishing he had brought a pocket calculator. "But no more than that."

"We have to prepare a bill of damages for that Mercenary Knight, whatever's his name," growled Murdan, amiably. He kept himself and his new Librarian busy as spring waned and summer began.

TOM chose to work in Altruance's huge rooms, just above his own in Middletower, scooting up the service stairway after breakfast to throw himself into organizing Murdan's library or sorting out Altruance's great mass of papers, surveys, contracts, and drawings, or putting some order to Murdan's own chaotic records.

Each morning after breakfast, Manda ascended the main staircase on her way to her own apartments. She was accompanied by her personal attendant, a bright girl named Mornie. The maid went tactfully on up but the princess, perched on a chair beside the Dragon's great drawing table, chatted while Tom pretended to sort piles of documents by subject matter.

She came each morning for just a few minutes, never outstaying propriety, and was gone about her own business too soon, but never before sharing a bit of castle news or telling Tom something about herself.

"What do you do while I'm imprisoned here in this rat's nest of ancient shopping lists?" Tom wondered.

"Oh, ladylike things, mostly. Mistress Plume comes to teach me my letters after breakfast. I used to hate it, but since watching you at work I've seen how important written words can be. I appreciate them more."

"I would have thought you'd learned your alphabet when you were a toddler, bright as you are."

"Oh, thank you so much, young master!" she cried, curtseying prettily. "I did learn *writing* years ago. Now I learn *what* to write. I pen beautiful invitations, neat and polite letters of regret, bright, pleasant notes of gratitude to a farmer for his gift of a sickling pig . . ."

"You mean 'suckling pig,' I think," Tom prompted.

" . . . *suckling* pig, then, and how to word petitions for redress of wrongs or bills for conveyance of real property.

Today we begin bequeathals and testaments."

"All that! Well, I expect it's good practice."

"My father, the king, has written me I must have a fair, round hand and proper grammar. I might be queen, one day, you know. A queen must be perfect in all polite matters, he says."

She bounced up to peer out a southern window to see if it was still raining.

"I used to worry about being letter-perfect, but I've learned to take it all with a few grains of salt. After all, Tom, if I'm destined to be Queen of Carolna, whether I will it or not, my people must accept me as I am! They have little choice."

"I can see where that might get you—and them—into a lot of trouble, down the road," Tom cautioned. "I've found it's better to let fathers and employers have their ways in little things. It's easier to get your way in the important things, after."

"Oh, Tom, you're a politician!" the princess laughed, a sound like silver bells. "You needn't worry about me being queen. In all likelihood the king, my father, will sire a son before too long and I'll remain just Lady Alix Amanda until I marry. If I ever marry. I'm very particular, they tell me."

"The king, your father, Manda—I know very little of him. Tell me something of him."

It had been a stormy night and summer rain still fell intermittently, stopping and starting every few minutes. Mistress Plume, who usually broke up their morning conversations when she puffed up the stairs to begin Manda's lessons, was late that morning. Manda settled in one of the old armchairs, ran her hand automatically over her long blond braid—she wouldn't let anyone call it a pigtail—folded her hands in her lap, and began to recite.

"Eduard Trusslo, the Tenth of that August Name to be King of Carolna, was born of the morganatic wedlock of Eduard Nine and Mistress Anne Selver, daughter of a wealthy silk merchant of Brant Bay. Upon the tragic death of his only son by an earlier marriage, Eduard Nine proclaimed his morganatic son, Eduard, his legitimate heir. Upon Eduard Nine's death in battle, Eduard Ten, then a lad of fourteen, was at once proclaimed king and crowned, according to the ancient and honorable rites of the royal succession, King of Carolna."

"That sounds like it came straight out of an encyclopedia," said Tom.

"If by encyclopedia you mean the *Official Proceedings of the Crown*, it did. It's part of my education to momorize . . ."

"Memorize," prompted Tom.

" . . . *memorize* huge parts of the *Official Record*, so that if I become regnant queen, I will know exactly what I must do in all circumstances."

"What of your own mother?"

"My lady mother was named Seacorde. She was the daughter of one of Eduard Nine's knights. Mistress Plume, who was at court in those days, says Father and Mother were very much in love, but Mother died shortly after I was born, poor thing!"

"I'm sorry, Manda, dear. I didn't mean to give you pain."

"Oh, I don't feel pain so much. Confusion sometimes, Tom. I never knew my mother at all, and the king, my father, only a little better, because I was sent away to be raised by my mother's brother, Sir Peter of Gantrell."

"I thought you were the ward of Murdan, though."

"You're getting ahead of my story!" she chided. "Gantrell was accused of interference with royal will by my—by the king, my father—about ten years ago. He was forced into exile."

"Was he?"

"Was who, what?"

"Was your Uncle Peter guilty?"

"Oh, yes. He was—is still, I suppose—a very cold, impatient, ambitious man, my poor mother's older brother. He thought he would make a better king than my father, and said so, too many times."

"But he was—what? Good to you?"

"I suppose. I seldom saw him, either. With Uncle Peter in exile, actual responsibility went to my other uncle, Mother's younger brother, Granger of Morningside. Granger has two sons just my age. Peter, who is unwed and childless, hoped to marry me to one of Granger's sons, to get the Gantrell family firmly seated on the throne, you see."

"All very, very complicated—like a Russian novel. Never mind that! I'm trying to find out," said Tom, a bit

exasperated, "how *you* fared in all this convoluted mess
of fathers and mothers, uncles and brothers and . . . Were
you happy? Did they treat you well?"

"I was . . . happy enough, I suppose. They all, Uncle
Peter and Uncle Granger and Aunt Phyllis, treated me well.
After all, I was their path to power. They, or Peter rather,
had been pried away from the crown when my mother died
so young. If anything happens to me—no power and no
crown through marriage!"

Tom put down the stack of papers he was sorting and
regarded the beautiful young lady with amusement and
compassion.

"Yet you seem to have adjusted well to it, this strange
life. Were you loved?" he asked.

"I am greatly beloved, by many wonderful people. My . . .
the king, my father . . . came to see me at Morningside as
often as he could. These are unsettled times, but he came
and he sent wonderful presents. When I wrote to him my
very first letter, he wrote back at once. He still writes. Or
would, if he knew where I was. His letters are always filled
with love."

She considered her next words very carefully.

"Father is a most considerate, sympathetic man, interested in such things as how peasants' wives bake bread and
what makes some flowers blue and others red. Interested,
too, in what a young daughter thinks and does and likes to
talk about. Most men consider him a very good king, just
and wise. I love him very much, both because he is my
father and because he is a most kind and gentle ruler."

"Things could have been a lot worse, I guess," observed
the Librarian.

"Much worse!" she agreed.

"What do *you* see in your future, Manda?"

"Lots and lots of things, all mixed up, usually," the girl
said with a small, sad laugh. "As for my father, I hope to
get to know him better and see him more often for longer
times—to live near him would be wonderful. I think I could
help him be happier. He's often quite sad."

"He's remarried, though?"

"Yes, and he was so good as to ask my permission! Given
the choice, I told him, I would not care to be Queen Alix
Amanda Two. I know it's selfish of me but I don't think I'd

make a very good queen, I said. If he should remarry and if his beautiful new wife were to bear him a son, I would never allow anyone to use me to stand in the little prince's way to the throne."

She looked very solemn and Tom reached out to touch her hand gently, reassuringly.

"So he has remarried, with my truly heartfelt blessing. I've heard his new queen—her name is Beatrix—is very beautiful and charming. I hope to meet her next Fall, when the court returns to Lexor for Session. Murdan has promised to take me with him, if the king, my father, sends his permission."

"One more thing," asked Tom as Mistress Plume's gray topknot appeared above the stair landing. She climbed slowly because of arthritic knees. "How can your father not know where you are? How came you here to Overhall?"

"I ran away from Uncle Granger! Mornie and I slipped away from his travel party when it passed close to Overhall on a roundabout way to Lexor. I threw myself on Uncle Murdan's mercy. Murdan is my father's favorite half brother, always has been, and could have great power, if he chose. I love him dearly. Always have!"

"Child," said Mistress Plume, sounding a bit testy, "I didn't climb four flights of stairs to listen to your gossip. We must speak of dusty wills and dry bequeathals now or we will never do it."

"I'm coming, mistress," said Manda, politely. She seemed fond of Plume's wife, who was probably irritable because of her sour husband, Tom thought.

Tom wasn't overly fond of the dry little accountant, either. Mistress Plume, at least, whether through unsuspected kindness or arthritis, allowed them these few minutes alone together each morning.

They had to thank her for that, at least.

TOM worked very hard and the time flew. Just when he began to hear anguished rumblings from the region of his stomach, the great flight door was flung open to the rain and wind and Retruance Constable flopped ungracefully through the opening. He shook raindrops from his wings before folding them loosely at his sides.

"How goes the book work?" he asked.

"Lovely! I have adapted the Dewey decimal system for cross filing by subject, title, and author, and it's making things go much faster. What have you been at?"

"Oh, well," sighed the Dragon. "I'm concerned about my brother Furbetrance. He's not yet appeared."

"I recall Murdan called him to come at the same time as he called you from your search for your father. Where was he, do you know?"

"Somewhere far to the south and west, I think. I was sure he would come to Overhall by now. I'm going to ask Murdan to let me go looking for him. He's my younger brother, you know, and I feel responsible."

Tom waved at the piles of books and manuscripts on the huge table.

"Murdan isn't likely to let me go adventuring with you, but I'll ask him."

"A Dragon needs a good, smart Companion," agreed Retruance. "It won't hurt to ask!"

"I'm starving!" Tom cried. "Let's go surround some lunch, first."

"Right!" Retruance Constable agreed with enthusiasm. Tom paused to pull a heavy velvet cloth over the piles of documents on the table, to keep them from blowing away, then settled himself on the Dragon's rain-slick head, grasping Retruance's ears firmly.

Retruance hurled himself out the great door and plummeted toward the rocks below, snapping his great wings out, deflecting upward and inward at the last moment, enjoying the rush of rain-filled air. He banked sharply, dropped twenty feet, and landed gently outside Great Hall.

Soldiers, household staff, and the master himself were about to sit down to a light lunch of fresh white loaves, newly churned butter, crisp green salad, and savory broiled pink prawns.

Manda had come down earlier to help Housekeeper Grumble, a vast mountain of a woman with a girlish giggle, inspect the laundry, the kitchen, the scullery, the butchery, the bakery, the kitchen garden, and flower gardens, and the weaving sheds, all places and things she needed to know well if she were ever to be a successful castle keeper.

Now Manda sat demurely to her uncle's right and greeted Tom with a worried frown.

Tom took his place on the Historian's left and wished a good afternoon to all at the head table. Murdan signaled his servants to begin.

"Something amiss?" Tom asked Murdan at the first opportunity. "You and Manda look unhappy."

"I *am* unhappy!" growled Murdan forking a tender prawn into his mouth. "Rosemary and her children are long overdue! Word has come that they've not yet reached Ramhold, which was to be their next-to-last stop on their journey home."

Rosemary was his beloved only child. She and her children had been visiting at Overhall when it was captured but had escaped, Tom remembered, a skip and a hop ahead of the Mercenary Knights. She'd fled across Snow Mountains to her grandmother's Achievement until she learned Overhall had been retaken.

Everyone spoke well of Rosemary, especially Manda. Tom was prepared to like her at once, when he met her.

"Rosemary?" called Retruance, who was outside the Great Hall, except for his huge head which was "seated" at a special place at table, near the door. "What about Rosemary?"

"No one knows!" Murdan replied in an anguished voice. "Talber at Ramhold sends that he expected her to come over Summer Pass days ago and there's yet no sign of her, though the ice on the road is long melted."

"Talber will surely send a party over the Pass to inquire for her," said Manda. "She may have had a good reason for leaving late from her grandmother's house."

"Too many things could have gone wrong!" exclaimed the Dragon, greatly concerned. "I'd better go and see what I can find out. At least, if she is safe, I can get word to you and to Ffallmar faster than any rider from Ramhold."

Ffallmar was Rosemary's husband, one of Murdan's liege men, with a small Achievement some miles to the southeast of Overhall. He'd been with Murdan in Lexor when word of the capture of Overhall had come and had taken part in the siege with his levy.

"Would you, please?" begged Murdan, and the fact that he asked rather than demanded showed how worried he truly was.

"Shall I go with the Dragon?" volunteered Tom, shoving back from his place.

"No, no, Companion," said the Dragon. "I'll go much faster alone on this flight. I'll fly very high and very cold. More cold than you could take without several hours of packing."

"Yes, stay with me here," ordered Murdan. "If anything has gone wrong . . . Retruance Constable is the best to send on such a mission. If it's sickness or injury to Rosie or one of the little ones, he can bring them back in mere hours, rather than days."

"I'm off, then," said Retruance, withdrawing his head from the Great Hall. They heard him snap his great wings up and crash them down in a powerful takeoff that rattled the panes of the castle windows.

Manda smiled at Tom wanly, and Murdan grunted thanks for his offer to accompany the Dragon. The household finished its meal in glum silence. Rosemary and her children were great favorites.

All save Master Plume, Tom noticed. The accountant was spooning soup rapidly into his prim, purse-lipped mouth. He seemed for a brief moment before he felt Tom's eyes on him, to be smiling.

✦ 8 ✦
One of Our Dragons Is Missing

MURDAN sent for Tom after Retruance had been gone for a day and a night. Deep lines of worry etched the Historian's face.

"I've had word on the matter of your sudden appearance in this world," he began. "It's more complicated than I thought. All they can tell me is . . . a powerful spell was worked the day of your arrival, but so far no mage can tell me who wove it or why."

"I . . . I must admit that I am not pressed to return home," admitted the Librarian. "I'm enjoying my work and Your Grace is a good employer. But I wonder . . . ?"

"Presumably someone, somewhere, schemed to work some powerful spell and, as a side effect, it brought you here. Or you may have been intended to be a danger to us, or at least a confusion."

Tom sat forward in his chair. These thoughts had been in his own mind for several days.

"If it would serve, sir," he said, "I'll leave your service. I don't want to bring danger on you and the king . . . or his daughter. I can find work elsewhere."

"It's a tempting solution, I admit," growled Murdan, but he shook his head. "No! I judge you to be a gentle, honest man. You're a hard and effective worker, most pleasant to have about. And Princess Manda would certainly be most upset if you were to leave. No! I'll not drive you out of my house just because of some imagined threat."

He stood and walked around his desk to lay his hand on Tom's shoulder.

"I trust my judgments. I say you're a good man to have on our side. Stay, Bookminder. We need you."

"I thank Your Grace, most sincerely," replied Tom.

"Whatever it is, this purpose in your arrival, I feel it has a connection with myself, and more especially with Manda. She is—I don't know how else to say it—in love with you."

"And I with her, sir. I didn't intend it. It . . . just happened."

"Well, as I recall, that's the way love usually comes. Knowing our enemies," the Historian said, thoughtfully, "I can't think that stealing Manda's heart was what they had in mind. That and becoming so firmly bound to a Dragon, either. They may have brought you here for mischief, but perhaps you have unwittingly confounded their plans, just by being who and what you are. That's my belief at any rate."

Tom nodded wordlessly. The two shared a silence.

"So! We'll proceed with our lives and plans, keeping your situation in mind, nevertheless," decided Murdan, returning to his seat. "There are several other matters, my boy, which concern me at the moment."

"Retruance's absence? Your lady daughter's disappearance?"

"Those, primarily. And the fact that Peter of Gantrell has written to me, demanding that Manda be returned to his brother's household."

"Manda has told me of her uncles. I don't think she will agree to go. She has put herself under your protection, sir."

"I'm damned well aware of that! Don't get me wrong, Tom. If she were just an ordinary girl, say the daughter of an ordinary friend, an ordinary family, I would stake my Achievement on her wishes. The king, her father, has secretly agreed that she remain here with me, but he is in too dangerous a position—he has not yet an heir to provide his kingdom a future king—to defy the very wealthy and powerful Gantrells."

"Why should he, a king, fear his brothers-in-law? After all, Peter of Gantrell is in exile!"

"So we believed, but the king's agents abroad have sent word. He has returned to Carolna! For Eduard to enforce his decree of exile now would cause dangerous rebellion, what with Peter's web of influence and favor spread all over the kingdom."

"His brother Granger?"

"Granger of Morningside is an enigma. At one time he was entirely under his older brother's thumb, but fifteen years of association with Princess Alix Amanda and her father may have changed that."

"I can easily see how Manda would have a powerful influence on almost anyone, but . . ."

"I've discussed him with Manda, who should know best. For example, I don't believe she and her maid could have escaped to Overhall as easily as they did, if Granger had not willingly turned his eyes away. He may even have wished her to escape, in order to rid himself of responsibility for her. I think he is no longer his brother's man."

There was a knock on the chamber door and, when Murdan called "Enter," Manda slipped in, looking apologetic.

"My ears were burning," she said, taking the chair beside Tom's. "You have been talking about Princess Royal Alix Amanda of Carolna, haven't you?"

"We have," admitted Murdan, "among other things. I was about to send for you, but Tom and I had a matter between us to discuss first."

"I see. The matter, I suppose, of his strange appearance in our world?"

"That's right, Manda," Tom said. "I've said that, if I pose a danger to you or your father, the king, I would leave at once, go where I couldn't be used against you, if that's why I was brought here."

"Leave me not!" Manda cried indignantly. "I warn you, Murdan! If Tom goes, expect me to follow, even if you prison me at the top of Aftertower!"

"Calmly, love!" Tom said, taking her hand. "The Historian refused my offer in no uncertain terms."

"He'd better have!" snapped the princess, but then she smiled brilliantly at both. "Because he knows I love you!"

"Well, now that's been settled, for good or ill, I'll abide by it," promised the Historian. "You both know there are ruts in any road, especially one paved with good intentions. I don't intend to let our enemies dictate where I go and who rides with us."

"Well put," Manda approved.

"We were, at the moment of your knocking," said Tom, returning to business, "speaking of your Uncle Granger. Do you feel he is still under his brother's thrall?"

Manda thought of this carefully before replying.

"I am quite fond of Granger, I must admit. He never did me harm or treated me less than as his own daughter. His goodwife, Lady Phyllis, by all her actions and demeanor, has been as my own mother!"

"His sons? Was there not talk of marriage to one of them, to cement the Gantrell family to the crown?" asked Murdan.

"Long since, yes. I learned of it from the king, my father, some months ago. I love my foster brothers, but I could not consider either of them as consorts if I became queen. They are both outgoing, sweet-natured young noblemen but not as husbands for me."

She leaned far forward and lowered her voice.

"I'll tell you a secret, Murdan. A while ago I called both Robert and Richard to me one day where we could speak unheard. I told them what my father had said. They both swore to me that they knew nothing of it and would not countenance such an alliance against my will. They will resist their uncle on the matter, they promised me."

"A short while ago?" asked Murdan.

"Yes, and even before that I sensed a change in Uncle Granger's attitude, a stiffening in his resistance to Uncle Peter. Will Uncle Granger go against his own sons' wishes and promises? I think not, Lord Historian! Not even for fear of Peter of Gantrell."

"Yes, but Peter *is* a power to be reckoned with, even for his brother," Murdan pointed out. "And a month ago Peter was far off, in exile, was he not?"

"And now he has returned, secretly? Well, a close-by Peter might explain why Granger and Phyllis let me flee to Overhall. He certainly went far out of his way to bring me near here. Morningside is south of Lexor, not west."

"That's what I was thinking," the Historian agreed.

"What's to be done, then?" Tom asked.

"As I said, I won't let my foes dictate my course. In the Fall, three months off still, I'll take Manda to Lexor to Sessions. Your father, the king, has agreed to it. By then, the queen will be delivered of their first child. The omens say it will be a strong, healthy boy-child."

"Oh, I hope so, for everybody's sake!" breathed Manda.

"It'll solve Manda's problems," Tom said carefully, "but probably create others."

"We'll conquer them as they come, though," decided Murdan. "Right now, however, there is another problem that requires action."

"Retruance Constable and my good friend, Lady Rosemary," stated Manda.

"Yes. At the longest, I expected to hear from Retruance about Rosie by this noontime. There has been no word. In fact, Talber sent a message by carrier pigeon, arrived this morning, that he had personally ridden to my mother's Achievement north of Summer Pass and found that she had sent Rosemary and her babies with a strong escort south a week past!"

"Oh, no!" cried Manda, echoed by Tom.

"Retruance has either been waylaid or has had to go off somewhere, tracing Rosemary's true path," guessed Tom. "Hard to think of anyone waylaying a Dragon, though."

"It's not easy, but not impossible, given the right magic," Murdan said. "The fact is, the possibility of magic is very strong in this, too."

He stroked his close-shaved face in thought while the others waited.

"I've decided that I will wait until noon tomorrow. If there's no word from Retruance by then, I'll send someone to look for him and for Rosemary."

"Who has magic strong enough to counteract?" wondered the princess aloud. "I have no one to recommend. A Seeker of Beymera, perhaps? Or one of the Recluse brothers? They are said to be available for such work although their fees are exorible."

"*Exorbitant*," whispered Tom.

"Well, then, *exorbitant!*" amended Manda.

"I've a better choice in mind myself," interrupted Murdan. "When it comes to confusing magics, a human is ideal, and we have one on hand now."

Manda's eyebrows shot up. She turned sharply to the young man at her side.

"You!"

"Me?" cried the surprised Librarian.

"The antidote for a powerful poison," quoted Murdan, smiling grimly, "is its opposite."

"You're the best one to look for Retruance, my Tom," said Manda. "And for poor Rosemary and her babies, too."

"But . . . I know absolutely nothing of magic," Tom protested.

"Pay attention, boy!" exclaimed the Historian. "It's just that quality that makes you the ideal searcher. You don't know any magic. Therefore a magic maker has almost no hold over you, almost no power to change you or baffle you. Magic is a part of our lives from birth. We know what it does and have some idea how it does it. Therefore, it has great influence upon us."

"Tom, why do you think my father's father was allowed to legitimatize a son born outside noble ranks? Everyone knows that a common-born child has greater resistance to magical powers! By making my father king, the kingdom was assured of a sovereign who would not be subject to all sorts of magic influences, enchantments, or spells. He has both the power of the royal line in him, and the common sense and resistance of the hardworking, tough-minded merchant who was his maternal grandfather."

She paused, looking earnestly at him.

"I see, I think. It makes some sense," Tom said at last. "I will, at least, not be terrified by what a wizard or a magician might do, because I have no idea what it could be."

"It's a lot more than that," said Manda, positively. "But never mind. To explain it too closely would be to adulterate it. Take our word for it, Tom."

She turned to the Historian.

"What is true of Tom is also true of me. I am almost as magic resistant as he!"

"Oh, no, Princess! I cannot . . ."

"You have no choice, Historian. Tom must not go alone. He doesn't know our ways, the means, the geography, the history, the lore. I can help him in many ways. We *must* recover Rosemary before Uncle Peter can use her to blackmail us."

"But you are a Princess Royal! If I were to let you wander . . ."

"You have no choice!" repeated Manda, slapping the desktop with her hand. "I will go!"

The Historian turned away to hide his hot anger and cold fear. He glared out the window behind his desk.

"Well, if you choose to go, I cannot stop you, although I will be blamed if anything happens to you, Manda."

He started to turn back to the young people on the other side of his table, but stopped short and looked out the window again.

"Ah, but maybe it will not be necessary, after all! There comes Retruance!"

They rushed out onto the broad entry court between Foretower and the battlements to watch the Dragon glide down from the blue sky, circle the castle once, and land in front of them.

"But . . . but that's . . . ," began Manda.

"Hello, Princess! You sent for me, Murdan?" the Dragon asked. When he spoke, Tom knew at once this was not his friend.

"You must be Furbetrance!" he cried.

"I am Furbetrance Constable," said the beast. "I haven't had the pleasure of meeting you, sir. Murdan will shortly close his mouth and introduce us, I guess. Hasn't my brother arrived yet?"

"Been and gone," said Murdan. "Thank you for coming, Furbetrance, but what in blue blazes took you so long?"

"Well . . . ," began the Dragon, looking sheepishly at his foreclaws. "I was a long way away and . . ."

"Makes no difference!" cried the Historian. "I have—we have—a great need of you right now. Your coming is most welcome."

And he began at once to tell the story of his misfortunes from the fall of Overhall up to the disappearance of Retruance. The Dragon listened carefully, only nodding to Tom when the Historian introduced him, but making no comment until the story was told.

"After a bite to eat, and a few hours' sleep—I've been traveling for days and days without stop," he said at last. "I'll be refreshed and ready to go look after my brother and your daughter, Historian. To carry the little princess and my brother's Companion will be an honor."

The three led the beast to the Great Hall, where Murdan shouted up a huge meal for the travel-weary Dragon, sending servants and soldiers scurrying. While Furbetrance ate and discussed with Murdan the details of the disappearances, Manda and Tom rushed off to prepare for the journey.

EVEN so, it was dusk by the time they were ready to depart.

"Dragons don't need much sleep, usually," apologized Furbetrance when he met them on the terrace. He'd had his nap by then. "But twelve days is about my limit for being awake, let alone flying at top speed."

"Fly first to Ramhold tonight," the Historian recommended. "Rest there and go on by daylight."

"Just out of curiosity," asked Manda, "what *did* take you so long getting here?"

"It's a bit embarrassing to admit," said the Dragon. He was actually blushing green. "I was looking for our lost father, you know, and followed a lead someone gave me about a Dragon seen on the isles off the Mantura coast. We'd better get going, now. I'll tell you the tale after we're aloft, lady and gentleman. It'll help pass the time as we fly."

Murdan gave Tom a flat packet bound with broad canvas straps.

"Maps," he explained. "I arranged them with the nearest lands at the top. Furbetrance has a good idea of the layout of the land hereabouts, as he was hatched not far away, but beyond Ramhold he says he's not traveled before."

"North and west were Retruance's sectors of search for Papa," explained the Dragon. Tom attached the map case to a harness Furbetrance had furnished from among his brother's tack. It provided comfortable saddles for riders, and loops, thongs, and pockets sewn in thick leather to hold luggage and equipment.

"Well, be off!" shouted Murdan. "I'd go myself, you can be sure, but I'm expecting a visit any day from Peter of Gantrell."

"Well, you can tell him I've run away again, to avoid his dragging me back to Morningside," said Manda stoutly. "Don't do anything to make him comfortable, I say."

"Be nice, now, Princess!" the Historian chided her. "Be sure he will not overstay his welcome by a single minute. Mistress Grumble has a particularly prickly spot in her heart—and her guest rooms—for Lord Peter. She knew him in Lexor, I understand."

This thought made him cheerful again. After his riders had climbed aboard, the Dragon waved a quick farewell to the watching crowd and threw himself over the battlements, to swoop at once into the darkening sky with a dramatic flourish even Retruance hadn't shown, tilting his wings from side to side and letting out a white-hot stream of burning gas from his nostrils. The flames roared satisfyingly.

"Well, now about this adventure that made me late," he said, once they were high and smoothly headed very fast west by north. "The Dragon I thought might be Papa lived in a big cave in the Cliffs of Obsidia. Just the sort of place Papa would love to live in, I thought, but when I arrived there was nobody at home. So I made myself comfortable, thinking the Dragon, Papa or whoever, would return shortly."

He beat his wings with a sound like canvas flapping in the wind, and went on: "I stayed several weeks but no Dragon came. I passed the time exploring the cavern, and one day I discovered a Dragon's treasure. It was quite a find! Not all Dragons have them. Retruance has one started somewhere,

I don't know where, but personally, I haven't really been interested.

"This one was huge, and some of the stuff was incredibly valuable! I began to suspect the inhabitant of the cavern could not be Papa, after all. In the first place, Papa is not the collecting kind, and in the second place, he has not been gone long enough to have collected so much."

"Where does a Dragon get a treasure, anyway?" asked Manda, fascinated by the Dragon's tale.

"Oh, mostly fees for jobs taken under contract," said Furbetrance offhandedly. "Most Dragons like collecting jewels and golden trinkets and pick them up wherever they find them. Not many refuse a Dragon when he asks for a jewel or some such odd thing. I never really understood why. I prefer to collect places and people myself, you know."

"Yes, I've heard you're a talented artist," Manda said. "I'd love to see some of your works, one day."

"We're going in the wrong direction to see anything, which is just as well," said the Dragon, obviously pleased with her compliment. "They aren't all that good."

"Not what I heard," said Manda aside to Tom.

"Anyway, they're too large and too far off the track to be seen easily," added Furbetrance. "I usually use sides of mountains or great cliffs for my best stuff. But if you really are interested, Princess, I'll take you to see them one day."

"About the Dragon in the treasure cave?" prompted Tom.

"Oh, yes! Well, I had about decided this Dragon couldn't be Papa. For one thing, indications were that this was a she-Dragon. Certain things like perfumes and ointments that lady Dragons use, you know?"

"Oh, dear!" cried Manda.

"Yes!" said Furbetrance. "Now you begin to see my situation. Why I was late."

"I don't understand. I'm not that familiar with Dragons yet," Tom objected.

"Lady Dragons are . . . well, *ready* only once every century or so," explained Manda. "This one . . ."

"This lady returned home to find me sleeping in her bed and eating her larder and naturally assumed that I was a . . . suitor, I guess you could say. Once she got that idea in her head, nothing I could say or do would convince her otherwise. Nothing would do but that we would . . . er, mate."

"And you had to stay until the eggs were laid?" asked Manda, delighted by the idea.

"More than that, I had to stay and tend the Dragon lady while she brooded our clutch! That takes four whole years! I fed her and talked to her and rubbed her back. She had strange cravings. I went completely across the Quietness to find the proper kind of pickled beets for her. She *must* have them, or she would die, she insisted!"

"Poor Furbetrance!" Manda sympathized, but with a giggle.

"Don't get me wrong! I was pleased to be her mate and this is my very first brooding! Even Retruance has never had the honor to be selected. But it *is* time consuming!"

"We'll have to meet this wife and mother," said Tom, winking at Manda. "What is her name, if I may ask?"

"Oh, of course! Hetabelle is her name. I'll bring her and the children to visit, once they are old enough to fly this far."

"I'm surprised you left the nest, even now," said Manda.

"We heard Murdan's calling and I left as soon as the eggs were opened and the little ones safe and cozy with their mother. Normally, I would have stayed a year or two longer and enjoyed teaching the kits fishing and hunting and flying, all the good old Dragon things. But Hetabelle insisted that I should answer the call. She's a stickler for duty, I'm proud to say."

"Those kits must be adorable!" cried Manda, clapping her hands. "I forgive you for being late, Furbie!"

"Thank you, Princess," the Dragon said, blushing even more brightly green around the chin and throat. "I knew you would understand. I'm not so sure about Murdan, however."

"Oh, he's not as bad as all that," scoffed the girl. "His bark's much worse than his bite, believe me."

"It's so, especially if you're a Royal Princess," said Tom.

"Or a valuable Librarian and a Dragon Companion," countered Manda. "And a rare human, to boot."

"I *thought* the Companion was a bit unusual!" exclaimed Furbetrance. He tried to roll his eyes about to examine Tom

more closely. "That weird hairstyle! I should have realized!
Now I see, also, why old Murdan sent him on this journey.
With a commonsense princess and a human gentleman, we
can't be beaten!"

By the time they swung about and down to land at
Murdan's sheep station Ramhold, the pair were just a bit
weary of the Dragon's endless talk of his new-hatched
children.

"Four girls, and a boy!" he repeated for the seventh time.
"I'm thinking of names for them, still. Retruance, after my
brother, and Alix Amanda, for you, Princess. Or perhaps
Tomasina. It's good luck to name a child after a Companion,
of course."

Manda and Tom put their heads together and came up
with a number of suggestions—such as Altruanza, after
a Dragon Tom particularly admired, and Phyllis, after
Manda's foster mother.

They'd been flying by full moonlight over an endlessly
rolling plain of grass for some hours when they spotted the
lights of the station ahead. By the moonlight they could see
a long, low main building of grassy sod, which formed
one side of a triangle of smaller buildings, evidently workshops, stables, kitchens, and storehouses. The station was
almost invisible against the rolling plain, its grass-grown
roof tucked against the side of a slightly taller hill that
protected it from the winter-chilled winds that blew steadily
from the northwest.

To announce their arrival Furbetrance emitted a shrill
scream—like a locomotive exhausting its steam chest at
one blast—before he dropped easily into the center of the
triangular court.

The sound tumbled shepherds from their bunks at once
and they rushed out into the midnight dark, clutching strung
bows, long, heavy crooks, and guttering torches to see what
had come upon them so suddenly.

Furbetrance lowered his head to allow Manda and Tom
to dismount, then gave a short snort of flame to light the
scene. The shepherds and their women fell back a pace.

"Hello! We come from Overhall," called Tom, eyeing
the drawn bows uneasily. "I am Lord Murdan's Librarian, and this is Princess Alix Amanda, whom you must
know."

"Welcome to Ramhold," called one of the sheepherders, striding forward then. "I am Murdan's Factor, called Talber."

"We seek the Lady Rosemary, of course," said Manda, graciously responding to the factor's low bow. Tom shook the broad-shouldered, tough-looking man's leathery hand.

"And the Dragon Retruance Constable," he added. "This is his brother Furbetrance, who brought us."

The Dragon nodded in greeting. "What news of the Historian's daughter, Factor?"

Talber raised his hand respectfully to the Dragon. "Come inside, out of the chill," he invited. "The large barn should hold your bulk easily, Sir Dragon, if you wish cover. It will snow before morning, I think. Spring comes in fits and starts here."

"I'll just tag along and listen at the window for a while, but thank you for the courtesy, just the same," replied Furbetrance.

Once within the main house, with a fire stirred and fed fragrant turves of peat to warm the common room, Talber had them brought mulled cider and big sugar cookies while he answered their questions.

"I rode over the pass to Old Place, Murdan's mother's Achievement, and just returned yesterday. Summer Pass is clear of ice and snow, and there were no tracks I could make out to tell where Lady Rosemary's party went astray; whether she was taken by some force or merely wandered off the track, which is always possible in those parts."

"The Lady Murtal, Murdan's mother," he went on quickly, "confirmed what we feared. The party left over a week ago, just as the snow melted from the highest places in the pass. She is most distraught, you can believe."

The fifteen station men and women gathered about to listen and contribute what they could.

"The latest news? Not much, Sir Librarian, Lady Princess, Dread Dragon! Yesterday late, a fur trapper came over the pass and asked to spend the night. It's our custom to give such countrymen who come to our door hospitality— for their news and despite their calling, which is at odds with ours."

"He is here," someone said, and the crowd pushed to the fore a grimy and very gamey-smelling young man with a black beard, great mane of uncombed black hair, and wary eyes.

"He's unused to crowding people," Talber apologized softly. It was evident the trapper was reluctant to speak before all these strangers.

"Well, let's get you all back to bed now," urged Talber to his own people, waving them off, genially. "A sheepherder has to be up before first light!"

When he'd cleared the room with promises that everyone would hear the outcome in due time, Tom and Manda were able to draw the fur trapper from his quiet bashfulness.

"You came down from the north?" asked the princess, smiling encouragement. "Tell us what you saw, please do. We're looking for my cousin and her party. They came from Old Place."

"I know it well, mistress," said the man, accepting a mug of hot cider. "I stopped at Old Place for two nights earlier and saw Lady Rosemary and played with her three cubs. Fine woman! Lady Murtal's always welcoming to us woodsmen, you see."

"What did you find of Lady Rosemary, though?" asked Tom.

"Well, sir, I went north for a week after that to collect my traps and take them up for summertime. That was around the lakes when the first thaw was over," the trapper said, not to be hurried through his tale.

"So I came back south toward Summer Pass by a different way, over the lakes. I've a cabin there, where I often over-winter, you see. Snug, with good flowing water and lots of game for the larder."

"Yes, I'm sure it is delightful—but lonely, too," said Manda with interested sympathy.

"Yes, mistress. Quite lonely but that's the way I like it! When I got there a week back I found someone had stopped there recently. Which is all right with me. It's empty land, you are right. When you get guests, you take them in, no matter who they are, and ask no questions, either."

"These guests, though," he went on, warming to the subject, "were not very nice. They ate all my stores and never left payment or replaced a bit of them! Never heard of such goings on! Their horses ate all my fodder and hay, too!" he added, greatly aggrieved by some people's lack of manners.

"I'd have given them no more thought than a suitable curse or two, however," he said, shaking off his anger. "One reason why I prefers to live alone."

"I certainly understand," said Tom. "Did they steal anything else from you?"

"No, left my pelts alone, which surprised me. Must have been city or castle folk. Woodsmen gone bad woulda stolen the whole lot and beggared me! A whole year's work! But pelts are smelly and greasy to such kinds, and I figure they didn't know their value. No, they stole my hospitality, my food and fodder, is all, nor ever left a word of thanks."

"Who might they have been?" asked Talber. "Mounted parties are not that common in the lake country. Most travel there by water."

"True, Factor!" said the trapper, whose name was Clematis. "It was a considerably large party, mistress! Fully a dozen horses and a half as many mules, by the sign they left. I judge at least eight or ten, in all, some of 'em women."

"But no sign of who they were?" urged Manda, refilling the trapper's mug and pushing the cookie plate closer.

"No, mistress! But one thing . . ."

"Yes?" they asked.

"I found this." Clematis plunged a hand into a huge coat pocket. "Behind one of the bunks, it was."

"Oh, my dear!" cried Manda, snatching the object from the trapper's hand. It was a soft-stuffed rag doll neatly dressed in blue-and-red gingham, with bright button eyes and brown yarn for hair. Manda burst into tears.

"Molly's doll!" she sobbed. "I made it for her myself before the Mercenary Knights came. I can be absolutely sure of it! See, Tom? The buttons I cut from the old shirtwaist I wore when I ran away from Granger!"

"We begin to make some progress, then," said Furbetrance from the doorway. "Tell us, which way did they go when they left your house, trapper sir?"

"West, mostly," Clematis told them. "Toward the ocean."

✦ 9 ✦
Tracks in a Broken Land

WHEN they awoke, snow had frosted the flat prairie like one vast sheet cake, hiding the single track and merging the sod station even more than before with its landscape.

Manda found Tom and Furbetrance helping the station hands clear three inches of feathery snow from the courtyard and off the station roofs.

"I slept longer than I planned. I'm sorry!"

"No problem, missy," said Furbetrance. "I've been up and about for only a few minutes myself. Found these people shoveling the snow and offered to melt it all away for them—like this."

He gulped a great breath and blow-torched the ice and snow from the area before the factor's door, burning off last year's dry grasses as well, leaving the ground hard and dry.

He flapped his wings vigorously to fan the smoke and steam away. The shepherds laughed and cheered but scurried back to their chores when Talber appeared, scowling in the bright sun on the snow.

"Good morning, Princess, Librarian, and Dragon!" he called. "Breakfast is served. Will you come?"

"At once!" cried Furbetrance. He plowed his way through a remaining snowbank to the dining hall wall and thrust his head through a window thrown open for him. "What's cooking? Smells so good!"

"We work hard and eat hearty," said Talber. "Flapjacks and syrup, bacon and eggs, honey butter, bread, and raspberry tea. Plenty for all!"

A bell clanged overhead as Tom and Manda took their places beside the Factor, and shortly the large hall filled with people, shedding their warm coats and mittens, talking and laughing to each other, greeting the guests, especially the

Dragon, cheerfully and politely.

"You've a happy lot, here," commented Manda in approval. "It's a good sign of a well-run establishment."

"This is the sociable time of year for us," explained Talber, spearing a stack of pancakes and drowning it in maple syrup. "Much of our spring is spent moving the sheep from winter to summer pastures. First comes lambing— we're hoping it won't get too cold again. Ewes who drop their lambs early have to be found out. Wolves and coyotes can be a problem."

Manda listened as she ate, making interested sounds around the tasty breakfast.

"Your people won't see home for months at a time this summer?"

"That's the life of a shepherd, Your Highness. Next week we'll shear, now that the coldest weather is past. They'll go up to pasture in the hills, and shepherds and their dogs will stay with them all summer long, moving them as needed until they bring them back down in the fall."

Tom sought out the fur trapper. Someone must have suggested he improve his appearance—and odor. He was newly bathed, clean shaved and wearing clean clothes. He looked much younger clean than he had dirty, but was still rather shy. Tom found him seated by himself at a table in the back of the hall.

"Come up and sit with us while we break our fast," he invited. "I'd like to ask you some questions I'm sure only you can answer."

Unwilling to refuse a great person, Clematis nodded reluctantly and carried his heavily loaded plate to the head table.

A robust shepherd's lass brought Tom sausages and pancakes, bumping him good-naturedly with her hip as she served him, laughing when he turned to see who was there.

Manda flashed a smile at her young man but continued her conversation with the Factor, learning all she wanted to know about sheep.

"Now what will you do?" Tom asked Clematis. "Summer is your time to trap?"

"No, sir! The best furs are the winter pelts—so winter is my busy time."

He attacked the plate of eggs and bacon, eating furiously.

"What will you do now, I wonder?" repeated Tom gently.

"Well, sir, haul my winter's take to market."

"And that is where?"

"Over west, to Wall," admitted the trapper.

"I don't know the country myself," Tom told him. He hauled out the Historian's thick packet of maps and together they studied a selection as they ate. "Where is Wall? On the coast?"

The trapper paused, his fork half-raised, before he nodded and pointed with the little finger of his fork hand.

"Ships come in the summer to buy raw pelts. Pay in cash. I buy supplies, take care of any business I have with bankers, lawyers, get drunk once or twice with old friends, then go back to Broken Land. Live in peace and quiet, repair my gear, maybe make some new traps, do some hunting for winter larder. Things like that."

Tom allowed him peace to tackle his second helping of everything within reach.

"The men who used your cabin went west, you say. Toward Wall, would that be?"

Clematis considered this for a while, chewing strongly, then bobbed his head.

"Likely. There isn't much else in that direction. No guarantee they went on west, however. Could have turned north. Not likely," he added after second consideration. "Nothing up north but a thousand miles of lakes and trees before you run to Everfroze country, where the ground never thaws."

"I'd like to make you a proposition, Master Clematis . . ."

"Call me Clem, for short," interrupted the other, and for the first time he smiled, if only very briefly. "Mother named me for a flower, you know. I'd rather be known as Clem."

"Well, Clem, then. Call me Tom."

"A business deal, Tom?" asked Clem.

"Yes. Suppose you came with us back over the mountains to your cabin. Could you track the kidnappers of Lady Rosemary and her children?"

"Could," admitted Clem. "Going that way, anyhow. I can't leave my winter take overlong. Skins rot. Bugs get into 'em, too, if they're not cleaned and dressed early."

"We can work that out. We need to know where the kidnappers went with Lady Rosemary."

"I can track anything that walks and most what crawls, anywhere, even across hard rock if needed. Those weren't countrymen. City bullies, I suspect. They'd leave a trail a half league wide through woods."

"If you lose any money by guiding us, Historian Murdan will pay you generous compensation."

"I'd be obliged. Good! I'll track for you, Librarian— Tom, that is. Those babies were a pure delight. It burns in my heart that they be stolen away."

"Good!" cried the Librarian. "We'll take off as soon as yon Dragon finishes filling his stomach."

"Take off? You mean . . . *fly?* Like we saw you last night? Through the air?"

"Don't worry. It's safe enough. The Dragon is a very good friend. He's here also to locate his brother, who went before us to find the lady and her children, you see, but hasn't been heard from since."

"Not at all sure about this flying," said Clem, shaking his head in doubt.

"It'd take us days to reach your cabin afoot," put in Manda, who had learned all she wanted about birthing lambs. "By Dragon, we'll be there in a few hours, over mountains and all."

"You've made a good point, m'lady," Clem admitted, unwillingly. "Fine enough! I'll chance it if you will! Make quite a story to tell over the first jack of ale when we get to Wall!"

Full of good breakfast and good wishes from the herdsmen, bundled against the chill in sheepskin jackets furnished by the Factor, the party gathered in the center of the station triangle, ready to mount the Dragon and fly.

"I'll send word by pigeon to Lord Murdan," Talber assured them. "He'll hear you've been here and hired yourselves a reliable guide who knows the north country."

"Very good of you, Factor," said Manda. "Tell him we believe we've found the trail and are going to follow it, wherever it leads."

Talber and his people waved and called good-byes as the Dragon stretched his wings to full extension over his head and brought them down with a thunderous clap. He and his passengers shot into the morning air. A great cloud of dust and powdery snow flew about them and by the time it had cleared, the Dragon was almost out of sight, arrowing north.

"RATHER lonely place," commented Manda, seated close to Tom. Clem was perched behind them, gritting his teeth and holding on to two rearward ears with a death grip. "But wonderful people! So helpful and friendly."

"Once I traveled in our own West," Tom recalled, "and the people there were friendlier the further I got from crowded cities."

"I'd like to live at Ramhold for a time," mused the princess aloud. "My father would like it, too. He should have been a farmer or a herder, instead of king."

"They say a good king is the shepherd of his people," replied Tom. He was checking a map. "Look! We're coming to the Snow Mountains!"

The Dragon circled to gain altitude and leveled out just at the top of Summer Pass. He would have gone on, except that Tom and Clem, after a brief conference, felt that they should take a closer look at the road leading over the pass.

Furbetrance swooped low over a narrow, rocky track. Clem forgot his fear of flying enough to kneel and lean far forward, scanning the ground with squinted eyes as they skimmed slowly along.

"There!" he shouted, minutes later. "Set us down, Master Dragon. Where the path crosses that stream."

Furbetrance backed his great sails and dropped to the pathway with amazing gentleness for one so large. Clem and Tom slid to the ground. The wind made the air bitingly cold.

"Be a muddy mess in an hour," predicted Clem, indicating the thin, frozen soil underfoot.

"What did you see?"

The trapper pointed but held his tongue until he had gone down on his knees to examine the ground at the shallow ford.

"They was here, the lady's party. They rested for a while under the overhang there, from the climb up the mountain. You can see the burn of a large fire."

"Now that you point it out, yes. How do you know they were Rosemary's people?"

"Iron horseshoes like only the blacksmith at Old Place makes," muttered the trapper. "Woodsmen use hardwood shoes they carve over summers. Last almost as long and lighter to tote."

He ranged over more than an acre and followed the pathway downslope a hundred or more yards while Tom stood shivering under the overhang. Furbetrance moved into its shelter with Manda still in the saddle and blew flame at the cold stone to make a comfortable if temporary nook.

"Two groups of riders met here. Kidnappers from the south. The lady's party from the northeast. Might as well go on to Broken Land," said Clem at last. "It's the same bunch here as stayed at my cabin. Recognize the hoofmarks, especially the mules."

"Let's go, then!" Tom called to him, willingly retreating to the Dragon's warm niche.

"One thing bothers me," said the trapper when he caught up.

"What's that?"

"How many in the lady's escort, could you say?"

"A half dozen mounted men, I heard Talber say," Manda told him as they climbed back onto the Dragon's brow. "Why?"

"I seen sign of twelve horsemen, here. Some of 'em never reached my cabin. Question is, where are the missing horsemen?"

"No sign of struggle?" wondered Furbetrance.

"None here."

"The kidnappers may have seized Rosemary or one of the children and forced the escort to surrender under threat of harming their hostage," Tom figured. "The attackers outnumbered the defenders by two to one, anyway."

"Keep your eyes peeled," suggested Clem, resuming his kneeling position, the better to see the ground. "Fly low and slow for a while, friend Furbetrance, so we can see."

Furbetrance did so, adding his own sharp eyes to the others'.

"Two parties rode back a way, together," said Clem shortly.

"And there they parted company!" called out the Dragon. "Want to take a closer look, tracker?"

"Down," agreed Clem.

On the ground he again went to his knees to examine the faint signs of the passing of horses and mules.

"Who furnished the escort, I wonder?" Tom asked Manda. "Certainly they were not Murtal's men, or they would have returned to Old Place."

"I've no idea," said she, looking cold and worried. "Grand-Aunt Murtal has a very small Achievement. She keeps not many servants and only a few men at arms. I can't believe they'd betray their mistress's grand-daughter."

"They left her here, whoever they were," insisted Clem. "Not Old Place shoes on their horses. Can't say for sure, m'lady, but it's possible Lady Murtal contracted with some local lordling to provide escort. Lady Murtal wouldn't strip Old Place of armed men. She's too wise a castle keeper for that."

"Hadn't thought of that," muttered Manda. "I think you're right."

"We can fly over to Old Place," Furbetrance suggested. "Take but a few minutes from here."

"No, let's go on to Clem's cabin. We can trace Rosemary's escort later, if need be."

"I wish we'd thought to bring carrier pigeons," said Manda. "We could exchange word with Murdan and Murtal, too. If the escort deserted or betrayed Rosemary, someone is going to pay!"

"Later," Tom insisted. "Finding Lady Rosemary and her children comes first."

"You're right, as usual," sighed the princess. "Go on down the mountain! It's bound to be warmer in lower places. I'm fairly turning blue."

"Pink and blue," chuckled Tom, teasing to cheer her up. "Very becoming combination for you, my princess."

Furbetrance flew faster now, as there was little the tracker could add to the story he read in Summer Pass. Their way ran diagonally across the north-facing slopes of Snow Mountains, a land deeply scarred by numberless vertical-walled valleys cut by snowmelt torrents plunging off the mountains each spring for thousands upon thousands of years.

"It's really quite beautiful," commented Tom, looking down at the seemingly endless pine forest.

"I find it somber and melancholy," Manda disagreed. She shook her head. "There's a desolation here that the prairie around Ramhold didn't have, though it's just as empty."

"It's the dark color of the trees, I think. Besides, you miss the touch of mankind on the land, don't you?" Tom guessed.

"I am, after all, a child of comfortable castles and crowded towns. I like my landscapes cluttered with plowed fields, with knights on horseback, and hunters in the forests and fishermen on the lakes. And mothers with children, spinning wool yarn before their doors."

Clem gazed at her in surprise.

"My lady, you must forgive me, but I feel just the opposite. Knights mean loud noises and sudden violence. Their horses have forgotten how to run silently in the forest. They frighten every little critter they meet."

He looked wistful. "I do agree with you about mothers and kinder, though. A family has been denied me, for what good woman would share solitude with me, I wonder?"

"There will be someone, somewhere," said the princess, consoling his wistfulness. "But as for me, give me some population."

"I'm in the middle," said Furbetrance. "I like people, but I like the peace of the high open skies, too."

"That's probably what we have in common, you Dragons and I," suggested Tom. "I can take 'em or leave 'em, alike. And I think this is beautiful country."

"You, Tom, are a poet at heart—and so are the Dragons. Could you live here as Clem does?" Manda asked.

"Well, not exactly. I don't have the skills."

"Not the skills, perhaps, but they are easily learned," agreed the fur trapper, "if the desire and the understanding are there, sir."

"That is true," Tom replied.

Clem hunched himself forward, saying, "Hi! My cabin is just ahead. Dusk is near, Dragon. If I'm to see signs, I'll need the light of morning. Besides, Princess and Librarian are weary. Set us down there."

He pointed out a tiny clearing among uncounted miles of trees. At first his companions couldn't see the cabin, so hidden was it under the eaves of the forest, but as the Dragon wheeled steeply down, they spotted it against a dense wall of pines.

Before it a low cliff overhung a stream playing cheerfully between sharp rocks and mossy banks, plunging over tiny waterfalls and racing from pool to pool, reflecting the orange-gold evening clouds and the pointed tops of the conifers.

"Home!" exclaimed Clem with a pleased grin. "Or the best of my several homes, at least."

The sturdy, well-chinked log house was clean, roomy, and comfortable, enough even for castle-bred Manda. Across the front, facing the cliff edge, the river below, and the treetops beyond, ran a wide, roofed-over porch furnished with rustic chairs and split log benches. Within, it was divided into four rooms—a combined sitting room and kitchen with a massive stone fireplace and chimney, two smaller bedchambers, and a storeroom smelling strongly of damp fur and slightly tainted meat.

"You must forgive the smell," said the trapper. "That's why I need to move my pelts before it gets warm, you can understand."

Manda wrinkled her nose and stayed away from the storeroom. Tom set about toting in wood from a great stack outside, for the evening promised to be cold, and Clem began to saute sliced onions and forest herbs from his stores in a huge, black iron skillet. The mouth-watering smell of cooking onions filled the cabin and overwhelmed the odor of the pelts.

Being in his own home brought out latent instincts of a host in the shy trapper. He prepared a good dinner of smoked game hen from his larder, found a jug of beer in his springhouse and managed to produce clean blankets and even wild-goose-down pillows for his guests.

"I'll sleep here on the hearth," he said. "Mistress, please endure a night in my own bed if you can. Tom, the other bedroom is not as clean or as neat. The last ones to use it were the kidnappers."

He bustled happily about like a housewife, and made them surprisingly comfortable when they retired for the night.

The Dragon disappeared into the forest on his own business. When Tom rose with the sun the next morning, he

found the great beast curled protectively about three sides
of the log structure, snoring peacefully despite a morning
hoarfrost that whitened his scales.

After very welcome baths in the trapper's ingenious bath-
house down by the stream—water warmed by the night
fire was led down to it through wooden pipes that, Tom
realized, represented many a summer day's work of drilling
and fitting.

Furbetrance splashed in one of the larger pools and proclaimed himself completely refreshed and ready to fly.
During all this Clem found time to bake loaves of bread,
prepare breakfast, and pack a hearty lunch.

"You know of my pelts?" Clem took Tom aside to ask,
diffidently.

"Yes, and smell them, but it isn't too bad, I guess. It
didn't spoil my sleep or my appetite, anyway."

"I'd wish to carry them with us, if we could. They're a
whole year's labor for me, and quite valuable, delivered at
Wall."

"I did say we'd make arrangements for them, didn't I?
Yes. Well, let's consult our winged friend."

Furbetrance, whose olfactory passages were inured to
strong smells of sulfurous fumes and flammable gases, had
no objection to packing the ripe furs behind his shoulders.

"Providing they can be securely fastened so as not to
interfere with flying," he said.

"Tie 'em as far aft as possible." He whispered to Manda,
"If the odor is offensive to you, Princess, I'll shake them
loose."

"The good man deserves our help, even though we've
promised to pay for any losses," decided Manda. "I can
stand it for a few days, I guess."

Clem led them out of the cabin, closing the door behind
him with the latch string hanging out, in case anyone else
came looking for shelter. A faint track ran under the trees
along the clifftop and here the tracker pointed to signs of
the passage of several horses—and mules, he insisted—in
half-frozen mud.

"Sixteen riders, I make it. This road leads only east
and west. The Snow Mountains are too high to climb,
especially as they're still snowcapped. To the north the
going is too wet—ponds, streams, and bogs at first, then

the long, narrow lakes in Lake Country. Good for trapping but bad for traveling, except in midwinter, when 'tis frozen solid."

"Then it should be easy to follow the trail from the air," said Furbetrance.

"They had no choice but to go toward Wall, I'd say. There they'll hope to take ship, most likely, or follow the coast down to Mantura or Obsidia, barren lands both. There are a few poor ports on midcoast but they're never pleasant to visit, I hear. Don't take much to strangers."

"I've been thinking," said Manda as they clambered to the saddle on the Dragon's head. "If I were kidnapping Rosemary to use as a hostage against Murdan's interference with my Uncle Peter, where *would* I take her?"

"You know better than I," said Tom. "What have you decided?"

"Not decided, but suspected, my dear. Look around you: the land to the north of here is, Clem says, inhospitable to men, especially men on horseback."

"That last is certainly true," agreed Clem. "Trade horses for boats and you'll do better in the Lake Country in summertime."

"Unless I'm very wrong, if the captors are Uncle Peter's hirelings, they'll have access to the ocean. Many Gantrells are sea captains and merchant sailors."

"What is their blazon, mistress?" asked the fur trapper. "I'll tell you if they ever come to Wall. I do business with many such each year."

"Blazons? I'm not sure what you mean."

"Gantrell's flag shows a great black bear reared on its hind feet, mouth agape, paws spread," put in Furbetrance as he ripped through the bright sky, following the westward track. "It's his ancient family ensign, the Standing Bear of Gantrell."

"Ensign, blazon, they're the same thing, m'lady. Blazons are brightly painted on mainsails and sewn on large sea-going flags, you see, so ships will be known by those who meet them at sea. A bear upright, eh? I've seen several with that sail marking over the years, come to think of it."

Furbetrance flew swiftly now, covering distances in one morning that would have taken the party days on horseback. The land, true to its name, was broken, twisted, and sharply upthrust, slashed by uncounted streams and rivers, creeks and rills, all of them roaring freshets at this season, carrying melting snow from the mountains.

"If we don't overtake the kidnappers before they reach the coast," said Clem, "we'll find them in one of the ports along the Sea Wall."

"I thought it was a town called Wall," Manda said.

"From far northwest, south to where the mountains meet the ocean, the coast is one long, high cliff with its feet in the sea. At places the top is a thousand feet above the water. Quietness Ocean beats at its foot with constant thunder. Wall is the best and largest of many ports along the Sea Wall," Clem explained patiently.

"How then do ships take on cargo?" wondered Tom.

"In some places the beach beneath the cliff is just wide enough for a town to get a toe in a crack. Traders load their holds from small craft that are practiced at plunging through the wild breakers to and from the ships at anchor in deeper waters."

"How do they get such a great bundle of furs down to the beach?" Tom wondered.

"Lowered by winches! Everything—furs, horses, supplies, and even men. Closest thing to Dragon flying I've ever seen and not nearly so comfortable or safe!"

He went on, "Wall is the one exception. The Sea Wall is mostly slippery black slate, easily shattered, but at Wall it's breached by a great slump. This allows foot and horse traffic down to the waterside."

"Sounds delightful," shuddered Manda. "Isn't a slate cliff very dangerous?"

"Very!" cried the woodsman. "Every year men die when the stone breaks away or a horse slips over the spill. I drag my pelts on a sledge and never trust a horse myself. Sell the sledge for firewood, too, rather than haul it up again!"

They paused only long enough to eat a cold lunch on an island in the middle of a long, narrow lake of magnificent beauty, set like a jewel between mirrored, thickly wooded hills.

"Be in Wall afore nightfall, I reckon," Clem told them. "Dragon flying has its advantages. Used to take me a week to cover the distance hauling a sledge!"

He had Furbetrance stop every hour or so to check the trail. By now the trapper could almost call each mount by name and its rider also. At one stop he brought them a rag of blue silk he'd found beside the path.

"Rosemary has a gown of that material," Manda confirmed. "It's been cut, but rather roughly, not torn. Is that a good sign or a bad, Clem?"

"I can only guess, mistress. Perhaps Lady Rosemary cut the cloth from the bottom of her gown to make it more comfortable riding."

"I believe you're right," said Manda with great relief. "It's the sort of thing our Rosie would do."

"I hope so," said Furbetrance to Tom. "We can only guess at the behavior of her captors."

"If they'd intended to slay her, they would have done so long since," Tom said. "No, they have a purpose in keeping her alive."

"We must be careful," Furbetrance cautioned hurriedly. Manda and the trapper were returning within earshot. "If they're startled by our sudden appearance, no telling what they might do in panic. Kidnapping is a hanging offense!"

After they'd resumed their flight, the Dragon suggested that they waste no more time checking the trail.

"I agree, sir Dragon," said Clem, nodding his head vigorously although there was no way Furbetrance could see the gesture. "They've come this far along, they can be headed for nowhere but Wall."

By late afternoon, with but an hour of sun left, they saw the sharp, black line of the Sea Wall, and the dark blue of Quietness Ocean beyond.

✦ 10 ✦
Over the Wall

THE Slippery Slate Inn offered the best accommodations in Wall. To it came the more successful trappers or seamen, the first fresh from Lake Country; the others, officers from the ships that called at that out-of-the-way spot to buy pelts.

It offered clean beds—you paid four times more if you wished a whole bed to yourself—plain yet hearty fare, leaning heavily on shore and sea foods—roast beef cost a fortune. Its roof was sound. Its taproom was a popular gathering place.

Most important, the inn had a bathing room with hot water and plenty of strong lye soap and rough towels, and its owner, Master Gregory Squiller, knew when to look the other way and never asked embarrassing questions.

"Set us down at the front door," directed Clem as Furbetrance circled high above the seaside town. " 'Twon't do any harm to let 'em all know we came by Dragon, I guess?"

Manda and Tom agreed. The Dragon swooped down on the Slippery Slate like an angry hornet.

A small crowd of patrons gathered outside the inn to have a drink in the cool evening air—drinks were cheaper outside than in—gawked in stunned surprise when the Dragon landed on the broad cobbled yard in front of them. Some cried out in alarm and fled, but most stood their ground but kept their hands well away from belt knives and pocket bludgeons. Dragons had sharp eyes as well as hot breath.

"Innkeeper!" shouted Clem, sliding off Furbetrance's head. "Innkeeper! Rooms for the night!"

Master Squiller burst from the inn like a cork from one of his bottles, wiping his sweaty palms on a stained apron and bobbing his head in welcome.

"Sirs! Er . . . sirs and madam! The Slippery Slate, at your service! I be Squiller, your host. What do ye require?"

"Let's see," said Tom. "Two of your very best rooms, side by side. Fresh-laundered sheets. Board for three and fodder for the Dragon, who'll sleep outside, but nearby."

"Easily, dear sir!" exclaimed Squiller, practicing his obsequiousness. "The estimable Dragon can sleep right beneath your windows, if he will. My stableman will provide—oh, say, fifty bales of fresh salt hay?—for his easy repose. Will you step this way, lady and sirs? In out of the night chill . . ."

He led them inside, leaving the outdoor drinkers to stare at the enormous Dragon in awe. Furbetrance gave them all a polite little bow and turned to look for the hostler and his fifty bales of salt hay.

Squiller wrung his hands in eagerness and greed, adding up the price he intended to charge this important-looking party. Manda, in her best lady-of-the-castle manner, sat in dignified silence, looking about regally, while Clem and Tom spoke to Squiller about their accommodations.

"I can let you have the two best front rooms—the left-hand one is really a suite, has a parlor and dressing room—for a hundred-fifty silver vols the night—"

"Say rather two hundred and a half in silver *the week*!" cried Clem in outrage. "I've rented your sitting room–bedroom for a third of that and felt cheated."

"Ah, you've been here before?" asked a deflated Squiller. "Yes, I didn't recognize you without your ten day's beard and trapper's aroma. Clem of Broken Land, is it not?"

"Then you'll know I'm a man of my word. I pay my bills in cash and on time," snapped the trapper, still angry. "We'll pay thirty a night for the four of us and take our meals in our rooms. None of your added-for-this, added-for-that!"

"Sir! Sir! The hay alone will cost that much! Fifty bales of finest salt hay!"

"Let me tell you, friend innkeeper, it had better be top quality, even at my offer. I know this Dragon. He's used to the very best and'd burn down the whole port if he found he'd been cheated of even a half bale!" growled Tom, getting into the spirit of the haggle.

"Well, well, of course, there's that to be considered," the

innkeeper sighed even more deeply than before. "Forty of silver, and that's my best offer, sirs."

"Dear innkeeper," interrupted Manda, softly. "Look out the window, please."

When Squiller went to the front window he saw the drinking crowd outside had grown tenfold, so far and fast had the word spread of the arrival of a Dragon.

"You'll make fifty times the price of our rooms just in beer and ale," Manda said. "Thirty vols for all, and that's *our* last offer!"

"Well, well, and well," sighed the innkeeper. "Thirty-five, in advance, little lady."

"Thirty, and we pay when we leave, if the service is good," retorted Tom.

"Done!" cried Squiller, quickly. "Come! Let me show you to your rooms."

They followed him up a broad staircase to the upper floor of the inn and along an open balcony to the front, where he opened two doors, side by side.

"The lady will wish the parlor-room suite," Squiller decided, ushering Manda in with polite ceremony. "This door communicates between the two rooms. It can be locked from either side, you see, if you desire."

"Leave it open for now, and open all the windows, too," directed Manda. "This place smells like the barracks in Murdan's Overhall. Send your maids up at once to sweep and dust and scrub the floor. It's filthy!"

Meekly agreeing to her demands, Squiller prepared to leave.

"Light supping at any time, gents. Dinner is served at eight of the clock. Tonight's baked salmon brought down fresh from the lakes, way up north. Gourmet delicacy, that is."

"Bring some tea while the maids clean the place up," sighed Manda, with a glance at Tom and Clem. "The Dragon, by the way, eats as much as five men, and he'll share our table. Place it by that large window."

"F-f-five men!" gasped Squiller, seeing his profit margin swiftly dwindling to less than two hundred percent. "I had thought Dragons were vegetarians. Ate grass and things like that."

"Not *this* Dragon," said Furbetrance through the open

window. "The closest I come to being a vegetarian is tossed salad, so see that I get plenty of it, innkeeper!"

"As you wish," sighed the resigned Squiller. "Welcome to Wall, again, madam and sirs . . . and Dragon! I am at your beck and call at all times."

He had a small worried frown as he turned away and Manda felt sorry for him.

"Give Master Squiller one night's tariff," she told Tom. The Librarian opened his purse and counted out thirty silver coins into the grateful host's hand.

"Now, the cleaning maids, soap and water and mops and brooms!" cried Manda, "and the pot of tea, if you please."

"Serve a round of your best ale to everyone in the bar," added Clem, who was enjoying playing the rich man for once. "And tell them I'll be down after a while to answer all their questions. And ask some, too."

Squiller bowed himself out of their chambers and dashed down the stair calling aloud for his wife, his chef, his barman, the maids, and his stabler.

Over hot tea minutes later, Tom asked what their next move was.

"I'll go down and talk with the boys in the taproom," said Clem. "Many of them I know. They'll have heard of any mounted party coming here. I'll butter up our host, see what he knows, too. Squiller may be sharp when it comes to vols, but he's an honest man, or he wouldn't have lasted all these years in Wall's rough company."

Said Manda, "I'll ask for a dressmaker to run up some things for me. Dressmakers go to many different houses in a town and hear all sorts of interesting things. Also, I've been wearing these mannish clothes long enough."

"I'll go have a walk about the port," Tom decided.

"There're rough, bluff people hereabouts," warned Clem. "Wall has no law, save the strength of a man's arm and the quickness of his blade."

"I don't intend to get into any brawls," scoffed Tom, "just look for the Gantrell blazon on the ships at anchor. None of them know me from Adam," he added. "I can go without creating suspicions."

FURBETRANCE, when Tom came to him in the stableyard, was asking the hands about his brother.

"Bigger'n ye!" exclaimed the head stabler. "Green and gold? If anyone has seen that, we'd have heard. Ye can't keep such a beast a secret, now can ye?"

"One would think not," said Furbetrance, "yet he's completely disappeared somewhere between here and Overhall."

He greeted the Librarian worriedly.

"I would have thought we'd have at least heard about Retruance being about. As the man says, it's next to impossible to hide a Dragon."

"Well, keep asking and looking," Tom advised, patting his huge friend on a paw. "Retruance told me Dragons are nigh impossible to kill."

"That may be right, but on the other hand, Dragons like Retruance are pure innocents when it comes to evil magicians and wicked witches. He may have been captured or enchanted or . . . I don't know! He may even be nearby and hiding, which is entirely another thing from being hidden by someone else. I'll wait until moonlight and fly about a bit. If I don't see a sign of him, he may see me."

"Good idea!" exclaimed Tom, who was as worried as Furbetrance about the missing Dragon. "For now, I'm going for a walk while it's still light enough to see blazons."

"I'll come with you," Furbetrance offered.

"No, you can do more from the air. I'll shout if anything happens," Tom promised, and he turned on his heel and marched out of the stableyard onto the street, rather grateful to be walking for a change.

The street was the only true passage in Wall, all the rest being narrow, crooked, dank, and fish-smelling alleys. Most ended at the water, for the whole town was built on a narrow strip of slate that ran from the cliff out to sea a mile or more. The street was lined with less-expensive inns, taverns, food shops, and wretched hovels that seemed to be mostly the business places of sad-looking women in bright but skimpy clothing.

As the Librarian passed on, the buildings became more imposing; wood-and-slate structures fronting low warehouses presumably filled with outgoing pelts or incoming staples the fur trappers would buy at inflated prices.

Tom examined everything closely.

• • •

MANDA closeted herself with the innkeeper's plump and cheery goodwife, Flavia. Mistress Squiller assured the princess she was by far the best seamstress in Wall, and proceeded to prove it by whipping together gowns and accessories at an amazing speed, talking all the while.

"Don't get much call for finery like this," she warbled. Manda stood in her shift on a low stool to allow Flavia to measure, poke, prod, and suggest to her heart's content. "I'm that happy to be of service. Haven't forgot my skills, have I? No, ma'am!"

"You have very few ladies, then, in Wall? Not by land nor by ship?"

"Occasionally one of the ship's captains brings his wife (or so he *calls* her, if you take my meaning, ma'am) on his voyage. Not many, no. Turn to the right, dearie. Ah, so, that's fine! Let me just take a tape to yer bosom. Remind me, now! Is it the fashion to wear the bodice low or the collar high, these days? I'm that far out of knowing, here."

"Rather more high than low," replied Manda. "I'll be frank with you, goodwife. My friends and I came to Wall seeking my cousin and her three young children, kidnapped by a troop of eight or ten unknown horsemen some days ago. Have you heard of them, at all?"

Flavia shook her head in outrage and dashed a kind tear from her eye, being careful not to dislodge a mouthful of straight pins as she did so.

"I'm that sorry, mistress! No, I've not heard of such a cruel deed!"

"Let me tell you the story," said Manda, deciding to trust the woman. "Then perhaps you and Master Squiller can advise us what to do."

She spoke steadily for a half hour while the seamstress worked, interrupting only with cries of dismay and anger.

"The poor, poor Lady Rosemary! And three wee ones, too! What evil men would do such a thing? There are wicked men aplenty here in Wall, lady, but none *that* sunk down in depravity."

Clematis, already well known in town, was the favorite son of Wall that early evening.

Word spread quickly that he was standing for drinks in

Slippery Slate's taproom. Outsiders crowded in to share the largess and regulars made room for them at the bar, tables, and benches. The rough seamen and rougher woodsmen listened to Clem's tale, and tried to answer his questions.

"I'll be frank with ye, lads," Clem stage-whispered, "my mates and I, we're looking for more than a Dragon. We seek a kidnapped lady and three little ones!"

The crowd moved as close as they could to listen.

"She be Lady Rosemary, daughter of king's Historian Murdan, of whom ye've heard many good things."

"We all know well of Murdan. He's the king's favorite, I hears," someone called out.

"Aye, and has made enemies in the good king's service, ye can wager," cried Clem. "Lady Rosemary was waylaid in Summer Pass and the trail leads here to Wall. Tell me now, has anyone here heard of a dozen armed and mounted strangers? They'd be maybe to the number of eight or so armed riders, castle folk, plus the lady and the kidlets."

There was a great deal of speculation and some rumors of this or that stranger being seen, but no solid information. While the ale flowed freely Clem listened intently but all the time kept a keen eye on the taproom comings and goings.

He didn't miss seeing one young dandy with an ornate sword slipping out the door into the darkness, alone—only short minutes after he'd entered looking very much like a man with a great thirst. But he'd never sipped a taste of Squiller's good brown ale.

"Anyone know that fancy youngster, just left?" he asked his companions. "Didn't even stop to take advantage of your hospitality, barkeeper!"

"I noticed him, but who was he? Does anyone know?"

No one did. Strangers came to a seaport town both from sea and mountains, and nobody thought much about them.

The potboy stationed near the outside door to the barroom came to Clem after a while.

"That there younker who didn't drink?" he asked.

"Aye, laddy. What of him? Do you know who he is?"

"No, sir, but did you see the badge he wore on his sleeve?"

"None of it," said Clem, pushing his jack away empty and wiping his mouth on his cuff. "What was it?"

"Seen it before as a blazon," said the potboy, thoughtfully. "A Standing Bear."

"Ha!" cried Clem. "The blazon of Gantrell ships?"

"Yes, so I believe. Not sure of the name but I've seen the blazon more than twice."

Clem raised his voice to still the loud laughter and talk about him, loosened by the free-flowing ale.

"Hoy! Hey! Any of you dogs seen a ship blazoned with a Standing Bear? Gantrell ship, I think?"

A sailor near the back of the room stood and waved his hand.

"Three lie at anchor well offshore. I wouldn't have noticed it save they send no hands ashore, though they've been in port for a week. I felt sorry for their sailors, I did."

"I'll take a look at her," decided Clem. "You boys have another drink on Master Tom and me while I'm gone."

"Better take a lad or two to help ye," advised the barkeep. Clem crooked his finger at three of the closest; two old friends from the deep pine woods and a dock roustabout he knew. The foursome slipped out the back door of the taproom, hardly missed as the barkeeper began drawing from a new keg just then.

FURBETRANCE circled slowly over the long cliff and out to sea, flying slowly and gliding silently in the clear moonlight. He turned his eyes and ears on the scene spread out below him, selecting those places where a Dragon might choose to hide . . . or be hidden.

At his furthest arc over Quietness Ocean's chop he was attracted by three great square-rigged ships anchored on the very edge of the harbor before the bottom became too deep to drop anchor. While the dozen or so other, smaller ships in the roadstead tended to huddle as close inshore as they could, these three stood alone. They showed no lights.

"Bad manners, at least," muttered Furbetrance at this. "Lights should be required."

With no sound at all the Dragon lowered almost to the wave tops and skimmed alongside the three vessels, passing them just out of bowshot. He could hear the creak of cordage as the ships rocked in the long swell, and the low sounds of voices. A bell clanged the half hour.

Furbetrance smelled the salt seawater, and most of all the musty odors of gulls and terns, but under these he caught the scent of cooking, of men in confined spaces, and . . . what was that?

He turned and passed downwind of the ships again, sniffing carefully.

It was the smell of a woman; mingled perfume and the scent of a gentler soap than sailors ever used.

"Could be a captain's woman, come along for the ride," he mused. "Or it could be Rosemary."

Again he swooped close to the restless waves and flew as close as he dared to the darkened ships.

The aroma of woman came again. And the sound of a child whimpering in uneasy sleep. A woman's soft tones, answering and soothing.

Furbetrance shot straight up, keeping his body well clear of the direct moonlight path as seen from the decks, below. He made his course directly back to the Slippery Slate, so fast the wind keened as it rippled over his scales.

"STANDING BEAR?" asked one of the four watermen huddled about a tiny fire at the seaward point of Wall. "Yes, young sir, I know it. Standing Bear's sail come here, once in a while. They're common in the fur trade, I believe."

"Is there one in now?" asked Tom, holding out his hands to the flames.

"Haven't seen one," said the eldest of the boatmen. "Ask my son Jamey there. He has the good eyes in the family."

"Not one, but three," said Jamey. "Funny thing, too. I was hired to carry passengers out to one of them early this morning. Foggy it were, ye recall, Daddy?"

"Aye," said his father, puffing on his long-stemmed pipe. "Not see a hand outstretched, I swear."

"They sent me packing in a rush, once these people had boarded the biggest three-stick. Wouldn't let me stay to get return passengers, as is the custom. Told me to shove off and keep me distance!"

"Passengers? Tell me about them," the Librarian urged. He placed a single silver vol on the ground near the fire where it glinted and gleamed in the firelight.

The elder man leaned forward, picked the coin from the

sand, examined it carefully, and slipped it into a waistcoat pocket, nodding to his son.

"Thank ye, sir! Most generous of ye! Well," continued the son, "They numbered six in all, if ye count the tads."

"They went willingly, did it seem to you?"

"Hard to say, master. The young woman, she wasn't too happy about it, I thought, but the little dandy who paid, he sat up close to her with his arm tight about her. The kidlets clung to her cloak. I thought they were afraid the chop would toss them overboard."

Tom fished a second coin from his pocket and laid it by the fire.

"I said to them kidlets, 'Don't be afeared, little fry. Jamey is the second best boatman on the Wall after me Daddy. Ye'll be safe.' "

"Did they answer?"

"No, just looked fearing and tearful, master. Thank ye, again! Now, that fancy, the one dressed like a castle dandy, yapped at me to shut my face and row, so I did. Paid well, I must say."

Tom considered the matter. It surely was Rosemary, her children, and her captors. The dandy? Who might that be?

"Did you know these ships at all?"

"No, sir. The big one had her name covered with a tarp, come to think of it. I never recognized a one of her sailors that I saw, either."

"I'll tell you why I ask," said the Librarian. "Some friends of mine and I are looking for a kidnapped lady and three children. These were most likely who you saw, I would say."

"Nobody else like that come to Wall in recent days, at least," agreed Daddy.

Said Jamey, "They come by fog and dark of morning, and never stopped at any inn, I think. They all still smelled strong, to a waterman like me, of horse sweat and fresh manure."

"What I wonder is why have these ships stayed here so long?"

"If what you're telling us is so, and I see no reason to doubt you, for the shame of it all," said Daddy, "I would guess the first three days they were here waiting for this shore party to arrive."

"But they're still out there?" Tom asked, gesturing seaward.

"Tide's high with the full moon. Dangerous waters along Sea Wall at such times, especially in fog. Fog lifted just this afternoon, ye'll recall."

"And perhaps they saw no reason to hurry their departure," guessed Jamey. "Did they know you and your friends pursued them?"

"I don't think so," answered Tom. "Well, I've got to get back to my party and report on this, friends. If I return in an hour, will I still find you here, in case I need a boat out to these ships?"

The boatmen assured him they'd be on duty until well after midnight. The last of the sailors on shore leave from other ships in the roadstead wouldn't roll down to the strand before then and business would be brisk for a while thereafter.

Tom stood, brushed sand from his trousers, and headed back up the spit toward Slippery Slate.

"WAIT a moment, young bully," came a file-rough voice from the shadows of an alley as he passed. "We needs some drinking money and've elected ye to loan it to us!"

"Here, catch," said Tom instantly. He flung a fistful of vols into a pool of moonlight at the side of the road. There was a breathless scrabbling and a ragged arm shot out of the pitch-black alley to scoop up the money.

"Ah, a willing donor," cried another voice. "Wait, maybe there's more where that come from, Salty!"

"Enjoy your drinks," called Tom, moving at a fast walk up the cobbles.

"Here!" cried one of the thieves.

"Ho, let him go!" said the other. "Let's find a crib for the night, mate."

Tom slowed down when their voices fell well behind him. No need to make himself conspicuous by running, he decided. The town that had seemed so quaint in daylight had become sinister in the dark.

Within hail of the inn four hulking figures back-lit by the inn's bright windows, stepped in front of him from the side of the street. Tom slid to a stop and took a great breath to call out to the Dragon for help.

"Here, here, we're friends!" called Clem, holding his hands up to Tom. "In fact, we're about looking for you, Librarian."

Tom let his breath sigh out in relief and joined the fur trapper and his friends.

"Lady Rosemary is aboard a Gantrell ship far out in the roadstead, I believe," he told them. "I came back for help. They might sail at any moment."

"Tide doesn't turn for over an hour," said the longshoreman. "Although if they was spooked, they might shove off before. Take their chances with the Shoal Races."

"So, Standing Bear ships are really here!" cried Clem.

Tom told him of his conversation with the boatmen.

"Know Old Petros and his son Jamey," said the roustabout. "They been lightering to and from ships for as long as I've been in Wall. I'd say you could trust their word."

"What's that!" cried one of Clem's trapper friends. He pointed to the sky.

"Just a Dragon," shrugged Clem.

"*Just* a Dragon!" cried the other trapper. "*Just* a Dragon! Ye're traveling in strange company these days, Clem!"

Furbetrance, hearing their voices echo in the empty street, changed course and thumped down beside them.

"There are three suspicious ships in the roadstead," he said at once. "I swear Lady Rosemary is aboard one of them. I didn't see, but I could smell her and I heard a child whimper!"

"I found it out in another way," said Tom. "You confirm it."

"And so did I," Clem added. "A little man in fancy clothes came into the bar. Had the Standing Bear blazon on his sleeve. He left as suddenly. We set out to follow him to his ship, we four."

"If your dandy boy is from one of the Gantrell ships," said Furbetrance, "he'll warn them of us."

"We've got to move fast!" Tom exclaimed.

"Likely they'll up-anchor, rather than come for us," Clem said. "How long for him to get back to his ship?" he asked the taller trapper.

"He left here, what? Five minutes ago? Did you see anyone when you came up the street, Librarian?"

"No one at all in the last five minutes."

"Then he had a boat bring him ashore near the inn, I'd guess," said the other man. " 'Twill take him a half hour's rowing in the turning tide, at least, to reach the far roadstead."

"Fastest way to get to the ships is Dragon-back," said Furbetrance. "Mount up, men!"

"Wait, now, how about Manda?" asked Tom.

Cried the Dragon, "She'll be safe where she is, trying on dresses and all. There's likely to be a bit of fighting where we're headed."

All five men sprang to the Dragon's head and shoulders, two perching in front of Clem's pack of furs. Furbetrance launched himself into the air once more.

"Let's take thought, now," Tom cautioned. "I don't doubt we can get to the Gantrell three-masters before they get under way, but what then?"

"We'll demand they release their captives or we'll sink all three ships. I can do it with a belch or two," exclaimed Furbetrance. "Ships burn beautifully."

"But so do Historian's daughters!" Tom objected. "They'll know we won't burn the ship that holds Lady Rosemary. They are the counters for any demand like that, ready to the scoundrels' hands."

"Right! Right!" admitted the flying Dragon. "What then?"

"Seems to me," put in Clem, "that craft and stealth are called for. If you put me and Tom aboard the big ship quietly, we can rescue lady and kinder before they knows it."

"Here's what we'll do, then," Tom decided. "A bold diversion out front, and a sneak attack from the rear!"

He pointed out the boatmen's fire. "Land near that as quietly as possible so as not to startle them."

Once on the ground, he approached Petros and Jamey, asking for their help.

"Take these three out to near the Gantrell ships and make a ruckus of some sort," he ordered, once a price had been agreed. "While they're looking at you, Clem and I will fly with the Dragon to the ship and take Lady Rosemary and her children right from under their noses."

"Done!" cried Petros. "Come along, Jamey. We'll take my boat. It's a bit larger than yours, and we both will row.

Give us a quarter hour, rescuers, and we'll be close aboard her, kicking up a dandy fuss."

"You lead the way, when we get aboard her," said Tom to Clem. "Rosemary doesn't know me but she'll remember you and come with no hesitation, I think."

"Fine by me," Clem agreed. "Wish we had better weapons, though."

The Librarian carried a sheath knife, more useful for dining than fighting, and the trapper carried a thinner, sharper, wickeder skinning knife that he was never without.

"Improvise," yelled Tom as the Dragon launched into the air once more. "In a last resort, we've got our Dragon. That's weapon enough for me."

"You can bet on it!" chuckled Furbetrance. He beat his wings for altitude, but silently.

"It'd be useful if we managed to claim a captive of our own—an officer, if possible—who could tell us what this kidnapping was all about," Tom added, clinging to the Dragon's forward ears. "But Rosemary and her children come first!"

"Agreed!" said both his companions.

"WHERE are my menfolk and my Dragon?" wondered Manda to Squiller. Mistress Squiller had disappeared into the innkeeper's quarters at the back of the inn to "run up" the new frocks and skirts.

"Well, I wasn't informed, you see," apologized the innkeeper, "but one of the potboys told me that the trapper left the taproom with three friends a while back. He watched them go. They met the young Librarian on the street outside and a moment later the Dragon joined them. They all flew off, he said, but he didn't see where."

"They've found Rosemary!" exclaimed the princess. "Why else would they leave so suddenly. And without me, damn it!"

She returned to her room, ate a light supper alone, and sat at her window, listening to the night sounds of the seaport.

I wish they'd taken me! she thought angrily. *But probably it's just as well. I'm not much at hand-to-hand fighting. Oh, Tom, be careful! You've less training in rough doings than even I!*

• • •

"I HAVE only one further question," called Furbetrance over the wind rush of his flight. "Where is Retruance? I scoured the area and saw no sign of him."

"It begins to look," said Tom, "that he never got as far as Clem's cabin."

"Woulda seen sign if a big Dragon had landed within a mile of my place," agreed Clem. "More later, friends! There's the Gantrell fleet."

The moon was as high as it would get that night and unless someone aboard one of the ships looked straight up, he would not notice the Dragon overhead, circling in declining loops toward the topmasts, still in eerie silence.

"Ahoy!" came a voice from the dark sea. "Ahoy the ship!"

"Who goes there?" shouted the officer of the deck. "Stand off, you drunken swabs! Clear away! Clear away, I tell you!"

"That's our diversion," whispered Clem. "Now, Dragon!"

In the open boat, Petros cupped his hands to bellow, "Hoy, I say! Permission to put alongside! We've a man here wants to board ye!"

"You think Freddie is with them?" someone on the ship's poop deck asked a shadow that appeared from the companionway. "He's not back yet."

"Damned little snot!" snarled the new arrival. "He took the gig ashore more than an hour since. But why would he come out in a waterman's skiff?"

"Knowing our Freddie," said the first with a sniff, "two drinks and he forgot the gig. Loves the booze too much and too often for my liking, does Freddie."

"Careful what you say," warned the other, the captain. "He's a bad reputation with that sword of his, the squeak!"

"Ahoy, ahoy!" someone in the open boat was yelling. "Permission . . ."

"Ho, the boat!" shouted the ship's commander. "Come up slow and lay off until I say to hook on. We've archers here with arrows nocked, waiting for a false move!"

"Coming on very slowly, Captain!" came Petros's voice over the dark water. Just then the moon chose to slip behind a bank of clouds, plunging the sea into ebony blackness.

"Get them archers up on deck," rasped the captain to his mate. "Keep 'em quiet! Something's not right, here."

FURBETRANCE slid ever so lightly into the smoother water in the lee of the ship's stern. He lifted his head level with the ornate gallery outside the great cabin windows but let the rest of his great body sink under the waves.

Clem leaped onto the narrow gallery outboard of the stern windows and found the nearest port standing partly open.

"*Hssst!*" he called to the Librarian. "Come on!"

The Librarian almost slipped on the scales of the Dragon's head but managed to get a grip on the rail, then hook his left foot. In the meantime, the trapper had swung the diamond-paned transom full open and stepped cautiously over the sill into the big cabin, his knife drawn. Tom quickly followed.

"No closer!" called the captain to the skiff. "Bring a light to see who they are."

"The lad is a bit the worse for grog," hailed Petros with a laugh. "Toss a rope down and ye can hoist him aboard like a sack."

He laughed again at his own joke and the officers on the deck swore luridly.

"Someone fetch a bull's-eye!" shouted the First Mate. A seaman scrambled down a hatch.

"Wait!" said the Captain. "I spy another boat out there, coming this way. Too dark to see . . ."

"Make 'em all wait 'til we sort this out," suggested the Mate.

"Good idea!" the Captain snarled. "Hoy, the boat. Stay where you are now!"

"THAT'S a ship's gig," Jamey whispered to his Daddy. "Man in the sheets and two at oars only."

"We'll take 'em," decided Clem's tall woodsman. " 'Tis the dandy hisself what ran from the Slate."

"Lie low until they come alongside," ordered Petros. "When I speak to them, jump!"

" 'Ware the boy-child's sword," said the short fur trapper.

"Not much he can do with a long knife in a short boat,

though," said Jamey in a hoarse whisper. "Quiet now, hearties!"

TOM went at once to the door of the saloon that stood open to the companionway leading to the open deck past several closed doors.

"One of these cabins, I'd guess," said Clem in a low voice. "They'd not put a lady in the chains, I think."

"You'd better be right about that," muttered Tom. He stole down the corridor and silently swung the outer door to, sliding bolts across to lock it securely from within. "Now!"

He rapped on the first door softly. A man's voice answered sleepily.

"Ye're called for on deck, sir," called Tom softly. He stepped to one side. In a moment the door banged opened and a tousled, half-dressed officer stood blinking in the stronger light in the hall.

"Hold there!" snarled Clem, pressing his skinning knife to the man's throat. "Just step quietly back inside, won't you?"

He pushed the man backward onto his bunk, forcing him to sit down, mouth agape.

In a few quick moves the trapper sheathed his knife, spun the man on his face and lashed his hands behind him with a strip of his own blanket. A moment later he had gagged his victim and bound his feet.

"No sound and ye'll survive the night," he growled in the captive's left ear.

He stepped back out of the tiny sleeping cabin and closed and bolted the door from the outside. Tom rapped on the next door but when there was no answer, he swung it open. Empty.

"Next!" whispered Clem. "No great rush. It'll take 'em ten minutes to bash down that outside door."

"I hope!" said Tom. He knocked on a third door. No answer. Empty! Then the fourth and last.

A woman's voice cried out in alarm and a child whimpered sleepily.

"Lady Rosemary!" Tom shouted aloud. He slid back the bolts and opened the door.

"Here's old Clem the fur trapper and friends, come to

rescue you, m'lady!" called Clem, showing himself in the doorway.

"Clem! Of all people!" exclaimed the woman. "Come on, children! We're escaping these vile men. Quickly and quietly, all!"

In a moment the four captives were in the saloon, dressed in their nightclothes and looking more than a bit frightened and confused. When they spotted Clem the children smiled tentatively.

"How do we get out of here?" asked Rosemary. "They'll be all over the deck if we go out!"

"Through the windows," urged Tom. "There's a Dragon you'll recognize outside, to fly us away!"

Rosemary had the quick wit of her father. She neither hesitated nor asked further questions.

"Take the boy," she told Tom. "Valery! Go through the window to the Dragon and find a place to sit and hold on. Come on, Molly," she added to the second little girl. "I'll help you climb over the coaming. There!"

Tom scooped up the smallest child and trotted after the mother.

"I'm Eddie. Who are you?" asked the boy, a lad of four or five years. "I don't know you, do I?"

"Not yet, you don't. I'm a servant of your grandfather," Tom told him. "Are you afraid?"

"I'm not afraid," said Eddie stoutly. "Who's the Dragon?"

"Furbetrance Constable," Tom told him. "Do you know Furbetrance?"

"He's my friend," said the boy, clinging to Tom's neck as the Librarian swung his legs over the rail. "Mama! I'll be a Dragon Companion now!"

"Yes, dear, so you shall. Hang on to this ear for dear life!"

Clem swung through the after-windows just as a great pounding began on the companionway door. Voices shouted angrily.

"Time to go ashore," said Clem. "Took 'em less than the ten minutes I figured," he added ruefully.

"All settled down?" asked the Dragon from beneath them. "Here we go! Up, up, and away, as we Dragons say!"

Several heads appeared at the poop rail above their heads,

bowmen drawing strings to their ears.

"Back!" cried the Dragon in a shrill, terrifying voice, accompanied by a jet of brilliant flame that lit the stern and the sea around them.

The archers fell back from the flame in fear. An officer screamed at them to return to the rail and shoot.

"Forget it," advised Furbetrance. He sent another, white-hot stream of fire at the cabin windows. Glass shattered and the casements exploded inward. Drapery and upholstery caught fire and black smoke began to pour through the broken lights, blinding the archers leaning over the poop rail, above.

Someone on deck shrilled in fear, "Fire! Fire!"

"They're away!" shouted Petros, watching as the flames rose from the stern of the Gantrell ship and began to lick at the tarred rigging and furled sails. "Time for us to haul off, too."

Their prisoner squirmed in the bottom, tied with his own velvet cloak, crying pitiably for mercy. Nobody paid him any attention. The two oarsmen from the Gantrell ship sat on their thwarts, looking shocked and helpless.

"Shove off there," Petros said roughly. "If you hurry you can make it back to your ship before she burns to the waterline with the rest of your mates."

"Hell with that!" cried one of the oarsmen. "We'll go ashore if you'll let us."

"Follow us, then," cried Jamey with a laugh of pure excitement. "Give way, Dad!"

The lighter, followed by the gig, spun about and headed swiftly for the dock at the end of Wall.

✴ 11 ✴
Unfinished Business

ROSEMARY'S return to Overhall was a gala occasion, reminding Tom of a Fourth of July in Iowa. The three towers were draped with bright bunting. The roofs were studded with dozens of flagpoles, each flying a different banner, pennant, streamer, or burgee.

The meadow before the castle was fresh-mowed and carpeted with spring flowers. Sconces usually holding smoky pine-knot torches were stuffed instead with daffodils, irises, jonquils, and trailing strands of dark green ivy. Tapestries that in winter warmed the halls within were hung from balcony to balcony to flap gaily in the breeze. Everything was scrubbed spotless and every vestige of Gugglerun's overflowing had been cleared away.

Even the swallows, doves, and wrens that nested under the castle's eaves flew excitedly about the towers, calling, cooing, and singing with pure joy.

Furbetrance Constable, with a fine sense of the dramatic, plunged out of the blue sky and swooped to a daring landing on the lea, putting his precious load of passengers down on the wide road to the foregate.

Both sides of the path were lined ten deep with Murdan's and Ffallmar's retainers, neighbors, crofters, farmers, foresters, freeholders, servants, pensioners, and men-at-arms, cheering and waving and calling out in welcome and happy relief.

When Tom and his group reached the foregate and had crossed the drawbridge over Gugglerun moat, they were showered from the battlements with flowers and gaily colored ribbons. The guards snapped to attention and the castle band played a fanfare.

Ffallmar rushed forward to gather his wife and children into his strong arms and Murdan hovered about the group, clucking like a great mother hen.

"My boy!" he shouted, clapping Tom on the back and hugging Manda tightly, "My princess girl! Well done! Well done!"

There were tears in his eyes and the smile on his face was wide enough to take in the whole world as he led them to the inner bailey, where tables loaded with all sorts of wonderful foods and drinks had been set under striped awnings.

"Everybody! No protocol! Dig in and eat and drink, for my only child has been restored to us! Ffallmar's goodwife and children are back in his arms, where they ought to be!" cried the Historian, quite full of himself.

Everyone seemed transported with joy. Except for two men, Tom noticed. Comptroller Plume hid a sour grimace behind an overflowing flagon of foaming ale and turned his back on the celebration.

Is that man just a crab by very nature? wondered Tom. *Nothing seems to please him!*

The other sour face was more to be expected. A rumpled and besmudged young man wearing a Standing Bear blazon upon his torn sleeve, Fredrick of Brevory, trailed the fur trapper, tethered to him by a long leather rope. Even he was greeted by the crowd as much with good nature as with jeers. When Clem loosed his tether, someone handed Freddie a jack of ale and he drank of it deeply.

"Eat, drink, and be merry, for my family is safe and sound!" shouted the Historian. "Princess, come sit by my right hand. Librarian, you've earned my undying gratitude! Furbetrance Constable, eat me out of castle and home, if you want. You and your family are ever welcome at the Overhall table!"

"I hope you don't regret that," muttered Furbetrance, burying his nose in a huge vat of savory beef, onion, and tomato, highly spiced salmagundi the way Dragons best like it. "We Dragons eat sparingly most days, but not at parties."

"Since when have Dragons eaten lightly of anything, anywhere?" scoffed Murdan.

"I worry about my brother," continued Furbetrance. "Our family has a penchant for disappearing, perhaps. I wonder where Retruance could have gone?"

"We'll tackle that problem, soon, I promise you," said Tom. "He's my Mount and I'm his Companion. We're a team when we're together and lost when apart."

"Retruance has sworn fealty to me personally," said Murdan soberly. "Think not that I'm indifferent to his fate. Yes, tomorrow morning we'll take up his case and set out to find him, trust in me!"

The crowd cheered lustily. Lady Rosemary and Lord Ffallmar, her husky, handsome husband, stood to drink their healths in gratitude. The party looked to go on for hours and hours, but nobody much minded.

SOME hours later Tom, unable to keep up with the Carolnans in dining and drinking, looked about for Furbetrance and found him seated beside the Gugglerun cistern in the upper court, happily blowing red and yellow smoke rings to amuse a giggling gaggle of castle children, including little Eduard of Ffallmar and his sisters.

"Where's our dandy?" Tom asked.

"We got so tired of his dour, sour, whining face that Murdan stuck him in the tip-top cell under Aftertower's roof," replied the Dragon. "Come on, children, catch that one! Ho, Eddie! That's the boy!"

Tom watched the fun for a while, then went to rescue Manda, who was seated still at table, toying with a confection of whipped cream and minted custard, looking bravely interested in a long and flowery speech by a slightly tipsy cottager.

"Let's go up and sit on the battlements," she whispered when she saw Tom. "I need a little peace and quiet and a hug or two. We've had little time to ourselves lately."

They climbed the narrow stone stairs to the top of the wall and perched on an out-of-the-way cornice, watching an evening rainstorm sweep across Overhall valley in the far distance, holding hands and speaking little.

"We must go find Retruance," she said at last.

"I must, yes. Will Murdan allow you to go, also?"

"He'll want me out of the way, or at least out of sight," Manda said, smoothing her skirt about her knees as a cool, rain-scented breeze puffed about them. "It'll be no problem getting his permission. Uncle Peter is coming to Overhall, you know."

Tom nodded.

"Yes, I remember. He wants you, Manda. You're his ticket to power over your father and . . ."

"It's the 'and' that worries me most," the princess confided with a shiver. "He believes if he holds me, he'll gain the kingdom. He'll try to marry me to one of his nephews, or someone like that nasty little Freddie of Brevory, and force Session to have him made co-equal sovereign with me."

"He'll try, certainly. Many powerful men will oppose him in that."

"Including you," she said with a sudden grin.

"I . . . I don't consider myself powerful," Tom objected.

"On the contrary! Tom, you don't realize your own power. First of all, I love you, and that can't be ignored. Secondly, you're human, which makes you an unknown quality in this broth of politics."

"Say 'unknown ingredient,' rather," prompted the Librarian.

"You know what I mean!" she cried.

"Not really. I really don't know. Why should I be an 'unknown power'? I certainly don't feel powerful."

"Uncle Murdan should explain it to you. Maybe I can make you understand a little."

She gazed thoughtfully at the curtain of rain across the valley.

"Tom, ours is a world in which magic, sorcery, wizardry, witchcraft, spells, and enchantment are commonplace. Only a few of us, like Murdan, comprehend a different scheme of things, in which great deeds are done and difficult tasks accomplished *without* the use of magic."

"Well, I guess I see . . . ," Tom said hesitantly.

"Take Overhall, for example," she went on. "You know very well it was built by a Dragon. You must know that Altruance, bless his fiery soul, designed and built it in a few short years with the help of some great magicians. Some used their powers to quarry, hew, and fit these very stones. Others levitated heavy beams and great vats of mortar as high as the tallest tower top."

"The point is, they were all skilled craftsmen in their fields. They had studied long and hard to learn how to do things like change the course of underground Gugglerun to flow into the castle and through the moat, there."

"Hmmm!" murmured Tom. "If that was so, why didn't Murdan simply hire one of them to cut off Gugglerun, when the Mercenary Knights . . . ?"

"You must see! Not every wizard can do such magic. And they all take time. Murdan would have had to send far off for a wizard powerful enough to change the flow of Gugglerun, set by strong magic in the first place. Unlike many elf folk, Murdan hoped to retake the castle by strength of arms, to save time and expense. Others would have thrown up their hands in despair.

"Why, though? Despite the cost . . ."

"If he had, Uncle Peter, who is many times richer than Murdan, would have just brought up his own specialists, fought magic with magic. There would have followed an expensive series of stalemates, you see, at best."

"You're saying that nobody would have thought of plugging the outlet and forcing Gugglerun to back up inside the castle?"

"What seemed to you a simple and logical solution to the problem might not have occurred even to Murdan for months! Remember, too, that Uncle Peter isn't really interested in Overhall. He wants to gain control of your sweet little princess and to destroy Murdan's power to assist the king."

"Without his keep, Murdan would be less powerful, I suppose."

"Without his keep, his people, and the wealth within his castle, too," Manda said with a nod. "And at a great loss of time! Time is the most precious coinage of all, my dear. Murdan could have grown old in the attempt. I would have *had* to marry someone *suitable*—or risk not having a royal heir. If Queen Beatrix failed to produce an heir in time, and if Peter Gantrell held me in thrall . . . well, you can see time would be on Gantrell's side."

"But, my dear, what did *I* do to change all that?"

"Peter never expected Murdan to use a human—your powers, reason, common sense, I guess—to solve the conflict. It just didn't occur to him!"

"It seems sort of farfetched. I can't believe no one would have said, 'Forget magic! Let's do something direct and simple!' "

"Well, turn it around, can't you? If you had built Overhall, would you have said, 'Forget stonemasons, forget carpenters! Let's try magic'?"

"Well, uh, I see what you mean. . . ."

"It wouldn't have occurred to you to hire a magician to lift stones to the top of a wall like this one. You'd have hired . . . whatever it takes to do it in your world."

Tom leaned against the cool stone and thought about her words for a while. The rainstorm passed majestically down the middle of the valley but no rain fell on the castle itself. Had someone woven a simple spell to keep the rain away for the gala celebration? *Rain, rain, go away! Come again some other day.*

"It does explain some things I've wondered about," he said at last. "For example, why didn't Murdan recover Rosemary by magic?"

"But, you see, that's what Uncle Peter *expected* him to do. Then he could block any efforts to rescue Rosemary using his own mages. As it happened, you were on hand to act in your un-elfish way."

"I see. That's why the kidnappers never bothered to cover their tracks."

"Exactly, beloved! We were amazed by your methods. Getting Clem to go with us and read the signs seemed a stroke of genius. Still does!"

She threw her arms about him and kissed him soundly.

"Thank goodness love isn't different here," said Tom. He kissed her back and they clung together, breathless for a long, lovely moment.

"What's to become of us?" he wondered, pulling back to look into her wide, bright eyes.

"Well, I had a talk with Rosemary about us while we stopped at Ramhold. You thought we were playing with the babies."

She slid backward and hopped to the battlement pavement. Tom followed her down the stair to the crowded courtyard. Everyone was still having a marvelous time, singing old Carolnan wassail songs at the top of their voices and in several different keys.

"She said what?" prompted the librarian under cover of the noise.

"I said, I supposed in the end I would have to do what was best for Carolna, if I became queen. She laughed and told me, 'The secret is, do what is best for you and it will be best for the country. If you're happy, the kingdom will be happy for and with you.'

"She told me her father had balked at her wishing to marry Ffallmar, when they first met and fell in love. Raised all sorts of Ned, he did! Threatened to shut her up in a tower, even."

"Sounds like my hot-tempered Historian, all right!" laughed Tom. "Lots of bluster and noise. But . . . ?"

"In the end he came to his senses and realized that he couldn't be happy if Rosemary wasn't happy. As simple as that, yet something Uncle Peter will never understand. Although it helped that Ffallmar is such a good-looking, hardworking, devoted, loyal sort."

The discussion stopped there, but they returned to it many times in the coming weeks.

"WE'VE happily recovered my daughter and my grandchildren," began Murdan the next morning. "Gantrell sought to hold them hostage against my support of King Eduard, we know. Brevory has admitted as much."

"We have this Fredrick of Brevory to hand," commented Furbetrance. "He will confirm our suspicions?"

"Before witnesses," replied the Historian. "Guard! Bring in the prisoner."

Fredrick of Brevory was still a sorry sight, not because he was worn or torn, but because he wore a sullen hang-head look and a sneer. His gorgeous clothes had been cleaned, mended, and pressed, yet they had a tawdry, secondhand look in the morning light streaming through Murdan's study windows.

He tried to strut before them but spoiled the effect by cringing fearfully when Murdan leaned forward in his chair to see him better. And he kept casting fearful sideways glances at the Dragon in the window.

"You . . . you can't hold me long!" he shrilled. "I'm a man of—"

"Peter of Gantrell?" asked the Historian.

"Gantrell will ransom me, and right soon," screeched the dandy without thinking how he gave his lord away. "He values my services too highly to—"

"I should think so!" cried Manda. "Who else would he find so base as to kidnap a helpless woman and three small children?"

"I but carried out his orders. If there is blame, it is Lord Gantrell's."

"No excuse!" Tom told him indignantly. "Wicked leaders have ever claimed their underlings misunderstood or acted without orders. And underlings have ever said they but did as ordered by their superiors."

"True!" said Murdan. "And both are revealed as being without honor."

"I will repeat your words to Lord Peter when I next see him," sneered Fredrick. "We will bring down vengeance on you and your house, Murdan!"

"I would expect naught else," chuckled the Historian, "from such as you . . . and he."

He ruffled a thin sheaf of papers before him.

"To business! It is my intention to forgo the usual ransom on such a wine-cellar rat as you, Brevory. The profit would hardly justify the bother. No, it is my intention to bring you before Fall Session in October. Let the king hear and judge your part in this, and Peter Gantrell's, too."

"You are *duty bound* to ask my liege for a worthy ransom!" yelled Fredrick. "It's the law!"

"Hardly," Murdan demurred. "It's *customary* only in cases between gentlemen in *honorable* warfare, I remind you. You were apprehended in the commission of serious and venal felony. It's my will as well as my duty that you be brought to trial for kidnapping Rosemary of Fallmar and her children."

The prisoner began to snivel piteously but his accusers showed no clemency. He tried another tactic.

"What can I do to indemnify my crime?" he whined, holding out clenched hands. "I'll do anything!"

"All you can do is wait and see," Murdan told him. "I will carry your poor carcass to Lexor for trial. Don't think of rescue. I'd welcome open battle with your liege."

"There must be some way I can mitigate your anger.

Slake your thirst for revenge. It's not me you seek to confound. It's Peter of Gantrell, isn't it? Let me pay for your clemency with information and cooperation!"

"Your sort I do loathe," said Murdan, glowering darkly. "Criers! Beggars for mercy! Snivelers! Cowards! You've nothing we need so much as to accept in payment for what you've done. We know who you acted for and why. Just because you were a tool won't lessen your just punishment, when it comes."

He angrily laid his right hand upon the hilt of his broadsword, which lay between them on the table, but drew it back.

"In the meantime, you'll be treated well but kept in a tower top with only a few bats and a jailer to tell your troubles to."

He waved to the guards to take the prisoner away. Fredrick of Brevory was dragged off, shouting hoarsely now of dire vengeance until they could hear him no more.

"I don't think we got much out of that exchange," observed Tom into the following silence.

"On the contrary," replied Murdan with a satisfied look. "We all heard him admit his orders came direct from Peter. I'll expect you to testify to that before the King. Now," Murdan continued with a wry shake of his head, "let us take up more pressing matters. There are two."

"My brother?" the Dragon asked.

Declared Murdan, "We must move at once to find and assist him."

"As Retruance's Companion, I claim that task," said Tom firmly. "I'll leave at once, accompanied by my friend Furbetrance."

"Not without me!" exclaimed Manda.

"Well, now, my dear princess . . . ," began Murdan.

"You don't want me here when Uncle Peter comes to claim me," said Manda. "I have no wish to put either of us in such jeopardy. Gantrell is legally my guardian by royal decree. To withhold me from him will appear, to those who don't know the full story, an act of treason."

"Of course, you're right," sighed the Historian. "It would weaken our case when we place it before Session, if Lord Peter had demanded you and I refused. 'Twere better if

I could truthfully say you had fled. You are, after all, a Princess Royal. Even I cannot hold you against your will."

"It's settled then," said Furbetrance, cutting off more debate. "We'll leave this afternoon."

"But where will you look for Retruance?" wondered the Historian.

"Best that you don't know," said Princess Royal Alix Amanda.

"What of Master Tom's status as your Librarian?" asked Captain Graham, who had listened until then in silence.

"He's a Dragon Companion. His first duty ever is to his Dragon, of course, regardless of other allegiances," Manda pointed out. She knew her law.

"He's not my liege man, anyway, although I intended to ask him to become so, soon," Murdan said thoughtfully. "He's only my contracted employee. As such, I cannot be held responsible for his actions, if Peter Gantrell seeks to use Tom's actions against me."

"Even Gantrell has to admit that a Companion is primarily responsible to his partner," said Furbetrance. "It's one of the most ancient provisions of our law!"

"I was referring rather to him carrying off a Princess Royal," responded Murdan, impatient now. "Peter will try to make it out that I ordered Manda's removal."

"Let him!" cried Manda. "I can testify for myself if it comes to that. The main thing is not to weaken *your* position, Uncle, on behalf of the king and before the law."

"I could take the obvious path and release you from my employ," Murdan said directly to Tom, "but I disdain to take that cowardly route. You go to find your Dragon with my blessings. If the princess chooses to accompany you, for her own ends, I can't stop her going anywhere she pleases. Only her father can attempt to do that."

"Good luck to him in that!" Manda exclaimed. "He would urge me to go."

"So be it!" declared Murdan, striking the hilt of his battered old sword with his clenched fists. "When Gantrell arrives, I'll be as innocent as spring flowers but tough as rawhide, too! I mean to take him to task about the Mercenary Knights, although I can't prove that he hired them, when you get right down to it. With any luck, I can keep him unbalanced long enough to slow him down a bit. That's my role."

"And while you play it, we'll seek my dear brother," said Furbetrance with a nod.

"Do you have any idea where to begin?" Tom asked Furbetrance Constable as he folded a few items of clothing and toiletry into his rucksack. Manda had gone up the stair to her own apartment to do the same.

"You're in charge of the smart thinking," said the Dragon. "I can't think of a thing. Murdan says asking even the best doom caster would be futile if Retruance is being held by minions of Gantrell. Even if not, it would take weeks, probably, and no guarantee of results, even then."

"We last saw him flying north by west from these very walls," said the Librarian. "We'll do the same ourselves, as soon as my lady runaway completes her packing. Any tips on finding Dragons when you want them?"

"Ah! Well, as to that, a Companion can usually make himself heard."

"A way Retruance didn't tell me about?"

"Dragon calling is a secret between mount and rider, and I've never had one. I guess Retruance didn't have time to instruct you. Too bad!"

"Anyone else we could ask?"

"Let's see! It's a tough question you ask. Arcolas is the one to tell you."

"I don't want to involve Murdan's people any more than I have," decided Tom. "The less they know of our going, the better for Manda."

"My name is being bandied about," said Manda, coming down the stair followed by her attendant, pretty Mornie. "What's the need?"

"We need to get going," said the Dragon. He prepared to take the ladies aboard his head while Tom swung open the heavy flight doors. The day beyond was warm and still. The sky was dotted beautifully with puffy balls of cloud in neat rows, moving on upper-air winds from west to east in precise ranks.

"Here's a tracking expert," said Manda. The fur trapper Clem had arrived, easily carrying his own pack.

"If you can't use me further," he said, apologetically, "can I beg a ride home? If you're going that way, that is."

"Pay for your passage by telling us where we could ask about sighting a Dragon," said Tom, making room for the trapper.

"Now we're ready at last!" cried Furbetrance, and he flung himself and his four passengers through the door into the air above the castle.

He went so suddenly and so fast, no one saw them depart.

✴ 12 ✴
The Crossbeak Migration

"I KNOW that Dragons can talk," Tom said to anyone who would listen. "But can birds?"

"They can, among themselves," said Manda. "Dragons can speak their song-language."

"I learned it at my mother's knees," said Furbetrance. "Well, actually Retruance is much better than I am. I can make myself understood, however."

"Wizards learn the language, but it's very difficult, they tell me," continued Manda.

"Nonsense, ma'am!" scoffed Clem. "Begging your pardon, too. I can bespeak most birds and I taught myself to do it. Birds are generally pretty flighty. The problem is to get one to sit still long enough to start a conversation."

"Which kind of bird might have seen the flying Retruance?" asked Tom.

"Any flocking bird," Clem replied. "They usually travel further afield than solitary pairs. They all migrate north or south, of course, depending on the season."

As they were talking, a flock of crows rose from a plowed field ahead of them and Furbetrance accelerated quickly to catch up with them before they could scatter.

"Crowtalk is easier than most," observed Clem. "We're lucky to find a flock this soon."

The lead crow was a huge specimen with striking white markings on her shoulders and under her tail. Otherwise she was coal black, except for her bright yellow beak. She and her flock of fifty eyed the Dragon cautiously, but didn't seem particularly frightened of him.

"We seek information," the Dragon called to them. "Will you stay and talk to us?"

"I'm not afraid of you, Dragon," the lead crow cawed raucously. "Come ahead!"

The Dragon drew even with the flight and bobbed his head carefully in greeting. His passengers clung to his harness and ears with both hands and saluted the lead crow with polite nods.

"On my head are, in order of preference," began Furbetrance, "the Princess Royal Alix Amanda . . ."

"I'm honored, Princess," said the lead crow, impressed despite herself.

"I'm truly charmed to meet you, also," replied Manda, when Clem had quickly translated the crow's words for her.

"I beg your pardon, however. I should be more polite," said the crow in Common Tongue. "I should bespeak you in your own language, as you don't know ours."

"I would love to learn Crow," said Manda, sincerely. "A princess and a queen-perhaps-to-be should know as many of her subjects' languages as she can, out of respect to them."

"I would be honored if you would allow me to give you some lessons in Crow," responded the bird.

"Wonderful!" cried Manda. "As soon as our current quest is fulfilled, come to Overhall and ask for me. We'll begin lessons at once."

Furbetrance introduced Mornie and the two young men to the lead crow and they exchanged polite amenities. The crow, whose name was White Shoulders, seemed unimpressed with a Librarian—she couldn't read, as it turned out—but she knew of the breed of men who trapped fur animals. She approved of what they did for a living.

"Nasty beasts, the ermines, the stoats, the weasels, the minx. Steal eggs at the drop of a feather!" White Shoulders shuttered in revulsion. "It's splendidly ironic that they should end their days keeping some lady warm, come cold weather."

Furbetrance tactfully waited until they all felt comfortable with each other before he broached the subject of the missing Dragon. The relatively short-ranging crows settled down in an oak copse standing by itself in the middle of miles of greening pastures, and the Dragon discharged his passengers nearby.

"We seek my noble brother, Retruance Constable," he began.

"Oh, yes, I know Retruance Constable quite well!" cried White Shoulders. "He flew this way quite often and often stopped to chat."

"Can you tell us of his whereabouts, now?" asked Tom impulsively. "He's been missing for weeks and we fear he has fallen into trouble of some sort, Lady White Shoulders."

White Shoulders cocked her head to the left and squinted at the man with dawning understanding.

"Ah, now I see! You're the new Dragon Companion! Your Dragon friend here did you an injustice by not using your title."

"I am so very sorry," apologized Furbetrance. "It slipped my mind, entirely."

"No harm, though," continued the crow. "It's a very great honor to meet a Companion. Retruance Constable told me of you, when last he passed this way. Said to assist you if I were asked."

"He talked to you since he and I met?" asked Tom. "Then you've seen him since we last did."

They explained the entire matter of the missing Dragon to the crows, all of whom perched on limbs of the oaks and listened in uncharacteristic silence.

"Of course, Retruance Constable told me of the Lady Rosemary. I told him I had seen her fleeing from Overhall, but not seen her return. That's all I could offer him at that time."

Manda told of how the Librarian, the woodsman, and the Dragon had rescued the Historian's daughter.

At the end of the story White Shoulders sat on a branch near Furbetrance's head and considered matters quietly and seriously.

"No, I neither saw nor heard of Retruance Constable after his brief stop here," she said sadly. "Migrant birds might have seen him, but they're all in the Far North by now, or close to it."

"Can you think of anyone, bird, beast, or man, who might have heard word of the Dragon?" asked Clem. "For example, some rodents pass news over considerable distance through their connecting burrows."

"Unfortunately," said White Shoulders, shaking her black head, "we are not on the best of terms with *rodents*."

She shook her head again, more slowly. "No, I just can't think of anyone . . ."

A much smaller crow flew to White Shoulders's branch. They conferred in quiet Crow before the smaller bird flew away, shyly.

"My little friend there," said White Shoulders, "has just given me an idea worth exploring, I think. As you know, birds either stay put all year 'round, like we crows, and the owls, or migrate north in summer and south in winter."

"We're aware of that," said Furbetrance.

"But my young friend reminds me that a certain breed of birds migrate east in summer and west in winter! The crossbeaks! They got into the habit centuries ago, my mother once told me, because they are so at cross purposes with each other and with other birds too."

"I've heard of the breed," said Clem, "but not of crosswise migration."

"They do it at the same time as the north-south movements, so nobody notices them moving *across* the current, as it were," the lead crow told him, chuckling. "But 'tis true!"

"Where are they now, then? Let's see, they go east in summer?" asked Furbetrance.

"Yes. They have been passing through our north-going brethren for some weeks now," said White Shoulders. "If you will wait for an hour or so, I will send scouts out to see if any are in the area."

Although it was early evening, the travelers pitched their tents in the grove for the night. The crows showed Tom a tiny spring among a jumbled heap of stone nearby and Mornie and Manda gathered dry, dead oak twigs for a cheery evening fire where Clem prepared their meal.

White Shoulders's flock settled in the trees above as twilight arrived, but no word came from the scouts. White

Shoulders joined them briefly for a supper of bread and cold meat before she went off to check her sentries for the night.

"Go to sleep, friends," she suggested. "There will be word by morning, I'm sure."

The five of them—the young people sitting about the dying fire, the Dragon curled protectively around them, fire and all—sat awhile, talking of this and that, mostly of the comparison between castle life and life in the wilderness.

"Not that I say this is true wilderness," clucked the trapper. "There is water and food here, easily to hand, if you know how to find it. I've been in places where even air was hard to find!"

Manda and Mornie crawled into their tent, saying good night to the men. Tom and Clem decided to sleep in the open, as the summer's night was mild and dry, and soon they were sound asleep, too, leaving the Dragon and the crow sentries to watch over them.

The great beast seemed to sleep also, but the crows who, out of curiosity, came close to examine the strangers noted a tiny glint of red fire showing in the Dragon's slitted eyes. The very arrow tip of his tail swung back and forth slightly every once in a while, like that of a puppy in its sleep.

"THIS is a crossbeak," White Shoulders said, introducing them to a medium-sized gray bird whose bill crossed itself strangely, giving the bird an unhappy, contentious look. "He's agreed to help you."

"For a *price,*" insisted the new bird, tartly.

"What price?" said Furbetrance, raising his eyebrows in surprise.

"I and my people will help you in return for undisputed rights to all the kingdom's mosquitoes and flying beetles. That's our proposal. Take it or leave it!"

"I don't see how we can give any one kind of bird unlimited rights like that," objected Manda heatedly. "All birds have rights, you should know!"

White Shoulders perched on Manda's shoulder and whispered in her ear.

"Oh, very well, in that case," said Manda to the crossbeak. "As Princess Royal I agree to your demands—providing that what you have to tell us is of assistance in our quest."

"Fair enough, Princess," said the crossbeak. "Ask me what you will."

They explained their interest in the movements of the missing Dragon, and when they had finished the gray bird sat in deep thought for a long while. Furbetrance cleared his throat with a burst of blue smoke, fearing the bird had fallen asleep.

"Yes!" cried the crossbeak with a start.

"Yes, what?" demanded his listeners.

"I've heard word of the Dragon flying west some days ago," the bird told them. "I didn't see him myself, mind you, but word of him passed up the line."

"There's nothing more you can tell us?" asked Tom.

"I'll have to check with my flockmates," snapped the crossbeak irritably. "It'll mean flying far ahead. Those who actually saw the Dragon have already passed this point."

"How long will that take?" asked Manda. "We're in a hurry, in case harm has befallen the good Dragon."

"Less than a day," the bird assured her. "Check with my people tomorrow morning. They'll know if I found anything for you."

THE crossbeak fluttered off eastward more quickly than his kind usually flew.

"What changed your mind about the mosquitoes and beetles?" Tom asked Manda over breakfast.

"White Shoulders said it was a meaningless concession. The crossbeaks just want to brag about it, she said. Crossbeaks eat mostly nuts and seeds! She saw no harm in the concession."

"Well, we'll have to wait for the crossbeaks to report, then," sighed Furbetrance.

"I think we should proceed to Ramhold, anyway," said Tom. "From what this crossbeak said, their news will reach us no matter where we are tomorrow morning. We know Retruance flew that way. We'll be getting closer by traveling ourselves in that direction."

"I agree," said Furbetrance, and the others had no objections.

Twenty minutes later they said good-bye and thank you to the lead crow, reminding her to come to Overhall for a feast and language lessons.

"No thanks necessary," said the crow waving a wing negligently. "Fare you well, friends!"

"We should reach Murdan's Ramhold in an hour or two at most," the Dragon said. "If that's where you think we should go now."

"Ramhold it is!" cried Manda. "Besides, Talber may have some word, too, of our missing Dragon."

BUT Talber wasn't at the sheep station when they arrived, although his people made the travelers welcome and comfortable.

"The herds are on their way up into the mountains," said the Factor's aide, in charge while the Factor was away. "We're just finishing shearing. If you'll excuse me, I must return to that work."

"Of course," answered Manda. "We'll watch, if we may."

They spent the afternoon—after a big farm lunch—in the open-sided sheds watching the shearers clip the ewes and rams, relieving them of the thick wool of winter and making it more comfortable for them to bear the heat of summer.

The following morning just before dawn a crossbeak flew in at Tom's window and awakened him with the loud, rasping call of his kind.

"Wake up, sirrah! I've news from the crossbeak flock for you and your princess."

"Come with me, then," Tom told him. He pulled on his trousers and marched across the hall to knock on Manda's door. She was already awake and, sitting on a bench beside the window, was combing her hair before plaiting it.

"The Dragon was last seen flying high on the south-facing slopes of Snow Mountains," recited the bird, perching on the top of the mirror before Manda. "He was a day and a half of moderate flight beyond Summer Pass road where it begins to climb."

"How far is that in miles?" asked Tom.

"I have no idea. I don't think in terms of miles," snapped the crossbeak.

"Probably Clem can tell us pretty well," said Tom. "Go on, good bird!"

"The wings of the great flock that came through that area two weeks ago say that they saw no sign of the Dragon. If he had continued westward, he would have been seen by them."

"So, Retruance flew at least as far as that, and either landed or turned south or north?"

"You've understood, Princess. If he had turned east or continued west, we would have had report of him, but he drops from sight after our sighting."

"Well, good!" said Manda. Turning to Tom, she said, "We're beginning to narrow it down."

They thanked the bird, offering it breakfast with the shepherds, but it refused indignantly, saying it preferred grass seed to table crumbs, and flew off to rejoin its flock.

"No one knows the south slopes better'n Talber," said the Factor's assistant over breakfast. "You ought to go to him, first, and let him tell you what to expect to the west. I hear it's bad country."

"A good idea," said Tom with an emphatic nod. "It's not out of the way, and could save us much time searching."

"I don't say Master Talber knows everything about the area," warned the assistant Factor. "It's terribly wild for the most part. And vast! You could hide whole cities in a fold or a canyon there, or a half dozen Dragons."

ROCKY hillsides were awash with fresh white new-shorn sheep for as far as the eye cold see. Furbetrance circled quietly for several minutes before he spotted the small group of shepherds and their dogs following the vast flock.

As they came in to land, the shepherds waved in greeting, and the sheep pretended to be terrified and started to bolt.

The four sheepdogs were off with hardly a signal needed, to head off the stampede before it could get started.

"Sorry to be such a nuisance!" called Tom.

"Not a problem at all," Talber said, grinning, pleased to see them again and hear their news. "The dogs know what to do. The sheep are merely having springtime friskies."

When they had shared morning tea with the herdsmen, the rescuers told what the crossbeaks had said of Retruance.

"That land is certainly among the most desolate in the kingdom or anywhere, for that matter," Talber said. "In the old days outlaws fled there to hide. It's still called Hiding Lands. Come to think of it, Gantrells are not unknown there."

"How do you mean?" asked Manda, looking up quickly.

"The sire of the present Gantrells, old Owen Gantrell himself, led the troops that chased down the outlaws, fifty years since. It brought him much favor with Eduard Nine, and made his family's fortune."

"And set us up for trouble in this generation," said Manda, making a wry face. "Which is unfair of me, for most Gantrells are decent folk. It's just my overambitious Uncle Peter . . ."

"So you think Gantrell might have knowledge of these Hiding Lands?" asked Furbetrance. The herder nodded in reply.

"I wonder, then," said Manda, "why Freddie of Brevory didn't carry Lady Rosemary there, after he captured her in Summer Pass?"

"Several reasons occur to me," replied Talber. "For one, Summer Pass is much closer north than Hiding Lands is west. It would have meant carrying m'lady Rosemary overland almost twice as far as taking her to Wall, you see."

"Also," put in the Dragon, "from what little I know and what the crossbeaks and others tell me, Hiding Lands is no place to take a lady you want to save as hostage."

"Do you want to guess what I think?" said Clem, smacking a fist into his palm. "I think our Retruance reached the top of Summer Pass, found the signs we saw there, and, knowing the Gantrells had knowledge of Hiding Lands, gambled that Brevory would take Rosemary there, instead of Wall."

Said Tom, "I don't see friend Freddie as a desert rat."

"Ha!" Manda gave an unladylike snort. "Anything dry would be anathema to Freddie the Sponge!"

"No more help you can give us on landmarks and so on?" Clem asked. "I've heard tales, but few men of the north ever see the south slopes. What would be the use?"

"There's said to be gold and silver, even diamond mines there. Men go into the lands regularly, looking for them. They seldom come out," said Talber, ominously.

"Let's not forget we're looking for a Dragon, not a man," said Tom. "I for one can't imagine any desert dangers that would phase Retruance, or prevent him from coming home to Overhall—or sending word, at least."

Furbetrance sniffed. "Yet the fact remains, he went in, and didn't come out."

"Magic, then?" asked Tom.

"Magic, perhaps!" answered Furbetrance Constable.

THEY talked to the veteran sheepherders, hoping that one of them would have an idea where Retruance might have alighted in Hiding Lands.

"My pappy went that way once, as a youngster," said the oldest of the herders. He blew a cloud of rank tobacco smoke from his stubby clay pipe before he went on.

"Told us it were desolation doubled and tripled! Leagues and leagues with nary a drop of water and not a living animal nor plant. The mountains shade the land from the rains from the sea, he said. It rains there maybe one day in five, six years! When it does, the hills melt away like sugarloafs and slip down into the canyons. Dangerous place, said he, and I believed him so well I never went there myself."

Asked Tom of the old-timer, "What could the Dragon have seen and where was he headed, can you guess?"

"Pappy said there were a few, tiny water holes in deep canyons where water was to be had and a few trees and some grass could grow. Seems to me one of these must be the place the Dragon was headed, if his quarry were men. After all, men need water, even if a Dragon don't."

"Look for spots of green deep in cracks in the land," said Furbetrance. "That sounds like a sensible way to proceed."

"In a spot of green, ye might find your Dragon or some trace of the passing of his quarry," the veteran agreed. They thanked him and prepared to go their way again, heeding the factor's advice to carry extra bottles of water.

Tom and Manda approached Clem then, saying, "We can put you over the mountain at your house in the woods, Clem, if you want to go home. This is not your work to do, if you don't want to. We'll understand."

The trapper drew himself up proudly.

"I'm committed to serve and help Master Tom and you, m'lady! And to help you and this fair lass." He gestured to a suddenly blushing Mornie. "Face the terrible desert without my being there to ease the ordeal? No, thank you muchly, ma'am and sir! Order me away, if you wish, but unless you do, I signed on for the full portage."

"We had to offer," said Tom, pounding the trapper on the shoulder in his delight. "We could think of no better, braver companion, old man!"

"Oh, we would be quite lost without you, Clematis!" cried Manda, and Mornie kissed him on his cheek.

"You may become lost even *with* me, ladies," he protested. "But I'll feel much better about myself knowing I'm along to help you."

"If you people are finished being mawkish," sniffed the Dragon, "I would like to get under way. We have less than six hours of daylight before we must stop for the night out there on the desert."

"Do Dragons cry, I wonder?" Manda asked nobody in particular as they shot aloft in the warm, dry afternoon sky.

"I haven't the faintest idea," replied Tom. "But it wouldn't surprise me a bit. They are like Murdan, in a way. They like to appear tough and self-reliant, but underneath they're softhearted and kind and extremely sensitive."

"*Huh!*" snorted Furbetrance. "*Hah!* Your experience is limited to two Dragons reared by the same Dame, my gentle mother. Wait 'til you meet a really tough, bad-tempered, terrible, man-hating Dragon with chronic dyspepsia and sharp clinkers in his gut!"

"I can wait for that," said Manda with a laugh. "Oh, look, that must be the beginning of the Hiding Lands. How desolate it is!"

✦ 13 ✦
Search for a Dragon

THE summer after his college graduation Tom had traveled in an ancient truck all over America's Far West, from Texas and the Gulf Coast to Montana's Big Sky country, from Pike's Peak to the Golden Gate.

He was enthralled by the dry, high desert. At the very bottom of Death Valley, almost three hundred feet below sea level, he'd stood alone on a dune and turned completely around. He saw not a single living being, animal or plant! Not even an insect in the sand or a bird in the sky.

He never decided if he loved the desert—or hated it.

As Furbetrance bucked in the first hot updrafts over Hiding Lands, the memories returned to him. This land, too, was flat as a pancake—a uniform yellow-tan pancake. No trees, little shrubbery or even dried weeds. No creature stirred anywhere within the fifty-mile circle of horizon.

In a way, this place made Death Valley seem almost hospitable. Death Valley at least had a road and motorcycle tracks to show that men had once been there.

"Yet, it has a beauty," he said quietly to Manda. She was staring at the desert over the Dragon's nose. "The colors are subtle. The stillness is overwhelming."

"I prefer greenery with noisy people," the princess answered shortly. "How can you say it's beautiful?"

"I prefer forests with lakes myself," said Clem to Mornie.

"So do I, really," answered the maid. "But I can see how Master Tom thinks it is . . . well, starkly attractive here."

"If you were down there, afoot and without water," observed Furbetrance glumly, "you'd soon learn to loathe it. And I say that when it's much more to a Dragon's liking than many places I've been. I was brought up on such a desert."

"It really lacks only a little rain to be a garden," said Tom, dreamily. "I've seen whole great valleys abloom where men brought water to the American desert."

"I won't say I hate it," said Manda, reasonably, "nor that I cannot see why it might attract you, my love, but I do say I wouldn't like to live here."

"Even if I built you a green garden and a blue lake to reflect the stark mountain peaks?" teased Tom.

"Well, I suppose even this desert could be made livable, if one had the means and time."

"It's the challenge," replied Tom, "to make it livable and yet not spoil its setting."

They flew straight into the heart of Hiding Lands until the Dragon judged they had come to where the crossbeaks had seen the Dragon. Then he angled north toward the Snow Mountains. Through air void of all moisture, Snow

Mountains appeared sharp and clear, as though modeled in blue clay on a tan tabletop.

For hours the Dragon flew straight toward them without seeming to get any closer.

"Distances are hard to estimate in this clear air," Furbetrance worried aloud. "I wonder if the birds were able to judge accurately?"

"Well, but their words are all we have to go on," Manda pointed out.

"Ah, well, yes," sighed Furbetrance. "I intend to go only a little farther. I can stand the dry and the heat below but you'll need shelter from the cold of night and it would be nice to find a little water."

He flew swiftly on. At last the Snow Mountains began to rise up over them rather than just being a ragged edge to the skyline. His passengers had been silent for some time, hypnotized by the rhythm of wing beats and the monotony of the scene.

"Wake up!" Furbetrance called. "I need your eyes here! Help me find a patch of greenery. Green means water."

The four on his head stirred like sleepers awakening. Where the mountain wall swept abruptly toward the sky the Dragon turned at a right angle to it and flew east, dropping lower and lower as he went, barely skimming the higher desert floor at the foot of towering cliffs.

"I see water courses but they're all quite dry," said Manda, scowling into the fierce afternoon glare. "Gads! It's hot here!"

"Shade, shade is what I seek," sang Clem under his breath, "and cool, clear water." He leaned further forward until Mornie grasped his belt in back to keep him from tumbling off his perch.

"There! Up that canyon!" shouted Tom. "Hey, go about! I'm sure I saw a glint of green and sun on water."

Furbetrance banked steeply, made a tight turn, and glided slowly into a vertical-sided canyon whose perfectly flat floor was covered with rippled sand.

"There!" cried Manda, pointing. "That's water!"

"Further, further," urged Clem, nodding in satisfaction. "There must be springs in the rock here. Ah!"

He guided the gliding Dragon lower until they were no more than fifty feet off the canyon floor, just room enough for Furbetrance to beat his wings. They passed over short stretches of stream that were filled with an inch or two of murky water, but no more.

"Beware the corner!" shouted Tom to the Dragon.

"Got it!" replied Furbetrance, easily. He banked to make the curve around a jutting rock. "Look at that! What did I tell you?"

Before them the canyon, now fully a thousand feet deep, widened to a thousand feet. Down its center, a long, narrow lake filled most of the floor. Its banks were choked with dark pine and light willow, as closely set as jungle. The Dragon's reflection shot across the still water with him, perfectly mirrored on the surface. The place was absolutely silent. They saw no birds at all in the air or in the trees.

"Well," said Tom, "I think we can camp on the shore, don't you, Furbetrance? There seems to be no danger."

"Don't be too sure," said Manda. "It's much too quiet. You'd think there'd be birds, at least. . . ."

"Only birds who would live in a place like this," Clem reasoned, "are kinds who could fly high enough to escape over the canyon rim. That leaves out most of 'em, except maybe eagles and falcons—and vultures."

Furbetrance picked a smooth rock beside the lake upon which to land. On the ground they all sat in place for a long moment, savoring the peace and beauty of the spot and looking for signs of life—and danger.

"Lunch!" cried Mornie, sliding from the Dragon's head, feetfirst.

"I'll gather some firewood," said Clem and he went off to the edge of the wood to find fuel.

"Well, I must admit, *this* is beautiful!" Manda said after looking about for some minutes in silence. "If someone were to build me a comfortable castle above this tarn . . . say over there? A few dozen loyal retainers and servants. A marvelous place to get away from the bustle and clamor of court life, I do say, and to be alone."

"No need for a fortress here," replied Tom. He jumped from his perch and helped her alight.

"True enough, Princess," said the Dragon. "No one could bother you here. A handful of men at arms could defend the narrow places for years, as long as there was water and food."

"I prefer to dream of it as a sort of . . . well, retreat," Manda said with a pleased laugh. "I wouldn't want it to be a fortress."

Tom went down to the lakeside and scooped up a handful of water to taste. The ripples of his touch spread as far as his eye could see in wonderful, even patterns, changing direction and constantly overlapping as the waves struck the rocky sides of the tarn, echoing back upon themselves.

He called to Manda and they watched the show silently together.

"I feel as if I've broken something," said Tom. "It'll take hours for the lake to be as still as it was when we came."

"It'll be still again," promised Manda, softly. "It will always return to stillness."

Mornie and the trapper returned with armfuls of fragrant cedar and dried pitch-pine boughs for a fire. In a few minutes a thread of blue smoke was rising straight as a ruler into the unmoving air, scenting it pleasantly with cedar and pitch. Mornie boiled water from the lake for tea and Clem carefully sliced cold meat brought from Ramhold, to go with biscuits he was baking in front of the hot coals.

"He does it all so easily!" Mornie marveled. "Cooking is a pleasure and a necessity, I know, but he makes it an art even here in the middle of nowhere, I vow!"

"The best part is, no matter what he cooks or where, it always tastes good," said Manda, clapping her hands.

" 'Tis because when you're eating my cooking," chuckled the trapper, "you're always famished from healthy exercise!"

"Maybe," laughed the princess, "but few of my Uncle Granger's highly paid and much-honored chefs can match you, Clem!"

"Just good, fresh ingredients and sensible preparation," said he, modestly. "The biscuits need to be turned end for end, my lass," he said to Mornie. "To cook 'em evenly on all sides. A campfire is not like an oven in your castle home!"

They sat on the smooth, cool rock in the shade of one enormous willow at the water's edge and ate lunch cheerfully together.

"If there is *this* place," said Tom around a mouthful of tender, buttery biscuit and cold roast lamb, "there may be other such hidden oases in other valleys and canyons. And perhaps signs of Retruance are hidden in one of them."

"I suppose we can investigate them all, in time," sighed Manda. "Thank goodness for Dragon-flying. It'd take a century on horseback!"

"There're not really that many canyons to explore, if we stay in the area indicated by the crossbeaks," Clem reasoned. "We can fly over them as we come to them. Should be able to spot sign of Dragon when we come to it."

"Yes, you've said Dragon-sign is hard to miss," said Furbetrance. "Well, I suppose that's because we never had any reason to hide our comings and goings."

"That's as I sees it," agreed Clem. "Ho, lassy! Let's set things aright here and put out the fire. We'll return the place as it was when we came. That's a law of the forest."

As the pair worked, laughing and talking privately, Manda walked along the lakeshore, studying the trees, the calm water, and the smooth, water-rounded stones with equal interest. The Dragon rested, his eyes closed against the brilliant sun, lying on a flat rock in the full sun, soaking up its heat, as Dragons do to recharge the furnaces within.

Tom leaned back in the shade and built, in his imagination, a castle in air for Manda upon the far shore. This place greatly appealed to something within him. He had always loved lonely places.

He must have dozed off, for the next thing he knew, Manda was calling softly to him. He popped his eyes open and found she was bending over him, smiling lovingly.

"Come down the shore a way," she urged. "I want you to see something beautiful."

She led him around a bend of the shoreline, into a tiny cove overhung by huge, old willows. In the deep and crystalline water around their roots swam a thousand or more tiny, golden fish, swirling and turning, weaving patterns and breaking them apart to make another.

"Isn't that wonderful!" Manda exclaimed in a whisper. "They're called sequins, but I've never seen so many at once or such magnificent ones! My father has a pool for them in his courtyard in Lexor, but he has only a fraction of this many! What a richness they are!"

The pair knelt side by side, watching enchanted as pattern after pattern, no two alike, were formed by the little golden fishes.

"You like my fish?" said a deep, dry voice behind them.

They spun about, caught completely off guard, tangling arms and legs.

Manda gasped a small scream and Tom drew breath but couldn't muster a shout. Before them at the edge of the wood sat an enormous, magnificently muscled, smoothly furred golden cat with black-tufted ears and gleaming, sharp teeth exposed in a sardonic smile.

"Er, ah, oh, yes!" stuttered the Librarian, smiling back rather weakly. "Splendid show, the fish."

The cat sank to its stomach and blinked back at them, comfortably.

"Ah, I'm Princess Royal Alix Amanda," said Manda, gathering her courage.

"I am pleased to meet you—ah—*Princess*," said the cat, her tone implying a measure of disbelief, cynicism. "I am called Julia, for some reason I have never quite understood. I am a jaguar!"

This last was dropped into a silence as deep as the pool at their feet.

"I, ah, I've never seen a jaguar as large or as beautiful as you, Julia," Tom said politely. "Most jaguars where I come from are a third your size."

"Well, yes, we do grow large here," admitted the cat, beginning to groom her ears with a forepaw dampened with a rough, pink tongue. "What is your name, please?"

"Oh, I'm sorry! I forgot my manners in my surprise," cried Manda. "This is Thomas the Librarian of Overhall, Achievement of Murdan the Historian."

"My, how you elfin-kind do love your fancy titles," mocked the jaguar. "As for me, the only title I need is 'cat,' and everyone knows who and what I am."

"That's very true! I've always thought," said Tom, "the only title I need or want is 'Librarian.'"

"I could do without 'princess' myself," added Manda. "It's more a big nuisance than anything I can think of."

"Modest to a fault!" chuckled the jaguar, shaking her head. "What do you want here, eh?"

These words were shot out unexpectedly, snapping at them like a whip crack. The cat's eyes had suddenly turned cold and cruel.

"Come, come! I asked you a question and I expect an answer," Julia snarled. "You come here into my private canyon coveting my fish and my forest! Account for your actions. This is *my* territory!"

"We came looking for a friend lost in these mountains," said Tom, swallowing his fear, despite the fact that the great cat was lazily running her claws in and out, tearing daintily at the moss that covered the rock upon which she lay.

"As he isn't here, we'll be leaving any minute," promised Manda.

"Only if I allow it!" purred Julia. "You must know that we jaguars are carnivores."

"I would have guessed it," said Tom, diplomatically.

"Meat isn't too easy to come by here in my little box canyon. I have all the fish I care to eat, of course, and an occasional desert hare wanders in—stringy, dry, bitter critters they are, at best."

"It explains why there are no birds," Manda whispered.

"Birds? If I can catch them, I eat them," said Julia, with the most wicked smile imaginable. "Unfortunately, they've learned to stay away from my canyon."

"So these sequins are your larder?" Manda asked, shivering despite the desert heat.

"What? Of course not! " cried the cat, jumping to her feet. "Destroy such beauty? Never!"

"I'm so sorry!" cried Manda, jumping back to the very edge of the lake.

"I am a cultured creature," said Julia coldly, swishing her tail angrily. "I don't eat beautiful things, my dear self-styled princess. I must point out, therefore, that I wouldn't hesitate to devour you. You aren't so pretty as all that!"

"You may not think me pretty," Manda retorted, anger in her eyes and her stance, "but I *am* a princess and I won't allow you or anyone to deny me that!"

"Well! Fire in the royal eye, eh?" the great cat jeered. "I've decided that you are what you say you are, after all. Welcome, Princess Alix Amanda, to my hidden lair. I've never had a real princess for dinner before."

"We've just had lunch, and we've got to be running along, now, very sorry and all that," Manda said hastily. "Maybe some other time!"

"What, running away already? How distressing!"

"We must find our friend we told you about," said Tom, taking Manda's hand and edging off up the way they had come. "Retruance may be in danger!"

"Too bad for him!" sneered the cat, moving forward on her belly after them, gathering her hind legs to spring. "What's a *retruance,* anyway?"

"A Dragon!" said a very slow, thunder-deep, sulfurous voice from high overhead. "A large, fierce, fire-breathing, foul-tempered Dragon half again as big as me, who isn't particularly fond of cats of any size."

Julia leaped up, startled. Her jaw fell open. She cringed back, flat against a willow's trunk.

"Retruance is also my brother," continued Furbetrance, more calmly. "And I take most unkindly to anyone or anything standing in the way of rescuing him."

Julia rolled over on her back, wriggled her hips and shoulders imploringly, and stuck all four paws in the air, claws well retracted into her pads.

"D-d-d-dragon? How interesting!" she gulped. "Bigger than you, eh?"

"Much bigger!" breathed Furbetrance, charring half a willow and sending it into flame. "Introduce us, Princess. If I have to incinerate this haughty feline I'd like her to know my name."

Manda grinned in relief and made the introductions quite formally. The huge cat remained on her backside, paws in air, but nodded politely to the Dragon leaning over her, breathing tiny puffs of acrid smoke.

"Very pleased! Wish I could stay to chat, but must run along," Julia purred jerkily. "Understand you have urgent business in hand yourself, Master Dragon!"

"Oh, get to your feet!" sniffed the Dragon. "I hate a groveler!"

"It seemed best to do a little groveling rather than a little smoldering," said Julia, regaining her feet and showing her most pleasant smile. "Nothing personal, beautiful Princess Alix Amanda and handsome young Librarian! Well, nice to have made your acquaintances, all!"

She started to draw back into the trees, bowing and smiling warmly at them as she left but keeping her eye on the Dragon towering over the trees at the water's edge.

"Wait a minute!" Tom called after her. "Have you heard of any unusual happenings in this neighborhood, Julia? A Dragon flying overhead? Anything at all to help us find Retruance?"

The jaguar paused just within the trees, sat on her haunches, and scratched her muzzle thoughtfully.

"Come to think of it," she said, "I've been hearing strange rumblings from over to the east a ways. If it weren't so far over the hot ridges and rocks, I'd have gone to investigate, out of curiosity. But you know what they say about curiosity and cats."

"I do indeed," replied Tom. "Thank you, Julia. We'll listen for these rumblings."

A moment later the cat had disappeared. Furbetrance scooped the young couple up and placed them atop his head in front of the maid and the trapper who had watched the confrontation with the jaguar with more glee than concern.

"This is not Overhall or Lexor," the Dragon chided Manda and Tom severely. "No more wandering off! Lucky for you we were ready to go and came to find you just then."

"She didn't seem so very wicked," Manda protested now that she was safe. "I might have liked her, you know!"

Furbetrance snorted derisively. "She might make a good friend, providing she wasn't hungry."

"You have to make allowances for an animal's nature," Clem admonished them. "We men are meat eaters and don't hesitate to kill for food. Why should we be surprised when a jaguar kills to feed herself?"

"I wasn't surprised," wept Manda, burying her face in Tom's shoulder and clinging to him. "I was terrified!"

"And will not wander off again without telling me where you're going, eh?" asked Furbetrance.

"Yes, Furbetrance Constable," the princess answered meekly.

The next two canyons were dry as old bones and about the same color. The third, which they reached very late in the afternoon, long after the sunshine had ceased to reach the canyon's floor, was graced with a small, tangled copse of greasewood and stunted cedars around a spring of sweet water that tinkled from a cleft in the rock and fell into a rock basin barely larger than a horse trough at Overhall.

"No big, hungry carnivores, here," announced Clem after a careful scout. "It's a safer place to spend the dark hours than the other one."

They set about pitching tents and making a good fire, for the barren canyon, as soon as the sun's rays left the bottom, turned quite cold.

"Small hungry beasties we *do* have," said Tom. He pointed to several pairs of yellow eyes watching them from the dark. As they turned to look, the eyes blinked and disappeared.

"Come on in and share supper with us," called Clem, making clicking noises with his tongue, as men call a dog. "Here, girl! Come, boy! Supper is ready to eat."

But the shining eyes didn't reappear, nor did their owners come to supper.

"COMPANION!" hissed Furbetrance, urgently shaking the Librarian by the shoulder. "Hoy! Wake and listen, Tom!"

Tom shrugged off his blanket. The cold night air awoke him at once.

He crawled from his tent, being careful not to awaken the trapper or the Princess and her maid in the other tent. No moon shone, at least not in the slice of sky visible from the canyon floor, but a million stars provided enough light to move around the edge of the pool to where the Dragon waited, his head lifted, listening intently.

"What?" asked the sleepy Librarian.

"Wait! Something I heard a moment ago. Maybe it'll repeat itself."

They stood in the cold starlight for a long time, hardly daring to breathe. Tom began to shiver.

"What was it?"

"The strange sort of rumblings the cat spoke about, I think. It sounded familiar, somehow."

"Well, I'm turning to ice," said Tom at last. "You listen all you want, but I'm going back under my blanket."

He had just turned back to the tents when he heard it. It reminded him of a distant someone rolling a grand piano over the stone floor of a vast and empty warehouse, bell-like, musical in tone. The Librarian and the Dragon listened as it rose and fell and finally faded away entirely.

"Well, what do you make of that?" asked Tom. He'd forgotten his chill.

"I've heard that somewhere before," mused Furbetrance. "I have the merest recollection. . . ."

"It was familiar to me, too," admitted Tom, mystified. The two sat on a broad rock beside the tiny pool as dawn began to light the thin strip of sky overhead. The sound didn't recur.

THE next morning they checked into three more canyons, finding each dry and short, none extending more than a mile or two back into the mountain range's flank.

Now that they had some idea of what they sought, the Dragon didn't waste time backtracking to the desert after exploring each valley, but soared over intervening ridges and dropped down only when they decided a canyon was worth investigating.

"Too narrow, you see?" called Clem, who had the best eye for distances and proportions. "A full-grown Dragon would have trouble squeezing through that cleft, wouldn't you say, friend Furbetrance?"

Furbetrance eyed the narrow gap. "I am sure *I* couldn't get through there," he said, "and Retruance is bigger'n me."

"Try one more before lunch," urged Tom. "We've covered a lot of ground this morning, fellows! Don't lose heart!"

Manda wet her handkerchief with water from a canteen and wiped her eyelids and lips. The hot desert air made their eyes sting from grit and cracked lips painfully in a few minutes. "I must look a true fright!"

Furbetrance climbed over the next knife-edge ridge. Mornie burrowed in one of the rucksacks she and her Princess had brought along, at length finding a small stone jar of ointment.

"Try this, ma'am," she said, handing it to Manda. "It may help your lips, at least."

"Thank you, Mornie!" cried Manda. "Oh, they feel better already."

She passed the jar on to Tom and then to Clem, who declared it was better than goose grease, which was used for the same purpose, up north.

"You use it, too, Mornie," Manda insisted.

"There is so little in the jar," protested the maid.

Manda examined the jar bottom closely and shook her head.

"This is a lotion prepared by an old household sprite who served my Aunt Phyllis. The jar itself has a spell that keeps it ever filled."

"Handy to have on a trip like this," said Clem, approvingly. "Your sprite could make a fortune out here providing canteens that never emptied."

"I'm afraid, yes, that we are overusing water supplies," agreed Tom. "Furbetrance, unless we find clean water in this canyon, we may have to turn back to the spring where we spent the night."

"It's not all that far," said the Dragon. "Look this one over," he added, referring to the next canyon. "It looks like a deep one and long, too!"

He banked to follow the run of the new canyon. His passengers peered down into the shadowy depths of the great rift in the mountainside. If it has been earlier or later, they could not have seen the bottom at all for the shadows, but now, near noon, the sun shot its rays straight down into the deepest part.

"Water!" cried Clem. "Not a little but quite a bit, friends. See there?"

The new canyon ended in a sheer, blank wall over which a steady stream of water fell, dashing itself to silver spray in a deep catchment below.

With the spray and the water, a fair grove of oaks, aspens, and larches had taken root in the canyon bottom, and grass dressed the sand-and-gravel flood plain of past springtime freshets. The miniature meadow was covered with a thick blanket of yellow daisies.

"Go down," cried Manda. "That water looks so good!"

Furbetrance alighted softly in the midst of the daisies and his passengers tumbled off his head to run and taste the water of the stream. In a few moments they all were splashing gleefully under the fall itself, washing away days of accumulated dust and fatigue.

"Let's have lunch!" cried Tom, exhilarated by the cold water and the odor of the flowers that perfumed the soft air of the box canyon.

"My turn to cook," claimed Manda and, together with Mornie, she set about laying out lunch for the four while the Dragon sauntered off to explore the lower canyon from ground level.

"Quite a lot of water comes into the canyon," observed Tom after their meal. "Where do you think it goes when it reaches the desert? It doesn't all evaporate, does it?"

"Probably," answered Clem. Manda and Mornie had gone to the edge of the brook to wash the lunch dishes and repack them for another flight. "The sand of the desert is very loose and porous, however. It's possible the water sinks in and runs down to Carolna River, way to the south, without appearing aboveground again. Never been there, but I hear to the south of the river are swamps and jungles. Place of crocodiles and hippopotamuses, they tell me. Not many people live there— or at least, not the civilized sort."

"Manda was saying that the new young queen—Beatrix, I think she is named—came from that part of the country."

"I believe that's right," replied Clem. "What's that noise?"

Tom sat up to listen. Down by the stream Mornie and Manda stopped chattering and rattling pans to listen, too.

Tom said, "It sounds like . . . the sound we heard last night! Rumbling, sort of, but with a musical tone of some deep, bass sort."

Manda waved her hand and shouted, "It's just our talented Dragon, vocalizing."

Furbetrance appeared from downstream, making the noise until he stopped in embarrassment, realizing that the others were listening.

"Just enjoying the echoes and acoustics," he explained sheepishly. "If it bothers you, I'll forgo the experiment."

"No, no!" cried Manda, rushing over to hug the Dragon's foreleg, or as much of it as she could reach. "I love to hear people singing. It makes me happy!"

Tom was looking at Clem, speculatively.

"Did you hear the sound last night, Clem?"

"Aye. As I was about to sleep, I heard it and heard you and the Dragon speaking of it. Yes."

Furbetrance, noting their seriousness, strolled over, munching a clawful of daisies.

"That singing, just now," began Tom.

"I've apologized," huffed the Dragon.

"No, no, old fire pot," said Clem. "When we first heard it, before we saw you coming up the creek bed, it sounded just like the rumble bumble we heard last night, and it couldn't have been you then."

"Didn't sound like that to me," protested the Dragon.

"It's the echoes off the canyon walls," deduced Tom. "They make the sounds quite different, more sustained, deeper, sort of mixed together."

"Very interesting," commented the Dragon. "Shall we mount up and go on?"

"You're missing the point altogether!" cried Tom. "The sound we heard last night was *almost exactly* the sound you made, just now."

"But I didn't make any sound last night," objected Furbetrance.

"*That's* the point! If *you* didn't make the Dragon sounds last night, then who *did* make the Dragon sounds last night?"

"Only one other Dragon in these parts I know of," prompted Clem.

"*Retruance!*" shouted Furbetrance, leaping fifteen feet into the air and clashing his wings together. "We heard Retruance *singing!*"

"If we heard him, maybe he can hear us and tell us where he is," exclaimed Manda. "Let's return to last night's camp!"

"Come on!" shouted Furbetrance, and as soon as the lunch things had been replaced in his saddlebags and his passengers were aboard, he flung himself at the sky and headed west.

IT wasn't as easy as all that.

"These hills and ridges change their appearance as the sun moves," Furbetrance complained. "How many canyons did we pass over without looking, this morning?"

"Five," said Manda.

"No, six," contradicted the Librarian. "I counted, just to be sure."

"I hate people who're efficient," exclaimed Manda. "How many do you say, Clem?"

"I would guess, only, and I would guess—six or maybe seven," said the trapper. "Now, that one looks familiar."

"Not to me," wailed the Dragon. He began to speed.

"A bit slower, old boy," warned Clem. "It'll be easier to see landmarks."

"Sorry!" said the Dragon, and he applied his air brakes and soared instead like a giant kite, sliding down the slopes of warm air rising from the rocky ridges.

"That's better!" shouted Clem. "Me, I watch landmarks, and I swear that pinnacle over there is at the head of the canyon we left this morning."

"You're right," called Mornie.

"Fly that way," Manda told the Dragon, pointing. In a few minutes they arrived at the pinnacle in question only to find no canyon.

"Could it be magic? Is someone fuddling our eyesight or memories?" Mornie wondered.

"No! Not magic," the fur trapper said emphatically. "This sort of thing happens all the time in wilderness. I'm still looking for a peak that is twin to the one we saw a moment ago. There! To the south and a bit east. Yes, our canyon was not as long as we thought."

This time they found the right valley and followed it to the spring, the tiny pool, and its runoff.

"Now what?" asked Furbetrance. "I don't hear the singing now."

"Noise, singing, whatever," said Tom. "Perhaps if Furbetrance sang in the narrow part of the canyon, it would produce the same effect in reverse. If it's really Retruance, maybe he'll hear and answer!"

"I'll try," said Furbetrance. "Wait here."

"Stop every minute or so, so we can hear if there's a reply," advised Tom. The Dragon nodded his understanding and trotted off down the stream bank and around a corner, out of sight.

In a moment they heard him humming in a deep basso voice and, now that they knew what it was, they could recognize an occasional word. The hard, flat, vertical walls distorted and rearranged the echoes and timbres of the Dragon's song.

"It sounds like somebody rolling a big empty barrel down the aisle of an empty church," murmured Manda, slipping her hand into Tom's.

"Or a piano being rolled in an empty room. That's what I thought of last night when I first heard it. There, he's stopped!"

Silence for a full minute.

The song began again and went on for a much longer time.

Silence again.

"Keep trying!" called Manda. And the singing, roaring, mumbling, rumbling, humming, whispering, keening resumed.

"Changed his tune now," said Manda. "I think it's 'A-Milking We Went,' isn't it, Mornie?"

"More like 'A Changeling's Tale,' " replied the maid, tilting her head to one side, the better to hear.

"I don't know either of those," said Tom, softly.

"I learned them from my mother," said Furbetrance's voice, coming nearer, "and I'm sure Retruance did, too."

"Furbie! That's not you singing now?" they all cried together.

"Not me! I heard Manda call something and came to see what it was she said. Words don't carry well here, although music does, it seems."

"That's Retruance's voice, I'm sure of it!" cried Tom. "I *thought* it was familiar."

"I'm sure, also. Where is it coming from?" Furbetrance said in anguish.

The singing faded away and Tom signaled the Dragon to resume his recital. "Try something you both know well, so he can be sure it's you, and we can be sure he is hearing us. We'll try to work out where it's coming from."

So as the Dragon sang, one by one, his Dragonet songs and nursery rhymes, filling the canyon with deep, strumming, humming, and rolling vibrations, something between a bass viol, the lower register on a harp, and a mellow tuba, the others spread out, listening carefully whenever Furbetrance fell silent.

Tom climbed the end wall of the box canyon near where the spring gushed forth. The sound seemed clearer, closer.

Manda hiked up her skirts and waded across the pool, keeping her ear close to the water. The sound was no louder here than elsewhere, she thought.

Clem, his ears undulled by years of noisy crowds in towns and castles, stood in the very middle of the pool, near the soft splash of the tiny in-flow, letting it soak his trousers to the knees.

He called, "The sound issues from the spring, itself!"

Tom waded into the icy water. Manda came behind him. They stood listening. Mornie and Furbetrance stood on the bank, saying nothing.

"Retruance, old friend!" shouted Tom, with his mouth close to the spot, a mere crack, from which the water issued.

Very, very faintly they heard a reply from deep within the rock.

"Is it you, Librarian? I knew you'd come sooner or later!"

✦ 14 ✦
Murdan Wins the Draw

MURDAN the Historian, Lord of Overhall Achievement, rose early and was looking from Foretower window with a worried and ill-pleased gaze. Graham, the captain of his guard, knocked on his chamber door and entered.

"He's there, now," Graham puffed and huffed—the two-flight climb to Murdan's apartments was getting more and more difficult as the years caught up with him.

"He won't come within the walls?" asked Murdan, not turning.

"No, sir! Said he preferred the open air to a falling-down, musty old pile like Overhall."

"Damned young puppy!" swore the Historian. "Well, the better for us, then. 'Twould be a messy, noisy, nosy Gantrell crowd if they all wanted shelter within. I wonder if Arcolas could raise a good rainstorm while he's here, living in that gaudy palace of a tent."

"He's already demanded the release of the Sponge," Graham said, pulling a wry face.

"Well, in a different case I'd give him up and gladly, but that pale, hungover worm kidnapped my only and beloved daughter and my grandchildren! I'll see him before the king! It's time that Gantrell lordling learned that Carolna's ruled by law, not by the whims of men."

"Yes, sir!" replied the soldier, standing at ease.

"I'll tell Gantrell about it myself this afternoon. Turned down my invitation to lunch, even, did he?"

"That he did," answered Graham.

"His loss, not mine! No camp cookie can prepare a meal like my castle chefs can."

Murdan leaned over his worktable. He scribbled a note to speak to Mistress Grumble about lunch.

"I'll lunch on the parapet above the main gate. You and all my staff will lunch with me. Grumble can arrange something really spectacular and make sure all Lord Peter's people see us enjoying ourselves. After lunch, I'll go down and sit in my gold armchair on the drawbridge exactly halfway across the span. And I'll wait. If Peter of Gantrell wants to bespeak me, he'll have to come to the draw—and bring his own chair if he wants to sit."

"Sounds all sort of . . . well . . . childish," said the straightforward Graham.

"Of course it is! But the alternative is to stand on the battlements and yell at each other. He pretends he won't come inside our gates out of fear, but what he really wants is to make me look ungracious, disrespectful of his rank, and personally ridiculous."

Murdan made a note to have his hair cut before lunch.

"He's said nothing yet about the princess?"

"No, Historian. Only asked for Fredrick of Brevory."

Murdan peered again from his window.

"I'm wondering who sent him word of the captive," Graham said.

"Peter's no fool. That's the tragedy of this vicious, ambitious infighting. He'd be valuable to the crown, would he agree to work in harmony with the king."

"There've been other ambitious lordlings," recalled Graham. "Some have succeeded, I think."

"Conflict's a way of ensuring a strong nobility and an effective royalty. But Gantrell's ambitions are not for Carolna, but for himself alone. Not even for his children—he has none! He has little interest in his brother's offspring, Manda says."

"Between us old friends, he may be more able than you or I would like to acknowledge. Without our opposition," observed the soldier, holding the Historian's cape out to him, "his ambitions would be poorly thwarted."

"Well, perhaps. I really just don't like Peter or his attitude or his methods. He's already made a lot of enemies for the crown, and Eduard needs all the friends he can get these days."

"You refer to the Barbarians?"

"Don't sneer! I've fought them, Graham! With halfway capable leadership they could overrun us all in less than a year."

"They've absolutely no idea of military tactics!" scoffed the other as they left the apartment and descended the stair to ground level together. "A well-disposed and well-trained army a third their strength would beat the Barbarians anytime, Lord Historian!"

"History shows, time and again, outsiders learn to play one inside faction against another and when the dust clears, the outsiders are the ones on the throne. Man, that's how the Trussloes came to power in Carolna, ten kings and a queen ago!"

"Not the same thing!" cried Graham. "Trussloes were minor northener earls before they offered to help old King Cristol. They weren't Barbarians, sire!"

"It depends on your definition of 'barbarian,'" growled Murdan. "My mother's Great-Great-Grandsire used to tell how he personally had to teach Eduard Two himself which fork to use at table and not to belch after. And their practice was to expose unwanted female babies, I recall."

"Not in modern times! And from Trussloes came Alix Amanda, the Queen Alone!" objected Graham, waving his hands in agitation. "If Trussloes held women in such low regard—as Barbarians invariably do—why would they allow a Queen Alone on the Throne, let alone almost worship her?"

"Trussloes are, above all, political realists," Murdan told him. "Most Barbarians are. We'll have to deal eventually with this new batch of outsiders, and I don't want them assisted by internecine warfare between the king and his brother-in-law."

Graham turned to go about his business, but halted to ask one more question.

"Have we of the king's party considered dealing with Granger of Gantrell? From what I hear . . ."

"Manda also asked that. My answer to her was that Granger is too much under his brother's thumb. He has shown too few signs of thinking or acting on his own principles—if he has any. We'll watch him closely, as the princess thinks he may be on his way to independent thought. She's a good judge of men. Well, she's a Trussloe!"

"She has the best of the two bloodlines, I would say," said Graham, saluting in farewell. "I go to inspect the guard. Everything must be exactly right, and there must be no compromises with security, with Gantrells close to hand."

"I don't want any Gantrells sneaking into my castle," Murdan barked after him. "That's how the Mercenary Knights managed to overcome your guard, remember?"

"Not bloody likely to forget," muttered the embarrassed captain of guards. He went his way, highly determined to learn from past mistakes.

Yet, thought Murdan to himself, pausing to pinch faded blossoms from a pot of red geraniums, *it would be no sort of life to lead if we have to give up the old traditions of hospitality for fear visitors will overpower our soldiers and lower the draw after midnight. And it's men like Peter of Gantrell who, unwittingly or otherwise, turn such fine amenities into foolishness!*

He sent for his barber and submitted to having his iron gray locks trimmed, combed, and perfumed while he conferred with the cook and Mistress Grumble about the lunch on the parapet and the meeting on the drawbridge afterwards.

Everything must go well. Gantrell was a formidable opponent, even in peaceful converse. He'd take full advantage of the smallest error of deed or tongue.

His thoughts turned to Princess Alix Amanda and her father and her stepmother.

Eduard, I've been keeping one thing from you, feeling that I should not add to your burden just now. Manda is in love and it seems to me, an old hand at such things, that this is quite serious. The Librarian must be reckoned with. Our Manda won't allow anyone to cross her in matters of the heart. She already knows what manner of queen she will be, if it comes to that. For her sake, I hope you and your new bride are successful in giving the crown a male claimant!

As he began his lunch on the breezy, hot parapet, he mused aloud on the matter.

"Manda may be queen, and a good one. Tom may be her consort. Will he insist on a crown? Will she want it for him? I'm willing to bet she'll insist on making him co-ruler. In truth, they'll both be much happier if Beatrix bears a healthy boy-child.

"How easily we condemn an unborn innocent to a lifetime of frustration, anguish, and perhaps physical danger! We're not very civilized, after all, are we? The Barbarians don't allow their rulers to force their sons and daughters upon them. They *elect* the best available leader and live with the results, or die with them."

"Not the worst way of governing," Graham concluded.

"Pass the salt, you, there," Murdan growled. A page jumped forward from his place to move the salt within reach.

By turning his head and looking out over the parapet, the Historian could see the Gantrell encampment, just about where he'd camped himself while besieging his own castle. Before Thomas came.

Brightly costumed figures in front of Gantrell's vast tent were having a picnic, the Historian noted.

"My own game, played back to me!" He laughed aloud. "Well, Peter, I was playing this game when your grandfather was a wee lad playing with lath sword and paper buckler."

Five minutes before he planned to appear on the drawbridge, Murdan sent for Graham again. This time they met in Foretower bailey, surrounded by soldiers and Overhall retainers, each in his or her very best and brightest costume or uniform.

"Well, I'm ready to go out. Any word from your watchers?"

"What looks like a holiday party from afar is in reality an armed squadron," said Graham grimly. "He's even dressed some of his men in dresses and skirts, to make it appear a pleasure outing. They're nervous, too, to judge by the reports, all a-fingering of swords and daggers and talking by jerks and starts."

"A good sign! He realizes he stands on loose turf, then, and is trying to put a bold face on it."

"As I see it, yes," replied the old soldier. "He's to be accompanied hither by a dozen of his best, their arms hidden beneath their cloaks."

"The span of the drawbridge allows no more than that. I'll go out unattended, except for you, Captain. Your shirt-waist is pulling out from your trousers, there. Oh, well, don't fret about it. I'll not put on such a show as Peter. You have your signals straight with the bowmen above?"

"If I push you to the ground, they'll know to shoot into the Gantrell crowd. We should have time to get inside and drop the portcullis, under the cover of their shooting. Did you wear half-armor under that blouse, as I recommended?"

"No! Too damned bulky and would slow me down, if we have to run for it," snorted Murdan. "Besides, Arcolas has produced a pretty good spell of warding that should protect you and me for long enough to get inside."

"If not, your people will be pledging fealty to Ffallmar of Ffallmar, tomorrow," said the blunt soldier.

"I trust Peter Gantrell no further than you do, Graham, my friend, but I don't think he's ready for open warfare, just yet. Well, let's see what he wants to talk about, and make him listen to what we have to say."

"One more thing," murmured Graham close to his ear.

"Say it quickly, then."

"A man was seen to leave the Overhall postern against orders, very early this morning."

"A swain aching for his beloved? A farmer concerned about a sick cow?" teased Murdan, laughing.

Graham remained grim, not meeting the Historian's joke with a smile.

"No, sire! The man who went out to visit Gantrell's camp before dawn and returned soon after was your comptroller."

"Plume? That slimy, skinny worm! I haven't trusted him

since he came. He doesn't laugh or even smile when he should. Keep an eye on him! In the meantime, he's the best accountant I've ever paid to do my arithmetic."

"You don't want to arrest him and perhaps ask him some pointed questions, then?" asked Graham.

"Hardly! Better to let him think he's getting away with something than have to discover who his replacement might be. Speak softly and carry a long spear, I say!"

"As you wish, sire!" agreed Graham. "Ready?"

"As I'll ever be," agreed the Historian. He turned to his gathered minions and called, "On your toes, everyone!"

"Raise the portcullis! Lower the draw!" shouted the captain, and with a great rumble the counterbalanced grille and the heavy bridge moved, opening the main gate wide.

"DEAR Historian, how good to see you!" said Peter of Gantrell. "I am pleased that you regained your Achievement so easily from the wicked mercenaries."

"Yes, I don't doubt you in the least, m'lord. Fortunately," said Murdan, smoothly, rising halfway from his golden chair to greet the young nobleman, "the Mercenary Knights proved no match for Graham's soldiers once we got home."

"I hear your pet Dragon had something to do with the defeat of the invaders," said Peter, gesturing for his footman to place a red-lacquered chair facing the Historian. The needlepoint cushion showed a Standing Bear.

"Please sit down and let us talk," said Murdan before the other could seat himself without being asked.

Gantrell sat, looking displeased for just a moment, and opened his mouth to begin speaking.

Murdan got in his words first. "I regret to inform you that I am holding a criminal, a man attached to your house. Brevory by name."

"We can talk of him at a later time," said Peter, waving in dismissal. "He is of no importance to me."

"Then I'll not mention him again," said Murdan, quickly. "Except to say that I intend to hold him for Session in the fall. He'll be charged with kidnapping a lady of high degree . . . my own daughter, as it happens."

"Er, I'm so very pleased that Lady Rosemary was able

to escape her captors, then," said the magnate.

"You've heard about that? Hardly an escape, really. She was rescued by two young friends of mine before any serious harm could be done. Your man, Fredrick of Brevory, will be held responsible for the crime and the insult. Perhaps he acted on his own. I'm sure he'd quickly inform on anyone putting him up to it, when the king asks," Murdan said innocently, smiling broadly at the thought.

Peter of Gantrell scowled. "I want justice done to such a wicked young man."

"Of course you do! Have no fear, Lord Peter. The king will hear the case, I am assured. His will be the judgment . . . and the punishment, too, if I remember my law."

"The king himself! You surprise me, Historian. A terrible waste of the royal prerogative to insist that Eduard sit in judgment of a minor felon like this Brevory fellow."

"Not minor to me!" snarled Murdan. Regaining his composure quickly, he went on, "You can understand my feelings, I'm sure. Rosemary is my daughter, my only child. Her son, Eduard of Ffallmar, is my only male heir. If I seem overly angered by this terrible act, I must be forgiven by all fathers and mothers."

"I am neither myself," snapped Peter. "But I am so sorry, old chap! I have led us off on a side issue. . . ."

"Not at all! I knew you would be interested to know the fate I have in mind for this Brevory person. By the way, m'lord, where's the Brevory Achievement, anyway? I don't know of it."

Peter turned several shades darker crimson but answered calmly, as though it were of no importance, "He is, as you have noted, a distant relative and a former liege man of mine, holder of a poor, small Achievement not far west of Lexor. If you weren't going to try him, I'd have done it myself. Wicked! Perverted!"

"Yes, I'm sure you'd like to have a hand in his just punishment," agreed Murdan, somewhat smugly. "I'll let you know if he says anything under interrogation that might interest you."

"Kind of you, I'm sure," Gantrell ground out. "Now . . ."

"I am so sorry. You had something you wished to discuss with me?" said Murdan, raising an eyebrow.

"You know, my good Historian, that I was appointed the legal guardian of Princess Royal Alix Amanda? Appointed by King Eduard, of course."

"Oh, I am very well aware of it! I understand she has been in the actual care of some lesser magnate for some years."

"Hardly a lesser magnate," snapped the lordling. "My own younger brother, Granger, has been raising her with his own two children. She has had nothing but the very best care, believe me!"

"Oh? I wasn't aware of that," lied Murdan. He gestured to one of his servants to bring him a drink. The sun on the drawbridge was quite fierce. Certainly, Lord Peter was perspiring freely. The Historian didn't offer him a drink.

"I thought you might have heard it from her, when she visited you recently," Lord Peter said pointedly.

"Princess Royal Alix Amanda? Here? I've been away at court, as you were, also. When I returned, my castle had been stolen from me and I had to devote a bit of time and attention to remedying that. No, I haven't seen the Princess Royal, bless her heart, since . . . well, for some time. Beautiful child! Quite bright and well mannered, too. Your brother Granger must be doing a good job raising her."

"I must have been badly misinformed, then," Peter said through clenched teeth. "I was told she was here until four days ago, and left with one of your servants, riding on one of your Dragons."

"You were misinformed, of course," Murdan chuckled smoothly. "For example, I have only one Dragon in my service and he hasn't been here for some weeks. Certainly I would have known it, if a Princess Royal had been in my house."

"I am not sure you're being entirely honest with me . . . ," began Peter, his eyes narrowing in the anger he was finding increasingly hard to suppress.

"Easy, Lord Gantrell! You of all people must know what trouble it can be to accuse a peer of being a liar. Are you prepared for such a confrontation?"

There was silence on the bridge except for the gentle murmur of Gugglerun in the moat beneath them. Not a man

at arms in the open gate or on the battlements above moved
a hair. Everyone within earshot had heard the implied insult
and the specific challenge.

The game had reached a dangerous point.

Peter of Gantrell took a deep breath and slumped a bit
in his chair.

"I am understandably upset, of course, Lord Historian.
The princess is my responsibility, and that of my family.
We must recover her soon or face the king's justifiable
wrath and Session's certain censure."

"You haven't told Eduard of his daughter's disappearance, yet?" asked the Historian in mock consternation.

"Not officially, no," said Peter. "I had hoped that we
would find her here, and . . ."

"Well, if I see her, I will send her to you, or rather to
Granger. Better yet, if she comes to me I'll bring her myself
to Lexor. That way she'll be held safe until she sees you and
your brother again. And her father, of course."

"Have *you* told the king of her absence?" asked Gantrell.

"How could I, when I didn't know she had disappeared
until you told me, just now? I'll write to His Majesty at
once and tell him of our conversation and that I will take
every step to locate his missing child. He's not to worry
about her, of course."

"Of course!" replied Gantrell with a resigned sigh. He
rose abruptly and stood, uncertain whether to break off the
conversation or drive conflict deeper between them.

"Is there anything else?" asked Murdan, smiling in a most
friendly way, showing he had forgotten the lordling's insult
of a moment before.

"No, no, no . . . I think we've reached an understanding
on these matters. You wouldn't consider turning Brevory
over to my own marshal, would you? I could bring him in
to Lexor for trial."

"No, I am committed to keeping him safely in custody," said the Historian bluntly. "He might be dangerous
to you, m'lord. Better wait until he comes with me to
Lexor."

"Oh, well, yes," muttered Peter, his manner distracted.
"On the matter of the girl . . ."

"You mean the matter of Her Highness, Princess Royal
Alix Amanda?" said Murdan stiffly.

"Yes, yes. One hopes nothing untoward happens to her. The future of the kingdom hangs upon her safety and well-being. No one would want her harmed, certainly not accidentally or . . . otherwise."

"I take your meaning," responded Murdan. "I'll convey your feelings to the lady, if and when I see her. Which may not be soon, of course."

"Oh, by the way, I've heard you've taken a new Librarian into your service," said Peter as he turned away. "You are most fortunate."

"Even more so than you might think," the Historian told him. "His name is Thomas and he is, wonder of wonders, a human!"

Gantrell's back, turned to the Historian, jerked violently at this and he glanced back over his shoulder.

"A human, you say! How droll! Do you actually believe in human beings, Historian? I eschewed such myths when I was a baby."

"Oh, there are humans, albeit very rare. Thomas the Librarian is a rare individual. He's been very useful to me already in the few short weeks since he came to Overhall."

"If you tire of him," said Peter with a frosty smile, "send him to me and I'll give him plenty of work to do."

"Perhaps we can share his expertise one day," suggested Murdan pleasantly.

The lordling stalked away, followed by his dozen men, their concealed weapons causing them to shuffle awkwardly. Their departure might have been dramatic, had not Peter's footman forgotten to take along his red lacquered chair and scurried back, much to the amusement of the Overhall garrison, to retrieve it and scuttle down the path after his master.

Murdan laughed as loud as anyone, partly in relief.

"All in all," he told Captain Graham, who had stood silently by throughout, "I believe we won that skirmish, hands down."

"Excellent, sir!" said the soldier.

"Next time it'll be a battle of spears and swords, not sneers and words, I fear," sighed Murdan, shaking his head sadly. "That is a stupidly proud man. Or proudly stupid man. Who can say which?"

• • •

"SHE *was* here, I swear it!" cried Plume. It was dark beyond the Gantrell pavilion, and only dimly lit inside. The comptroller stood, shaking in his dusty, scuffed boots, before Peter of Gantrell, seated at table with a deep silver cup in his hand. "I saw her with my own two eyes, m'lord!"

"I don't doubt your eyes," Peter snarled at the Overhall accountant. "But you can't tell me where she is now, can you?"

Plume hung his head in fear and shook his miserable head slowly from side to side.

"They never confided in me, m'lord!"

"Yet you say you are among Murdan's chief advisers, privy to all his secrets, eh?"

"So I believed, Lord Peter."

"But not so deep in the Historian's trust he will let you know when a royal guest has departed his house? Who cannot see a conflict here, Plume? The question is, now, does Murdan suspect you of running to me with tales for a few vols of silver?"

"I truly believe not, master! He consulted with me only this late afternoon, about the receipts from his small holdings. He trusts me with all his money and investments."

"Well, perhaps you're right, Plume. We'll chance it, as nothing will happen to me if you're discovered. You, however, can expect painful punishment, I would think."

"Hanging would be the kindest treatment I could look for, m'lord!"

"Hanging, drawing and quartering! Being dragged behind horses through the streets of Lexor I suspect. Well, return to your post and keep sending me any plans the Historian hatches and tells you about. Will you accompany him to Lexor?"

"I imagine so, sir. He never goes to court without me."

"Is that right?" cried Gantrell. "But you weren't there with Murdan this past spring, but here at Overhall when it was taken. He may well be suspicious of you. Figure out who might have opened the postern gate to Basilicae. I wouldn't want to be in your shoes, comptroller dear, if it's found out. Well, that's your problem! Go then!"

The accountant bobbed a quick, grateful bow and backed out of the tent into the pitch dark of a cloudy night. A spat of rain was falling, increasing steadily, as the sneak made his way along the course of Gugglerun to where the stream flowed through into the moat by a water gate.

A sudden flash of lightning revealed him running on the narrow postern drawbridge, to the watchful eyes of three Overhall guardsmen.

"Report him to the captain, again," said the sergeant-at-arms, gruffly. "The sneak is back from the enemy camp!"

✦ 15 ✦
Under Snow

"NOW what?" asked an impatient Furbetrance. "How do we get brother Retruance out of the mountain?"

Tom sat down to consider the problem.

"Water on this side of the mountains doesn't run off on the surface, so it must come through under the ground in springs, like this one."

Seeing that they were confused by his deduction, Tom went on. "Look at the dry slopes above us. There's no running water on the surface as there is on the north slopes."

"Well, that's true," agreed the Dragon.

"Ah! Then, when the snowcap melts in spring, some of the water must flow down to the desert floor, *underground!*" cried Clem.

"That's what I believe," Tom said. "There must be a lot of subterranean channels under these mountains to account for the springs in these canyons. The meltwater must carve them, always seeking the lowest level and flowing out at the foot of the mountains here."

"If I understand you," said Furbetrance, beginning to get excited about water flow, "if we could follow this stream back under that rock, we *might* find caverns that lead to Retruance?"

"Perhaps," said Tom.

"But how do we get into the caverns?" asked Manda,

pointing to the inch-wide crack from which the water flowed.

"If we could find out how Retruance got inside, we could follow him," Clem proposed, spreading his hands wide. "Simple as that!"

"Maybe not so simple," said Manda gloomily. "We may need a good magician. The nearest wizard is days away."

"Magic? Well, perhaps, but don't give up yet, beautiful princess!" cried Tom. "If a beast the size of Retruance could get inside, surely we can get inside, too."

"But just how . . . ?" began Furbetrance.

"We might try asking Retruance," suggested Tom.

IT was full dark before the missing Dragon's answer was completely delivered, put together from distantly heard bits and snatches, much-shouted repetition, and careful listening.

With the puzzle all pieced together, Retruance had said, "I went to the top of the highest peak in the Snow Mountains as a lookout to see if the kidnappers left any sign of whether they had passed north or south of the mountains.

"I'd just caught sight of them from a pinnacle having the best view of Broken Land, when the ice crust under me collapsed and I slid down a steep incline into a gaping hole in the mountaintop!

"The hole was so narrow, I couldn't spread my wings wide enough to fly before I was deep inside the mountain. Plopped among a stand of tall stone columns in the middle of an underground lake. Jammed tight! I can't move my wings to break free! Trapped!"

"Use your shrinking spell, as you did to sneak into Overhall," suggested Tom, speaking through the deep-voiced Furbetrance, whose voice carried best through the rock.

"Can't," shouted the trapped beast. "Spell calls for a paw gesture—and I can't move a claw!"

"Ask him if the water in the lake is flowing," Tom told Furbetrance.

"Let me check," they heard the trapped Dragon reply, and it was some minutes before he called his answer.

"Yes, it spills from its basin, southward, I think, down a wide fall or rapid, and disappears under a low archway."

"It must be terribly dark where he is," Mornie said with a shudder. "How can he see?"

"Dragons have built-in torches," Furbetrance reminded her.

"Oh, of course!" cried the princess's maid, hitting her forehead with her palm in chagrin.

Tom paced up and down while the others waited patiently for some practical plan to take shape in his human mind.

At last Tom said, "Flying to the top of the peak to find Retruance's cave-in won't help. More rock might slip and we'd just bury the poor Dragon! We've got to get at him from below. If we can drill or blast into the mountainside, we might find the stream's course and follow it up to the under-mountain lake. There must be a clear, open connection, or we'd not hear Retruance as well as we do."

"I can do some pretty powerful blasting," said Furbetrance. "Noisy, at any rate. Stand back, please!"

"Wait! Wait!" cried the Librarian. "First tell Retruance what we're going to do. He should be ready to shout or burn a flare or something, to guide us once we're inside."

"Excellent thinking!" exclaimed Furbetrance. He shouted to attract his brother's attention.

"We'll blast our way in," he called. "Keep an ear open for us when we get close to you, brother! We may need you to blow some flame to light our way to you."

"Be careful!" came Retruance's faint reply.

Everyone except Furbetrance retreated beyond the first curve in the canyon. They sat down on the creek bank, ate a late supper, and watched and listened.

Furbetrance huffed and puffed a dozen deep breaths until his internal furnace was roaring and white hot. He gave off a brilliant scarlet-white glow that lit the canyon end, reflecting from the walls and overhanging cliffs.

The waiting party heard a tremendous clap of thunder. The reflected glare from around the corner was bright enough to read by, if they'd wished to read.

Darkness fell as suddenly. They blinked into it, seeing ghostly afterimages of each other before their eyes.

Again and a third time the Dragon blasted away at the narrow cleft in the rock, sending monstrous chunks of stone tumbling and flying like chaff from a threshing machine. A vast column of white steam shot up into the night sky. The

rumble continued for several minutes after the actual blasting ceased, with cooling rock snapping and cracking like
rifle shots. The stream beside them bubbled and steamed.

"Any luck?" called Tom to the Dragon.

"Getting there," Furbetrance responded. "One or two
more puffs should do it!"

Twice more the Dragon shook the very fabric of the
mountain with his blasts.

"They must hear that as far away as Overhall," exclaimed
Clem. "It'll scare the birds at roost in Broken Land, I'm
positive!"

"Better wait for a while, now," Furbetrance cautioned,
coming around the curve with a weary tread, his spear-
pointed tail dragging in the coarse gravel.

"It's delightfully warm," cried Manda, dipping her hand
into the water. "I'll have a bath while it lasts. Can you find
our soap, Mornie?"

"Of course, m'lady!" said the maid. She rummaged in
her pack for soap and emollients suitable for a princess,
even in the wilderness.

The ladies retreated further downstream, lighting their
way with a firebrand.

The younger Dragon gave one last puff of smoke and
fell over on his back, feet in the air, utterly exhausted.

"Sleep for an hour or two, friends," he muttered. "By
then the rock will have cooled. . . ."

Tom and Clem sat on the gravel bank until the ladies
returned, freshly bathed and looking rather pink and damp
in a most attractive way.

"Let the Dragon sleep," decided Tom. "A few more hours
won't hurt us or Retruance. The business of climbing about
inside a mountain will be pretty strenuous. Maybe we'd all
better get some sleep while we can."

They agreed and settled down in their blankets beside the
creek, where the water ran almost boiling hot for several
more hours.

THE slice of sky over the canyon was fading from indigo
to pale blue when Tom awoke. Clem was up before him,
stirring up the campfire for breakfast tea. Furbetrance still
snored mightily—shaking the rocks slightly with each exha-
lation—a short way off. Manda, wrapped in her blanket, had

rolled close to him during the night as the creek cooled and the air became chilly once more.

"Wake up, lazy Dragon!" the Librarian called. "Enough of this sleeping when there are daring deeds to do!"

"Huff! Mumble? Gruff!" said Furbetrance without opening his huge eyes. "Wassit? Whoesser?"

Manda woke with a smile and a laugh, rousing Mornie with a playful pebble. She exchanged a good-morning hug with the Librarian and began to help prepare their meal.

"Need a good fast-breaker," said the trapper, skillfully propping his heavy iron skillet over the hot coals. The rousing fragrance of smoked bacon wafted to the Dragon's nose and he was at once fully awake. After a pound and a half of bacon from Overhall's larder and fifteen large flapjacks from Clem's secret recipe, he declared himself fully recovered from his blasting.

When they walked upstream to examine the Dragon's handiwork, they were surprised and impressed. Not only had Furbetrance torn a long, deep, high-arching tunnel into the mountainside, but he'd rounded off all its edges, channeling the stream into a shallow, polished oval pool of bedrock, where once again it ran ice cold, cooling the air and making it fragrant.

"You share some of your great-grandfather's talent at building," Manda complimented Furbetrance, to his delight. Everyone paused at the sparkling pool for a long drink before they faced the entry into the mountain.

"I'll come last," decided Furbetrance, "and provide light for our going. The path turns rough all too soon, I'm afraid. It seems to be large enough to walk through once I shrink myself to your size."

They went two by two, Manda and Tom, then Clem and Mornie, hand in hand. At first, Furbetrance's tunnel was easy going, level and smooth as a pavement. Their steps echoed and reechoed off the polished rock, so loudly that it wasn't until they reached its end and debouched into a rougher, natural cavern that they could stop and call out to Retruance that they were on their way.

"You've a long way to come, yet," shouted the imprisoned Dragon. His voice was clearer and louder now that they were inside the mountain and away from the sounds of moving water and wind. "I'm just fine, if a bit confined, you know. I can hear you quite easily."

An hour passed and a second. Without the younger Dragon's flare behind them they would long since have become completely lost, as the cavern branched and rejoined, the stream parting and coming together again, sometimes like braids, in several separate courses.

Toward midmorning they reached the bottom of a water stair and the way became a difficult, cold, and wet climb, moving from rock to rock by leaps and bounds, sometimes having to wade knee deep through swiftly running water.

"Thank goodness for a stout pair of boots!" panted Manda on reaching the top of the rapids. She reached back to pull Mornie up the last drop. They stood gasping for breath, waiting for the Dragon.

"It gets worse," said Clem, returning from a forward reconnaissance. "The ceiling gets lower. I had hoped it would get higher so we could fly."

"At least there don't seem to be any great waterfalls between us and Retruance or we'd hear them," puffed Tom. "Well, we'll have to find the way, one way or another."

They all gazed about in wonder as they continued. Here the cavern was low ceilinged and the stream wandered between what appeared to be an endless forest of stone trees, rooted in the rock underfoot and stretching up into the darkness above. When Manda commented on them, wondering how they grew, Tom passed the time explaining stalactites, stalagmites, and flowstone.

NOONTIME passed. They paused on a ledge beside the stream, now rushing along a polished, jade green channel as straight as an arrow. It made hardly any sound at all, but from in front of them they could hear the muted sound of other rapids.

"How do you explain that this morning we heard Retruance speak so clearly, but now his voice is all but drowned by the water sound?" Mornie asked Tom.

"I don't explain it," said Tom. "I wonder if we've taken a wrong turn, however."

The thought bothered him until he realized there were places in the tunnel where it was so quiet you could hear yourself breathe and the sound of their clothing stretching and bending. Yet, round a corner and all of a sudden the roar of water might be almost deafening.

In quiet spots, they paused to chat encouragingly with Retruance, who was invariably cheerful and encouraging.

"I've long since decided the trap I fell into was natural, not the result of any sort of magic," he commented. "Unfortunate, but not a fatal mistake, I say."

"I wouldn't know how to tell," said Tom, shaking his head, although the Dragon couldn't possibly see the gesture. "Think about how we can help you get free once we find you."

"I'm pretty well tied up," said his mount. "However, with your help and that of brother Furbetrance, I'll easily break free once you get here."

Shortly after they resumed their trek, now over rough, shattered stones beside the river course, they turned one of those unexpected corners to find themselves on the shore of a vast, underground lake, stretching as far as the eye could see to the left, right, and ahead, until it faded into the darkness. They couldn't see the far shore.

"Swim it?" considered Furbetrance. "That's good! Dragons are as at home in the water as in the air!"

He folded his wings tightly along his flanks, worked the spell that restored his size, and invited his friends to clamber onto his saddle. Once they were comfortable, he waded out into the inky waters. After a half dozen steps, he began to swim as the bottom dropped off steeply.

"What was that?" wondered Manda very softly. Something about the place made them fall unconsciously into whispers.

"What did you see?" asked Tom, who was busy tightening the harness that held their saddle arrangement to the Dragon's broad forehead.

"A ripple, circling about us!" Mornie squealed.

"That's what I saw," cried Manda, throwing her arms about the Librarian. "There's something alive out there."

"Advantage of having a Dragon as a carrier," said Furbetrance, calmly. "It's just a cave fish, albeit a big one. He's curious, only. And fearful, too."

The shape in the water circled for some minutes. The Dragon plowed on, now walking on the smooth, gravelly lake bottom, now swimming when the water got deeper again.

A smaller, more rapid chevron of ripples crossed in front

of them. Furbetrance paused, one foreleg lifted.

"Hello!" he called cheerily. "We're friends, just passing through, you know."

A soft answer reached them.

"Who are ye? Who are ye, great behemoth of the deep? Have you come to destroy our home as you did the outlet? How hot your body is! We fear it, fear it, fear . . ."

"No need to fear, friend fish," said the Dragon. "We won't harm you or your lake, believe me."

The ripples stopped abruptly and a dead-white fish head, round of snout, with long, flexible whiskers all about its lips, broke the glassy surface of the lake.

"It has no eyes!" exclaimed Manda, clutching Tom's arm.

"I've heard of cave fish without eyes and without color," Tom said, to comfort her fear. It was not easy, for the sight of the eyeless white fish head was unnerving.

"You must be related to the beast who fell into the Hall of High Columns," observed the fish, politely. "I feel your size and heat and it's similar to that beast's feel."

"He's my brother, Retruance," explained Furbetrance, setting his foreleg down carefully, so as not to make waves. "We intend to rescue him."

"Thank goodness!" exclaimed the blind fish, giving his head a sharp shake. "He's been disturbing our poor sprats for some time with his singing."

"He fell into the mountain by accident," Tom said, leaning forward to see the fish better. "He can't get free of the columns without help."

"Yes, we've seen that," answered the fish. "Unfortunately, we were not able to offer our assistance to him. He's like a fish in a net, tangled in those columns as he is."

"Have you bespoken him, then?" asked Tom.

"No. No purpose. We've felt sorry for him but knew we could do nothing for him, so we left him alone to expire in peace."

"Is he far from us now?" asked Furbetrance.

"Far? I would say not. Only an hour's swim, against the current," replied the fish. "How long it would take you to get there, I couldn't say."

"But at least tell us what lies between, please," requested Manda. "Beyond this lake?"

The fish considered his answer. Several other blind fish gathered some distance away, slowly waving their white whiskers, sensing the Dragon from a safe remove.

"We've decided the best thing for us to do, to hasten your passage and the end of your turbulence," said the fish at last, "is to guide you to your brother. The way is an easy swim but rather complicated to tell in words."

"We'd be much obliged if you could do so," said Manda. "Perhaps we should introduce ourselves, friend fish."

"It would be nice to know your names," agreed the other. "We don't meet many outsiders, of course. I am Albiola Bespeaker. My people selected me to speak for them on such occasions as this—although, thankfully, such occasions are rare."

Furbetrance said, "My own name is Furbetrance Constable. On my head is Princess Royal Alix Amanda of Carolna, and Thomas the Librarian of Overhall. Behind them are Mornie of Morningside, the princess's maid, and a fur trapper of Broken Land, Clematis."

"My honor!" cried the fish. "A princess royal! I learned about kings and queens and princesses in our school!"

After that it would not do but the entire shoal of blind fish would accompany the travelers on their way across the lake and up the river beyond.

"I thought at first, when you began to call him from outside, that the other Dragon had several voices," explained Albiola, swimming alongside, close enough to talk with the riders. "Comes from not seeing, you understand."

"You can't see, even under the water?" Manda asked, very curious about these cave-bound fish.

"In a way. It's more a matter of listening, although we're aware of light and dark. We remember, way back, when our people could see as well as anyone. But seeing is a lost art here under the mountain."

"A mighty long time ago, I guess," said Tom, and the fish agreed. "You live a most quiet and peaceful life, then. I don't imagine there're too many predators to bother you, Albiola?"

"None whatsoever, except for an occasional bear or wildcat, wandered into the caverns by mistake and gotten lost. They're always hungry but they're also so noisy they're easy to avoid."

"And ultimately they will starve to death, I reckon," observed Clem. "That's the way of the wild."

"Actually, we often manage to show them a way out, when they get hungry enough to be reasonable," said the fish. "It's much the same as helping you find your Dragon. It benefits us all to cooperate, don't you agree?"

They entered a broad, slowly flowing stream on the far side of the lake. It flowed through an underground canyon of its own. The walls were lapped by the water on each side, and the ceiling was far, far above, lost from sight. Here the Dragon could have flown, but it seemed easier to wade up the sluggish current, following the ripples of their sightless guides.

The voice of Retruance sounded clearer and closer than ever. Tom asked him to release a burst of flaming gas as a beacon but after three tries, he told the Dragon it was no use. They could see nothing, not even a reflected glow.

"But I feel you are very close," said Retruance, cheerfully. "Keep up the good walk, old friends!"

"We come to a shallow cataract ahead," Albiola soon told them. "Around a sweeping curve. We won't go much farther with you but it's a short way beyond the cataract to the Pool of Columns where your friend is captive."

The cataract rose like a shallow stair before them, curving, as the fish had said, gently to the right and out of sight.

"We could swim up the cascade, of course, with much danger and exertion, but once you reach the top, you'll sense the pool and the Dragon," Albiola said, shortly. "If you wish, we can continue."

"Not necessary, I believe," said Furbetrance. "We'll find the way."

"Is there anything we can do for you and your people in return?" the princess asked, politely.

"I can't think of a thing—except leave as quickly as you can. Your vibrations disturb our sprats, as I said, and they shoot off in all directions. It doesn't hurt them so much. Actually, they enjoy it. It provides them an excuse to skip school."

"Youngsters are the same everywhere," commented Tom with a chuckle. "We're very sorry to have caused any trouble for you, Albiola."

"Not really trouble," said the blind fish, waving a fin in

farewell. "Speak well of us when you get aboveground. And leave us to our dark peace thereafter, we pray."

The ripples and flashes of white scales disappeared. Carrying the young people, Furbetrance quickly climbed the watery stairs and rounded the corner, lighting the way with a thin stream of fire as they went.

"*Ho!* I can see your light!" called Retruance suddenly. "You're only a mile or so away now."

He ended his sentence with a bright yellow jet and they could see him at last, hanging in midair.

The stalagmites that filled the center of the pool were smooth and straight, looking like huge marble spears. With the light from the two Dragons' flares the travelers could see, across the wide, shallow pool, columns of swirled, pastel-colored stone randomly scattered about, rising forty or fifty feet into the air, tapering to rounded points high above.

In the middle of the pool the spears were crowded quite close together, and where they were thickest, jammed down among a dozen of the closest-set, hung Retruance Constable, his great leathery wings held fast, a bit like a fly impaled in the jaws of a Venus flytrap, Tom thought.

"Poor Retruance!" cried Manda. "Are you hurt?"

"Uncomfortable, but unhurt, Princess. Nothing broken, bent, or breached, thank goodness! Took some hard blows in the ribs when I came down, but that will pass once I can move about a bit. Hello, everybody! Welcome to my bed of nails!"

Furbetrance maneuvered himself under the trapped Dragon and stood in the shallow water staring up at Retruance, puzzling out their next step.

"We at least have the advantage of light," said Mornie. "I'd hate to be working in the total darkness."

They all agreed. The problem was how to lift the trapped Dragon from the spires.

"Is the hole in the roof open still?" asked Tom.

"Yes," answered Retruance, curving his long neck upward. "I would say so. Yes, I can see it as a spot of light when I look up. If I could just flap my wings a few times . . ."

"While you're wishing, wish for magic to help us," sighed Manda.

"There are other ways," Tom claimed. He leaned forward to speak to Furbetrance, "Can you take off in this space?"

"No reason why not," replied the Dragon. He had found a part of the pool only inches deep.

"Fly above Retruance and hoist him off the spears, enough to free his wings. Then we'll either go straight up though the hole in the roof, if it's big enough, or retrace our steps to the desert."

"I can do it, but you all had better wait for us here," Furbetrance decided, after giving it some thought. "My brother is half-again as heavy as I. It'll take all my strength to lift him."

"Put us ashore over there, where it is fairly dry, then," said Manda. "We can wait for you there and be out of the way, too."

The Dragon lowered his great head to the shelving beach to one side of the pool. They easily hopped ashore.

"Now for it!" cried Furbetrance, taking a deep breath. "Be back in a few minutes!"

They could follow the rescue operation even at that distance by the flaming breaths of both Dragons. Furbetrance shot up between columns where they were farthest apart, near the cataract, and climbed swiftly over Retruance's head.

"Be easier with a cable of some sort, but we'll have to make do without," they heard Furbetrance call to his big brother. "It seems to me the best way is to haul you up by the tail."

"Ouch!" cried his brother. "Be careful! My tail is very tender."

"It might hurt but it won't do any harm," declared Furbetrance. "Here we go now!"

They watched the younger Dragon hover over the other, reaching down with his powerful hind feet, beating his wings strongly but steadily over them both. The downdraft stirred ripples on the pool's mirror surface.

"Up! Up!" urged Retruance. "A bit to the left. My portside wing is twisted around that pillar there, as you can see. Ouch! There! It's free! Ouch!!"

"Up you come, big brother," gasped Furbetrance. "Up! Up!"

Suddenly the trapped Dragon was free. There was an

exciting moment when he spread his wings and took the first, thunderous flap.

Furbetrance gave a shout of triumph and warning. They collided in midair, almost losing airspeed, and began to tumble before each Dragon swung away from the other, beating thunderously to regain control.

With an exhilarated rush of wings the two beasts swooped down to the narrow beach, loaded the four young people on their heads, and flew to the ceiling far above.

The opening seemed much too tiny for the flying Dragons, but they popped through with room to spare, into the bright, cold afternoon sun. They soared triumphantly up, high into the sky, before gliding slowly in lowering circles toward the rolling foothills to the north of Snow Mountains.

THE nearest place to be sure of food and shelter for the coming night was Clem's cabin in Broken Land. They arrived just before an approaching rainstorm and by the time it began to pour, all were well on their way to being warmed, fed, bathed, and comforted in Clem's homey house.

Furbetrance and Retruance, too large to put even just their heads through the cabin door, remained outside, enjoying the show of lightning, thunder, and pelting summer rain. Retruance demanded a telling of their adventures, both seeking Rosemary and looking for himself, and his brother gladly complied.

The others, wrapped in warm blankets and furs, sat in front of the cabin's fire drying their clothing, still wet from wading in the underground river.

"What next?" asked Clem, handing around a pitcher of hot mulled cider before he settled down on the warm hearth beside Mornie.

"Return to Overhall in the morning," Manda told him. "Murdan and I will go to Lexor for Fall Session. Murdan intends to bring charges against the nasty little Freddie. He'll need all of us for witnesses."

"That one deserves to be hung up somewhere to dry out," barked Clem. He was particularly fond of Rosemary of Ffallmar and her three children. "I'm sure the Historian has something like that in mind."

"Murdan wants to discredit my uncle Peter, at least for

long enough to get my stepmother through her pregnancy and birthing. Goodness! I do pray it is a boy-child."

"In one way I agree," said Tom, thoughtfully. "But it seems a terrible burden to place on an infant, being a king whether he likes it or not!"

"What other way can you get a legitimate ruler?" wondered Mornie. She yawned hugely. "Not that my opinion matters. I don't decide such things."

"But perhaps it should be decent, honest people like you who decide," said Manda, sitting up to gaze thoughtfully into the fire.

Tom put his hand in the small of her back to help support her position.

"There are other ways to find a good ruler," he said softly. "I'll have to tell you about them one day. Or perhaps I shouldn't interfere."

"You have my respect, and that of Murdan," said the princess. "Your words will be heard, I believe."

They sat on the warm hearth together, speaking less and less as sleep overtook them.

"Furbetrance will go to his family. His Hetabelle and their kits live on the Obsidia Cliffs. Retruance will carry us to Overhall. What will you do, Clem? It's full summer now," Tom asked.

"Not too late to ready myself for the next trapping season, if I work fast," said the woodsman. He was silent for a long while before he went on.

"But, if you need me, you and Manda . . . I could go east with you. See the great nobles at Lexor, for once. I'll miss my empty and beautiful wilderness, of course, but . . . a man needs to expand his vision, I believe. See new places and people now and again. It makes such good telling over a pint of autumn ale in some cozy inn."

"And there's Mornie," suggested Manda with a mischievous glint in her eye, "who's already sound asleep here on your floor before your fire. Better gather her up, Clematis, old wallflower, and we'll put her to bed beside me in our room."

"Aye, the hearth'll grow cold before morning," agreed the ex-trapper. He gently scooped the maid into his strong arms, as easily as though she were a bouquet of flowers. She stirred slightly, murmured his name, but didn't awaken.

Manda knelt before Tom, put her hands on his shoulders, staring for a moment into his brown eyes.

"There's the matter of you and me, too," she whispered. "What is to happen between, to, and for us, beloved?"

"Good and bad, of course, for that's what life is made of," replied Tom, feeling warm, sleepy, and philosophical all at the same time. He kissed his princess and she returned the kiss at once. For a while there was no sound in the cabin except the drumming of rain on the cedar-shakes roof and the hiss of raindrops falling into the fire.

"Carry me, also," said Manda at last. "A maid should not have better treatment than her princess, do you think?"

✦ 16 ✦
Discussion, Decision, and Departure

THEY bade a loving and rather tearful farewell to Furbetrance, who said he was needed at home.

"I've completed my mission," he said. "Here is brother Retruance, safe and sound . . ."

"My tail will long be painful from your hauling," moaned the older Dragon with a comical grimace.

" . . . and I promised fair Hetabelle I'd be home before Flight Time."

"Flight Time?" wondered Tom.

"It's the traditional time for teaching Dragon hatchlings to fly," explained Retruance. "Early summer is the best Flight Time. It's something every kitten remembers fondly, ever long after. A most happy time for a Dragon family."

"Kitten?" asked Manda with a laugh.

"Well, you wouldn't expect us to call them 'calves' or 'puppies,' would you?" protested the proud father.

"No, no! Kitten is just perfect," Manda replied, struggling to contain her bubbling laughter. "Why not, say, Dragonette, though?"

"A Dragonette is a half-grown Dragon. Sort of equivalent

to a teenager," Retruance told her.

"Give our love to the beautiful Hetabelle, brother! Persuade her to visit Overhall in the fall, when the kits can make the trip."

"My good mate is rather shy but I think I can convince her she should visit the East, if only for the children's sake. Once she arrives, she'll love it, I know."

He lifted his black, leathery wings, called good-bye once more, and hurled himself into the clear sky over Broken Land, angling into the updrafts breasting the Snow Mountains.

The rest of the party, perched on Retruance, left shortly thereafter, heading east.

"We could make it all the way to Overhall easily," the older Dragon told them, "but we should stop and tell the good people at the sheep station that I am found again."

"They were most helpful," agreed the princess. "I wonder if we should also stop by Old Place and reassure Lady Murtal. She has few visitors, I know, being far from other castles or towns."

"Easy enough to do. It's almost on our way," Retruance said, catching himself about to nod his head. "We'll stop there for lunch and go south to Ramhold for the night."

They soared. The Dragon's passengers enjoyed the wide view while Clem pointed out landmarks, recalling stories of ancient and not-so-ancient exploits that had taken place here or there.

Old Place appeared below in less than two hours and their welcome was warm and cordial.

"My Lady Princess!" cried Murtal when she rushed to meet them at her gate. "I'm so glad to see you safe and sound! My son has written me everything that happened and how you rescued my granddaughter and her children from that rogue, your uncle Peter's henchman."

Lady Murtal was a plump, jolly grandmother who embraced the entire world, willingly and happily, seldom speaking anything but good of anyone—except Peter of Gantrell, it seemed.

She swept them immediately to her private sitting room and called for cool drinks and hot tea, with lunch to follow in an hour. Retruance excused himself to go off and speak to the sergeant of Murtal's small guard.

Lady Rosemary's escort, the sergeant told him, had been provided by a local piecework mercenary named Trout. He'd surrendered without a struggle to Brevory's armed band in Summer Pass—and now had run from Murdan's certain wrath. Not a man of the hired band had been seen in weeks.

"If I may ask, ma'am," Tom said after he'd gotten to feel quite at home with the Historian's mother, "why do you choose to live so far from your son and the center of Carolna?"

"It's a long, long and sometimes sad story, Master Librarian. Someday when it's snowing, blowing, cold, and gray outside, I'll tell it in absolute detail. Enough for now to say—Old Place was the scene of my happiest and most loving years. Here my sons were born. And here lived, 'til his death, my good husband and beloved friend. Here I intend to stay until I, too, die."

"I hope it will be many years before that happens," said Tom, sincerely, for he had at once come to love the sprightly elderly woman with her very direct manner and violet eyes.

"As do I, Grand-Aunt Murtal!" cried Manda.

"That's especially nice, coming from you young people. May I ask a question, in my turn?"

"Of course! Anything at all!" promised both.

"Am I just a lonely old woman with too-vivid imaginings? Or do I sense between you two . . . ?"

"You are perfectly correct," said Manda, blushing crimson. "We love each other, Grandmother!"

"We do; that's as true as sunrise," Tom admitted, unable to keep himself from coloring, also.

"My! My! Don't be embarrassed by your love, children! What a splendid thing to share. I remember . . . but, as I said, that's a story for a long, wintery evening. I'm so very pleased for you both! Tell me, does my son know of this?"

"I think so," Tom told her. "We've made no effort to hide it. Should we have?"

"Of course not!" snorted Murtal. "Publish good news at the top of your voices, say I!"

"We foresee, however, some serious problems arising," Manda said, hesitantly.

Murtal nodded soberly and then spoiled the effect by chuckling—in a younger lady it would have been called a giggle.

"There are always problems, child! Don't concern yourself about them, at least not yet."

"But if Queen Beatrix—"

"I'm familiar with the situation as regards a royal heir," interrupted the old woman. "I am not *that* isolated here!"

"Of course you aren't," murmured Manda. "But I can't help worrying about it. Frankly, I'm torn between my love for Tom and my feelings toward my father and our kingdom. If I *am* to be queen, how does Tom fit into my life?"

"Child, children, listen to me! Carolna has been around for more than seven centuries, through all sorts of kings and queens, interregnums and dual monarchies, anarchies and rule by merchants' committee, and even no rule at all. There're a lot of conflicting procedures and customs of the past, but every monarch, believe me, makes his own rules, when it comes down to that."

She reached out to ring for her servant.

"Whether you become queen or not remains to be seen," she continued. "Horatio, serve lunch in the garden, please. Find that big Dragon and ask him to join us there. I always liked Retruance," she confided to Tom. "Some Dragons I've met have been, well, rather too uppity. I gather it comes from being so large. But Constables have always been good friends."

She led them into her garden, a place of fragrant greenery and early summer blooms, lilacs in the cool shade of a fringe of poplars, and late iris and early daylilies, beds of bright cutting flowers, delphinium and gladiolus, just beginning to bloom, resplendent in the full sun.

The manservant Horatio, almost as ancient and fully as sprightly as his mistress, served them a delicate salad and a compote of fruit preserved from last fall's orchards, and a chocolate cake with swirled sugar-butter frosting.

"A great deal will depend on your power base," said Murtal, suddenly resuming her earlier discussion over dessert. "You'll have Lord Gantrell and his sycophants arrayed against you . . . actually a small number of men, taken all in all, but overproud and arrogant in their wealth. A great many others will sit on the wall, you realize."

"You mean, watching which way to jump?" asked Tom, accepting his second helping of cake, the first he had encountered in this world.

"Exactly! They'll swing their support to whichever side appears to be winning. Which is why, you see, my son is determined to bring Rosemary's foul little kidnapper to trial before the king. If his guilt is proved, the matter will cast doubt over Gantrell's ability and suitability. The undecided faction will go over to the king's side, especially if the matter of the royal succession is clear."

"I understand the king already favors Murdan and Manda," said Tom.

"True, but a king has to consider other things than friend-ship and kinship—if he is a good king. Eduard Ten is above all a responsible ruler. Would it be better for Carolna *as a whole* to be ruled by a mere slip of a giddy girl? A girl, in this case, very young and—so far—unmarried, inexperienced, kept virtually hidden away by her uncles since the sad passing of her mother? Would Their Lord-ships obey her willingly, support her policies if she has the scholarly Historian as chief adviser? That's why Peter wants to hold Manda close and away from Murdan. That way he controls what is known, believed, and expected of her by the wealthy and powerful on whom the ruler must depend."

"Plus," added Manda, "if Uncle Peter controls me, he'll gain the support of all those who don't really know— or care, it seems—what's going on, just because I'm my father's daughter, not a son."

"A lot of people think Gantrell is preferable to Murdan as regent for Manda," said Murdan's mother, sadly. "They don't know my son as we do. Gantrell is wealthy, holds many Achievements, and controls others because he's bought their owner's support . . . or gained it by promises or by threats."

"I guess it's easier to see the situation clearly if one is an outsider," said Tom with a sigh. "I'd oppose any ruler who uses threats and terror, even murder, to gain power. I've never met the man, but I have a hearty dislike for this Uncle Peter already."

"Suppose you had arrived suddenly in this world of ours,

as my son told me, and were hired by Peter of Gantrell
instead of Murdan the Historian. Peter can be a delightful,
charming man when he wants to be. Many, who never see
his darker side, think he's the greatest man in the kingdom,
not even excepting Eduard Ten!"

"At the very least it would have taken you some time to
form an honest opinion of my Uncle Peter," agreed Manda.
"Even if you, in the end, decided he was not to your liking,
he would have tried to poison your mind against the king,
against Murdan, and against me!"

"I suppose so, although . . . I'd like to believe I'm po-
litically mature enough to see behind the posturings and the
promises. In my country—in the land of my birth, I mean—
politics are no less convoluted. The form of our government is such that everyone must try to read a politician's
innermost character—or get a destroyer instead of a leader.
That's why, long ago, we chose a government modeled of
laws, not just of men."

"You've put your finger squarely on our problem there,"
exclaimed Lady Murtal, her forefinger thrust at Tom in
emphasis. "Peter of Gantrell, for all his wit and charm, is
ultimately a destroyer, a driver. Given unrestrained power,
would he have the patience to lead? Or would he rather
drive us to wherever he wishes us to go?"

"And Murdan hopes to convince enough people of the
fact that they must not stand idly by and allow Gantrell to
force himself onto the throne?" asked Tom.

"That's what the lady is saying," put in Retruance, who
until then had kept his silence.

"What effect on all this will I have, when it becomes
known that Manda and I . . . well, are, well . . . ?"

"It depends," Retruance considered. "Many will hesitate
to support a queen just because she is a woman alone.
You would gain support for Manda in that quarter, I think.
Others, remembering Alix Amanda, Queen Alone, might
object if the queen had a commoner for consort and—let's
be frank about this, Companion—an *Outsider!* The fact that
you are a human will enter into it, too. Many will fear your
influence on the queen for that reason alone. Others will
believe, as I do, that a human is a handy sort of person
to have at one's side. You've already proved your worth
in that regard."

Tom digested more than just lunch as they departed from Old Place with Lady Murtal's farewells and blessings.

"If I would be a hindrance . . . ," he began.

"No, it won't make any difference. If, and I say *if*, you were my husband and if, again *if*, I were offered the Trusslo throne, I would not be queen of a people who would not respect my choice of consort. I won't be sold to anyone in exchange for political position or gain! I decided that years ago, my dearest. Your coming merely confirmed my determination."

"You would give up the Crown if it stood between us?" marveled Tom. He remembered the sad case of a king of England, not so long before, who had done the same brave—some said foolish—sort of thing. He spent the time it took Retruance to fly from Old Place to Ramhold telling her that story.

"This Edward," decided Manda, "from what you say, preferred not to rule, despite all the laws and traditions pressuring him?"

"That's about it," said Tom.

"I can understand that," said Manda emphatically. "I tell you truly, my own love, that I would . . . I will, if necessary, do the same."

"But if it means abdicating the throne to your Uncle Peter?" asked Retruance, who, with Mornie and Clem, had listened in interested silence to the discussion.

"Well, I'd have to find a way to prevent that from happening," said Manda.

"*We* will have to find that way," Tom amended. "You and I and the Historian, and Retruance, too. Lots of people will be working for and with you, Alix Amanda."

"I'm not the least bit concerned," she replied. "Except as it affects you and me. There are too many other people who would make good Kings of Carolna, including you, or Murdan, or even Clem here. I've decided," she said with finality, "that I *won't* be *forced* into queensness under any circumstances."

"Queenship, rather," prompted Tom.

"Well, right! Queenship, then. Is my decision terrible?"

"Lady Murtal evidently doesn't think so," the Dragon answered her question first, "nor do any of us, Princess. There's Ramhold!"

"I really am looking forward to a Ramhold supper!" said Tom, and behind him Clem laughed his agreement.

THEY walked hand in hand, that evening, over the golden-green grassland surrounding the sheep station, mostly without speaking, very content just to be together, to be in love. A half moon rose in the east, a silver bowl slightly tipped.

"It means it will rain," said Manda, pointing at the moon. "It's a bowl pouring its contents over the land. A good sign!"

"Talber says winter and spring weather have been good for farmers. There are going to be what Iowa farmers call bumper crops. The ewes bore healthy lambs at the right time and their milk was rich, so the lambs grew strong in a very few days," he said.

"You're starting to talk like a farmer yourself," Manda teased him.

"Well, I was born and raised in a small farming town. My sympathy is with farmers, always."

An amazing thing happened, just then. A fiery meteor streaked through the evening sky, and with a distant roar and hiss, it crossed the face of the moon and disappeared in the haze on the western horizon. Its blazing flight lasted ten heartbeats or longer.

"Wow!" cried Tom in wonder, hugging his princess closer. "I haven't seen anything like that in a long time and never so big!"

"A shooting star? We see quite a few of them in springtime here. Not many that bright, however. They say they're a good omen for lovers."

"I accept that!" Tom laughed aloud.

ON their return to Overhall they found the Historian highly pleased by their adventures in the west, for he really did like the Dragon very much, no matter how hard he tried to hide it. But he was also rather gloomy. Tom at last found an opportunity to ask him about it.

They were sitting on the balcony off Murdan's parlor, letting the evening breezes cool the first really hot day of August. Manda had gone off to see about her wardrobe, which was scant, since she had left her Uncle Granger rather suddenly. She was already looking forward to the fall journey to Lexor with anticipation.

"Manda found letters from her father waiting when we came back," Tom noted, ending a companionable silence.

"Aye," responded the Historian. "She hasn't told you yet what was in them?"

"No, I said you ought to see them first, under the circumstances."

"Well, he is worried . . . about a lot of things, but mostly about his queen. She'll go into childbirth pangs any day now. Although she is healthy and well protected by the best medical spells money can buy, he fears that Peter Gantrell will somehow find a way to interfere."

"What? Harm the child, you mean?"

"Or harm the queen and thus the unborn child. Beatrix is not as well loved as Manda's mother was, being a daughter of the far South. You may have heard."

"Does that make her disliked?"

"Unfortunately. In public she often seems cold and distant, they say. She speaks with an odd accent, they add. We who know her know she is a good-tempered, well-spoken lass, but still unsure of herself. Afraid, even."

"Poor lady!" Tom could not help exclaiming.

"Eduard is deeply in love with her, I must say, and she with him, which makes me optimistic about her prospects. But for now, too many of our good northern petty nobles are suspicious of anything that comes from the Swamps, as they call the south coast."

"An unfortunate burden for Eduard to bear. Is that proper? I mean, my referring to him as just Eduard?"

"A king needs no other title than his good name, my boy. When you meet him, you'll address him as 'Your Majesty' and 'Sire' and 'Lord King,' but in person he won't object to simply, 'Sir' . . . after you get to know him."

"I want to meet him," said a thoughtful Librarian.

Murdan stood and paced back and forth, thinking, while his Librarian sat silently watching, respecting his reverie.

At last Tom said, "Sir, what bothers you?"

"Just what we were talking about now," said Murdan, stopping to rest his elbows on the stone baluster. "The king and queen and this unborn child of theirs—of ours, in one way of looking at it. I'm trying to anticipate all the wicked things Gantrell might do to upset the even course of events this late summer and fall."

"Manda and I have discussed it a lot," admitted Tom. "Will you hear my opinion?"

"I would value it!"

"Then, this: It's far better to act than to wait. If nothing else, it keeps your opponent off balance, makes him hesitate in some of the things he might otherwise do."

"I have people watching Gantrell very closely. Friends are poised to counter any sudden moves he might make."

"But he knows that, I am sure."

"Oh, I am sure of it!" Murdan grunted.

"If Peter does anything, it seems to me, it will be underhanded, secret. There are a lot of things that can be done seriously to upset a mother-to-be. Did you see the great shooting star two nights ago?"

"No, but I heard of it. I was already abed when it passed."

"Manda says such things are considered omens, for good or ill."

"Yes, most people would agree."

"What I'm getting at is the role of superstition in this world. It's much stronger than in mine, and God knows it's strong enough in Iowa! Black cats are still taken as bad luck. Brides refuse to see their grooms on their wedding day. Finding a four-leaf clover is good luck. Spilled salt and broken mirrors are bad. Things like that."

"Those are believed strongly here, too."

"A bad omen could be cruelly upsetting, taken as ill news by many of Eduard's people, wouldn't you say?"

"Peter is fully capable of manufacturing an evil sign or two," agreed the Historian. "And, being from the south, Beatrix is even more susceptible to what you call superstition. Yes, Peter might arrange it. Nobody could point any blaming fingers at him, certainly."

"No, and there must be a hundred things he might try. Carried out ruthlessly, it could be a severe shock or a terrible fright to the queen."

"I can think of dozens of omens that would do the trick," Murdan agreed. "The king has the best magics available, as I said. But if the ominous events were manufactured, their magic wouldn't have any effect!"

"I've been studying this business of being human. It seems to me that a human here is regarded much as a wizard or a witch is regarded in my world. In Iowa it's considered very good luck for the mother to see an elf or a fairy while she is carrying an unborn child. Nobody admits they believe it, but they do! Some mothers will go a long way out of their path to make sure they meet a magi, a wraith, a fairy, a wizard, any magical being."

"So . . . ?"

"What if Queen Beatrix were to have a real, live human near her during the last weeks of her term? That might counter the *effect* of any bogus omens, in the eyes of the people of Carolna. 'A wave of this hand, this very hand,' " Tom half quoted someone he had once seen in a movie, "and the evil sign is neutralized! Or so the superstitious might believe."

"Ah!" was all the Historian said for a long while. The two of them stood watching the evening activity in the castle courtyard.

A stable lad carried a saddle from the saddlery, freshly cleaned and polished. He whistled cheerfully.

A gang of castle children, scarcely ten years old, perched on the stone verge of Gugglerun moat, throwing pebbles at the fireflies that skimmed over the water, zig-zagging back and forth to dodge their missiles. Children's laughter rose to the watchers on the balcony.

"Manda . . . , " began Tom.

" . . . must remain here until I escort her to Lexor," the Historian said flatly.

"Oh."

"It's extremely important she make the right sort of entrance into the city and the royal court. She is a stranger there, too. Everyone will be watching with critical eyes, forming opinions of her for the first time. She'll be very busy for weeks, making clothes, planning parties and celebrations. She must write to her friends and relatives, picking her maids of honor. Jewelers will arrive to design and make her tiara and her other regal adornments. Besides, you realize that if she leaves Overhall now, she is herself vulnerable to any last-minute machinations Gantrell might devise to repossess her."

"If I must, I will go alone," said Tom.

"Not alone. You'll take your Dragon, of course."

"I wouldn't consider going without Retruance Constable, no," agreed Tom.

"And I should think that young woodsman who I see mooning about Manda's maid, these days. What's his name?"

"Clematis? Good man to have along, I'd say."

"Take him with you. These Broken Land people are a tough and resourceful lot, to a man."

"I am to go, then, but with what excuse?"

"Leave that to me. I'll send you with a letter to the king, who is with the queen now until the babe is born. I'll tell him what we've just talked about and suggest that he introduce you to the queen as my personal emissary. It'll be up to you to settle her mind, make her a friend."

"It's done that way?" asked the Librarian, gathering up his cloak before leaving the Historian's balcony. He wanted to speak to Manda before she went to bed.

"It is now," said the Historian. "When can you leave?"

"In the morning."

"Oh, I've sent that pesky Dragon of yours off on an errand. He begged me for something to do. Getting bored, he said. He won't be back for two or three days, I judge."

"No matter, sir. I'd like to see something of the country from ground level for a change. Meet people. Talk to them while they're not goggle eyed about a fifty-foot dragon. There is so much I don't know yet about Carolna."

"Good idea, I say! I'll send the Dragon after you when he returns, then."

Captain Graham arrived to report the setting of the evening watch. Tom asked to be excused and went off to climb Middletower, hoping that Manda was in her apartment working with her needlewomen and tailors by lamplight and not yet retired for the night.

"Let Master Tailor, here, take your measurements, Tom," the princess greeted him. "You'll need suitable clothes, hose, shoes, boots, hats, capes, kerchiefs, everything to your underclothing, for the royal court."

"I'm not sure I can afford such luxury, Manda," Tom protested.

"If you promise not to ask who pays for it, I promise not to tell anyone," she giggled. "Do you like this red velvet?

It gets cool at times in Lexor on fall nights. It may snow before we come home again."

"You plan to return to Overhall after sessions?" Tom said in surprise. He hadn't thought that far ahead.

"If I can, I will," she replied. "If I have my way, Murdan will be declared my guardian until I reach twenty years—two years off yet. Master Tailor! Here, to my side! This young man needs a wardrobe, as I told you."

The thin, lank tailor came with his tapes, chalks, pad, and pins. Tom submitted to the most careful measuring he had ever had, even to the length of his fingers and the width of his palms.

"Gloves are in this year, Rosemary says," chattered Manda happily.

"I'll have to have a week or ten days to run up the suits and doublets," the tailor was saying at the same time. "Shall we set a first fitting for a week from Tuesday?"

"Wait! Wait," cried the Librarian. "I won't be here after tomorrow. You'll have to make the clothing and bring them to me at Lexor in time for the Opening of Session."

"Tom!" cried Manda. "I need you here. I was hoping we could spend the rest of the summer together at Overhall."

"Remember what we discussed, Manda? I've just come from Murdan and he sends me to your father, the king, as soon as I can leave. I told him tomorrow."

Manda looked so disappointed that Tom thought for a moment she would cry. Seating herself on a chair, carefully so as not to puncture herself with any of a hundred straight pins scattered everywhere about her person, she said:

"I need to hear about this. Ladies! Master? Kindly take a few minutes of rest. The cook has a buffet laid in the parlor. Go over and have a bit to eat and a stoup of Overhall ale. We'll be working until past midnight, I think, especially as Master Tom is leaving tomorrow!"

The seamstresses and the tailor and their assistants gratefully departed. They had been at work with the princess since lunchtime and it was well after dark by now.

"A little supper will be welcome," hinted Tom.

"Tell me first what you and Murdan agreed upon, and then I'll let you eat," Manda growled. She patted the chair beside her and Tom took it, admiring the flustered, flushed look of her.

"You remember my talking about superstitions?"

"Yes, of course. What has that to do with Murdan?"

"Not Murdan, but with Queen Beatrix."

"Explain, please."

He did so and when he was finished, she sat back, stretched her shapely legs straight out, and sighed.

"I would like to go with you to Sweetwater Tower."

"Sweetwater Tower?"

"My stepmother's castle on Brant Bay. Pretty place, for all it is often foggy and damp. You'll be going there, for there she will be delivered of my half brother or half sister."

"Ah! I had assumed she was in Lexor."

"It's a short ride southeast of Lexor."

"You and Queen Beatrix are friends?"

"I haven't seen her since her wedding three years ago, but we've written to each other, rather stiff and formal. I think I like her, although she's perhaps rather too quiet and withdrawn."

"Murdan says that's because she's frightened, alone in a strange part of the land."

Manda picked at the unsewn hem of her skirt, a richly brocaded, deep orange affair that suited her magnificently, even in its unfinished state.

"He's probably right. I was really still a child at the time, so I hadn't thought of her as being just plain scared. It fits, however. Perhaps now I understand her better."

"But you feel you'd be unwelcome at Sweetwater Tower?"

"Murdan says it would be folly to give Uncle Peter a chance to blame anything that went wrong on me. People expect me to be jealous, he said, even if I'm not at all. I do wish it weren't so. I would like to get to know Beatrix better. One day I shall."

"Of course you will! But for now, I must go alone and you must be a princess and prepare for Session. I'd like nothing better than to have you travel with me again. You know that!"

"I know, beloved. And I also know my duties and responsibilities, so I won't make any fuss—at least not in public—about losing you for two months. But tell me, what will you do in Sweetwater Tower?"

"Get to know your father the king, for one thing. It's important that he like me and trust me, wouldn't you agree?"

"Absolutely so! What else?"

"There's this business of having a human nearby—with all the supposed powers of a human. It may—will, Murdan insists—make it very difficult for Gantrell to fake an evil omen, perhaps to cause a miscarriage."

"Yes, I see what you mean. Yes, having a human like you as an attendant and friend would help offset any wicked tricks Uncle Peter might be tempted to try. A good plan, I say."

"I suppose what I'm supposed to do is, when the king's magicians and wizards try to ward off evil with spells, I'll reinforce them with common sense."

"*Human* common sense, which has served us very well recently. All of Fredrick of Brevory's wards against being caught stealing Rosemary were brought to naught because they were intended to ward against our own magics. You used human sense and won through. And the matter of Retruance being trapped, also. If we'd sent for a divining sorcerer, we'd likely be baking and freezing on that canyon floor, still!"

Mornie and Clem brought them sausage, cheese, and bread from the buffet. All four sat amid the bolts of cloth and piles of laces and brocades, tapes, scissors, and packs of needles and pins, to picnic at midnight.

Tom asked Clem if he would go with him to Sweetwater Tower. The trapper merely nodded his head and asked when they were leaving.

"After breakfast," Tom told him.

"Might not it be better to leave before dawn, by the postern?" Clem asked around a fistful of grapes.

"No, I want everybody to know I'm gone and where. We want Gantrell to know about it as soon as possible."

"Who will tell him?" asked Mornie.

"Probably the comptroller, Plume," said Tom. "He seems to be in regular touch with the Gantrells."

"A spy in our midst!" exclaimed Manda. "Why doesn't Uncle Murdan clap him in Aftertower with that slime, Fredrick?"

"Because a known spy is of more use to us than he is

to the enemy," observed Clem. "I've got a bit of business
with the sour-faced number juggler. He has yet to pay me
for my services as tracker to Wall."

"You didn't lose your furs at least," said Manda, sym-
pathetically. She knew, now, how much work it had been
to collect pelts all the previous winter.

"They brought a good price, as we were among the first
to come to Wall this season, thanks to the Dragon. As for
the tracking, I didn't want to charge anything, but Lord
Murdan insisted. He gave me a piece of paper instructing
this accountant to disburse cash to me. I'll go to him first
thing tomorrow, before breakfast, and demand payment. I'll
put the money aside for our future, Mornie."

"Ah, yes! And you'll accidently let slip the information
that you go with me to Queen Beatrix and King Eduard?"

"Exactly."

"In which case, to make it seem more authentic, maybe
we *should* leave quietly and before first light—as soon as
you've got your money in hand," decided Tom.

"Thank goodness we'll be too busy to miss you men,"
said Mornie, making a face. "Will you write me, Clem?
Can you write anyone at all, Clem?"

"Saucy miss! Of course I can and will write! My spell-
ing is not that good, but you'll be able to ferret out my
meanings, I'm positive."

The dressmakers trooped back into Manda's sitting room
and soon were hard at work, leaving the young men with
no more to do but say good-bye and go to their beds.

THE cocks in the roosts in the top bailey had yet to make
a sound when Clem pounded heavily on the comptroller's
door, deep under Foretower. After a long wait and two
more bouts of pounding, Mistress Plume, looking quite
disheveled in a faded old nightdress, opened the door to
admit the ex-trapper.

"I must see your husband, mistress," said Clem. "I depart
in minutes for the east and may not return for a quarter year
or more. I will need my money."

"I'll awaken the old rat," said Mistress Plume. She seemed
to relish the idea of disturbing her husband's sleep more than
regret the loss of her own. While he waited in their bleak
parlor, almost bare of furniture except for a large, high desk

and a shelf of heavy, leather-bound books, Clem heard the lady rousing her sleeping husband with ungentle words.

"Going off on your own then?" asked Plume when he appeared, buckling his belt and rubbing the sleep from his small, close-set eyes.

"No, comptroller. I go with Master Tom, the Librarian, my friend."

He handed Plume the Historian's order. The other examined it closely as if suspecting a forgery.

"Well and good, then," Plume said at last. "All's in order. I am happy to serve you, Master Clematis!"

He tried very hard, but failed miserably, to seem cordial and helpful. He asked questions about the proposed journey.

"To carry a message to the king?" he repeated, pausing in his counting of silver vols into Clem's hand.

"I wouldn't know about that," replied Clem, watching in distaste the way the accountant lovingly fingered and caressed each coin. "Master Tom is to serve the queen, I hear, in her remaining weeks before childbirthing."

"He is a physician, too, then?" cried Plume in some surprise.

"I have no idea. He is, after all, a human. Humans have some strange and useful ways, they tells me. Thank you, comptroller! I apologize again for awakening you so early. We depart at once."

And he took his heavy bag of cash and his leave, noting as he shut the heavy door on the comptroller and his wife that the former seemed rather excited, while the other showed signs, clear to the sharp-eyed woodsman, of distress . . . and disgust.

✦ 17 ✦
The Heartland

SOUTHEAST of Murdan's Overhall the rolling countryside, checkerboarded with newly plowed fields, and square woodlots, was pleasantly studded with stone farmhouses and sturdy frame barns, all surrounded by freestone fences—the small Achievements of freeholders whose forefathers had combined a sweet soil, careful husbandry, and hard work to build moderate wealth on grains, cattle, pigs, cheese, butter, and draft horses.

The day was hot but breezes blew from the northwest, promising a rain shower by afternoon. The sun glinted brightly off ponds and streams every few miles. Foals capered about their dams in the short-cropped grass of pastures on either side of the wide roadway. Their mothers stood watching the passersby with calm eyes, sometimes nodding in greeting as they passed.

At one freehold after another, the travelers called polite greetings to farmers and their field hands, but didn't pause. Their first destination was Ffallmar Farm, where they planned to spend their first of five nights on the road to Sweetwater Tower.

The two young men swung along the smooth dirt road at a good pace, chatting of this and that, mostly of the scenes through which they walked. They had agreed to travel lightly, so each carried only a thin backpack containing changes of linen, toilet articles, and a fresh shirt or two. They both wore swords at their belts, balanced on the right by scabbarded knives.

"We'll have to find a place to get lunch soon," Tom observed, peering up toward the late-morning sun. "I'm getting hungry, aren't you?"

"A woodsman is always hungry," replied Clem with a

broad grin. "There's a village just ahead. I saw it from the last rise."

"They'll have an inn, perhaps," said Tom, remembering the Slippery Slate at Wall. "They can give us something to eat, I suppose."

"These inns are required to have provender for men and beasts alike," Clem told him. "By the king's law."

"A sensible law," Tom said. "From a sensible king, do you think?"

"I never thought much about such high persons," Clem admitted, kicking a stone into the ditch without breaking his stride. "Those of us who work for our living have little time for discussing our betters."

"But surely you would have heard opinions over a pint of ale of an evening, perhaps in Wall?"

"Just gossip!" cried the trapper. "I pay no attention to that guff."

"But others do speak of kings and such, do they?"

"More than you would believe!"

"What, then, do these others—these gossips—have to say about the qualities of King Eduard?" Tom asked, pushing the issue.

"That he is a good man. That he seems to be sensible, if you like! That he is handsome—that from the ladies, of course—and that he is strong of hand and sharp of eye— from the men. They have no great complaints about the king. . . ."

"But the new queen?"

"I know you spoke of her with Princess Amanda, Tom. What do you want me to add?"

"What your friends think or what you've heard them say. We'll shortly be in her service for some months. I'd like to know how she is perceived."

"Perceptions are chancy things," observed the trapper. "Well, since you insist . . . Beatrix of Knollwater is a very beautiful woman, they say, but a quiet one, who seldom speaks out in public. Most men think she's cold and distant, maybe uncaring. Women say she is unhappy—or afrighted."

"Thank you, Clem. I know what Manda says, and Murdan, but I value an outside opinion. There's that village ahead!"

•   •   •

SPREND lay astride the roadway. A slowly winding, clear brook, known locally merely as the Brook, ran north to south through its middle. Just across the stone bridge stood the Babbling Bass, a substantial, rambling two-story inn fronted by an elm-shaded dooryard and backed by spacious stableyards and an apple orchard. The trees were already heavy with young, green fruit.

Along the Brook, on pilings driven down to hold back slips of sand or soil from the stream, a dozen men of all ages sat, fishing poles in hands and lines in the water.

As Tom and Clem came across the bridge, a youngster near the bridge suddenly jerked his line from the water and landed a flopping large-mouthed bass. He grinned up at the travelers and popped the fish into a reed-woven purse by his side.

"You've brought me luck, good sirs!" called the lad, while the other fishermen scowled, pretending to be displeased by the mere boy's catch and the interruption by strangers.

"Sell us your catch for our lunch?" Clem shouted back, leaning his elbows on the wide parapet.

"Gladly!" replied the lad. He grounded his pole and brought them his creel basket, in which the bass was still flopping on a bed of wet green cress. "The keeper of Babbling Bass will fry it up for you, quick as I can tell about it."

Tom paid him five new coppers for the fish and invited him to come dine with them at the inn.

"Ah, no, sir! I'm off to my own home, where my mother will have luncheon for me and a scolding for fishing instead of cleaning the henhouse."

"Wicked boy!" laughed Tom. "Here, have another penny. 'Twill make Mother feel the better for your playing hooky."

The boy thanked them, recommended them to the innkeeper, who now stood in the dooryard, his spotless white apron flapping in the breeze. Grinning from ear to ear, the lad dashed off, not forgetting his fishing pole on the bank of Brook. His fellow fishermen nodded at the strangers and returned their attention to their poles and lines.

They ate the freshly caught bass and found it delicious, in the dim, low-ceilinged common room of the Babbling Bass, and talked easily with the innkeeper, who, it turned out, was a retired guardsman of Murdan the Historian.

"Yes, I served him long before he built Overhall, even. We were young blades, those days, always fighting great battles and chasing beautiful ladies! I mind me one time . . ."

And he was off on a rambling tale of how Murdan had met his wife, the late Murielle, to which the travelers listened both because it was polite and because they learned a great deal about their Lord Historian at the same time.

"How did Murdan come to be so close to the king? They are related, I understand," Tom asked, pushing his emptied place away.

"They are half brothers and were friends from early boyhood. Shared the same tutors," said Fling, the innkeeper. "They fought the Barbarians, side by side in the snow. The prince, the king as he's now, was Commander of the Blue. His royal father was not at all in favor of his only son leading us in battle. We were ever in the center of every fight, proud and glory seeking, ye know! Ah, foolish, I might now say, what with all my years."

"A good commander, was Lord Murdan?" asked Clem.

"The very best! Old Gantrell, the young lord's father he was, was Commander of the Green. Much too stodgy! Wouldn't stray from a direct line for anything, they said. He did keep his men alive and well fed, however," added Fling, admitting, now that he was close to a hundred-fifty years, that this was a good idea, after all.

"We go to the king and his new queen," Tom told the innkeeper as they finished lunching and prepared to leave. "I'll give him your greetings, if you like."

"I would be . . . well, quite overcome with gratitude, sir, young sirs! Mayhap he won't recall old Fling, although we had some exciting times together—me and the king who was then Prince Royal, and the Historian, who I served as batman—as valet, as they call 'em these days. Give His Majesty Fling's love and fealty and good memories. And Her Majesty the queen, too, for I suspect she'll need all good wishes, poor thing."

The jolly innkeeper's honest well-wishings sped them on their way.

FFALLMAR was a tall, broad-shouldered man with a ruddy, square face and intelligent, thoughtful eyes who had a marvelous way of breaking into a sunny smile when he was pleased, which was often. His wife and children adored him, it was obvious, and his men and maids served his needs with friendly, cheerful willingness.

The broad acres of Ffallmar Farm were beautifully cared for, the dairy cows were pampered like household pets, and the orchards promised a great crop of tart-sweet pippins—those that make the best eating and cider pressing, according to Ffallmar, as he showed them about his place.

Young Eddie and his sisters—Valery, very much the young lady, and Molly, who hadn't decided yet whether she was tomboy or lady (and was some of each, in her delightful way)—followed them about, proudly displaying their own pigs, chickens, and ponies.

Their mother, Rosemary, supervised a gala supper and prepared a guest room for each of them in her spacious, spotless, low-eaved house. Hot baths and clean clothes were waiting for them when the farmer at last brought them inside. The imminent rain was beginning to fall, a blessing on the fields and apple trees.

"I can see why you chose Ffallmar for husband," Tom said to the lady of the house as they sat down to dinner. "He's a delightful, sensible man! I like him very much."

"And handsome, too!" added Rosemary, highly pleased at his words. She passed a pitcher of chilled cider to Clem and told her husband again how the wicked kidnapper Freddie had sniveled and sobbed when these two caught him at Wall.

"I rode a Dragon!" cried Eddie, waving a chicken drumstick aloft. "We flew over the ocean and over the cliffs!"

"Son, eat that leg or put it back on the plate," admonished his father, but he smiled at the boy's enthusiasm. "He wants to be a Dragon Companion himself one day. A fine ambition for a farm lad!"

"There could be many worse ambitions," said Tom. "Even this Companion will be happy someday to settle in such a place as this and make his land fruitful with grain and apples and healthy, happy children."

When Rosemary at last led her offspring away from table and headed them unwillingly for their beds, the travelers sat with Ffallmar on the farmhouse's broad porch, overlooking a pond where a flock of snow white geese was settling down for the night.

"Eduard Ten is all you've heard, certainly," said Ffallmar, lighting his pipe with a spill brought by a housemaid. "Honest, hardworking, faithful, and fair to his people, especially his countrymen, the farmers and the small merchants. His troubles come from a few great magnates, such as Peter of Gantrell and his noble friends, and a small group of wealthy commoners, mostly merchants and lawyers. They all feel they could rule, with a Gantrell as king, better than King Eduard can rule."

"But everyone seems to think His Majesty does uncommonly well as ruler," objected Tom. "Or am I just parroting what has been told me by friends of the king, men like you and Murdan?"

"No, I know some quite good men who don't dislike Murdan nor me but agree with Gantrell on this particular matter," said the young farmer. "Eduard Ten has powerful enemies, and most of them have gone to Gantrell's camp."

"Why do the rich merchants and lawyers oppose the king's party, then?" asked Clem, interested despite himself.

Ffallmar considered this while he relit his fragrant tobacco. His wife returned and, taking up some embroidery, sat beside him in the last light of day, stitching but saying little.

"These merchants don't want to pay the duties the throne demands, for one thing. Nobody enjoys paying royal taxes. No farmer, I can tell you, wants to pay money to support a distant, high-living court. But most of us realize it's necessary to pay for good roads and safe passage for our produce. For strong but fair royal justice, also, which is needed in matters in dispute. So most of us pay with grumbling, but we pay and on time."

"But?"

"But it seems very wealthy men love their money more passionately than others not so well off. They hate to see it go out. They can hire their own soldiers and sailors to protect their houses, carts, and cargoes. They claim they're paying twice for armed protection from the Barbarians, for example. A shortsighted view, but there you are! They think, because they have managed to make a fortune buying and selling goods or trying expensive lawsuits in the lesser courts, they're better suited to making decisions than a king born to the crown and its power!"

"Not a new story, I suspect," said Tom thoughtfully. "It sounds all too familiar to me."

"Nor will it go away when Eduard passes the crown to his heir," put in Rosemary. "Manda, if she is crowned queen, will have these and even greater problems. I mention it to you, Tom, because it seems you'll be close to her when the time comes."

"It worries both of us, of course," admitted the Librarian. "If it's left at that, Manda has the intelligence and the will to be a good ruler, I believe."

"I've no doubt of it, especially if she's lucky enough to have an intelligent, strong consort by her side to help her."

"*If* she is made queen," amended Tom.

"If not, what then for you two?" asked Ffallmar bluntly.

"An Achievement of our own somewhere, I think," answered Tom. "I would be most happy serving Murdan for years to come, but I must make my personal way. With a princess for a bride, I'd need more income than my wage from Overhall's library, I imagine."

"No doubt about it!" Rosemary chuckled. "But our Manda will be content with less than the king's treasury to buy her gowns and fill her stables."

"I believe so, also," said Ffallmar. "Bring a lamp, Hewy!"

They sat until full darkness, talking of farming and ruling, of crops and courts. And about Queen Beatrix.

"I don't know her at all well," Rosemary answered Tom's question. "I've only seen her twice, from a distance both times. That was when she married Eduard. My impressions—and I was little more than a lass myself at the time—is she was unhappy in the milling, overwhelming crowds, unsure of her dealings with powerful men and their rich, proud wives, who know everything and how to do anything, or seem to."

"Was she an only daughter, do you know?" asked Tom.

"Yes, I believe so," Rosemary answered. "Yes, that might explain some of her diffidence. And her young life was lonely, very isolated at Knollwater. Only children, as I can attest . . ."

" . . . and I can also tell you, being one myself," Tom inserted.

" . . . are often shy and, well, both quiet and spoiled. Fortunately for me, I early on found a husband who gave me the confidence to be a sure woman."

"I beat her regularly," teased Ffallmar behind his hand, loud enough so that all could hear. "It keeps her from being too spoiled."

"Nonsense! No one is more spoiled than am I!" cried his wife in mock anger. "Besides, you couldn't beat me at checkers, husband!"

THE next morning Clem and Tom set out on the next leg of their journey under cloudy skies and in cool, moist wind.

"It'll clear before eleven o'clock," promised Ffallmar, bidding them good-bye at his house gate with his wife and his children, all three of whom had begged to go along.

"I remember that adage from my childhood," cried Tom. " 'Rain before seven . . . ' "

" ' . . . Clear before 'leven!' " finished the children, having heard it so many times before from their father.

"We'll see you in the fall at Lexor," promised Rosemary, slipping a packet of ham sandwiches into Clem's pack. "Be watchful, gentlemen! Peter of Gantrell is not a man to forget or forgive, for all his smooth ways! He knows, you can be sure, who thwarted his plans to make me hostage against my father's support for the king."

Clem was silent for some time after they began to walk. At last he laughed aloud. Tom looked sideways at him with raised eyebrows.

"I've never been privileged to see a noble family this close," Clem confessed. "I find they are very little different from most of us lesser folk, from my own family."

"People like Ffallmar and Rosemary are what my father used to call the 'salt of the earth,' " Tom told him. "They make everyone else seem better for having them around."

"I've never thought much of having land and wealth," Clem went on. "But if I could be like them, it would be worth the while. Better'n looking forward to setting trap lines in frozen mud and blowing snow every winter for the rest of my life, perhaps. Not that I will ever lose my love of wild places."

"Nor should you!" Tom exclaimed. "Ah, I would think Mornie would be a happy helpmeet in anything you decided to do, Clem, farm or furs."

"I hope so," replied the trapper, blushing. "And I'll be worthy of her confidence in me, Tom. I really will!"

"As for that, I don't spend a moment worrying about it," Tom answered.

"WHAT'S that ahead?" he asked, some miles later.

It was another village—a town, rather—on the shore of a blue lake that stretched to the horizon.

"According to Murdan's map," said Clem, briskly, " 'tis called Lakehead. It's a Gantrell holding. We'll tread more carefully from here on."

The very pretty lakeside town was somewhat cheerier and less grimy and run down than Wall, the only other town of size Tom yet had seen in this world. The people were friendly, but they spent little time in pleasantries, rushing off on this or that errand before a visitor could begin to ask questions about the best way to go.

A short, red-faced, rather paunchy man wearing a tall felt hat decorated with a green feather saw them enter the town square and immediately headed importantly their way.

"A bailiff, by his feather," Clem warned in a quick whisper. "He'll be Gantrell's man, here. 'Twould be best not to say too much, sir."

"Mum's the word, then," agreed the Librarian, and he saluted the official pleasantly but with cool reserve.

"I am Kedry, Bailiff for Lakehead Town and Lakeheart County," the man announced pompously, with no preamble or greeting. "It is my duty to ask who you are and where headed."

"I am Thomas, Librarian of Overhall Castle," answered Tom. "This is my friend and traveling companion, Clematis of Broken Land."

"Broken Land, is it?" sniffed the bailiff, in a neutral tone. "Few of your kind ever come this way."

"I walk with my friend from Overhall, in order to broaden my knowledge of the kingdom," explained the trapper.

"We carry the greetings and letters of the Royal Historian, Murdan of Overhall," Tom went on. "I carry his letter addressed to His Majesty the king himself."

"What reason has that sly rascal for sending word to Eduard Ten?" wondered the bailiff aloud.

"I have no idea," protested Tom. "I am but the messenger."

"Messengers must beware, if the message is bad news," warned Kedry, frowning at them meaningfully.

"I can but assume that, as Murdan is Royal Historian, my master often has important words to write privately to the king," Tom said stiffly, giving the bailiff back look for look. "Few would dare to interfere with any letter addressed to the king, I think."

The bailiff stood back a pace, looking as though he might dispute this, but at last he glanced away and said, more respectfully, "You'll be looking for a ship going toward Lexor, then?"

Tom glanced at Clem, who answered with a shrug.

"If that would speed our steps, it would be the way we want to go," he answered the bailiff.

"Well, in that case, ask for Captain Boscor of *Maiden Skimmer*," Kedry said, already moving away into the busy crowd. "He sails within the quarter hour from City Pier, out there."

He disappeared and the two travelers followed his gesture to a wide stone mole that jutted into the lake from its rocky shoreline. City Pier was lined with boats and ships of all sorts and sizes, some of them passenger packets, Tom decided, but most small cargo and fishing vessels.

They asked for *Maiden Skimmer* and were directed by a fisherman to the far end of the pier. "She's that two-master there."

Approaching the ship, which was busy with all the preparations for sailing, they were suddenly halted by an elderly man in shabby clothes, with a heavy gray beard and reddened eyes.

"Ye seek to sail aboard *Maiden Skimmer*?" he asked, blocking their way with a stout cane.

"We seek a way down the lake to Lexor rather," answered Clem sharply. "Do you object to this *Skimmer*, Oldster?"

"Bonny lad!" said the man, more softly. "I wouldn't recommend Boscor's ship to anyone wearing the livery of Overhall. He's the haughty follower of . . . well, ye can guess, can't you?"

Tom looked over the man's shoulder to where the sloop was beginning to warp away from the pier, her sailors busy hoisting sails.

"I can guess, but we are peacefully traveling on our master's business to the king," he explained. "What would you have us do, rather?"

"Delay your departure an hour or so. I recommend you sail with a king's man known as Trover. His ship's down the shore a short way. Called *Pinnacle Flyer,* she is."

"And this Trover is more friendly to Murdan?" asked Clem.

"I can guarantee it, as over Boscor."

"Well, talking to you, old coot, we've missed Boscor's ship, anyway," said Clem. "I suspect your advice is good, however."

"If 'tis," said the ragged man, "I could use a penny or three, just to thank me for the tip. We are being watched, and I have the reputation of being a vile beggar, you see."

"Walk down the shore with us and talk to us," said Tom, "and perhaps—no, I guarantee—you'll get your tip."

"Done!" cried the man, who looked a heavy drinker, although he was quite sober at the moment. He led them off City Pier and turned eastward, down a narrow path that paralleled the pebbly lakeshore. The way was lined with shops, sheds, shipyards and sail lofts, ropewalks and chandleries, all very busy. Boats and ships of every description were moored close to shore. No one seemed to note their passing.

"Here in Lakehead, everyone minds his own business," explained the codger when Tom remarked upon it.

"Except you," Clem said quickly.

"It's my business to look after Murdan's business, here. I am his eyes and ears in Lakehead."

"Is it so?" asked Tom. "You saw his blazon on my sleeve and knew we would be in trouble if we took this Boscor's sloop?"

"Oh, I had word of your coming from the Historian himself. I ekes out me living, or so it seems, selling and buying

pigeons and doves. In amongst them are well-trained hom-
ing pigeons secreted. Murdan and I exchange little notes
now and again."

They had walked beyond the last of the shops and works
and rounded a bend in the shore. The dove man went
faster and straighter, no longer leaning so hard on his
thick cane.

"You be Thomas Librarian, who rescued the Historian's
daughter. And you, sir, are the doughty woodsman who
showed him the way."

"You've established that you are well informed for a
town drunk," said Clem, still suspicious. "Do you also sell
information to a certain bailiff here? Didn't the fat one set
you on us, just now?"

"I saw Kedry bespeak you, certainly, but he and I never
talk to each other. He suspects what I am—but then, he
suspects everybody equally. Maybe this will convince you,
youngster. Last night you sat at Ffallmar's table and ate roast
spring lamb with Lady Rosemary's best mint sauce. Is that
right?"

"Correct," admitted Clem. "How came you to know
this?"

"Lord Ffallmar sent a bird to me this morning, and the
menu was to be my proof of good intent, of course."

"I'm convinced, then," said Clem with a grin, giving the
man a clap on the back.

"You'll live longer in the east, if you're suspicious of
every man," grunted the pigeon breeder. "When ye've
sailed, I'll send a fast bird off to Overhall. I imagine old Murdan will be relieved to hear you went
with Trover, rather than Boscor. Incidentally, Trover
and Boscor are brothers, to muddy the waters even
more."

"There's an interesting story in that, I'm sure," said
Tom and, as they walked slowly along beside the lake,
the bird seller told them about the two captains who clung
to opposite sides in the old conflict between the Crown and
the Standing Bear.

They never did learn the pigeon seller's name.

"WITH the exception of the bailiff," complained Tom,
"everyone we've bespoken so far on this journey has been

attached to Murdan and the king's party or, at least, quite sympathetic with it."

"Do you misdoubt the king's party?" asked Captain Trover, surprised.

"I only want to hear what his enemies are saying about the king, about Murdan and about Princess Royal Alix Amanda. You can't know too much about your enemy's thoughts, can you?"

"I'd agree with that. Me worst enemy is me own brother, ye'll have heard from the dove lover, I warrant."

"Yes, he told us about that," said Clem.

"A good man, for all he talks way to much," said the rather dour lake captain. "Excuse me, Master Librarian, but I must see to me sails, now."

He dashed forward, shouting to two of the three men who formed his crew. The third handled the tiller.

Pinnacle Flyer skimmed along before the west wind, which carried them and a few brief showers of slanted rain with it. Once they had left Lakehead, the lake widened rapidly. They were almost out of sight of the northern shore while the south shore was already over the horizon.

The wind was warm and wet, not uncomfortable. They sat on a cushioned thwart just abaft the sloop's single mast. Captain Trover roamed back and forth, stepping over their legs to go forward and stand with his hand shading his eyes, gazing forward.

"Damnation!" they heard him swear. He stomped aft and stopped next to Tom and Clem.

"We're overtaking him, the slimy rat!"

"I assume you're referring to your brother," said Clem.

"Blast his eyes!" swore Trover. "He must have sailed late, rather than on time."

"No, *Maiden Skimmer* was just sailing when we met the dove seller on City Pier, two hours back," Tom remembered.

"He should have made better time than this!" the captain calculated. "Something must be wrong aboard *Skimmer!*"

"Will you go alongside her to help?" Clem wanted to know. His nature urged him to assist anyone, even enemies, when they were in trouble.

"I should let the mad dog sink!" growled Trover. He shook his head angrily. "But . . . he's me brother, for all his misguided ways."

He raised his voice to call, "Stand by to go about! Lively there, boys. Not too near, but close enough to cuss at the damned reprobate."

✦ 18 ✦
Lake Piracy

A FEW minutes later *Pinnacle Flyer* had run close enough to *Maiden Skimmer* to see she lay almost dead in the water, her sails in heaps on the deck and trailing over. They saw no one aboard.

"Ahoy!" Captain Trover hailed. "Ahoy, *Maiden Skimmer*! Boscor, you blacksnake, is this your idea of a joke? Ahoy, anyone aboard the sloop!"

No answer.

Trover ordered the helm put hard over, and as the wind spilled from her main, stay, and jib sails, *Pinnacle Flyer* rocked to an uneasy stop half a length from the silent barkentine.

Trover stood beside his helmsman, staring out over the water at his brother's vessel, taking in every detail, studying how she lay, how she rolled in the swell.

"Break out the sweeps," he ordered in a subdued voice.

His lake men unlashed long, slim oars from under the gunwales on either side of the cockpit and set them in oarlocks on the rail.

The tallest and huskiest of his three men seated himself on a thwart and dragged the long oars through the water. In five strokes he sent *Pinnacle* toward the derelict.

"Easy!" cautioned Trover, signaling to his helmsman with his hands. "A bit to port, lad. Midships now."

Just as it seemed they would ram the other ship broadside, he ordered, "Back water!" and the oarsman pushed heavily on his sweeps, slowing the tiny ship to a halt. *Pinnacle*'s bow scraped softly along *Maiden* amidships, swinging slowly to come to rest parallel to her length.

The distraught captain scrambled onto her deck, eighteen inches higher than his own, while his crew made lines fast between the two ships.

"Can we help you, Captain?" called Tom.

"Right! Come aboard her, then, sirs. You lads stay at your posts and be ready to cast off if I say so."

The travelers from Overhall joined him on *Maiden*'s empty deck.

"No one," noted the lake captain, puzzled and worried. "I'll look below. Better come with me, sirs, just in case. Keep your eyes open."

The main cabin, five steps below the deck, was a shambles. Papers and clothing were scattered over the whole. Broken glassware and spilled liquids made walking treacherous as they moved forward. In the tiny galley alcove half-prepared food had been left standing and an iron cookstove still smoldered, charred rags piled about it on the deck.

"Pirates!" howled Trover, wringing his hands. "My poor brother! What's been done here? Murder? Larceny?"

"Calm yourself, Captain," Tom soothed. "I see no signs of violence to men, at least. No blood or bodies. If these were pirates, they must have taken the passengers and crew off as captives."

"It appears to me," said Clem, kneeling to examine the charred rags, "that they hoped to burn her when they left. This tinder is still hot and smoking. It was too damp to burn well, is all."

"Toss it over the side," urged Trover with a shudder. Clem did so, and Tom and the captain followed him up to the deck.

"Captain!" called out a crewman. He pointed aft. "*Maiden* carried a skiff and a longboat, there and there."

"They've been kidnapped, then," cried Trover. He looked about in dismay. *Maiden* wallowed in the choppy waves pushed up by the westerlies. "They put everybody into her boats and abandoned her to burn. Even if she hadn't burned, she'd have drifted before the wind for miles and miles before she ran on shore."

"Is this usual?" asked Tom. "Piracy on Lakeheart Lake, I mean."

"Not in recent years," said one of the lake men when Trover wandered off, not answering. "Most every boat family on Lakeheart was lake pirates at one time. Including the Sacks. That's the captain's family."

Trover Sack returned, shaking his head, now recovering from his shock.

"If we read the signs aright, they didn't harm anyone. They'll send a demand for ransom soon. We must return at once to Lakehead and tell Bailiff Kedry. Not that he could do much. Wait for the ransom demand . . . and meet it."

"We'll stay with you until you recover your brother," Tom promised him. "Man needs company at a time like this."

"I . . . I . . . I thank you, from me heart," replied Trover Sack. "Ye're strangers here, but good king's men, I see. Thank you for your help and support!"

He quickly made arrangements for his first mate, the most experienced of his crewmen, to take command of poor *Maiden* and sail her home.

"If you'll be so kind as to lend me your hands," he said to Tom and Clem, "we can sail *Pinnacle* while the boys bring in *Maiden*."

Tacking against the stiffening breeze, the two ships struggled together back to Lakehead, arriving after dark and mooring at City Pier in *Maiden*'s usual spot. Even before they stepped ashore word had spread that something unusual had happened, and a crowd of lake sailors and merchants gathered.

"They know Boscor and I wouldn't sail together, unless something had gone very wrong," explained Trover. "Our fool feud is the talk of the entire town."

He sent a boy to fetch the bailiff from his supper. Kedry arrived, red faced and looking angry at the imposition, just as the sailors finished furling the sails and battening hatches against the rain and night.

"Ho!" shouted the burly official. "What is it couldn't wait 'til I'd finished dinner? You brothers had a falling out, is it? What have you done to him and his crew? And his passengers? I've a good mind to clap you in irons in the town jail!"

"Wait just a damned minute," said Tom in some heat. "You don't even know what happened out there and you're talking of irons and jail!"

"It's my judgment that counts," Kedry screamed back. "Every man here knows about Trover and Boscor Sack. At each other's throats all the time! Something like this was bound to happen in the end, I say."

The growing crowd was quite obviously polarized, half supporting the bailiff's guesses, the other half shaking their heads and muttering that he was being unfair.

"Hear their story at least," someone shouted. Tom thought it was the dove seller, on the back fringe of the crowd, but he couldn't be sure. Neither could Kedry.

"Well, then, tell us how you did it, Trover. Waited for him over the horizon and surprised him, was it?"

"No, bailiff! I just got this charter with these two young men. Otherwise I would not have sailed today at all! We . . ."

Kedry squinted at Tom and Clem, saying, "I thought I sent you to sail with Boscor, lads. Why did you change your minds, eh?"

"We missed *Maiden*'s sailing and a passerby told us about Captain Trover," Tom explained patiently. "We sailed with him aboard *Pinnacle*, and after an hour or so on the lake he sighted *Maiden* becalmed, her sails in the water, and nobody aboard."

"Pirates!" someone yelled, and the uproar over this kept anyone from speaking for several moments. At last the bailiff raised his voice in a harsh, wordless shout and the furor died away.

"Pirates, indeed!" he scoffed. "We've not had such in this lake for close to fifty years. It's a story made up by Trover to fool the law, believe me."

"Be of some sense, Kedry," said an important-looking gentleman, just arrived on the scene. The crowd parted to make way for him.

"Mayor Fellows!" the bailiff cried, almost bowing double at the waist to the newcomer. "Here's a mystery and a dispute, sir! I say Trover did away with his hated brother Boscor, and Trover and his passengers say it were pirates!"

"Let us get this inside out of the rain," said the mayor. He was a tall, middle-aged man, evidently of some position and respect. He wore a gold chain of office about his neck and his doublet was discretely embroidered with the Standing

Bear symbol of the Gantrell family, the first Tom had seen since Wall.

"Can you get a fair hearing in this town?" Tom whispered to Trover as they followed the mayor off the pier.

"Mayor Fellows is a good man, fair and just, even if he be a Gantrell creature. He'll control Kedry, at least. To Fellows, renewed piracy will be more important than a mere family quarrel."

Tom smiled at the man's new view of his brother. The crowd followed them all the way to Town Hall on the square, opposite City Pier. Those not quick enough to take seats within stood about the open doors and windows to listen.

"Now, then," began Mayor Fellows, "by virtue of my powers and duties and so forth, as Mayor of the Town of Lakehead and Justice of Lakeheart County, I declare open a court of inquiry under the laws of the king, Eduard Ten, whom God bless with long life, and the guidance of my lord, Peter of Gantrell, our liege lord."

He clapped his hands once and sat behind a massive desk carved with looping ropes and fouled anchors. There was a pause while someone hastened to bring out flags to place on either side of the bench. A crier rephrased the mayor's words with proper regard to ceremony, in a loud, high-pitched voice.

Mayor Fellows waited impatiently until this was completed, then slapped the desktop with his open palm and at once the crowd fell silent.

"Let the bailiff testify first what information he has, then," said he.

Kedry, looking flustered, stood in the center of the open space before the mayor's desk. To give him credit, now under oath, he made a straightforward statement of the facts as he knew them.

"Now, Captain Sack, let's hear your story of what happened," said Mayor Fellows. "Under oath, please."

Being sworn, Trover Sack related for the court what he had done, and when, down to taking his brother's ship under his care and returning to harbor.

"I understand you dispute Trover Sack's testimony, Bailiff Kedry?" inquired the mayor when Trover had finished and taken his seat.

"Well, Your Honor, I may have been hasty in me words, although it seemed obvious that if our friend Boscor Sack is dead or missing . . ."

"No evidence of his death has been adduced," the mayor interrupted.

"Well, Your Honor, sir, I merely suggest an interpretation of the facts based on the known quarrel between the Sack brothers. They've been heard to threaten bodily harm to each other, ofttimes, even to threats of death! I can take witnesses from this very crowd, here, to those facts."

"That may be necessary, later," agreed the judge-mayor. "For now, I'd like to hear the witness of the two young men who were passengers aboard *Pinnacle Flyer*."

Tom stepped forward and was sworn in in due form. He identified himself and his companion, showing the mayor a letter of introduction that the Historian had provided for just such a purpose, should it arise. The mayor entered into the record that their identification was true and proper, as he recognized Murdan's signature and seal.

"Now tell us, please, what happened today, beginning when you entered Lakehead."

Tom told the story, ending with the discovery of the sloop *Maiden*, adrift and abandoned on the lake.

"Do you have any reason to believe Captain Trover Sack planned to intercept his brother's ship while underway?" asked Fellows.

"No, Your Honor. Although I'm not conversant with ships and sailors' ways, I have to say that when we arrived at *Pinnacle*'s mooring, which is some distance from the town, her crew was not prepared or even preparing to sail. They knew Boscor's *Maiden* usually sailed on schedule at noon. Everyone else knew it, it seems, including the bailiff, who recommended her to take us over the lake."

"Is this so?" the mayor asked the bailiff.

"It is true, Your Honor."

"Then," said Fellows, leaning forward in his chair, "had Trover intended to waylay his brother in open water, he would have departed his anchorage at least two hours sooner than he did, according to Master Thomas's testimony."

"It would seem so, Your Honor, sir," agreed the deflated bailiff.

"Then we can accept the matter as Trover and this witness testify, I believe. The barkentine belonging to Boscor Sack, I must believe, was intercepted, boarded, and captured by unknown pirates and her passengers and crew carried away captives."

"It would seem so, Your Honor," replied Kedry grudgingly. "And I apologize to Captain Sack for doubting his truthfulness."

The mayor called for the witness of Clem of Broken Land, and the experienced woodsman carefully described what he saw when they boarded the abandoned sloop, down to the charred rags and the missing boats.

Mayor Fellows heard corroborating evidence from the three *Pinnacle* sailors, who were all of good reputation in Lakehead, being sons of long-standing families.

Then the mayor-judge stood and spoke.

"The court believes piracy has been committed by a party or parties unknown upon the open lake, against the persons of Captain Boscor Sack, his crew, and six unknown passengers, although it remains to be seen whether all or some of said passengers were perpetrators or victims.

"The court orders the lord's bailiff, who is charged with prevention, apprehension, and punishment of the crime of piracy on our lake, to proceed at once to find, arrest, and bring to trial said pirates and to rescue their victims, if they still live."

Kedry signified his willingness to begin an investigation at once. He asked for permission to form a posse to carry out the search.

"I guess we'll have to wait for the pirates to send some sort of ransom note, then," said Trover wearily to the mayor.

"Kedry is an incompetent blowhard and sometimes a downright fool, but he's an honest, incompetent fool," said Fellows. "It's possible he'll locate where the captives are being held."

"Just barely possible," muttered the lake captain, shaking his head sadly. "I'm not sure Kedry could find his mouth with a spoon. Well, friends," he said, turning to Tom and Clem, "let me invite you to bunk at my house for the night. It's the least I can do for you."

They accepted his invitation and shortly, while the bailiff huddled with the two dozen men of his posse on how best to search out the pirates, the three of them retired to Trover's lakeside cottage for a late supper.

Over a Spartan meal—the lakeman was a bachelor—Tom turned Trover's thoughts from his brother's tragedy with questions about the king and the lord of Lakehead.

"Is Peter of Gantrell an evil man, Captain? Some say he is so, but others aren't so sure."

"I've heard the gossip and watched the man's actions from afar. I say that he's no better or worse than many men, just richer. He's very ambitious, it's obvious. He's said to have done cruel things, but I've read of kings who have been as cruel in the past, some for good motives, others for selfish ones."

"But you personally don't like Lord Peter, do you?" asked Clem.

"N-n-no, I must admit that I dislike a man with so much ambition that he forgets he can do great harm to innocents who might be in his way. Several years ago Gantrell—I mean Lord Peter, of course—was suddenly *given* Lakehead as a holding by our former longtime liege, one Beryl of Beryl. No one ever found out why Beryl gave up such a lucrative property. It was rumored that Gantrell forced Beryl to cede him the whole county as payment of a gambling debt. Unfortunately, Beryl died shortly afterward."

He paused to sip from his mug of birch beer.

"We were upset by the change, you can imagine. Beryls had been our masters for centuries. We prospered most of the time, despite outbreaks of piracy. The first two things Lord Gantrell did were, one, to appoint a respected local man as mayor. That was a good thing. Mayor Fellows is well liked and fair, as you could judge from his court of inquiry."

"Yes, I was impressed with how well he handled it," responded Tom.

"The second thing he did was not as popular. He made this man Kedry his bailiff. Kedry is a long-told joke. He's tried his hand unsuccessfully at a half dozen different trades. He lost his father's two ships—bad luck, he claimed; bad judgment, his creditors said! He opened a chandlery, but lost all when he lowered his prices to beat his competitors, and went bust. Another time he tried bottling lake water and shipping it to Waterfields, where he heard the water was rank and bad tasting. Imagine! Shipping bottled water to a place as wet as Waterfields!"

They laughed at Trover's description of the fiasco and foolishness.

"As bailiff, he uses his office to punish those he feels drove him out of his businesses. Last year we all signed a petition against him, and the mayor took it to Lord Peter. Lord Peter laughed it out of his house! And it was signed by fifty of the staunchest Gantrell supporters in Lakehead!"

"That was when you turned to the king's side?" Clem guessed shrewdly.

"I had my doubts long before, but it was the straw that broke my back, I tell you. We deserve better from the man to whom we pay enormous imposts each year. Why else have lords?"

"Why, indeed?" Tom asked quietly.

"There are some very frightened sailors out there somewhere," Clem said as he prepared for bed.

"We may be able to help them more tomorrow," said Tom from the bed, already half-asleep.

"How so? Neither of us is a boatman. These pirates could be hiding in any of a hundred coves on either shore, or on a thousand islands between."

"You forget who will join us in the morning, if all has gone according to plan."

"Who's that?"

"Retruance Constable, of course," answered Tom.

✦ 19 ✦
Retruance to the Rescue

THEY were at breakfast when the sun, which was shining brightly through the east windows, suddenly was blotted out, plunging the room into shadow.

"What in . . . !" exclaimed Trover, leaping to his feet.

"Nothing to worry about," Tom reassured him, continuing to fork fried egg. "Just a Dragon arriving."

"My God!" exclaimed the captain, rushing to the window. "The size of him!"

Retruance lowered his great head to the window and peered in, eye to eye with the lake man.

"Is this the house of Trover Sack?" he asked politely. His head was at the house but his tail was splashing playfully in Lakeheart Lake.

Tom came to the window to greet his mount and, after Trover had thrown the shutters wide, he patted the Dragon fondly on the snout.

"You had no trouble finding us?" he asked.

"None at all. I stopped this morning to ask Ffallmar if he'd seen you. He'd received a note by pigeon saying you were staying with a sailor named Sack."

"Have you had breakfast, Sir Dragon?" asked Trover, swallowing his amazement long enough to remember his manners.

"Yes, thank you. I found the lake trout in your waters most delicious!"

He retreated to the lake—a Dragon finds few freshwater lakes large enough to actually swim in comfortably—while his companions finished breakfast.

"What's to do?" Retruance asked, when they appeared on the lakeshore, accompanying the captain. "Are we off to Lexor now, or direct to Sweetwater Tower?"

"We've got a task to do here first." Tom told him the events of the previous day. "We need to search out these pirates and rescue their captives, especially Captain Trover's brother."

"Shouldn't be too hard to find 'em," Retruance said with great confidence. "We'll go aloft and look for signs of 'em. If they're pirates, they'll probably stay near the water, I'd think. Boats are pretty hard to hide and harder to drag overland, aren't they?"

It took a bit of persuading to get Trover to climb aboard the Dragon's brow and fly out over the lake, but the thought of having to wait on shore for others to rescue his brother steeled him to do it at last. Shortly they were winging over the calm, blue water. The Dragon flew with his pinions widespread and almost unmoving, providing a slow and silent flight. Tom knew from past experience that the Dragon's blue-silver underside made him virtually invisible from below.

"*Skimmer* was just about here when we found her," said Trover. He had quickly adapted to the viewpoint, the result of years of reading charts, which were, after all, a kind of overhead view.

"Where would *you* go if you were in an open boat in the middle of such a sea?" Retruance asked.

"The nearest shore is sixteen miles north of here—but the road along the North Shore is rather heavily traveled by local merchants and those who can't afford lake passage. If I were a pirate, I wouldn't want to go ashore there," said Trover Sack.

He hunched forward in the Dragon's saddle, studying the scene below; lake, waves on the shoreline, and islands scattered over the surface as far as the eye could see.

"In fact," he said thoughtfully, "having given it some thought during the night, I've about decided that, if it were me, I'd head for one of the larger islands just over the horizon to the east. Bear Claw, perhaps, or Midlake— no, not Midlake. There's a fishing village there."

"How many islands are there?" asked the Dragon, serenely banking to head east again.

"No one's ever counted that I know of," answered Trover. "Fifty, perhaps. If you count the really small ones, ten times that number. Only a few are large enough to hide a handful of men and at least two boats, however. That leaves maybe twenty islands to look at."

"We've got the time and the Dragon," decided Tom. "Let's give them a good look from the air first. If we see anything suspicious, we'll investigate. If not, we can look more closely later."

"The south shore is mostly swampy and tangled," said the Dragon, who had flown that way many times. "It's an equal thing, whether the south shore or the islands would make the better hideaway."

"My own feeling would be to hide on an island. My grandfather, who dabbled in piracy in his time, I suspect, used to say, 'Stick to what you know best.' Pirates usually do best on the water, not dry land."

They flew over the first of dozens of green islets dotting the surface of the lake, some with narrow, rocky beaches,

a few with no beach at all. All had close-set central crowns
of pines and cedars.

"Bear Claw, over there," said Trover, pointing off to the
right. "It's one of the largest, but very rugged and steep
sided. Too steep to log, you see. Fishermen turn loggers in
winter when they can drag the logs through snow to open
water and float them home. Most of these isles are burned
clean of underbrush every few years to keep them from
becoming too tangled for dragging the trees out. Not Bear
Claw, however. It's without a safe harbor and too chopped
up for logging."

"We'll take a closer look at Bear Claw, though," said
Tom, and the Dragon swooped low over the rounded isle,
circling while they peered down at it from a hundred feet
in the air.

"See? No place to pull even small boats out of the
water," Trover said, shaking his head. "Hardly any level
ground anywhere, even if you could drag your boats up the
cliffs."

Clem, who was best at reading signs, nodded agreement.
The Dragon climbed back to a thousand feet and the search
continued.

"Would it do any good to ask the fishermen of Midlake
Island?" wondered Clem.

"Not likely! They're all likely to be related to the pirates
if not actual pirates themselves," sniffed the lake captain.
"They're a suspicious and closemouth lot at best."

"Maybe a fire-breathing Dragon could convince them to
talk," said Retruance, shooting a short, hot flame before
them to demonstrate, much to Trover's discomfiture.

"Hold to that thought, if needed," said Tom with a laugh
at the Dragon's pretended ferocity.

The search went forward until after the sun reached the
top of the sky and began to slide down the other side.

"We should have brought lunch," complained Clem. "I
was forethoughtful enough to bring a loaf of bread, in case
you're interested."

" 'Woodsmen,' " Tom quoted, " 'are always hungry.' "

"I can go as long as any man without victuals," huffed
Clem, "but in this case, if we're to have lunch, we've got
either to land and eat my bread . . . or go back to Captain
Trover's cottage."

"The lake's full of great trout," Retruance reminded them. "And Dragons are unsurpassed fishermen."

He chose a tiny, flat islet crowned with white birch, gray poplars, and dark green firs but with a gently sloping, shingle beach. While the Librarian explored the island on foot—its only inhabitant was a huge porcupine, asleep in the sun in the lee of a boulder—and Clem scrambled to the highest point of the island to look about, the Dragon quickly captured four fat lake trout. By then, the lake captain had a fire going and was ready to broil them.

When Tom returned, having failed in an attempt to rouse the sleepy porcupine and Clem slid down the rocks from the top of the island, the trout were sizzling cheerily in a black iron frying pan from Clem's pack. From the pack Clem also produced a large white onion and the loaf of bread. He sliced them both and, when the fish filets were ready, made trout-and-raw-onion sandwiches for everybody. To wash their food down they dipped up cold, fresh lake water.

"What next?" Retruance asked, his usual question after lunch.

"More scouting, I guess. Unless anyone has a new idea where to look," Tom said. His companions shook their heads.

"We should keep in touch with Lakehead, perhaps," thought Trover. "Kedry and his posse may have found something. And there'll be a ransom note delivered soon, I think."

"With Retruance's speed, we can return to Lakehead in a few minutes," said the Librarian. "We'll check there later in the afternoon."

"Work like this requires patience," Clem pointed out. "Don't give up yet."

The fire was doused. The Dragon carried them aloft once more and they resumed looking down at dozens of islands of all sizes, from square yards to a few square miles.

The sun was slanting down to the horizon behind them. A new gray cloud bank in the west, laden with rain and flashes of lightning, threatened to cut the long summer afternoon short. They'd gone thirty more miles across the lake until no more islands showed ahead. Tom suggested they turn back.

"Good!" cried Retruance. He made a wide, banked turn

and set a course toward the sun just as it reached the tops of the thunderheads piling up in the Carolna midlands.

"Aha! Hoy! What do I see!" cried Clem just then, pointing straight ahead. "Is that a whiff of smoke?"

"Probably one of the fisher villages," said Trover. He rubbed weary eyes and studied the faint blue trace of smoke rising straight into the unmoving afternoon air.

"No, no, a village would have more than one smoke," Clem insisted.

Retruance slowed his pace and dropped down to keep the thin apostrophe of smoke between them and the sun.

"Hook Island!" exclaimed the lake captain, recognizing it as they came closer. "No village there. We passed over it earlier, I recall."

"Carefully now, Dragon," cautioned Clem. "Slow, low, and easy. We don't want them warned of our coming."

Retruance glided silently down, as slowly as possible for his great bulk and wingspread. They seemed to be standing almost still, a hundred feet above the dead-calm water in the lee of the isle.

"It has the look of a campfire rather than a chimney smoke," thought Clem, aloud. Just then a breeze, stirred by the approach of the storm, came their way and they all caught the smell of wood smoke—and of frying fish and baking bread.

"I think we should look at this one very closely," suggested the lake man. "It could be innocent fishermen, or the bailiff's boys spending the night after a day's searching."

"Or pirates, hiding," said Retruance. "You see? There? The island has a neat little cove."

"That's why it's named Hook," explained Trover. As they dropped almost to the level of the tallest pines atop Hook Island, he started in excitement.

"Boats! Beached in the cove, under those waterside willows!"

"Veer away to the left, Retruance," Tom said quickly, but the Dragon was already changing course to the opposite side of the mile-wide islet. He made a tight circle below the level of the treetops and landed abruptly on a flat, smooth rock at the water's edge.

"I think it's best if you look more closely on foot," he said. "I'm much too big to sneak up on them, here. If they *are* the pirates, I fear they could harm their captives."

"My fear, also," said Trover, grimly. "Some pirates are bloody enough to dump captives in the lake rather than risk being caught with them."

Clem led them into the woods while the Dragon sank down among the rocks, ready to come if called. A deep blanket of pine needles silenced their footsteps as they circled the rise in the middle of the isle and followed their noses toward the cook fire. Under the trees it was getting darker by the minute, now that the sun had dropped behind the thunderheads. A fresh breeze smelled of rain as well as frying fish.

"There!" whispered Clem. He had crawled on his stomach up to the edge of a sharp rise, gently pushing aside the lower boughs of a young cedar. The others followed his example and peered over the hill, down into a hollow at the tip of the cove.

They saw the fire immediately, a bright eye in the gathering gloom. It took a few more moments to make out other details in the camp. Two figures hunched over the fire, doing things with pots and a frying pan set on the coals. Others worked to pitch tents well back from the fire, among the pines. The watchers on the hill heard the low murmur of voices and the crackle of the fire.

"Just fishermen?" whispered Tom to Trover, prepared to be disappointed.

"No, look off to the left, under that steep bank, between the two white birches," said the trapper. "What do you see there?"

His companions stared intently at the spot. Just then one of the cooks laid a piece of dry pinewood on the fire and it flared, momentarily lighting the tiny hollow brightly.

Between the birches five people crouched in a row, their hands behind them, their heads bent low, looking very tired. Before the light died, the searchers saw their wrists were bound behind them and they all were threaded on a stout line stretched between the two trees. The arrangement allowed them to sit or crouch, but not to stand erect, unless they all stood at once.

"The one on this end?" Trover said in a choked whisper. "That's Boscor!"

"And the other passengers from *Maiden*," answered Tom
with a nod.

"No, wait," Clem exclaimed. "There were five crewmen
on *Maiden*, right?"

"Correct, counting my brother as one of them," answered
Trover.

"And I heard six passengers. Nobody knew who they
were."

"That's what was said at the inquiry," Tom agreed.
"What's your point? I count eleven there, which accounts
for all."

"But *just* eleven, you see? No more than eleven, which
means . . ."

" . . . that either the crew . . . *or* the passengers . . . were
the pirates!" cried Tom, clutching Trover's arm.

"Certainly not Boscor!" grated out the lake man. "He's
tied up with the prisoners. And his crew has been with
him ten, twenty years. They're, most of them, our cousins.
They're the ones tied up!"

"Do you recognize the captors?" Clem wanted to know.

"Too dark!" replied the lake man with bitterness. "We'll
find out who they are, before we hang them."

"Back to the Dragon, then," Tom decided, sliding backward down the ridge on the slippery needles. "We need to
plan a bit on this."

As they moved silently back through the wood, rain
began to drum heavily through the dense pines, accompanied by jagged flashes of lightning and rolls of thunder.

Retruance, as the rain began to splash his back scales,
found a shallow cave—a mere overhanging rock, really—
that would shelter his friends. He gathered a clawful of
driftwood and laid a fire in a natural chimney at the back
of the alcove, ready to fire up when they returned.

He heard them coming—a Dragon has four very sharp
ears—and stuck his head and neck out of the shelter to hail
them between crashes of thunder.

"Who would go adventuring without a Dragon!" exclaimed Tom. The three were soaked to the skin. The
wind had chilled them, but in a few minutes the Dragon's
close presence and the small fire warmed them and dried
their clothes.

"We can be thankful for the rain," said Trover, wringing

out his socks. "If they were planning to leave any time soon, they won't now. This wind will kick up a wicked chop on the lake."

"Not to mention the lightning," said Clem. "We'll want to move against them at once."

"I see no reason for delay," Tom agreed.

"Maybe let them get settled down for the night," Clem said. "To tell you the truth, I'd just as soon get this over with and go back to your house, Trover! It's going to be very uncomfortable here if we wait very long."

The rain had been increasing steadily and the storm was moving closer and closer with each thunderclap.

"I don't have any sleepy spells to cast over them," said the lake man regretfully. "How about you, Sir Dragon? Got any amulets to make us invisible when we attack? They outnumber us two to one, and I think they're heavily armed. How will we get close enough to release the captives?"

"No magic amulets, but something much better," boasted the Dragon. He laid a foot-long claw gently on Tom's shoulder. "I have a human!"

Trover gazed at the Librarian intently for a short moment and then laughed.

"I *thought* there was something different about you, Master Librarian! I feel much, much more optimistic about rescuing Boscor, now!"

Tom shrugged self-consciously, not yet fully accustomed to being thought of as different. The Dragon's words had the immediate effect of putting him in sole charge of the expedition.

"What we'll do," he said quickly, "is use the elements we've got to hand."

"Elements? Oh, you mean the rain?" asked Clem.

"The rain . . . and surprise. We'll hit them in the worst of the storm, while they're huddled under their tents, wishing they could get dry and warm, hearing nothing but the rattle of rain and the roar of thunder."

The other two and the Dragon's head drew close as he outlined a simple plan. After a suggestion or two, it was agreed to and set in motion.

WRACKEY, the largest and strongest of the Bloodthirsty Band, as they rather vaingloriously called themselves, checked the bonds that held the prisoners before crawling back into a tent made of a tarpaulin stretched over a piece of line between two trees. The hollow was already inches deep in cold rainwater and what clay soil there was had turned to thick, slippery mud. First mate Splitter had neglected to lay a tarp under the tent to keep the inside dry.

The pirate chief cursed viciously and kicked Splitter, who was already sound asleep on one side of the skimpy shelter, oblivious to the wet and cold. Drawing no response, the captain launched several other, progressively more foul curses at the sleeping mate before settling down in a damp and smelly blanket.

Lightning blazed close by, making the pirate cringe. It was followed immediately by a tremendous crash. *A close strike!* the pirate thought. *Almost on top of me!*

Rain, rain, go away! An old rhyme came back. *Come again some other day! Wicked Wrackey wants to . . . sleep!* The thought, if not the rhyme, made the pirate grin uneasily into the darkness.

A DOZEN yards away, deep in the piney wood, the rescuers huddled under a spreading hemlock, as much out of the rain as possible. They had to shout to make themselves heard over the hammering of the rain.

"Give them a few minutes more to get to sleep," advised Clem. They had watched by lightning flashes as the pirate chief checked the prisoners. These unfortunates were left out in the weather while the pirate crew crawled into their tents near the drowning fire.

"Remember your assignments," Tom cautioned. "Clem, the far end of the picket line and cut it clean. Trover, speak to your brother and tell him to keep his fellows quiet, while you strip the tether through their arms."

"Understood!" replied Clem, drawing his sheath knife. He tested its keen edge for the fifth time since they had left the Dragon's cave.

"Aye, aye, sir!" replied a nervous but determined Trover.

"Quickly but quietly," cautioned the Librarian. "Don't take time to free their wrists until you get them away. I don't *think* their feet are bound."

The others nodded.

"The Dragon and I'll keep the pirates busy. If anything goes wrong, call for help in a loud voice and Retruance will come to your aid at once. Ready?"

Not waiting for a reply, he slid down the bank into the hollow, darted across the open ground about the drowning fire, and took station between two of the three tents, facing the prisoners.

If the captives noticed his dash, they didn't show a sign of it. They were either asleep, or blinded by the torrential rain.

Tom watched as two blacker shadows moved swiftly to either end of the prisoners' line and waited until he saw the glint of Clem's hunting knife in a flash of lightning. There was a faint murmur as Trover spoke to his brother, shaking him alert and awake. The rope slithered through the bound arms. All five were suddenly on their feet, shakily, but they followed Trover up the gentler back slope of the hollow. They disappeared at once under the confusing shadows of the wind-whipped pines. Clem turned to wave a signal.

"Now!" yelled Tom into the rain-filled air.

One of the pirates gave a snort and a grunt but before any of the six could squirm from soggy blankets and out of their tents, a green-and-gold Dragon dropped out of the sky falling across all three tents at once, snapping the supporting lines. The pirates within were squashed flat by a ton or two of hard, slippery scales pushing them into the pine needles and mud.

They screamed, choked, and struggled, but Retruance lay atop their shelters, grinning broadly and humming a cheerful country air under his breath. Wisps of smoke and flickers of fire came from his wide nostrils, lighting the scene like some version of pirate hell.

"When you're finished floundering about," Tom called to them in a loud voice, "the Dragon will release you, one at a time, to be disarmed and bound."

Most of the pirates began to beg for mercy, wailing piteously, especially those with enough of a view to see they were being squashed under a tremendous, fire-breathing Dragon. The leader who had checked the prisoner's bonds a moment ago lay sobbing in frustration and fear.

Clem returned to help Tom.

"You!" growled Tom, prodding the first pirate figure

with his toe. "Up and shed your weapons. Quick! Or the Dragon broils you alive. No tricks!"

One by one the pirates clawed their way from under the wet blankets and collapsed canvas.

When Clem at last coaxed Wrackley out from the last tent, they were sure.

Each of the six pirates was . . . a woman!

✳ 20 ✳
Judgment at Lakehead

BLEARY eyed, foul tempered, and more than a bit hung over, Bailiff Kedry drove his posse onto City Pier at six in the morning. They had spent most of the previous day picking flotsam and jetsam from the lake—what Kedry called "significant clues"—and the night drinking and talking about their adventures, mostly imaginary.

"Dear, dreaded bailiff!" called one of the back rankers, before the official had a chance to speak, "we were on the lake over twelve hours in rain and storm yesterday. It's pure, blind luck nobody drowned. Several of us lost valuable boats. Did we find *anything* that made it all worthwhile?"

"Of course we did, you damned fool pigeon seller!" yelled Kedry. "We found . . . ah, er . . . thirty-two pieces of rope, seven torn gill nets, forty-three glass floats of various sizes, a stove-in scuttlebutt, an empty beer barrel, and over a hundred empty wine bottles. That's not nothing!"

The posse wearily pretended to be impressed. They were paid five coppers a day to serve and were having a good time all in all.

The pigeon seller, always the gadfly, retorted, "What do these pieces of trash mean, Bailiff? Do you know where Boscor and his crew and passengers are being held?"

"Not yet," admitted the bailiff. "But we're working on it."

"Who," someone else asked plaintively, "is 'we'?"

"Listen up!" Kedry shouted him down. "Here are my orders for the day."

They would again search on the lake, he said, this time calling at every island. Where there were no inhabitants, Kedry said, search parties would fan out and examine every square foot of ground for signs of the pirates.

"Do you realize how many islands there are?" the pigeon merchant scoffed, incredulous. The posse murmured its agreement, but not too loudly.

"Police work takes time and patience," Bailiff lectured them, "and attention to the smallest details. Don't get discouraged! This is only our second day of the manhunt!"

Most of Kedry's searchers had been chosen from his close acquaintances and drinking companions. They had no objection to a pleasant voyage on a sunny day to visit island hamlets. It they were lucky, the fishermen's women would be alone and well stocked with the particularly potent liquor they distilled—or so the rumors said—against their isolation and lack of menfolk through the long days of the summer fishing season.

Despite the defection of a sensible handful, more than twenty posse men filed down to the end of City Pier and were scrambling playfully, like boys on a school picnic, into a sloop and two ketches Kedry had commandeered, when someone looked out over the lake and yelped in fear.

"Dragon! Dragon! A Dragon!"

The word flew through the crowd. A number of would-be pirate hunters immediately remembered promising their wives to clean their cellars that day and began to shuffle away across the square.

Kedry was so crowded in by his posse that there was no room for him to faint, fall, or flee. As a child, his mother had frightened him with tales of fearsome Dragons . . . and all the things she warned him never to do again or "the Dragons would get you," he'd insisted on doing, anyway.

Retruance came winging grandly out of the rising sun, beating straight for City Pier. His wingtips slapped the water on each powerful downstroke, flicking up towers of spray to sparkle in the backlight.

On the Dragon's scaly head rode four men—the two Overhall travelers, and another pair, recognized at once

as the long-feuding Sacks—although their fight seemed
now forgiven. They were grinning broadly, nodding to the
crowd, and clinging firmly to a Dragon ear.

Trailing the Dragon on long lines were the two boats
missing from sloop *Maiden*, skipping over the waves at
a breathtaking pace; Retruance's slowest flying speed was
considerably faster than anything a Carolna boat had ever
achieved before.

In their bottoms huddled a ragged, disheveled band.
Clinging grimly to the thwarts, as guards, were Boscor's
four sailors, grinning from ear to ear.

The Dragon, in a move that almost caused the bailiff's
demise from pure fright, settled himself in the water and
lowered his massive head to allow his passengers to step
dry-shod onto the stone mole mere yards from where Kedry
was rapidly turning to quivering, pink jelly.

"Ahoy! Bailiff!" called Trover in a jovial and carrying
hail. "We've rescued my beloved brother—the Librarian,
the woodsman, the Dragon and I. We captured the pirates,
too! Think of the trouble we've saved you!"

A ragged cheer went up from the onlookers. Towns-
people roared their approval at such a brave and daring
rescue. Posse men applauded the fact that they would not
have to spend the day rowing and sailing among a hundred
islands, chasing a fierce crew of pirates. They seemed, all
at once, glad to forgo their fees, the lonely fisher wives and
daughters, and their homemade booze.

The crowd surged forward, despite the nearness of the
immense Dragon, and carried their leader, willy-nilly, right
up to where the brothers Sack and the young strangers were
standing, modestly accepting congratulations.

"Er," said Kedry. "Ah? Ugh!"

"Words fail the bailiff!" shouted Trover to the crowd.
"He's overcome with gratitude and relief that all are safe
and sound."

This brought a loud laugh from the throng. Boscor clapped
the gasping bailiff on the back, as though he were choking—
which he was.

"You had no right . . . ," coughed the bailiff. "You had
no authority . . . you should have come to me, not gone off
on your own!"

"You were busy with your own search, Master Bailiff,"

put in the Librarian. "The opportunity arose to capture the pirates, and we seized it, knowing that to delay would be to allow them to escape with their prisoners."

"That makes great sense to me," said a new voice. Mayor Fellows shouldered his way to the end of the pier, smiling broadly at the rescuers. "I think they did just right," he said to Kedry. "You'd have done the same, in their shoes, Bailiff!"

"Ah, and well, er, Your Honor," gulped Kedry, lamely accepting the soothing compliment. "I suppose you're right, Lord Mayor!"

"Of course I am!" cried the mayor, and he shook hands cordially with the Sack brothers, and nodded cordially to Retruance, Tom, and Clem.

"Our sincere thanks and congratulations," Fellows called to the Dragon.

Kedry interrupted, struggling to retain a vestige of authority. "You say you *captured* these pirates?"

"Yes, Bailiff," said Tom, gesturing at the small boats still trailing offshore at the end of Retruance's tethers. "We brought them back with us, as you can see."

"Ah, yes. Tell me if I am wrong, Your Honor," said Kedry, gaining confidence, "but is it not a felony to fail to punish piracy by immediate hanging or drowning, or at the very least, abandonment on a deserted island?"

"The old law does say that, I'm afraid," the mayor admitted, shaking his head in regret. "You should have strung them up or left them to perish on some lonely island. The punishment for failing to do so is a year of imprisonment!"

The rescuers looked at each other in dismay and the crowd fell silent. Most Lakeheaders had great-uncles, grandfathers, even brothers who had been marooned for piracy. The bailiff was speaking the truth.

"As to that," said Clem into the silence, "we faced one small problem."

"What is that?" demanded Kedry, glowering, his confidence restored. "What possible excuse could you find . . . ?"

Mayor Fellows had stepped over to the edge of the pier and was gazing down into *Maiden*'s boats, which Retruance had now hauled close.

"Shut your gap, fool Bailiff!" he ordered, sharply. He pointed at the bedraggled figures in the boats. "They did right, after all!"

Kedry rushed forward and what he saw almost spilled him into the lake.

"They're women! Girls! Ladies! What is this? Some kind of trick? These can't be pirates!"

The pirate's captain, Mistress Wrackey, glared angrily up at him and sneered, "Why cannot a woman be a pirate? We're as good or better than your grand-uncle Foghorn, who was a pirate, Kedry! Successful for nearly seventy years!"

"Aunt Wrackey!" wailed the bailiff. "How could you? Piracy!"

"Well," said the lady pirate, allowing Tom to help her climb from the open boat onto the pier, "it were a more honest way to be dishonest than taking tax money on the pretense of being a guardian of the law, like some people I could name."

The crowd, which by now included almost every soul in Lakehead, cheered her words and applauded her forthrightness. Bailiff Kedry, after the reference to his great-uncle Foghorn, withdrew within himself and had little more to say. He tried, instead, to hide behind the full figure of the lord mayor.

Fellows was on top of the situation, however.

"We'll reconvene the court of inquiry, at once!" he shouted to the crowd. "All who want, come to Town Hall in half an hour, prepared to listen and be quiet until justice is served."

This had the desired effect. The crowd, in a jovial and excited mood, hurried off across the square to Town Hall, rushing to get good places.

"ELF," intoned Mayor Fellows from the bench, "is the name of our species. It means females and males together, as a race. The word in the law doesn't refer to sex, one way or the other. We are all 'Elf' however delightfully divided between male and female, as I see it."

"The law," argued Mistress Wrackey, pounding her fist into her hand to emphasize her point, "does not ever say a *female* is forbidden to be a pirate. You may declare it differently now, but you can't prosecute my band for doing something that wasn't a crime when we did it!"

The court of inquiry had been sitting for four hours without even recess for lunch, and tempers were getting short and frayed. Mistress Wrackey glared defiantly at the mayor-judge, and Fellows glared back at her just as angrily.

"A remarkable lady, your pirate aunt," said Tom to Kedry, who was trying to sink into the hard seat of the front row. "She's obviously prepared for this! I think she may win her case, although I agree with the mayor myself."

"I only wish none of this had ever happened!" wailed the bailiff miserably. "Everyone will think I winked at auntie's piracy. I never knew it! Last I knew she was teaching town's school!"

"Lots of guts, has Mistress Wrackey!" laughed Clem aloud, calling down on himself the glowering stare of the mayor.

"Have you something to contribute to this argument? If not, sir, I would prefer you remain silent."

Clem shrugged his apology, but Tom raised his hand for attention.

"Yes, Master Librarian?" asked the mayor-judge. "Can you be of any assistance in this matter?"

Tom rose and approached the bench. Noises from the crowd, which had slowly grown as the hours passed, diminished to silence once again. Something new was about to happen.

"I'm ignorant of the law in Carolna. Would it be a bother to the court to answer some questions?"

"I have a better idea," said the mayor wearily. "Let us adjourn for lunch and you can ask your questions over a bowl of my wife's leek soup."

"You're most kind to ask, Your Honor," Tom responded. "If I understood some points of law better, I may be able to suggest some solution to the present dilemma."

The mayor slapped the desktop before him loudly and proclaimed a recess for lunch. "Court will reconvene at . . . um, four this afternoon. Bailiff, incarcerate the accused in the town jail."

"Well, Lord Mayor, er, Judge," Kedry hemmed and hawed, reddening in embarrassment, "I don't really think—"

"I recall," the mayor interrupted, "and you are quite right.

Your jail is no place for ladies, even if accused of piracy. I order you to find a secure place for the accused, give them lunch, and have them back here at four."

"I'll take them to my own home and feed them at my own table," promised Kedry, gathering the pirate crew together.

"Your Worship, I strongly object!" cried the pirate captain, jumping to her feet.

"Object? As a matter of law, ma'am?" asked the mayor.

"No, as a matter of taste!" retorted the former schoolmarm. "I've had the misfortune to eat at the bailiff's table before, and it's surely quite cruel punishment for us, who have not yet been convicted."

"Objection overruled!" shouted the mayor over the laughter of the crowd. "The accused will be fed and housed at the bailiff's convenience, as the law requires."

After he'd stalked out into the square, he waited for Tom and Clem to join him, and invited the Sack brothers to dine with him also. Bored with the endless argumentations, Retruance had wandered off some time before.

"My wife, on the other hand, is one of the best cooks in the county," he told them. "Old bailiff's wife must be one of the worst and I'm not surprised. She's a timid mouse of a woman, afraid to raise her voice against anyone or anything. But Kedry is good to her, nevertheless, I must say."

Chatting thus, they climbed the street behind Town Hall to a pleasant, pillared, large white house on the brow of the hill, overlooking the harbor of Lakehead. Mistress Fellows, seeing their approach, met them at the door and made them welcome, then disappeared with several servants to prepare lunch for the five men to eat as they talked.

"What I want to ask," began Tom, "is whether you have to decide this case yourself or if there is a way of passing it up the line. It seems to me that piracy should be in the king's jurisdiction, rather than a local matter."

Fellows ate, chewing methodically as he listened.

"I understand what you're thinking, Librarian. Yes, there is a way to pass difficult cases into royal courts, but perhaps you'll understand why I am reluctant to do so."

"Unless it has something to do with politics, with Lord Peter's desire for power, no, I don't understand."

"Ah, but there! You've said it, of course. Lord Peter has

no wish to yield jurisdiction to the royal court. In addition, defendants—especially the guilty—would far rather be tried before a strange judge in a distant town. Justice, on the other hand, thus loses the advantage of local knowledge and understanding—often to the detriment of the accused, I must say, where the accused is really innocent."

"You're telling us that Lord Peter of Gantrell would be angry with you if you send these pirates to the king to try?" asked Clem in surprise.

"It's a political fact of life, my lad! This is Gantrell land, and his wishes must be considered. He is a formidable enemy when he feels betrayed."

"Would he have to give his permission to move the case to a royal court?" asked Tom.

"N-n-no," hesitated the mayor. "Actually, I am obliged only to inform him of such an action. Look here, gentlemen, I would love to push this case off on someone else! These women may be pirates, but they are also daughters and aunts and even wives of local freeholders. If I were to find them guilty and sentence them to hang, there would be an awful uproar. Maybe even armed insurrection, against me and against Gantrell. Law or not, local sympathies have always been with the pirates, not the victims or the judge."

"All the more reason to remand the case to the king's jurisdiction," said Trover.

"If I may?" interrupted his brother.

"Yes, of course, Captain Boscor," said the mayor-judge.

"Other than the fact that we five spent a most uncomfortable day and night, no harm was done in this case. I've got back my ship, thanks to my brother and these good gentlemen. I even got back my small boats. I lost no money in the matter, except maybe a day's charter. Sure, the ladies posed as passengers in order to capture me for ransom, but if they hadn't come along I would have sailed empty except for some local freight of no consequence. What if I merely withdraw the charges of kidnapping?"

"No help, however nobly intended," sighed the mayor. "Kidnapping is not even under consideration here. The county has charged them with piracy only, as that's the more serious crime. Thank you, anyway, Boscor."

The luncheon party fell silent until the servants brought

out milk and lemon cake for desert. Tom broke the silence
at last.

"You're caught in the middle then, sir. It's you who must
decide if the piracy law applies to females, and I don't
see how you can avoid ruling that it does. Otherwise, any
woman could commit serious crimes and escape unscathed,
until the law is amended. A most arduous task, I would
think."

"Too true," said Fellows, sighing deeply. "Am I condemned whichever way I decide?"

Observed the Librarian, "You can only do what you think
is right and suffer the consequences. Look at it this way,
Lord Mayor: If you rule that the ladies are to be hanged
or marooned, you'll bring great hardship and perhaps even
violence down on your community. On the other hand, if
you decide to send the case to the king's court, you risk
only one man's wrath."

"Hmmm!" the mayor-judge considered. "As you say,
hurt is inevitable either way."

"In my opinion," Tom said, "making hard calls is one
of the reasons a country has a king. Let *him* decide and
depose. He's better situated to withstand any furor the
decision might create than are you, sir."

"Yes, I see what you are getting at. But by sending the
case to the king, I may incur not only Gantrell's displeasure,
but the king's disdain."

"Do you believe the king would hold it against you personally?" asked Clem.

"Well . . . no, from what I know of Eduard, he'd be just
with me, also. Not unreasonable, like Peter Gantrell, is
Eduard Ten."

"Something for you to remember, if it comes to choosing
between them one day," murmured Tom. The mayor gave
him a quick, sharp look, but then nodded and smiled. He
bounded to his feet, his decision made.

"ACCUSED, stand forth. Yes, you may represent them, Mistress Wrackey. Yes, Bailiff, I *do* need you."

When the accused ladies and the law officer had gathered
before the bench, Mayor Fellows spoke to them in a loud,
clear voice that carried to the crowd in the square outside
and the Dragon perched on the roof.

"I have reached a decision in this matter. It may not be to everyone's liking, but it's all I can do under the circumstances."

He paused while one of the pirate ladies wailed and sniffed aloud. Someone rushed over to soothe and quiet her.

"This case hinges on a basic interpretation of king's law. I am not qualified to rule upon that."

The pirates and more than half the crowd gasped and chattered at the admission, and it was several minutes before Fellows could get their attention once more.

"As justice of the County of Lakeheart I willingly admit that I am not competent to make a decision in this case without advice and consent of royal authority."

The courtroom and the square fell deathly silent.

"I must, from the evidence, find the defendants guilty of piracy"—another, louder gasp from the audience—"and will forward this case with a plea for immediate review by His Majesty of the application of the law on piracy to females. As this may take months or even years, I hereby release the accused into the custody of the county bailiff. Bailiff, it is your responsibility to see to it that all six defendants are prevented from returning to a life of crime, and are available when called to retrial or sentencing, based on the king's ruling on the matter of law."

"But, but, but," stammered Kedry. His face drained of all color. Fellows beckoned Kedry closer and spoke to him privately.

"It's your *duty*, Bailiff, and don't let me hear you complain of it, or I will recommend to Lord Peter that you be removed and another appointed in your place!"

"No, no! I have no problem with your decision, Your Honor," squeaked Kedry. "I'll watch them like a hawk!"

"Like a pigeon, more likely!" laughed someone in the crowd. Tom thought it might have been a certain pigeon breeder, but he couldn't be sure.

WHEN the Librarian, the trapper, and the Dragon left Lakehead the next morning they were bade farewell by a large and friendly crowd of lake men, their wives and children, and the Sack brothers.

"Your quarrel is forgot, then?" Clem asked Trover.

"Not forgot, although I do believe Boscor is leaning a little toward the king, now," said the captain of *Pinnacle Flyer* with a dry chuckle. He punched his brother's arm lightly. "After all, Wrackey is not just related to the good bailiff. She's Boscor's wife's cousin, also."

"Yes," sighed the other captain. "We'll have to be careful not to hurt Cousin Wrackey's case by upsetting the king with overadherence to Peter of Gantrell!"

"I've not yet met His Majesty," said Tom soberly, "but from what I've heard and seen, he's perhaps the better man to follow than Lord Peter. Only time will show you if I'm right."

Clem and Tom mounted the Dragon and waved good-bye to the Sack brothers and their neighbors. On the edge of the crowd Tom saw and waved especially to a somewhat scruffy old man leaning on a heavy cane. He looked like an aged and molting dove himself.

"Murdan will hear of our work here, shortly" he said to the Dragon and Clem once they were aloft over the lake and heading due eastward. "Now, Retruance, don't fly so high and fast that we miss the scenery. Beautiful area, this! I envy those who live near a lake, as only a lad born on endless plains would do!"

✦ 21 ✦
Sweetwater and Tomatoes

SEVERAL days had been lost in looking for pirates and Tom wanted to fly straight to the castle on Brant Bay.

"We'll see plenty of Lexor in October," Retruance agreed.

"I'm eager to meet the king and the queen," said Clem. City or castle, either was enough to stir his enthusiasm. "And the Blue Ocean, too. I've only seen a bit of the Quietness Ocean at Wall myself."

Lakeheart Lake stretched more than a hundred fifty miles to the east, although it was seldom more than thirty miles wide. Its shores were heavily wooded, at first with pine and cedar, and later with wide-spreading oaks, towering elms, and sycamores.

Across the foot of the lake stretched an escarpment over which water plunged in a great fall, three hundred feet wide and a hundred feet high. In the mist beside the fall pool was a large town called Rainbow, where the travelers stopped for a midday meal. The people they met were cool and unfriendly, suspicious of travelers wearing Overhall insignia on their shoulders.

Retruance explained, "The Great Hall of Gantrell is less than three hours' horseback ride to the north. Lord Peter's rule is felt in a wide circle."

"But," said Clem, angrily, "is that any reason to serve us cold soup?"

"The soup is *supposed* to be cold!" Retruance laughed. "It's a specialty of the inn, you see. Lord Peter, they say, particularly likes it. Colder the better!"

"One more reason," Clem muttered into his spoon, "for . . ."

"For keeping one's mouth shut, unless one wants to stir up trouble," advised the Dragon. He was stretched out along the grassy riverbank outside the inn, enjoying the fall's perpetual cloud of cool spray. "We'll be better received at Sweetwater Tower. Are we ready to fly?"

"Don't leave a tip," growled the woodsman as Tom began to count out coppers from his purse. "Service was not good enough to earn it."

THE country between Rainbow and broad Brant Bay, which brought Blue Ocean waters to the outskirts of inland Lexor, was called Overtide. It was generally flat and watered by dozens of meandering rivers and shallow streams. The people who farmed and lived there, rather than build roads, traveled mostly by boat. Between the rivers, farms blanketed the low ridges while the manors of wealthy landowners were built on the highest points, with views of the falling land on either side.

Along the coast were vast wetlands into which the rivers flowed and were shattered into intricate networks of channels. A hundred varieties of birds circled and screamed there in vast flocks. Retruance picked a more inland course, where it was quieter.

It was three days before they were received by the royal couple. The Lord Chamberlain Walden, a tall, extremely elegant man with sharp, suspicious features and chill dignity, when pressed by the Dragon admitted that the king was in Lexor and the queen never received anyone in his absence.

"Her Majesty is feeling well?" Tom asked.

"She is feeling well," replied the Lord Chamberlain, who never said just yes or no to any question. "She has been informed of your arrival, Librarian, and has sent word that you are to make yourself comfortable."

Comfort was a meager word for the profuse luxury of Sweetwater Tower. They were assigned dark, heavily decorated rooms with only narrow-windowed views of the magnificent bay. Each man was assigned a deeply carpeted velvet parlor, a vast bedchamber with a high, soft bed, and a number of silent servants to see to their needs.

It was made clear that they were expected to wait in their apartments and not wander about the castle nor talk unnecessarily to courtiers or servants.

Retruance got along better—nobody told a Dragon where to go and to whom he could speak—and he brought news and gossip when he thrust his head through the midnight blue drapes of Tom's balconied window for a chat, which he did several times a day.

"Be patient," he advised. "The air of the castle is not that of its master or mistress."

"Then of whom?" asked Tom, rather piqued at being shuffled aside by officious flunkies.

"This overstuffed Lord Chamberlain, mostly. It's his way of protecting the king, the queen, and their soon-to-be-born from what he considers evil influences."

"Us? Evil influences!" cried Clem. "Why, I'd like to . . . !"

"Hold your horses, countryman," said Tom. "We'll make progress, shortly. A king and queen have a great deal of business to conduct every waking minute of the day. They don't yet see how we fit into that day, I imagine."

"You've said it better than I could," said the Dragon with a shrug of his enormous shoulders. "Say, fellows, if you're that bored, I can fly you out to the Point to watch the cadets drill and the ships come and go."

So on the second full day they went with the Dragon across the bay to the Point, a grimly fortified castle surrounded by unusually thick stone walls with their feet in the bay on one side and the ocean on the other. Fleets of warships and galleys anchored just inside the narrow entrance to the bay to protect Brant Bay, the city of Lexor, and the royal personages—not to mention, said the Dragon, a great number of traders and merchants of all kinds.

They were very well received. Retruance was a—detached—colonel of the Coastal Guards, treated with great deference and respect. Tom and Clem wished they had arranged to live at the Point rather than Sweetwater Tower, for the soldiers were outgoing and cheerful.

A day was all they dared spend away from Sweetwater Tower. When Retruance flew them back in the early evening, they found Lord Chamberlain Walden huffing and puffing impatiently with a message from the king.

"Their Majesties will receive you at ten tomorrow morning. If you had been here, sirs, you would have had a full day to prepare yourselves for the honor."

Tom gave the man a hard, long look and might have said something untoward had not Retruance, at the window, quickly thanked the official and sent him about his business.

"Dragons—and Companions—are not upset by mere Lord Chamberlains," he snorted, and flew off to take a hot bath.

"A bath, a shave, and a clean shirt," claimed Clem, with heated determination. "They're all I need to do to prepare for anyone, even a queen!"

They ignored the perfumed, pressed, and richly embroidered knee breeches and lacy, heavily starched linen shirts that had been laid out for them.

"Something underlies the bad attitude here," Tom murmured. "And I have come to the conclusion it is fear."

AT ten the following morning the young men were shown to a waiting room at the base of the tallest round tower. They kicked their heels alone and watched a steady parade of courtiers and servants climb up and down the winding stair on the far side of the vast room.

"I thought promptness was the 'courtesy of kings'!" Clem grumbled under his breath to Tom.

"Easy, lad! But I certainly would like to know what Murdan would have to say about the way his emissaries are treated. I don't care for myself, but if it's a reflection of royal regard for the Historian this country is in deep trouble."

"Nor do I care whether I sleep under a down comforter or on a hay-strewn floor," said the woodsman. "As you say, it seems a calculated insult to the Lord of Overhall. What does the Dragon say? He should know."

Retruance had gone off on an errand of his own. They hadn't seen him that morning.

"He's embarrassed. He doesn't know what to think about it. Himself, they seem to treat very well."

"Just plain fear of a Dragon, is why. Personally, I'd just as soon we were fishing for bass on a lake I know back in Broken Land," said Clem. "Ah! Here's that glum fellow, Walden!"

The Chamberlain appeared from a side door hidden by thick draperies and stalked toward them, chin held too high and eyes half-hooded.

"He probably would take out the garbage with the same look on his ugly dial," scoffed Clem.

"Exactly the same," agreed Tom. "Now be quiet!"

"Master Librarian and . . . er, Fur Trapper . . . your wait is to be not much longer."

With which he turned on his heel and stalked away through the same hidden doorway. Before it swung closed, they heard his footsteps climbing stairs.

An hour passed.

Clem pretended to sleep, slumped in his chair. Tom spent the time studying the rich tapestries that adorned the walls of the waiting room. They seemed to tell stories of a very ancient time but his knowledge of Carolna history and legend was much too limited to give him any clues to the events depicted.

Shortly before noon a highly polished and beautifully uniformed guard platoon marched through the waiting room and up the stairway without stopping or looking to either side.

"Change of the guard at noon," guessed Clem. Tom sat down and considered what they should do. Nothing occurred to him save rushing the stair and demanding immediate audience.

"But, recall, young Librarian," he scolded himself, "we're dealing here not only with highest royalty but also a lady pregnant for the first time, as well. Who knows? She may even now be in labor."

Consoled by his imaginings, he walked over to a mullioned window overlooking the castle's innermost garden. Gardeners were planting, trimming, pruning happily away. It was the most pleasant aspect he had seen since they'd arrived, so he watched for a long time, trying to put names to the flowers and shrubs.

Close to the tower the garden was rather English in style: large, free-form clumps of multicolored blooms, bordered by other, lower flowering plants, casually trimmed and trained. Grassy paths wandered among the beds and a tiny brook rippled over stones and twinkled into a pool filled with gold-colored fish.

Further off, beyond a low hedge, the gardens became very formal, with geometric beds of flowers in solid colors, separated by carefully aligned border plants from wide brick paths. Shady alleys of trees were punctuated with square, round, and oval pools and fountains. From a distance the patterns hardly seemed to be living plants at all.

Rather like a Persian carpet, Tom thought to himself.

"Their Majesties will receive you now," came Walden's voice just behind him. Tom jumped despite himself and spun about to see the Chamberlain stalking toward the stair without looking to see if they followed.

Clem shrugged his shoulders eloquently and fell in beside his companion as he followed the Chamberlain up the stairs.

At the next level they were scrutinized carefully by six heavily armed, silver-steel-armored guards. Walden paced on to the next flight of stairs without giving so much as a glance to the soldiers.

From somewhere above came soft music; strings and a flute. The stairs here were carpeted with rich maroon and gold pile. At the top of the flight another platoon of soldiers stood stiffly at attention.

"This way, please. Don't dawdle!" admonished the Lord Chamberlain. He stopped before a tall, double door with polished copper and brass fittings. When the two visitors stood beside him, he nodded to soldiers, who drew open the doors on silent hinges.

"Master Librarian Thomas Whitehead of Overhall! Master Woodsman Clematis of Broken Land!" the Chamberlain said in a loud, harsh voice.

He stepped back and disappeared, leaving the companions standing awkwardly in the royal doorway, staring at the scene before them.

In a vast bed piled high with pillows and cushions of pastel fabrics reclined a small, delicate, dark-haired woman with skin almost as pale as the sheets upon which she lay. Her hands fell limp to either side, palms up and helpless. Under the thick coverings Tom could make out her swollen figure. This was Queen Beatrix of Carolna.

Standing to the queen's right was a strikingly handsome middle-aged man of just above medium height with close-cropped gray hair. He wore a maroon uniform (that matched the carpeting) and a brightly polished silver scabbard at his side, a ceremonial sword whose hilt and pommel glittered like a jeweler's showcase. His face was familiar. Tom had seen it in portraits hanging at Overhall, and stamped on golden vols—and in the features of Princess Royal Alix Amanda, this man's daughter. This was Eduard Ten, King of Carolna.

Tom also saw, beneath the maroon velvet, the silver, and jewels, a worried, care-haggard husband.

"Welcome to Sweetwater Tower," Eduard Ten said in a clear, pleasant voice with bass undertones that surprised Tom, for the man was rather too slight for such a timbre.

"Thank you, Your Majesty!" they replied together, bowing from the waist.

An uncomfortable silence followed.

"We bear a letter to Your Majesty," the Librarian said quickly, trying to sound at ease and confident, "from your loyal servant and friend, the Historian Murdan of Overhall. And we bring his personal, spoken greetings and good wishes as well."

The king took a step forward and held out his hand, so Tom plucked Murdan's letter from his inner coat pocket and laid it in the royal palm.

"Thank you!" said the king. He glanced at the superscription and for the first time smiled, ever so faintly. "You are, I believe, Murdan's Librarian?"

"Yes, sire. I am Thomas. May I say it is a great pleasure to meet you."

"And a pleasure to me, also. My daughter has written to me of you, Master Thomas."

"I knew she intended to," said Tom, blushing crimson under the king's level gaze. "I hope she would . . . well, be complimentary, I guess is what I mean . . . but not just complimentary. Approving?"

The king laughed and the sudden sound in this somber place was like the pealing of large, well-cast bells.

"She was both approving and very complimentary," said the queen. Tom turned to her in surprise, having almost forgotten she was there until she spoke. Now she smiled wanly at him and nodded to her husband.

"May I present my wife? Her Majesty, Queen Beatrix. . . ."

"I . . . I . . . I'm *truly* honored, ma'am!" said the Librarian, stammering in spite of his resolution to seem bold and confident. The lady on the bed was really very beautiful, if much too sickly pale.

"This is my companion and good friend, Clematis of Broken Land," Tom went on quickly. "He claims no title but that of freeman of Carolna."

"We are ever deeply grateful for our freemen," said Eduard, nodding warmly to Clem. "Where we would be without their support and love, I don't dare imagine!"

Clem made polite, confused, pleased noises and bowed again to the royal pair. Eduard and Beatrix smiled at his bluff good looks and country manner.

"Please, take chairs here," the king impulsively invited. "Under normal circumstances, at this time of the year, I meet friends in the garden, but . . ."

"I was just admiring your beautiful gardens, sire," said Tom. "I've not had a garden of my own since I was a child, having lived mostly in places where it was impractical."

Gardens provided all four with a common subject on which to converse while they warmed to each other.

"I plant herbs and flowers as well as green and yellow vegetables in my own plot beside my cabin in the Broken Land," Clem told the king. "I live pretty much alone, so it's pleasant to have bright colors about when you work, not to mention the aromas. Besides, sire, some of the flowers are also herbs—and some of the herbs are flowers!"

"Where I grew up," said Queen Beatrix, showing more animation and a bit of color as she joined in the conversation, "my mother had the most splendid garden anyone had ever seen. You remember it, Eduard? She worked in it every morning before it got too hot, and sometimes in the evenings. I wish . . ."

She didn't say what she wished but said it with such wistfulness that Tom leaped to the realization that she missed being out of doors, in a garden, free of artificial restrictions. The queen had been a child of open places and wide waters. No wonder she was unhappy here, even to the point of sickness!

"What did your mother grow?" he asked, as it seemed to please her to remember her mother's garden.

"All sorts of flowers. Some that won't grow this far north, but many were the same as the ones our gardeners grow here."

She described the green shrubs and the herbs in her mother's garden, as well as the flowers her mother lovingly cut, arranged in vases, and put everywhere about the big Knollwater manor house. Then she spoke of the vegetables, especially fresh, sweet corn, green beans and yellow beans, and peppers of dark green, yellow, orange and bright red, both hot and sweet.

"And, oh! Tomatoes! Big, red, juicy, wonderful tomatoes. How I miss them!"

"Tomatoes grow in the north!" injected Clem. "I always had two or three rows just for myself, to home. They do wonders for a stew, ma'am!"

The queen looked forlorn, somehow both elated and saddened by the thought. The king hastened to explain.

"My Northerners have the idea in their heads that tomatoes are poisonous," he said.

"Who is that, sir?" asked Tom.

"Oh, the people of the northeast. Never grow tomatoes, they say! They ruin the soil! Never eat tomatoes! I grew up near Lexor and never tasted one until I visited Knollwater, the time I first met my wife. And I loved them, and her, at once!"

The queen blushed prettily and gave her husband a radiant smile.

"I would think," Tom said, boldly, "that a Queen could insist on having tomatoes on her table any time she wished."

"It's not easy to get your royal way, despite all the so-called privileges and powers," sighed the king. "Getting a bunch of local cooks to serve tomatoes is like trying to get blood from a turnip! I do believe I'd have to hang a few of them before they'd agree to serve a tomato, let alone cook with one!"

"Sorry if I speak out of turn," cried an indignant Clem, "but I think you *should* hang a few of them, for the good of the kingdom! Tomatoes are good for one, beside being tasty and cheerful to the eye as well!"

"I never thought of them as being cheerful," exclaimed Beatrix, beaming at Clem. "What a marvelous thought! They're cheerful!"

The king began to plan a garden for Tom, even though, as he said, they had no idea where it might be, as Tom had no land of his own. Clem and the queen added their ideas and soon they were, heads together, laughing and talking, interrupting each other to add some new flower or fruit, forgetting the stuffy formalities and protocols of a royal audience.

"Ahem!" said a new voice.

They looked up in surprise to find the Lord Chamberlain in the doorway, looking extremely upset to see the young woodsman perched on the side of the royal bed extolling his mother's recipe for rhubarb-and-strawberry pie.

"Majesty! May I remind you that you are to lunch with the Dowager Duchess of Corently," Walden intoned without expression. Tom happened to be looking at the queen when the chamberlain spoke and was shocked to see all the animation and color drain suddenly from her face. She sank back weakly into her pillow.

The king saw it, too, and he spoke sharply to his pompous servant.

"Tell the Duchess of Corently that I am indisposed and will ask her to lunch another time," Eduard ordered sharply.

"My dear!" cried the queen in a small voice. "You mustn't!"

"Nonsense! The Dowager Duchess is a crashing bore. I'd much rather sit here with you and talk about flowers and summertime and weddings and things like that," the king insisted. "Go tell her, Walden. And have lunch for four sent up."

The Chamberlain paled, aghast at the way the royal audience was progressing. Not at all according to his ancient ideas of protocol.

Said Eduard, "Anything special you'd like for lunch, my dear? Gentlemen?"

The queen shook her head weakly and closed her sad green eyes.

"Whatever's available," Clem said offhandedly.

"Well, I'd like a tomato, nice and ripe, sliced thick, with salt and lots of pepper, some soft cheese, and a sprig or two of basil," said Tom, inspired by a thought of the queen's happy memories. "Dress it all with olive oil and vinegar, please."

The Lord Chamberlain's chins all fell to his chest. He took on a stomachachy look, a little green about the jowls. It wasn't lost on the queen, who sat up, smiling again.

"Tomatoes!" Walden gasped. "But . . . good sir . . . tomatoes are rank poison!"

"Nevertheless," Eduard insisted, an edge of flint to his voice, "my guest has asked for tomatoes and it would be a blot on the royal honor if he were to be refused."

"But, sire, Your Majesty . . ." For the first time Walden seemed at a loss for dignity and words. "Tomatoes! I'm not at all sure we have any."

"Then get some," growled the king. "And report to me if my cooks can't find any nearby. Send away to Waterfields for them. I may send away to Knollwater for their cooks, too, tell them. Now, bring lunch!"

The queen was sitting straight up in her bed, gazing at her husband with a pleased and surprised expression. When the Chamberlain had withdrawn to see about tomatoes and lunch, she gleefully clapped her hands.

"My love," she said to the king, tenderly, "I have just had the most pleasant moment since coming to Sweetwater Tower. The way you spoke to that awful butler about tomatoes and made him jump . . . !"

"Chamberlain, not butler, my dear," prompted the king with a broad smile.

"Oh, Chamberlain, then! You made him buckle down and . . . and *listen* to you instead of always telling you what to do and say and think! I *loved* it!"

She gave him an impulsive hug and her eyes crinkled with suppressed laughter. The king bent down to kiss her on both cheeks, chuckling himself with pleasure to see her so lively once again.

"So I did! Well! I must do it more often. Do you think he can find any tomatoes?"

"He may have trouble, but keep after him about them," said Tom. "I think a large part of Walden's problem is he doesn't have enough to do. He has all those underlings who do everything for him."

"You may be right," said Eduard thoughtfully. "It might also be said of us, my dear. We decide things, we order things done, but we don't do very much."

"I'm sure of it, husband! Now, what could we do to change, I wonder."

"I am beginning to get some ideas," said Eduard, winking at Tom and Clem.

OVER a really fine lunch—no tomatoes; Walden almost wept when he had to report it—talk turned to Murdan the Historian. The king took a moment to read the letter Tom had brought. When he put it down he turned to the Librarian to ask him about the kidnapping.

"I don't know if I should speak about it before Freddie Brevory's trial," demurred Tom. "You'll need to make an unbiased judgment based on the evidence, won't you?"

"That's truly remarkable!" cried the king. "Most men would give half of all they possess to influence me before I hear a case in Session."

"I don't think that's the way to obtain or dispense justice, however," Tom responded. "I don't know what Murdan has told you . . ."

"Very little other than the bare facts," admitted Eduard. "A great deal of anger and insult, as you'd expect. Murdan agrees with your ideals about justice."

"So do you, Eduard," chimed in Beatrix. She'd called maids and ladies-in-waiting to slip a sea blue dressing gown over her rather dowdy nightdress and joined them at a table set in a round turret corner in the sunniest part of her parlor.

Afternoon sunlight poured in. A plump-breasted, older lady-in-waiting, a female Walden, drew the drapes, cutting off the sun and the view of the gardens. King Eduard stopped the woman with an abrupt gesture.

"Leave them open," he exclaimed sharply to the startled woman. "Her Majesty prefers sunshine to darkness, I believe."

"But the Lord Chamberlain said . . . ," the large lady-in-waiting squeaked, almost jumping out of her shoes in fright.

"Chamberlains don't banish disobedient ladies to their country seats," snapped the king. "Do as I say!"

"Yes, leave the curtains open, Lady Agnes!" said the Queen in a kinder tone. "I haven't seen sunlight for weeks and weeks."

"But Ma'am! The baby!" shrieked several of her ladies.

"A bit of sun never hurt a baby," said Tom. "Just the opposite, I'm sure. A child raised in darkness would be blighted, don't you think, sire?"

"No doubt about it!" cried the king happily. The queen waved her attendants out, causing many unhappy backward glances.

"More sunlight the better—well, at least within reason," said the king. "I remember when Alix Amanda . . . well, Manda . . . eluded her nurses and played all afternoon in the sand with a gatekeeper's son. Red as a beet she was! It was all I could do to keep from howling with laughter."

"You should have howled, sire," said Clem. "It's good for children to see their fathers and mothers howl with laughter . . . or anger. Provides a standard, you see. Teaches 'em what's right and what's wrong."

"I didn't know you knew so much about raising youngsters," Tom teased his friend.

"I was one o'seven," Clem claimed. "That qualifies me to have an opinion, at least."

"You know, I do believe you're right," said Beatrix. "My father yelled at me when I deserved it. I listened well, because it was so unusual for him to raise his voice."

"Which leads me to ask something I have been wondering, if you'll forgive my curiosity," Tom said to the queen.

"I promise not to take offense, Librarian."

"Why are you abed on such a wonderfully sunny, warm afternoon of midsummer?"

Beatrix glanced quickly at her husband and Eduard nodded his head, ever so slightly.

"Well, to be frank, Librarian, you know I bear the royal heir within?"

"I'm aware of that, yes," said Tom, trying not to laugh at her quaint phrasing.

"My doctors tell me I must lie very quietly abed most of the remaining days, so as not to harm myself or the child, you see. So much depends on us!"

"Such a pity," sighed Tom, shaking his head.

The royal couple looked shocked.

"To put such a terrible burden on one not even born yet!" Tom hastened to explain. "I feel sorry for the child as well as its mother. Forgive me, but it's so."

The king nodded sadly. "I remember when I first realized that I would have to bear the burden of a crown. Many men would kill and kill again to hold a tiny corner of my burden. If they only knew what it was like to *have* to bear it, willy-nilly, never to lay it down for a minute!"

"Why do you do it, sire?" asked Clem.

"Well, it was my father's burden before me. I was prepared to carry it from birth. Carolnans, not just the nobles and magnates, but all the people, need a good king. Have you ever read Carolnan history, young Clem?"

"No, sire. Oh, I've picked up bits and pieces here and there."

"There have been wretched periods when Carolna had bad kings, even wicked kings. Those were bad enough, but the worst times came when we had no king at all! No law! No justice! No safety in town or countryside! Every sort of crime and evil perpetrated on innocents who could do nothing about it, had no one to whom to appeal for redress or rescue! If I can prevent some of that suffering, I'll be king, no matter how painful. Wouldn't you?"

Tom nodded. "Under those conditions, yes, I'd submit myself to being king. But—"

"Young man, I've read my daughter's letters. Manda writes to me as honestly and fearlessly as no one else does. She says she'll have you as husband, no matter what happens."

Tom said nothing, but nodded his head.

"Life is filled with 'ifs,'" Eduard continued solemnly. "*If* the child dies or is stillborn . . . ?"

"Oh, Eduard!" cried his wife, pressing her hands to her mouth in horror.

"I'm as sorry as I can be, my dear, but it's true. *If* the child dies, and no other child is born to us? *If* the child is a girl? In all these cases, Manda will—unwillingly, I know, but she will—wear the crown and sit upon the Trusslo throne after I am gone. She'll be Alix Amanda Two, Queen of Carolna. If you, Thomas, are her husband, you will share her power and prestige—and her burdens, as well. Manda would not want it otherwise!"

"We've spoken at length about this, sire," Tom assured the king. "If Manda is called upon, I will be at her side and do what is required. But I won't allow anyone—or anything I can prevent—to hurt her under the guise of blind custom or senseless regulation. Sometimes you have to break the rules."

"Good for you!" cried Beatrix. "Like eating tomatoes?"

"Exactly! I may sound rather crass and green with youth, but I feel I know better than anyone what makes Manda happy. An unhappy king or queen makes an unhappy kingdom."

"I think I hear an echo of criticism of myself in those words," said the king, taken aback.

"No! Well, perhaps. I'm a stranger in your land, sire. I'm not a doctor. Yet everything I've seen and read and heard about babies—quite a bit, now that I think of it— makes me believe that Her Majesty's is not a happy, healthy pregnancy. I must believe it affects her health—and that of her unborn, within!"

"I'm as happy as I expected to be," Beatrix protested. "Eduard has worked very hard to make me so!"

"Not hard enough! You are far too pale, too weak! You're too passive, both of you. Mothers to be, where I grew up, were encouraged to walk in the sun, to keep their muscles in tone and strong. Eat well and sleep well! To be clean and happy and pleased to carry their burden. Are mothers here so different? Or is it the advice of your doctors that is different? Or are the motives of your doctors entirely unselfish?"

His last words descended like a wet, icy blanket over the luncheon party. The queen reached out and clutched

the king's hand, and even Clem looked at his companion
with consternation.

"Y-y-you," stuttered the king, "you're suggesting that the
queen's physicians are . . . ?"

"No, of course not! I've no idea of such a thing. Probably
the doctor, like the Lord Chamberlain, is so terrified about
what would happen to him, if anything harmed the queen
or her baby, he's overly cautious to the point where even
I can see it's foolish!"

"But . . . ," the king hesitated. "What can I do? I am not
a doctor, either."

"Filter the doctor's advice through your own common
sense. You've fathered a child—my Manda, bless her! She
was born healthy and grew up as perfectly as any father
could ever wish! Remember your own youth. Who's to say
you can't guard your wife's health as sensibly as any doctor,
unless something totally out of the ordinary happens?"

"There is much in that," admitted the king. The queen
nodded, vigorously.

"Listen, Lord King! Here's another thing. I've seen very
well how Peter of Gantrell operates. He's entirely selfish.
Convinced of his own rightness and worthiness to rule, no
matter who gets hurt. My God! He kidnapped a young mother with three innocent children and dragged them halfway
across the continent on horseback in an attempt to blackmail
Murdan!"

Tom rose and paced across the floor.

"Gantrell would suborn your trusted servants, your Chamberlain, your physician if he could. He doesn't want this
poor babe to be born. He fears it will be a male and thus
incontestably your heir."

"He has the nerve and the selfishness to do it," agreed
Beatrix.

"Peter wants Manda to take the throne. He knows a lot of
notables will object to a queen alone or a queen married to a
stranger, someone from outside their tight circle, Librarian,"
said Eduard. "He gained legal guardianship because I was
grief stricken when Manda's mother died. What would
sound more reasonable to many if he were to be regent
when she takes the throne?"

"Thanks only to Manda's good sense and courage, his
plan of guardianship failed," put in the woodsman.

"He'll turn his wrath on me next," Tom plowed forward, "as Manda's consort. He'll seek to poison her subjects against *me* . . . as he has so far managed to poison many hearts with slanders against your queen!"

This cruel truth brought deep anguish to the king and his queen. They sat holding hands and stared at each other for a long while. Neither Tom nor Clem moved nor spoke.

"Well, my dear," said the king at last, "I see it! Do you?"

"I'm only amazed that we didn't see it earlier. Why should the common folks in the markets so hate me? Why should my maids talk of us maliciously behind our backs? Who begins the foul rumors about stillbirthing and about foul spells and dire predictions?"

The king nodded. "But how to prove it!"

"Gantrell is behind it all, I'll stake my life on it," said Tom, "but, no, we can't prove it. We *can* guard against him, even counteract him, however."

"Yes, that we can do. We've the power as well as the desire," said Eduard. "Will you help us, you and Clem? You're both men of great common sense and uncommon abilities, I've seen."

"Murdan sent us here to help," said Clem. "Both of us would lay down our lives for you, sire, and for you and your child, ma'am!"

"I don't deserve such devotion," said Beatrix, "but it surely is comforting!"

"The first thing to do," Tom said, "is to get the queen some outdoor exercise—nothing strenuous, but hearty enough to bring the roses back that I suspect were in her cheeks when you first met her, sire."

"I remember so well!" murmured Eduard.

"I propose," continued Tom, "that she do a little walking abroad in this nice weather, for all to see. Who can hate a beautiful, happy woman large with child? Some work in the garden, maybe, when she is up to it. And tomatoes to eat. Tomatoes are very important!"

THEY did it in many nice and quiet ways.

First to fall was the Lord Chamberlain. Walden was no creature of Gantrell. The king and the queen—and the two young newcomers—lightly teased the too-dignified old man until he was near to showing anger, then loved him until he glowed, and then trusted him until he would do anything in the world for them, without a hesitation, even if it was illegal, immoral, fattening . . . and even if it were against cherished custom!

The queen soon called for a summer frock and a broad-brimmed garden hat and spent a half hour, much longer than anyone would have expected, conferring with the gardeners. Those worthies, who had grumbled that their hard work went unappreciated, at once became her most devoted subjects. She noticed what they accomplished in their gardens and praised them extravagantly for it.

They found to their delight she knew and loved gardening, flowers, vegetables, pruning, mulching, planting, hoeing, weeding, even plucking off leaf-devouring insects . . . how many fine ladies, they told their wives, got down on their tender knees, middles ungainly with child, to pick striped beetles off thorny roses?

The merchants who came to sell their produce to the royal kitchens were asked for red, ripe tomatoes.

"To eat?" they cried. "Tomatoes to eat! Me grandma told me tomatoes were certain death. We *never* eat tomatoes!"

When a scullery lad let slip that it was the lady queen herself who doted on ripe, red tomatoes, the shock turned to wondering murmurs. A delegation of weavers asked to address a petition to the king and used the occasion to tell him that someone was trying to poison the queen with deadly tomatoes!

"My good, dear, clever craftsmen!" the king said, shaking his head. "Haven't you heard the latest medical advice? Tomatoes are good for you! We should all eat at least one a day when they're in season, which is all summer, as you may not know. Try 'em on salad, or lay them atop a slide of beef or chicken or veal. We eat tomatoes every day, when we can get 'em, and they've made us feel like new persons!"

The evidence was before them to see—a robust, merry king and a glowing, laughing, pregnant queen. The weavers went home and spread the word. The king and the beautiful young queen ate tomatoes raw in salads, stewed or broiled, even in sauces on their meat!

• • •

FALLMAR of Ffallmar hailed a neighbor on the way home
from Lakehead who stopped to pass the time of day and
share the latest news.

Lady pirates were no longer the news, said the farmer,
chuckling. What was important was . . . tomaters!

"Tomaters!" laughed Ffallmar. "Those red things my wife
grows down by the pigsty? She makes a cough medicine for
winter from them, but I never have touched one myself."

"They tell me the royal court has sent orders to all ends
of the kingdom to buy all the tomaters can be found, at
almost any price. Everybody's eating them! They say the
queen and even the king eat 'em every day."

"And the queen with child!" cried Rosemary when she
heard of it.

"The Lakeheaders told our neighbor the queen was sick
near to death but someone got her to eat tomaters and
she's fit as a fiddle with the new baby due any moment.
They expect him to pop out and dance a royal jig for
her!"

"Now, I may be a gullible ninny, but I don't believe
that!" cried Rosemary. "Still . . . tomaters? I have always
been secretly fond of them. They just *might* be good for
you, you know."

Ffallmar threw his head back and laughed, long and loud.
But he and his children ate red tomatoes for supper that
very night. And the next day he sent off two mule loads
of Rosemary's best late tomatoes to Lakehead for fastest
shipment to Sweetwater Tower.

TOM and King Eduard had a serious and often heated
interview with Dr. Flabianus, the Queen's chief physician.

"Tomatoes, fine!" said the doctor, a short, fat man with
a cherubic expression and not-too-clean fingernails. "But
exercise? No, no! She should remain in bed, I insist."

"What do you fear? If she does not stay abed?" asked
Tom politely.

"Well, the obvious! Any shock! A bump or a fall! I
cannot be responsible for her health and that of the child
if she insists on *weeding* in a garden!"

"The good doctor fears my wrath, is that what it is?" the
king asked of Tom.

"One suspects that's one of his concerns. Even a blind man should be able to see the queen is already healthier for her daily walks, her gardening, and for meeting and talking to people."

"I have to agree with my Librarian there," the king said to Flabianus. "I see clear signs of better health in the queen that were absent before. Her eyes sparkle again. She laughs easily and often. Her cheeks are rosy with sun and wind and she delights in her new friends. She talks with a lilt I haven't heard since I brought her here. She's eager in her anticipation of the child and takes an active interest in the preparations for him—or her. What do you answer to these, Doctor?"

The learned physician wasn't blind or stupid, either. He rubbed his hands together briskly and carefully smiled from ear to ear before answering.

"I agree, sire, that Her Majesty is much improved. Perhaps it is the change in regimen; who knows? It's certainly worth continuing. Ah, under my watchful eye, of course."

Tom drew the physician closer to say, "All the kingdom watches the queen and sees her improvement. The credit will ultimately go to you, Doctor. Lesser physicians would pay handsomely to learn your methods. You could become a wealthy man, I should think."

"I . . . I hadn't thought of that, Master Librarian. Interesting! Do you have any further advice for me in this matter?"

"Yes," said Tom, pointing. "Wash your hands at least four times a day and scrape your fingernails, especially before you examine the queen!"

The physician became bright red with embarrassment, spluttering, "Actually, they're dirty because I was working in my new garden this morning when the king sent for me."

He wondered why the Librarian found his new interest in gardening so very funny.

✵ 22 ✵
Outcomes and Departures

IT begins to appear, wrote Tom to Amanda, *that your new stepbrother or -sister will arrive at about the same time you do, sweet princess. The doctor, his eyes opened to the miracles of fresh air and clean fingernails, estimates as much.*

HE paused to dip his pen. He was alone in his huge apartment in early afternoon. The weather outside was blustery, with a dark gray autumn fog rolling in from the ocean in great, slow billows.

Clem, bored with waiting for the royal birthing and Fall Session in Lexor, had jumped at the chance to travel west to escort the Historian's party to the capital in two weeks' time. Tom himself was busy and happy setting the Royal Library in order—it was almost as neglected as Murdan's—and training four bright young people to continue the work when he returned to Overhall.

In addition, he sat with the queen on days when she couldn't go outside, and on fine days worked with her in the garden or went with her into Lexor to shop or attend a rash of birthing parties given by her new friends of both high and low station.

She was a picture of happy well-being and, in her own words, as "big as a keep!"

I spend my days enjoying the company of the queen and the king, or at my work, or in the depths of missing you, Manda. This place needs your touch to make it the pleasant house it should be, for your father and your stepmother and their baby, too.

We refer to the child as "it," as if we hope to avoid influencing, either way, the sex of the newborn—which

*is nonsense. The sex of an unborn, I have read, is deter-
mined at conception, not at birth. I have trouble convincing anyone of it.*

RETRUANCE had been sent to the northeast frontier to inspect
the Frontier Guard. There were rumors of Barbarian tribes
moving southwest toward Carolna. The presence of the
Dragon would warn them away, the king felt.

*So, I am alone and lonely, despite the good friends I've
made. The best of them is your father, the king (now I'm
saying it—"your father, the king"!). I spend anywhere
from an hour to a half day with him each day, talking
of books and Dragons and babies, and daughters and
weddings. No, we aren't making any plans without you,
bride-to-be! We just talk about it and enjoy each other's
company.*

*As for the queen, I love her dearly! For all her appar-
ent frailty, she has shown she has grit and spunk! (I'll
explain those to you later, dearest.) I can easily see why
she was so instantly loved by your father. He was sure, he
tells me, that he would never love another after your lady
mother. Years later he happened to travel in Waterfields
and there met Beatrix of Knollwater.*

*Was it shallowness that he fell headlong in love with
Beatrix? Of course not! Both loves were, in their time
and place, sincere, strong, good, clear, and deep.*

HE stopped to reread his last paragraph and to think of what
he had said.

*I've seen no sign in you of jealousy or resentment toward
your parents, although I understand that such circumstances sometimes call forth these unreasoning, unworthy
emotions. I know you very well, dear heart, and I tell you
sincerely there is only one person more fortunate than
you. Me.*

HE added several more lines, the kind of silly, yet necessary, nonsense that lovers always put in love letters, and
signed his name with a flourish unknown at the Library of
Congress.

"Two pigeons' worth," he decided, weighing the letter in his hand. He went to a rear window in his dressing room, one that faced an interior courtyard where laundry maids hung linens to dry and blankets to air on clear days. Raising the sash, he called to a flock of pigeons in their cott under the castle eaves.

"On your way," said Tom after fitting each half of his letter into the carrying tubes of two birds. "I wish I could go with you."

"If you did," said a voice nearby, "I'd wager that would be the very night the baby is born!"

"Retruance! Come around to the front so you can put your ugly head inside. Welcome back! What news?"

"The Barbarians made a fast about-face and headed back to their fastness," said the Dragon. He slid his head through an enlarged front window and rested it on the sitting-room carpet. "Whew! What a trip! This storm's one of the more gusty ones I've known. Don't expect your letter to get to Overhall as quickly as usual. Your pigeons'll be heading right into it."

"Have you seen the King yet? He'll be relieved to hear the Barbarians have withdrawn from the frontier. It has preoccupied him of late."

"I'm on my way and stopped only to tell you I'm back," said Retruance. "Ah, well, duty calls!"

As he snaked his head out of the window again, carefully avoiding several priceless antiques, Tom called, "Come back and have dinner with me. A good night for sitting before a fire and talking!"

"I suppose," sighed the beast. "Even if one of us has to sit outside and get wetter and wetter and colder and colder!"

But the Librarian had returned to his work.

A WAIL sounded faintly through the central tower halls and down the winding stair. The king and Tom, who had been playing cribbage on the corner of a table the size of a tennis court, jerked bolt upright. The clock showed half past two in the storm-tossed morning.

"What do I hear?" cried the king, throwing down his cards.

A second cry sounded, faint but strong enough to be heard over the rush of the wind.

"Shall we go up?" asked the anxious royal father.

"Who's to say nay?" cried Tom, leaping to his feet. "You're the king and I'm the godfather!"

They rushed up the broad stairway to the third level, where they were met by an out-of-breath Walden, balancing a bowl of steaming water and an armful of towels.

"Dr. Flabianus sent me for more water!" he puffed. "Why, I can't imagine."

"To get you out of the way," guessed the king, grabbing the towels from him as they seemed about to slip to the floor. "Come along! We'll soon find out."

They rounded the end of an ornate carved screen that closed off the entrance to the queen's bedchamber. Beside her huge bed, the queen's physician stood watching while four experienced, middle-aged ladies-in-waiting worked feverishly over something tiny and squirming. The men caught a thankful glimpse of a pale but smiling Beatrix amid piled-up pillows.

"Your Majesty!" Flabianus cheerily greeted them. "Safely delivered with little discomfort to my patient, I'm proud to say!"

"The queen is well?" demanded Eduard anxiously. He rushed to one side of the bed and took Beatrix's tiny hand in his own. "Yes, she smiles, still the picture of good spirits and health, Tom!"

Tom walked to the far side of the bed where the ladies were drying a child after its—her—first bath. She had ceased her crying and slept.

"A girl, sire!" Tom announced gleefully. "A beautiful little princess!"

Then, in complete surprise, he looked at another newborn, laid on the counterpane, his legs kicking and his arms flailing, red and wrinkled and beautiful.

"And a boy, too!" Flabianus puffed proudly, as if he took full credit. "A manly little Prince Royal!"

"What?" cried Eduard, lifting his gaze from his wife to the Librarian.

Tom nodded. Beatrix giggled. Dr. Flabianus chuckled and the nurses managed to look both harried and proud.

"Twins!" cried the king of Carolna. "My God! One of each! A boy *and* a girl?"

"Beautiful and wonderful!" exclaimed Tom. "Beatrix, loveliest of queens, you did your husband and your kingdom proud tonight."

"Not just tonight," said Eduard, leaning over to kiss his wife on the brow. "Always!"

When things had settled down somewhat and Walden had shot off to post the double birth announcement and send riders into the capital with the news, Tom, the king, and the queen watched the two tiny babes, sleeping peacefully after their first dinner of mother's milk.

"We'll have to order a second cradle," said their ecstatic father. "But for now they look like angels together like that."

"Well, my dears, I am tired but not nearly as tired as I thought I'd be. Do you know, when I realized that I was about to deliver a second child, a strange thought came unbidden to me? It still bothers me, but not very much."

"What is it?" asked her doting husband.

Beatrix frowned a little frown and closed her eyes. "What will Peter of Gantrell do now?"

"Damn Gantrell! If I only knew," exclaimed King Eduard. "Don't worry about it, however. Tom, Murdan, and I will be thinking about it as soon as we get our breaths."

The queen smiled, nodded confidently, and fell asleep still smiling.

"He will, even more now than before, seek to put Manda on the throne, she being my eldest child," King Eduard stated firmly.

IT was later that morning, in the king's study.

"The boy Ednoll was the first of the two. If anything happens to me, Murdan will be his regent, of course, until he reaches twenty years. I'll make a binding decree to that during Fall Session. And you are to assist him, Tom. You and Manda, both."

"I'm honored," Tom said simply, "as Manda will be, also, I know. But that may never be necessary."

"I know and hope so, but we kings must plan for all contingencies if we can. Someday the boy will be king in my place."

"It will take a great load off Manda's mind," Tom said.

"And put one on Gantrell's," the king agreed, looking worried again. "What will he do?"

"I want your permission to take Retruance and fly to Overhall, at top speed," said Tom. "The Historian must learn of this twin birth before Gantrell, who is at his seat in Overtide, I hear."

"I agree. Ask Murdan to return with you. We must anticipate what our enemy will do and prepare for it. My imagination is filled with gambits Gantrell might spring on us."

"I'm off!"

King Eduard Ten saw the Overhall Librarian off on his flight, Companion and Dragon hurtling into the dark sky, accompanied by bolts of lightning and tremendous thunderclaps.

✦ 23 ✦

Snow Time

"OVERHALL looks different somehow," said Retruance.

They'd flown very high, where the winds were less turbulent. Tom shivered, clothed though he was in woolens and warmed by the Dragon's heat. Overhall was a mere speck in the foothills of the Snow Mountains below.

"What do you see?" asked Tom.

"Nothing . . . and that's what's strange," replied the Dragon, warping his great leathery wings to begin a spiral descent. "No flags flying, for one thing. Nobody abroad and it's midafternoon. I don't even see guards on the battlements, and that's not like Graham at all."

Tom peered worriedly over the Dragon's nose but they were still too high for him to make out details.

"Maybe it's just this sudden cold," he suggested. "Everybody's keeping indoors."

The Dragon snorted impatiently and plummeted toward the castle. Tom clutched the saddle's pommel with one hand and his knit cap with the other. The wind shrieked past his cold-burned ears and brought tears to his eyes.

The beast dived straight for Foretower, pulling up abruptly at the last moment, his wings booming and echoing between the stone walls. No guards called out challenge or greeting. No stableboys came running to help the Librarian dismount. The windows of the three soaring towers were slitted, empty eyes, seeing nothing. In spite of the chill, there was no smoke from any of the castle's myriad chimneys.

"Hello!" roared the Dragon as Tom slid to the frozen ground of the outer bailey. "Is anybody home?"

Echoes and silence . . . except for the icy mutter of Gugglerun in its channel.

"Even if Murdan's already left for Lexor," Tom said, heading for the Great Hall at a run, "*somebody* should be here!"

"Foul play!" muttered Retruance in a gush of blue-white flame. "Something's badly amiss, Tom!"

The Librarian tugged Great Hall's door open and rushed in. The hall was empty and still, as cold as the outside, its four fires extinguished. He circled the huge room, looking for any signs of the residents. Nothing appeared out of place or out of ordinary, save a total lack of occupants.

"I'll check the other towers," said Retruance, who had stuck his head through the door to watch. He dashed through the gate into the middle bailey, shouting hello in a voice that shook the stones.

In the empty courtyard Tom stopped to look about, listen, and think. A door to the guard's barracks against the far wall swung in a sudden gust of wind and banged loudly against its stop. Tom ran that way, drawing his sword as he went.

Inside, the scene was horrifying. Twelve soldiers lay in their bunks, either dead or deeply unconscious.

"My God!" Tom gasped. "Retruance! Come here!"

The Dragon's eye appeared in the open barracks door. He took in the scene at a glance.

"They're not dead," he declared. "Enchanted, I think."

"Frozen stiff!" cried Tom. "Look! They're blue from the cold."

"There's magic here, Companion," breathed Retruance. "I can feel it!"

Tom stood very still and it came to him at once, a tingling in the air, a twisting vibration, like the faintest echo of distant, derisive laughter.

"I-I-I can feel it, too," he said, shivering. "Gantrell's work, do you think?"

"Not Gantrell himself, perhaps, but someone, some magician or wizard, paid to do this. By Lord Peter, of course, who else? But why?"

"Manda!" cried Tom.

"She's not there," Retruance said, quickly. "From the looks of her rooms, she packed up and left before the spell was cast."

"Thank God!" the Librarian sputtered. "How about Murdan?"

He climbed to the Historian's quarters in Foretower and found everything in order there, too. Murdan's best court clothes and his satchels and trunks were gone.

The Dragon hurriedly inspected the other living quarters in the castle. He found the entire household as frozen in enchanted sleep as the soldiers: the cooks, scullery boys, blacksmith, hostler, saddler, carpenters, and charwomen, everyone who would have been left behind.

"The Historian and Princess Manda left for Lexor before whatever happened, happened," decided Tom, somewhat relieved. "They're somewhere on the road."

"They'll have gone by way of Sprend and Ffallmar Farm and on to Lakehead, then," said Retruance. "We flew too high and missed them. Their entourage would be large, especially with half the guard going with them. Fifty or so, I would expect."

"What's to do?" asked the distraught Librarian. "I can't think!"

He returned to the Great Hall and laid a fire in one of the fireplaces. Retruance, squeezing through the doors, set the kindling afire with a puff and in a few minutes the place began to recover some of its normal warmth—but none of its accustomed cheeriness.

"I'll see if I can find something to eat," decided Tom. "We'll both think better on full stomachs."

He lighted a pine-pitch torch and went to the kitchens, searching until he found a baked ham, some loaves of bread . . . and a frozen cook sitting slumped beside a cold range where the spell had caught him taking a midmorning nap.

He tried to slice the ham but found it, too, was frozen hard as stone. Putting it under his arm, and several loaves of bread under the other and a crock of mustard in his pocket, he hurried back to Great Hall. A blast of Dragon's hot breath thawed the meat and bread enough to cut and the two made a quick, lonely meal.

Retruance flew off, saying he wanted to check further afield. He returned after dark, as the Librarian was rolling himself in two woolen blankets on a bearskin rug before the fire.

"You'd be warmer in a smaller room," the Dragon suggested.

"Now that you're back, this is where I'll stay," Tom said, sleepily yawning. "Sorry! This warmth after being so cold makes me drowsy. What did you find out?"

The Dragon crept entirely into Great Hall, almost filling it and raising the temperature by forty degrees.

"I flew to Ffallmar, of course," he said. "Ffallmar and Rosemary are still there. They'll go to Lexor in a week or less, depending on their harvesting. Murdan, Manda, and their people, forty in all counting the soldiers and Freddie the prisoner, stopped overnight with them three days ago. Clem was with them."

"Thank goodness!" cried Tom. "They're safe then!"

"Wait! Ffallmar had word from our friend the dove seller, in Lakehead. The message said all the lake ships had been hauled ashore because of the coming storm."

"He'd seen Murdan?"

"Yes, Murdan reached Lakehead and then went on by the North Shore road when he found no captains willing to risk the storm."

Tom thought this over. The Dragon went on.

"It was getting dark by then and beginning to snow, so I came back to tell you what I'd learned."

"We'd better get some sleep, I guess," said the Librarian, sighing. "And start out early in the morning."

He punctuated his remark with another great yawn. The

bed he'd made before the fire was cozy and he'd been in
the cold wind all day. In a moment he was sound asleep.

The Dragon tried to sleep, too, but Great Hall was stuffy
with his own heat. He wormed his way out and toured the
whole castle once again. Everywhere he found the Historian's retainers and staff in the deep, enchanted sleep, in
their rooms or at the tasks they had been doing when the
spell had been cast over them.

By carefully inserting his head and long, supple neck
into the windowless basement of Middletower, he found
Mistress Plume asleep in her frosty bed, but alone. The
sour-faced comptroller himself was nowhere to be found.
Surprising, as Murdan had said he would not take Plume
to Lexor for Session as he had in the past.

"THAT slimy, sneaky old ingrate!" cried Tom upon waking the next morning. "Plume was selling our secrets to
Gantrell. He was the one who let the Mercenary Knights
into Overhall! We should have locked the double-dealing
old pencil-chewer in Aftertower!"

"Be that as it may, we've other problems just now,"
said Retruance. "It's been snowing hard all night, as the
lake men predicted. If we fly to Lakehead and along the
lakeshore road, we might find them. But their tracks will
be covered by the snow!"

"Worse luck!" exclaimed Tom. He heated slices of the
ham and made some toast and tea. "Can we do anything for
these poor people?"

"We'd better leave them as they are until we can send a
skilled wizard to undo the spell. Arcolas is with Murdan, of
course. I'll get word to someone I know who owes Murdan
a favor. He'll come as soon as the roads are open. In the
meantime, they'll be safe enough behind barred gates."

The temperature had dropped even lower and snow still
fell in huge, soft flakes, blotting out all sight and most
sounds.

"I've brought you a warmer cloak and your warm
Ramhold boots from your wardrobe," the Dragon added.

"You're one of nature's kindest creatures!" exclaimed
Tom in gratitude, pulling on the lamb's-wool-lined over-
boots given him by Talber of Ramhold that spring morning
long ago.

"Not to Gantrell!" snarled the huge flier. "When I catch that blackguard I'll char him completely and stomp his ashes into the soil as fertilizer!"

"Well enough, but we've got to find Murdan and Manda and the rest first. Then I'll help you char and stomp. Let's go see if we can find their trail along the lake."

They flew fast and high, over Sprend and Ffallmar Farm early in the morning, without stopping—"No need to worry them, just yet," Tom decided—and by noon they passed over a Lakehead buried in enough snow to cover more than a man's height. Only thin streams of blue smoke from smooth, white mounds marked the town at the head of the lake. The lake itself was a glassy expanse of windswept ice across which billows of blown snow drifted, twisted, and swirled.

Retruance flew almost at the tops of the drifted snow-banks, following the faint trace of the shore outlined by the water-edge pines. He and his rider peered down at the glaring white snow, but saw no sign of the passage-two days before of a party of forty.

After a while, Tom complained that the glare on the snow was giving him a headache, so the Dragon swooped down into the lee of a particularly thick stand of ship-mast pines. Tom ate cold ham and dry bread, and drank handfuls of snow. Retruance fanned his immense wings back and forth, sweeping the loose snow in a wide swatch across the shore road.

"Here's the road, I believe," he called after fifteen min-utes' hard work. "Just a path, really. The ground was soft before it froze, and look! There are hoofprints."

"Wish we had Clem with us," cried Tom, running over to where the Dragon had stopped blowing snow. "He'd know at a glance if the prints are those of our people, or not."

"Let's see," pondered Retruance. "They came at least this far before the snow started in earnest, I figure. As the weather got worse, they probably found a sheltered place to camp. Clem would certainly know to stop before the snow got too deep even for the horses."

"Cold comfort," said Tom, discouraged. A clot of snow as large as a wagon suddenly slid from an overhanging bough and dropped to the frozen ground with a loud *plump*, making them both jump in alarm. "Is it getting warmer, do you think? Will it get warmer? This is pretty early in the year for such a bad storm, isn't it? It isn't even October yet."

"I'd say so," the Dragon said doubtfully. "I never pay much attention to weather, being able to fly over it, usually."

They sat on a bed of needles under the pines, where the ground was clear. "Lakehead will be hours digging out, even if I helped them with the old wings or a few blasts of fire breath," declared the Dragon.

"Yes, otherwise we could expect Mayor Fellows, a good sort for all of being a Gantrell man, to organize a search," said Tom.

"With a change of weather for the better, Ffallmar could muster all the farmers to form searching parties, too. If we flew back to Sweetwater Tower, the king would do the same. But none of that does any good until the snow stops and it gets warmer."

"We can't afford to wait! Retruance, this storm was just *too* convenient. Murdan says Gantrell can afford to buy the best wizards and most effective magic. This snow and the sleeping spell at Overhall add up to expensive enchanting."

Retruance nodded sober agreement.

"Gantrell's captured the two people he most wants to miss Session, and rescued Freddie the Sponge, too. Freddie is not the least of Peter's concerns, even the king agrees. He said the kidnapper's trial would greatly weaken Peter's influence over the undecided nobles and even many of his friends."

"Let me guess," said Retruance, stroking his chin thoughtfully. "Gantrell will maintain the queen and Murdan conspired, captured Manda to keep her from declaring for her Uncle Peter at Fall Session. The king cannot hear the case of Brevory because key witnesses are missing. The king will be forced to bow to the demands of Gantrell and his cronies that a suitable guardian be appointed to care for little Prince Ednoll, as they did Manda. Who better for guardian than kindly, wise, rich old Uncle Peter? If needed, Gantrell can force Eduard with threats of harm to Manda."

"Whew!" exclaimed Tom. "What a mess!"

"Well, what's to do, now?" the Dragon sighed.

"We can't possibly track the captors in this stuff. We must go directly to the one person who knows where our people are."

"You mean, go to . . ."

"Exactly! To Gantrell and somehow force him or trick him him into revealing where he's hiding Manda, the Historian, and Clem."

"I'll go with you."

"No, this calls for stealth. A fifty-foot Dragon can't go sneaking about without being seen."

"I suppose I could shrink myself again."

"I need your speed more. See to it that Rosemary gets safely to Lexor. Remember, she's the real key witness. And ask the king to delay the trial as long as possible."

"Peter couldn't touch you while you were so highly visible at Sweetwater Tower. Be careful, Tom! You stole his royal pawn from him. He wants you out of the way, too."

"I've already thought of that. Perhaps his spies told him that a young man wearing Overhall's blazon rode to Overhall just before the babes were born. It was Clem, but Peter thought it was me! Or he thinks that the Librarian who rescued Rosemary is still at Sweetwater Tower."

"Where do we start?" asked Retruance, lifting his wings high to rid them of snow and ice.

"Peter will be at his Achievement in Overtide until Sessions begins, I think. It's a good place to start looking for him, at least. Take me there, then go quickly to report to the king."

"Hah!" the Dragon roared. "Let's be off!"

RETRUANCE slanted down over the watershed of Overtide, the river-laced tidal plain on the middle Blue Ocean coast. Retruance had spent their flight time lecturing Tom about Dragon riding. There never had been time before.

"The bond between Dragon and Companion is closer than friendship or even brotherhood," Retruance told him solemnly. "We're as close to being a single being as can be."

"That's how Murdan was able to call you and Furbetrance, when Overhall was taken," Tom exclaimed. "He's a Companion, too, isn't he?"

"His Mount is our father Arbitrance Constable. He's been far out of touch for some years, you remember. Furbetrance and I were searching for him when we heard Murdan's urgent call. We broke off our search and returned to Overhall as quickly as we could."

"Yes, I remember," said Tom thoughtfully. "Can I summon you like that, too?"

"Oh, yes! As our bond grows stronger, I'll be able to sense when you need me most. Unfortunately, it wasn't yet strong enough when I was trapped inside that mountain. I tried, but you didn't know to listen, I guess."

"When this business of heirs and babies and lost princesses is over, we'll go looking for your father again," Tom promised.

"Thank you, Tom! Dragons are family people and it's unnatural that Papa would stay away so long, willingly."

He pointed down with one long claw.

"There's a Gantrell Needle! It marks the northwest corner of Gantrell's Achievement. I'd best put you down here. Peter has armed guards about his house, I'm sure."

They landed in a dense copse of oak and maple near a tall, thin stone monument that towered over the trees.

"Call me if you need me! I can be here in an hour or less. Better take off that Overhall blazon. If anyone asks, you're a freeman scholar, on your way to observe Fall Session in Lexor."

Tom replaced his emblemed jerkin with a plain sweater, then slid off the Dragon's smooth head scales, landing on his feet in a thin crust of snow. The leaves were just beginning to change colors for fall, chocolate brown oak, flaming red-gold maple, brilliant gold aspen. Within view, on a distant ridge, was a two-story, steepled building of red brick and white trim. It bristled with dozens of chimneys.

"Gantrell House," Retruance said, pointing it out. "Good luck, Companion!" he called softly and launched himself into the afternoon sky again, beating away at once to the northeast.

✦ 24 ✦
Missing Princess

A DOZEN burly soldiers blocked Tom's path with their long pikes.

"Here! You!" yelled the sergeant in charge. "Where you going, youngster?"

"I'm on my way to the capital for Fall Session," Tom told him, bowing deeply. He stopped in the middle of the road and held his hands out, palms up, to show he wasn't going to draw sword or knife. "I'd hoped for the night's hospitality of yon great house, good sirs."

"Where be you from?" asked the sergeant, squinting suspiciously at the stranger, noting the quality of clothes, and his sword.

"From Waterfields, sir, in the far south."

"A Swamp Rat!" chortled one of the soldiers. "Not many of you Swamp Rats take to dry land, do you?"

"No, sir, but my master has ordered me to carry his loyal greetings and petitions to present to the king, come Session," Tom replied. "He makes his wishes known in the matter of the young princess who would be queen."

"You haven't heard? We've a real king now, born just three days or so ago." He obviously wasn't privy to Peter of Gantrell's innermost hopes.

"I heard rumor of it in Rainbow, gentle sir. My master says, better a baby king and a strong regent than a flighty, unmarried queen. If the regent is right, if you get his meaning, he says."

"Well, good enough for him, I say!" cried the sergeant in a more kindly tone. "Now, lad, Gantrell House is famous for its hospitality to *friendly* travelers."

The sergeant chuckled, waving him on. "Ask for Mistress Frabble at the kitchen door. She'll take you in, is the way it works."

Tom thanked them all profusely, and walked past the squad. Once more the sergeant stopped him.

"Now, water boy, take good advice. Keep to the road. Go straight to the back after you crosses yon moat, and don't be a-wandering where you don't belong. Lord Peter of Gantrell is bloody strict about strangers on his Achievement. Lucky for you you were on the road. If we'd caught you in the forest, we'd have trussed you up like a chicken and hauled you off to our jail. Wet and foul place, even for a Water Snake!"

His men had a loud laugh at this but they did no more to hinder him. Tom walked quickly down the middle of the broad sycamore avenue toward Gantrell's manor house.

Mistress Frabble, when he arrived in the kitchen yard at the castle's back door, was a thin, mean-eyed, purse-mouthed middle-aged woman dressed in rusty black from head to toe. She interviewed him sharply there in the door-yard.

"Waterfields, eh? What town is that?"

"Chutney Canal," Tom improvised, careful to be very polite, "ma'am!"

"Chutney Canal? Never heard of it! Nobody I know ever went to Waterfields, ever."

"The king once came to Chutney Canal," Tom lied cheerfully. "He was a great, grand man! Ten feet tall, I recall. He squired a young lady of Knollwater. Pa and Ma didn't take to that."

"What do you say?" asked the sharp-tongued matron. "You folks didn't like the king?"

"Not so much the king they didn't like, ma'am, as the lazy . . . Beatricksy, as they call her in the tavern jokes they tell and don't want the young-uns t'hear!"

Mistress Frabble became at once considerably more kindly to the visitor, and led him into the open-sided kitchen shed, where she screamed at a fat assistant cook to bring the newcomer a plate left over from the noon time meal.

"When you finish, sweet laddy," she cooed, her idea of an ingratiating tone, "I'll show you to a room over to the guest-house. Eat well and build your strength! You can tell me those dirty jokes about the queen, eh?"

She sailed off, head high and mouth set in a grim but anticipatory smile.

"Best eat up. You'll need your strength!" joked the chubby assistant cook, bringing a generously laden plate. "I hopes you knows what you're getting into with that ancient she-goat!"

"No, I'm not sure I do. What?" Tom asked innocently, digging at once into the cold food. The roast was badly overcooked, but tasty enough. The greens were greasy.

"Lord! She'll keep after you all night to tell her all the gossip from your parts. She'd rather gossip than eat or—"

He scuttled off suddenly as Frabble returned.

"What was that lovely lad saying to you, sweetheart?" she asked, attempting to sound honey-tongued.

"Oh, just that you are a hard but fair overseer, Mistress Frabble. He said you were a good woman to serve under."

"Ah-ha! Well so I am, although I never thought young Spiggott would say it, the lazy-butt! Are you ready, dear one? I've much to do, or we could have a nice long talk. His Lordship is in residence now and I must be there to see to him and his important guests when they return from the hunt. Come along!"

As the housekeeper led him across the wide courtyard to the guesthouse, there came a sudden rush and flurry of horsemen through the gate beside the Great House. The hunters had returned. Hounds bayed and jumped in excitement, horses stomped, eager for a rubdown and a ration of oats, and sweaty-faced men called for a drink to wash away the dust.

Lord Peter of Gantrell was at their head, the first glimpse Tom had had of Manda's uncle. He was well built, broad of shoulder, with a hard-visaged but handsome face, which was neatly framed by a coal black beard, cut short to highlight the outline of his jaw and chin.

All the hunters were dressed alike, in scarlet coats and tight-fitting trousers. Lord Peter's were more richly and carefully tailored, and while the others looked overheated, mud spattered, and wrinkled, Peter remained fresh and clean, unmarked by the rigors of the chase.

Mistress Frabble hurried her visitor into a long, low brick guest house and showed him quickly to a room at the back, away from the gardens and the courtyard.

"Make yerself to home!" she said distractedly. "Linen's

fresh. I'll send a boy with hot water if you care to bathe. The *necessary* is out that door. Stay here! Don't wander abroad too far!"

She rushed off without further ado, intimate gossip forgotten for the moment, to manage the homecoming of the Lord of Gantrell.

LEFT to his own devices, Tom pulled off his boots and heavy clothing—they were getting rather too warm now that the storm had passed—and after waiting a half-hour went off to the kitchen again, seeking the pail of hot water that Frabble had forgotten.

He bathed, changed, and lay dozing on the narrow cot for an hour, expecting the housekeeper to return for her gossip, but Frabble never reappeared. Someone sent a turnspit to call him to supper in the servants' dinning room. He sat with Spiggott, the assistant cook, while they ate.

It was by then early evening, not yet full night. Up at the Great House lights blazed and there came sounds of loud talking and laughter, the clinking of glasses, and orchestra music, full and lively, for dancing.

"Is it like this all the time?" Tom asked Spiggott.

"Ever! When the master is home, at any rate. Pretty quiet, otherwise, I admit. The food is much better when he is here, too."

"Who is here, beside the lord and his lady and their children, I mean."

"You *are* a bumpkin! Everybody knows Lord Peter is unmarried. He's said to be waiting for the Princess Alix Amanda to come of age . . ."

"I never heard that!" cried Tom. "Nor did . . . er, anyone else where I hail from."

"I don't say it's true, but old Frabble swears she heard it, up at Great House. *Overheard*, is more like it. That woman has ears as long as a jenny's!"

He allowed as how the guests that night were magnates going up to the city, Lexor, on their way north to attend Sessions.

"All they talk of is this princess and the king's baby son, and things like that, Frabble says. I don't understand most of it."

"If His Lordship marries this princess and she becomes

queen someday, Lord Peter will be king then?"

"Don't ask me! I just help cook his meals and stay out of his way!"

"He is a hard master, then?"

"It be worth my tongue to say anything against him, friend. Better to remain silent."

Tom changed the subject back to Mistress Frabble.

"She loves to gossip, I can tell. She seemed about to set down and get me to talk about my folks and what was said about the queen, but the hunters returned and she rushed off."

"She's forgotten you, I'll wager on that," said Spiggot with a laugh. "Old Frabble likes to be where His Lordship can see her. She'll rush about and order people to do this and that, as long as the quality are awake and drinking."

"They'll be at it late, then?"

"Usually are. Never hit bed until sunrise, them kind don't. You have people like that down in your swamps, don't you?"

"Oh, we have ones that'll drink and carouse, sing and shout at each other for days without rest," Tom boasted. "Waterfields folk raise bottomless boozers, I can tell you!"

He was grateful that Gantrell's servants were, like the soldiers on the road, ignorant of almost every aspect of Waterfields life and ways—aside from the fact that their queen came from there—because Tom, almost as ignorant, made it up as he went along.

Someone yelled "Time!" and the servants' supper was abruptly over. Spiggott hurried away, looking hard-pressed, but Tom dawdled on his way back to his room, studying the layout of Gantrell's country place.

Overhall was a heavily fortified dwelling, with tall towers and thick walls in concentric rings, all perched along an inaccessible ridge. Ffallmar Farm was a well-built, rangy farm home, with sturdy walls and steep-pitched roofs and rugged outbuildings of stone and timbers. Ramhold was a squat, practical, log-and-sod affair set into its protecting hill, looking as though it had not been built, but rather as if it had grown there, like a tree.

Gantrell House was grander than them all. It reminded Tom most of the mansions of wealthy Tidewater planters in Virginia. Begun as a plain, solid farmhouse, it still showed strong signs of farming. Its redbrick Great House, its appendage buildings, barns and storehouses, garden sheds and stables, were all set close together in careful husbandry.

The Great House may once have been a simple farmhouse, but the addition of a second floor, tall windows, wide verandas, soaring pillars and carved cornices, painted white, had made it almost a palace.

The whole was arranged sensibly in a roomy rectangle, with the Great House across the top, the kitchen, scullery, dairy, and bake house to its left, not connected to it except by a covered brick walkway, to allow serving boys to reach the dining room quickly and dry shod bearing heavy trays of food.

To the right of the House, also separate but with connecting arcades, were a chapel; then a small schoolhouse, now used for storage, it seemed; workshops for weavers, potters, and various craftsmen; and, at the far end, the guest house. All stood one story high but with tall, steep-pitched roofs, channeled to carry rainwater into deep cisterns, lined with carefully fitted stone, around the edges of the central court.

The fourth side of the square consisted of practical brick-and-wood farm buildings, centered on a lofty barn, in which were stored sweet-smelling straw and hay, against the coming winter.

Beyond the barn and the dairy, the pigpens and the chicken coops, was a fenced meadow for horses and another for dairy cattle. In sheltered places under a neat orchard of apple and pear, crusted snow still resisted the warmth of the fall evening.

After quietly making the rounds of the rectangle twice—pretending to be taking an after-dinner stroll, being careful to remain fully in everyone's sight—Tom returned at near darkness to the guest house. He undressed and lay down on the bed to wait.

A while later he heard someone try his door and open it a crack. Mistress Frabble's long, inquisitive nose poked through, sniffed in disappointment, and withdrew. The door closed silently and he heard the housekeeper cross the brick floor to the outside door.

He jumped from his bed, breathing a silent thank-you, and ran barefoot across the hall to where he could look from an open window after the departing woman.

He caught a glimpse of her reentering the house by a rear door. The noise and music of the party still rolled out over the otherwise quiet and peaceful scene. The clock in the tower over the front gate began to toll. He counted the strokes. Ten.

He returned to his room and lay awake atop his bed for another hour. The party showed no signs of winding down, although most of the farm hands and servants were long abed. A woman Frabble's age would not be able to resist falling into her own bed when her duties were at last completed, on toward two or three next morning, Tom guessed. He should be left to his own devices until morning.

He walked silently down the central hall of the guest house, passing the closed doors of other guests. At a few he heard low talking or snoring, but most of the rooms were quiet. He let himself out through a door facing the stables across a grassy exercise yard surrounded by white-painted fences.

If I'd captured twenty-five soldiers and fifteen servants, maids, and grooms and such, would I keep them all together? Probably not. Perhaps Lord Peter ordered the servants and soldiers held at some out-of-the-way place. Does Gantrell have holdings between Overtide and the north shore of the lake? He didn't know. Retruance might have known. The thought made him feel discouraged.

Of course, Tom mused, Gantrell would want to keep Manda close by, to produce her quickly if he needed. He'd want to supervise her captivity and Murdan's too. What better place than this vast farm?

"Manda, my princess, I bet you're close by, if I can but find you!" he muttered to himself. "But where are you?"

He found the dairy herd sound asleep, the chickens in their coops, and the ducks and geese in their hutches near the mill pond, also sleeping. Tom had sense enough to stay way from the geese. He knew from his Iowa boyhood that they made great alarm sounders.

He stole through the deepest shadows—*No moon tonight, at least, not yet*, he thought—to the far side of the barnyard, guided by a faint glow from an open-sided blacksmith's shed where the forge fire had been banked but still glowed.

Standing under the smithy's roof, feeling the heat of the glowing coals on his back, he studied the next building in line. It was, possibly, a large storehouse. Its doors were tightly closed, its windows barred and shuttered.

A movement caught his eye as he was about to step out into the open again. Around the corner of the storehouse marched a soldier with a pike over his shoulder, humming to himself.

An armed guard? Guarding what?

The soldier paused at the corner of the building nearest to where Tom was hiding. The Librarian faded back into the deepest shadows under the smithy's roof. At first he thought the man was staring at him across the fifteen steps between them, but the soldier dug something from his pocket and, walking right past Tom, he used a pair of smith's tongs to pluck a coal from the banked forge fire to light his pipe.

A cloud of aromatic tobacco smoke wafted past Tom; he almost sneezed. The soldier strolled back to his post, passing again within ten feet, leaned against the corner of the storage building, puffed his pipe, and gazed dreamily across the meadow to the fringe of trees.

Tom sank slowly to his knees to ease the strain of staying very still so close to the guard. But the soldier's attention was fixed on the edge of the trees long after he'd knocked the dottle from his pipe. Then he straightened, as though he'd seen something coming.

Tom, too, caught a flutter of white and heard almost inaudible footsteps in short-cropped grass. The soldier moved from the shadow of his building and raised a hand in greeting. A slight form slipped quickly over a stile in the meadow fence and ran to him. They embraced and Tom heard faint, soft words.

The lovers slipped back into the shadow of the storehouse. "Where's your mate, love?" he heard the girl ask.

"*Shhh!* Not so loud, damnit!" whispered her man. "He's asleep at the other end on a pile of hay. I told him we planned to meet and he promised to keep away."

"We're supposed to lie here? In the dirt and chicken droppings?" the girl protested, pulling away from his embrace, her voice shrill. "There's nettles here, too!"

"No, no, wait, Lucy! I've a good, snug place in mind. Across there in the barn. I left the back door unhooked, see? We'll slip up there and be very comfortable in the loft for a long while."

"Let's go then!" cried the lass with a throaty giggle. The two, clinging together, skipped swiftly across the open yard to the barn and disappeared within.

"Thank God for Lucy's healthy hormones!" Tom breathed. He waited several minutes more, listening and watching, in case the guard sergeant was wise to the soldier's intentions. No one came.

The storehouse was as large as two houses, with widely overhanging eaves on all sides, providing welcome shadow. There was just enough light to see where the end door stood closed and a light push showed it to be locked. Tom circled the building, moving away from the direction taken by the lovers.

A burst of cheering from the Great House made him pause. There was a loud crash and a shriek of laughter.

"Damnation!" said a voice almost in his ear. "They're still at it!"

"Be thankful," Clem's voice said from further away, within. "I've got a sackful to be dumped, now that guard's gone off to sample love's sweet secrets."

Shutters on a window a few feet away slowly opened and arms stretched out, emptying a feed sack of dry, loose dirt on the bare ground.

"*Psst!*" Tom hissed softly. "Murdan!"

"The devil! Why 'tis Tom Librarian!" hissed the Historian, pressing his chest tight against the window bars to see out. "Come to get us free, are you, Tom?"

In a moment they were shaking hands gleefully through the stout wooden bars.

"We're digging," Clem explained from the stygian darkness. "The hole's almost ready to crawl through. Only a short way to go."

"Chipping away at the window bars would've been quicker," Tom observed, drily.

"No tools," said the Historian. "We're digging with a piece of shingle. Besides, we're not digging out. We're digging in!"

"In?" Tom asked in surprise.

"Into the next room. Manda and Mornie are locked in there with no way to get to them, except under the wall," explained Clem. "Lucky the floor is dirt."

"Manda? Next door?" asked Tom.

"We've a plan," said Murdan. "We get into the ladies' chamber and hide. Our meals are pushed through a grille in our door but the ladies are served by a guard who brings their food right into their cell."

"Jump the guards. Bolt through the door together," finished Clem.

"But," Tom objected, "that won't be until tomorrow morning!"

"Best we can do, my boy," said Murdan. "Here, spread that dirt around so the damned guard won't trip on the pile when he comes around again."

While they went back to work inside, Tom scouted around the building, locating the snoring second guard some distance beyond its far end. If needed, he could be overpowered.

He inspected the door that led to Manda's cell and found to his delight that it did not boast a mechanical lock like the end door, but was barred by two sliding bolts. He returned to the diggers to inform them of his find.

"We're six inches from breaking through to their side," whispered Murdan. "Be quicker now to go that way, collect the girls, and you open the door for us."

"Agreed," said Tom. "Will we escape on foot? I know where the stables are."

"No time!" said the Historian. Tom could feel him shaking his head in regret, despite the darkness.

"Once we're away I can call Retruance. But it'll take him several hours to get here. He's at Sweetwater Tower by now."

"We'll have to trust to our woodsman to get us through the woods," said Murdan.

"Get you through the hole in the floor first," said Clem, arriving with a heavy sack of dirt. "I've broken through, but I'll have to widen it a bit more before an overweight Historian can squeeze through."

Tom stood silent in thought while the two miners finished their tunnel.

"Do you know any of Gantrell's guests?" he asked as the last bit of soil was dumped and spread on the bare ground.

"I know 'em all," growled Murdan, dusting his hands together disgustedly.

"Give me the name of one from somewhere nearby. I'll go to the night groom and order him to saddle the man's horses on the pretense he wants to leave. We've got to ride, if we can. Dawn is no more than three hours away."

"Might work," the Historian conceded. "All right! Man named Folderal is here. Came with three companions in the late afternoon. We were able to see him."

"Master Folderal it is, then! I'll open the door, then go to fetch horses. Wait for me here."

He slipped around the storehouse once more and quietly unbolted the door to the adjacent storeroom.

In a moment he was inside, being smothered with hugs and kisses from a shadowy princess and her maid.

"Tom! Oh, Tom! I knew you'd come get us!" whispered Manda.

"Not a thing in the world could stop me," Tom declared, holding her close for a moment more. "But we're not out of this yet, my heart."

The Historian and the woodsman emerged from a far corner of the room, covered with mould and dirt but beaming happily. Their dirty clothes didn't prevent them from receiving kisses and hugs, too.

"Listen," Tom whispered, gathering them all close so he could speak very softly, "I'm going to get horses—"

"I'll go with you," interrupted Clem. "It'll take two to handle four mounts and knock out the groom, if needed."

"Good, then. Manda, wait here. Keep the door closed."

"Much too risky," declared Manda. "The guard might be back any minute. Better to stay together!"

Tom reluctantly agreed and in short order the five were creeping through the shadows, giving the barn and its lovers wide berth, back to the guest house. Tom ducked inside to recover his weapons and knapsack.

Clem found the others a hiding place behind the paddock fence.

Tom walked boldly to the groom's office at the stable's

entrance, finding the man sleeping on a bare cot, fully dressed.

"Here, fellow!" Tom cried in an impatient, commanding voice. "Master Folderal wants his horses up to the house, at once!"

The groom grumbled and growled a bit but, more asleep than awake, found and saddled Folderal's four mares and gratefully turned them over to Tom and Clem so he could go straight back to his bed.

They mounted—Manda and Mornie on the same horse— and walked the animals quietly around the paddock, through the meadow, into the orchard. As they rode under the fruit trees, Clem plucked a double pocketful of fall keepers for their breakfast later.

"Which way?" Tom asked, the first time he had spoken in a normal voice in what seemed hours and hours.

"North by west," Clem answered at once, pointing the way. He'd already given it some thought. "I noticed when we were brought here, the trees and underbrush are thickest there. There're deep ravines we can hide in and still go in the right direction."

"Will you call your Dragon?" asked Murdan.

"Only if I have to," answered Tom. He took several minutes of the ride to describe what he and Retruance had found at Overhall, and what had happened at Sweetwater Tower before that.

"Twins!" exclaimed Manda, grabbing Tom's nearest hand. "Beatrix, bless her heart and soul, had twins?"

"A loud and lively boy, Ednoll, and an equally lively girl, Amelia," Tom told her. "I'm their godfather."

"What beautiful names!" cried Manda. "Well, then, we have our little kinglet, don't we?"

"It would seem," Tom smiled, a bit sadly. "It'll put a wrench in Peter's machinery, at any rate."

"Wrench?" wondered the princess.

"Never mind, Manda, dear! We need to talk it over, but we think, Retruance, your father the king, and I, that Gantrell will be defanged, what with you in our arms . . . ah, that is, hands . . . again, and Murdan free, and the trial of Freddie the Sponge ready to start."

"Defanged?" Manda giggled. "A perfect word! It suits Uncle Peter so very well!"

✦ 25 ✦
A Different Kind of Flight

THEY reached the edge of Gantrell House farmland. Fields and woodlots gave way to a jungly tangle of close-set trees, thorny brush, and tangled vines that at first sight seemed impassable.

"Leave the horses," Clem decided. "There's enough light now to make our way through this. Horses would take us through no faster, and leave traces a blind man could follow."

They dismounted. Clem shouted at the horses and flapped his cloak. They reared back in alarm and galloped off toward Folderal's distant farm.

"That'll perhaps lead any searchers astray for a while," the trapper said with satisfaction. "Now, friends, follow me closely and step as I step."

Clem knew how to move through rough country leaving no trace of his passing. He led them down brush-choked draws, through marshy wetlands, along shallow trickles between overgrown banks, through ever-thicker clumps of willow and white poplar, teaching them to leave neither footprint nor broken branch to show they'd passed that way.

"We could move a lot faster," he told them as the sun rose and full day dawned at last, "but they'd see exactly where we'd been and guess where we were going."

"No, no take your time! Slow and steady wins the race!" puffed Murdan the Historian. "I'm getting too old for dashing about in the woods."

Manda and Mornie, as the morning became hotter and more humid, suffered with him from too little sleep and too much tension over the past four days. Tom suggested to Clem he find a hidden place to rest, perhaps to sleep, until nightfall.

"Not quite yet," the woodsman disagreed. "We're only a short, fast ride from Gantrell House. You see? They're looking for us already!"

He pointed back and up the long slope they had been descending, keeping within a fringe of swamp birch. Along the top of the rise a troop of horsemen galloped swiftly by, rattling, jingling, and shouting to a baying pack of hounds in front of them.

"They're hunting us with dogs!" gasped Mornie in horror.

"That bunch will never see a sign of us," said Murdan, wiping his face with a soggy kerchief. "We were never near that road!"

"The dogs worry me more than the riders," Clem said. "They're old-timers at hunting, know the ground like their noses. We need a bit of woodland magic, just now."

They followed him as quickly as they could through the copse. His eyes swung methodically from left to right, back and forth, searching the ground.

"A-ha!" he said at last, going down on his knees in the leafy litter. He picked a handful of small, round leaves from a flat, gray-green plant beside a mossy rock. "Here's dogmaze! Great luck!"

He had them all sit on the ground right there and vigorously rubbed the soles of their boots with the thick, oily leaves.

"Dogmaze, eh?" commented the Historian, who considered himself something of an expert on herbs, spices, and woodland remedies. "It has a pleasant odor. Does it cover our own scent, then?"

"More than that," answered the trapper, applying the last of the leaves to his own boots. "The scent tells the dogs that we are friends and wish not to be found. The hounds'll pretend to lose the scent, run about as if confused. Actually they'll be covering our tracks for us."

"We must get some rest. We're all dead tired and stumbling," Tom insisted. Manda strove to appear fresh and willing to go on, but failed. Mornie, with a smaller pride to defend, let her exhaustion show in lusterless eyes, sagging shoulders, and ragged breathing.

"We'll go slowly for just a bit more," promised Clem, shaking his head in sympathy. "Nearer the Samber we'll be safe until Gantrell mounts a more careful search afoot."

"How far?" Mornie sighed, rising wearily.

"In miles? Two or three at the most. In time? An hour or two, depending on how brave you are and how strong your reserves, lovely maiden," answered Clem with a tenderness his drinking companions in Wall would not have recognized. He took the lass's hand and led her into the thickest part of the tangle, ducking down a muddy watercourse that appeared before them, into a low-lying scrub even more tangled than before.

"There's River Samber," gasped Murdan. He pointed to a wedge of open water seen momentarily between the trees.

"Samber? What a pretty name for a river," murmured Manda. Tom held her arm as they plodded on. She seemed almost asleep on her feet.

"It's the northern border of Gantrell's Achievement," Clem said, "according to maps I saw in Tom's library at Sweetwater Tower."

"The king's library, rather," said Tom with an enormous yawn. "What lies over the river, then?"

"I don't recall," replied Clem.

"I remember!" said Murdan, snapping his fingers. "North of Samber and almost all the way to Lexor is the largest of the royal forests, called Greenlevel."

"It's royal land, then?" asked Tom.

"Not just a royal forest, but the patrimony of the princess royal from her birth," said Manda.

"*Your* land?" Tom asked.

"Yes, of course," said his princess with a wan smile, "and I'd give it all now for a hot bath and a bed."

"We'd better make the best of what cover there is, Clem," Tom suggested again, "or we'll end up having to carry the ladies."

"Perhaps it's time to call the Dragon," said the Historian, stopping to lean wearily against a tree. "Unless we can hide somewhere nearby for the rest of the day. Once we're across the Samber and under Greenlevel, we'll be safe from Gantrell. Even if he brought an army, Manda's foresters could easily hide us and fend him off."

"There are things I don't know about myself," laughed Manda. "I have a forest, I knew, but foresters?"

Clem was unhappy with the necessity for resting but accepted it, finally, leaving them in the shade of an overtopping bank to scout ahead. Fifteen minutes later he led them to a hollow, entirely invisible from every angle and filled to its brim with a single, ancient, long-thorned bay bush.

"Under here," he directed. "Crawl low so the thorns won't stab you."

Once beyond the first screen of low-hanging boughs, they found themselves under a dome of aromatic, closely growing leaves. Only a dim, green light reached them. The air felt cool after the humid heat of the open woods. The floor of the hollow was covered with fine, dry sand.

"No fire," Clem warned. "We'll be hidden and safe enough here until dusk. If anyone comes close by, we can dash down that way, into the river in a few paces."

"Oh, a wonderful place!" sighed Mornie in relief, and she set about spreading their heavy winter cloaks on the ground. In less time than it takes to tell, both young ladies and the Historian were sound asleep.

"I seem to be fresher than you," said Tom. "I got a few hours' sleep at Gantrell's guest house last night. I'll take the first watch."

"Good!" Clem agreed. "Wake me at noon. Stay out of sight, especially from the ridge."

Tom crawled back under the bay, being careful not to disturb the leaves or snag himself on thorns. He found a raised bank of bare clay, which allowed him a fairly clear view of both the ridge and the river, and settled down to watch.

HE was wakened in the late afternoon, when the trapper crawled up to his perch and shook him by the foot.

"Fine wide-awake guard you are!" Clem teased. "I don't suppose you've seen or heard anything of interest?"

"Nothing," Tom assured him sheepishly. "Some commotion at the top of the hill a long time ago. Must be the main road, up there. Horsemen keep coming and going, in full view."

"Gantrell expected us to follow the straightest, shortest road to the river ferry," Clem said. "By now he's discovered his mistake and will start his people beating the bushes on foot. It'll take them hours if they start at the orchard. Less, if they discover where we dismounted."

He narrowed his eyes into the lowering sun through the bayberry's branches. "We'd better have something to eat and get started. As the Historian said, the sooner we get within Greenlevel, the better."

He produced the apples he'd picked when they rode through Gantrell's orchard. As the others awoke, stiff and sore but happy to be free, he sliced and passed them out. While they ate, he snaked out of the hollow and went scouting toward the river.

They were ready to resume their journey when he returned, popping out of the underbrush at the end of a completely silent approach.

"What news?" asked Murdan.

"We're a short walk from the river, mostly through marsh, which means we'll have to wade. I suggest we all remove our boots and wade bare of feet, for we'll want dry boots in the forest."

They followed him as he moved off, with their boots buckled together and hung about their necks, through dense undergrowth, picking a way to avoid sharp thorns and beds of stinging nettles.

"I haven't been barefoot out of doors since I was a little girl," whispered Manda, her good spirits revived after a sound sleep and a slice or two of juicy-tart apple. "My soles used to be hard as horn."

"You must have been a tomboy." Tom laughed at the picture in his mind's eye, and then had to explain the expression, for she'd never heard it before.

"In any case," she said when she understood, "now I have a Tom-boy!"

Twenty minutes of sliding down muddy banks and wading through knee-deep pools of warm, algae-black water, over sandbars carpeted with purple and blue flowers, and they came to a line of ancient willows, roots tangled and braided together into a barrier to the open river, which lay just beyond.

The refugees stopped to catch their breath and admire the slow, silvery river.

A band of men dressed all in dark brown, armed with staves, short swords, and long bows, dropped from the limbs of the willows and surrounded them.

• • •

EDUARD Ten, King of Carolna, in his most splendid robe of
state, marched solemnly down the four-hundred-foot aisle of
the Hall of Session in Lexor, and ascended the red-and-gold
Trusslo throne.

Nobles and freeman delegates cheered enthusiastically,
with all evidence of sincere admiration. A company of
young men-at-arms in highly polished half-armor, swords
drawn, preceded and followed the king, looking fiercely to
all sides, as ancient custom dictated. They were followed by
the queen's escort, twenty-four beautiful maidens dressed in
gowns of pastel colors, and ten imposingly dignified matrons
of honor in shimmering silks and satins.

Beatrix, now seen abroad for the first time since her
confinement, was greeted by even louder cheers and calls
of good wishes from the assembled Session. She smiled
brilliantly at everyone, even into the dark, disapproving
visage of the king's powerful ex-brother-in-law, Peter of
Gantrell, who stood, handsome and erect, at the foot of the
dais, just under the edge of its sea blue silk canopy.

Men searched his face as well as the young queen's,
looking for signs of unease at this meeting. Rumors were
flying everywhere—as they always did when the delegates
to Session came to the capital.

Those who knew Peter well saw he was under tension;
there was a wariness to his deep-set gray eyes that were
usually so arrogantly confident. He stood with the faintest
touch of slump, as if tired or bored. Gossips had no answers,
but all eyes watched him closely.

King Eduard, looking rested and fresh, waited until his
consort had gracefully mounted the two steps to the throne
and gallantly handed her to a gilt chair at its right, smiling
warmly at her as if to say, *This is as much your acclamation
as mine, my dear.*

Applause rolled over them, on and on. The king stood
facing the delegates until the din subsided enough to allow
him to be heard without shouting.

"Carolna!" he cried in a rich, carrying baritone. "Friends,
countrymen of high and low degree! We, your king and
queen, greet you with love and extend to you our wishes
for continued peace and increased prosperity."

With a few exceptions, notably Gantrell and his closest
adherents, they were all in very good spirits.

"The birth of our son, I warrant, has lifted from them all a burden they shared with us," Eduard said aside to Beatrix. She nodded happily and waved again to the excited throng.

The king waited again for the uproar to subside, then bent to pick up the Wand of Justice, laid at the foot of the throne and, raising it for all to see, called out: "I declare this Twentieth Fall Session of our reign hereby to be open. Let all men, of any and all circumstances, closely attend and be heard in all matters, that I, your king, may judge the right and render true justice, decide and dispose, for the good of each and all."

A choir of trumpets soared in a stirring fanfare. The king seated himself on the throne, and the business of Carolna in Fall Session began.

The king was firmly in charge. He set the pace, decided when to stop to rest, when to begin again. He selected those whom he would hear first, and who must wait. Sessions were expected to last for days, perhaps weeks, but few failed to attend every sitting.

Their evenings would be spent in celebration, at gala balls, in sumptuous private dinners, and public banquets. There would be merchant ships racing on Brant Bay, mock duels between heavily armored knights, and competitions between highborn ladies in needlework, poetry, drawing, and music.

Freemen flocked to archery tournaments, wrestling and boxing matches, and contests between woodsmen and among horsemen. They especially enjoyed horse races, horseshoeing, and exhibits of husbandry—and wifery as well.

In the first three days the king heard petitions from freemen and minor noblemen, and disputes between neighbors or members of the same family.

A father had died intestate. His eldest son claimed all his property and wealth. His other two sons demanded equal shares. The eldest had housed, fed, and made easy the deceased's last days. The other two, pleading lack of funds, failed to give the old man support, and stayed distant until his very last moments. Angry words had been spoken and threats made.

"What was the last wish of the deceased?" the king asked.

"He left no written will," the eldest testified under solemn oath. "But he told me I was to have all, as his other sons had deserted him in his old age."

"You would appear to deserve it," said the king, cupping his chin in his right palm to help him think. "What did he say of your brothers?"

"That they were churls and ingrates, Your Majesty," answered the eldest son, reddening, suddenly ashamed to say it.

"That was in anger, perhaps?" Eduard wanted to know. "He said that *before* he was certain of death?"

The eldest shook his head. He couldn't remember, he said haltingly.

"Didn't he say, in earlier days, that his sons were all precious to him and all three shared in his love, as well as his hard-won wealth, while he was alive?"

"Ah, I say, well," hesitated the eldest son, beet red now.

"Was it not so, sirrah!" demanded the king, sternly.

"Yes, sire, it was so. But . . ."

"You ask me to speak for your dead father," said the king, straightening in his seat. "If I'd known the man, perhaps I could judge better, but I can only think what *I* would have wanted, were you my sons. And that's clear. I am a father. A father, I know, may say things in anger and disappointment, but still love his sons—and his daughters— too much to wish them hurt when he is gone."

He turned to the royal recorder who sat on his left, and dictated his decision for all to hear.

"The eldest son will have an exact half of the patrimony left by his father, as reward for caring for him and supporting him in old age's infirmity.

"The other two sons will share equally the other half of the wealth of their father, carefully determined according to the law of the land. The king reminds them that they, one day, will be fathers who must divide their patrimony among loved and loving children. They are, he says, to enjoy the money and the land, but remember, every time they use or sell it, the love their father bore for them."

The three litigants, without prompting, fell into each other's arms at the relief they felt and wept away their past quarrels and hot anger.

"I've at least made the spirit of their poor father happy, wherever he rests," said Eduard to Beatrix.

"That's no small consolation," replied the queen with warm approval.

"I AM Alix Amanda, Princess Royal!" insisted Manda angrily. "How dare you doubt me?"

"Anyone can claim to be of royal blood, mistress," said the tall, wiry chief forester. "Any pretty girl could come along and say she was our liege, the Princess Alix Amanda. How are we to tell? Think of what harm it would do if we made a mistake, we of Greenlevel?"

He looked genuinely distressed and Manda relented from her sudden hot anger.

"Hear me, however! I am vouched for by these persons. Here is the Royal Historian, my uncle Murdan, Lord of Overhall. This young man is my betrothed, Thomas, Librarian to Lord Murdan, and this is his close friend, a freeman of the northern forests, not unlike yourselves, Clematis of Broken Land. The lady is my kinswoman and attendant, Lady Mornie of Morningside . . ."

"*Lady* Mornie!" gulped Clem, startled. "*Lady?*"

"Well, yes, I thought you knew about that," said the maid, smiling at his confusion. "Does it make any difference?"

"No, no, no!" cried her swain. "No difference! I never paid any attention before to what titles they gave you, Mornie."

Manda watched their captors closely. They were impressed by her words and manner, despite their deep suspicions, and by the byplay between the trapper and the maid.

"If I may?" begged Tom.

"Yes, sir," said the chief forester, brusquely.

"I suggest we retreat to the other side of River Samber before Lord Peter of Gantrell and his soldiers come looking for the princess and the Historian. They aren't far off."

"We've seen them riding the Ferry Road," agreed the forester. "But we've no quarrel with Gantrell."

"You do now, by God!" Manda exclaimed furiously. "He has held me captive against my will! Held my uncle and my friends in prison as well. We have just last night escaped his house!"

"There is much to sort out here, lady," conceded the

chief forester. "Perhaps it's better to pursue the matter in the safety of Greenlevel, after all."

He gave orders to his brown-clad bowmen and they hurried off downstream under the arch of willows, swiftly and silently leading the escape party in their midst.

A good-sized side stream entered the river, forming a cove, hidden from sight by the drooping willow boughs. On a tiny sand beach lay four bark canoes, light but strong and swift by the looks of them, Clem thought. The foresters of Greenlevel put the travelers into the boats and seized leaf-shaped paddles to propel the craft out into the slow-moving current, angling across to the far shore, a mile away.

"They'll see us!" objected Tom to the chief forester.

"Doubtful at this time of evening. There's nothing for it, anyway," replied the other, swinging his paddle in time with his mates. "If what your lady says is true, we must not let Gantrell find us on his land. He has great powers there, not to mention a large force of trained men-at-arms."

The canoes crossed unchallenged, however, and nosed into a grassy shore on the north bank. The land here rose steeply to the forest floor, where it became gently rolling under the cover of trees, without swamps or marshes to bar easy travel. In an hour the party was brought to a clearing in which stood four or five rustic log cottages with moss-covered cedar-shake roofs and tall fieldstone chimneys, from which spiraled thin threads of smoke.

"This is our southern headquarters," explained the forester. "We call it South Post, for want of a better name. You're welcome to our hospitality."

"*My* hospitality," insisted Manda, but with a smile. "If you wish to explore this problem, I ask only that we be given a chance to bathe and dine first. Five days as captive and a night and a day in the swamps of Overtide may account for my not looking very regal."

"So it shall be, for such is our usual hospitality," the chief forester agreed, and he turned to give orders to his men and their women, who came from the cottages to meet them.

"You are Strongoak," Manda said to him, remembering his name at last.

"I apologize for not introducing myself at once, lady! Yes, I'm Strongoak, Princess Royal Alix Amanda's chief forester in Greenlevel Forest."

"I seem to recall meeting you long ago," Manda said. "Didn't you bring a present to me on my fifth birthday?"

"No, that would be my father, of the same name," said Strongoak, shaking his head. "He passed away—"

"Six years back," interrupted Manda. "I recall the sad news coming to Morningside. Killed by a wild boar, as I remember."

"That's true. My father brought a pair of pups to the ward of Granger Gantrell," said Strongoak.

"No, it was my forest pony," cried Manda. "Adorable, gentle little Charade! I was so sad when I grew too big to ride him about Uncle Granger's meadows and gardens."

Strongoak listened gravely but said no more until, several hours later, he sat with them over a plain but hearty supper on trestle tables set under the oaks in the cooled evening air.

"I know no absolute way to confirm your identity," he began when they settled back to relax after the meal. "I must say I personally am convinced you are who you say you are, but feel I must have proof positive. I owe it to you, Princess, for I am responsible for the safety and management of your lands here."

"Even if I am not your princess?" asked Manda with a laugh. "Well, I can't think of anything more to say to convince you. I am who I say I am, and so are these others. We wish to be protected from my wicked Uncle Peter, and escorted to Lexor to join my father, the king, at Fall Session. You are aware of the importance of this Session, aren't you, Chief Forester?"

"Very much so," replied Strongoak. "I was about to depart myself to attend, carrying the fealty of my people, especially if Gantrell makes trouble for you, Princess, in the matter of becoming queen."

"Do you know where my desires lay on that?" asked Manda, suddenly.

"I . . . I have heard you do not wish to wear the Trusslo crown or to sit the throne," Strongoak hesitated.

"It's true, however. My father now has a son, Prince Ednoll, who is his clear male heir. Once Peter of Gantrell thought he could control the crown by holding fast to me, marrying me to one of his nephews or taking me as bride himself, perhaps. I ran away—to Overhall. All this will be brought out at this Session, you see, and Gantrell will be much reduced in power, perhaps even sent into exile again when the freemen and nobles hear my story in full."

"I can see why Princess Alix Amanda would hasten to Lexor," conceded the Chief Forester.

"The point is," interrupted Murdan, "that the proof of Manda's identity will come if you were to escort us to Lexor."

"No one should doubt you," cried Mornie, suddenly. "Anyone who met you should see that you are the Princess Royal!"

"But here is Strongoak, doubting me, even now!" exclaimed Manda. "Oh, if it were not for the life and happiness of my father and Queen Beatrix and the little babies and all, I'd say return to Overhall and let Gantrell have his way!"

She began to weep quietly, which disconcerted those who saw it, Strongoak most of all.

His wife, Ermine, who sat at the other end of the table, stood and came to Manda, putting her arms about her shoulders and calling out to her husband, "Stop your harassing the princess, husband! I, for one, believe her. You can no longer pretend to doubt!"

"My wife is my conscience," the Chief Forester said with a rueful grin. "And she is perfectly correct! I have not doubted, not since your first words. I am so sorry, Princess, but I felt . . ."

"It *was* your duty, I know," said Manda, accepting a handkerchief from Tom to wipe away the tears of frustration and weariness. "I cannot fault your faithfulness, Strongoak. I forgive your seeming doubt."

From the applause, even from the servants who waited upon their table, it was evident that all the foresters agreed with Mistress Ermine.

"Lord Murdan; gentlemen! I would feel better if you forgave and understood, also," begged Strongoak, rising.

"Nothing to forgive, forget, or misunderstand," said Murdan. "You have shown yourself a most faithful liege man, and that's much more important than mere words."

Tom, Mornie, and Clem nodded their agreement.

"Now, after a good night's sleep and perhaps a day of

rest here, we will lead you through the heart of your forest to Lexor, Lady Princess," promised Strongoak.

A forester came to them as they sat talking. He reported that Gantrell's men-at-arms, or so he presumed from their livery, were preparing to cross on the ferry and enter the forest.

"Bad news!" cried Strongoak. "We'll have to turn them back!"

"Just hold them for the night and morrow," suggested Clem. "That's enough time for us to get a good start, I think."

"I'll go down to the river ferry myself," decided the Chief Forester. "I can delay them, if you don't want us to outright fight them, Princess."

"Once we're away to Lexor, I don't think they'll bother you, Strongoak," said Manda. "But we do need a night's rest. Hold Uncle Peter's people with diplomacy at least that long. We'll ride on, tomorrow morning."

"LORD King," said a freeholder named Triple. "I yield my time and place to my lord of Gantrell."

"But you have entered a petition, I believe, that deals with a serious matter between yourself and the Fishermen's Guild," objected Eduard, leaning forward. It was the morning of the fourth day of the Twentieth Fall Session of his reign. Gantrell was making a move.

Triple coughed nervously and paled, but insisted that he would step aside for his liege lord, which was in accord with the rules.

"Very well, then, right after lunch," decided Eduard at last. "We'll hear Lord Peter on a full stomach, at least."

A few in the audience laughed aloud at his quip but most looked at each other with worried frowns.

✦ 26 ✦
Feints and Thrusts

"YOU realize," Tom said to the Historian, "that we don't have our prisoner anymore. He was released when Gantrell captured you and Manda?"

"Of course," snapped Murdan. They were riding side by side through endless aisles of oak, ash, elm, and lesser hardwoods of Greenlevel Forest.

"How can the king try Freddie if he doesn't have Freddie?" the Librarian asked.

"The important thing is the testimony against Brevory, and we can give him that," said Clem.

Tom shook his head in disagreement. "Even Freddie deserves to be present at his own trial and to speak in his own defense. Besides, I rather expect him to rat on Peter, if it came to that."

" '*Rat*'?" wondered the Historian.

"Squeal," explained Tom. "Uh . . . turn king's evidence. Testify against Gantrell to save his own neck."

"Ah, I see! *Rat!* Very good!" Murdan laughed.

"Under our laws, the King can try a felon even though he is uncaptured and not present," explained Manda. She had heard the discussion from ahead of them, where she was riding with Strongoak. "Freddie need not be there. I admit he probably would 'rat' on Uncle Peter, given a good chance."

"But this goes beyond the trial and its results," Tom argued, somewhat stiffly. "If Freddie is tried and convicted without being there to speak up for himself . . ."

"He deserves it!" cried Mornie.

"Well, yes, you and I know that," said Tom, "but what about the nobles and the people who are considering siding with Gantrell against your father, the king, Manda? Or feel that a grown, experienced Regent like Peter is better than

287

a huffy old Historian? If they're convinced Eduard . . .
er! . . . diddled . . . Freddie and your Uncle Peter, it will
strengthen support for Gantrell. A free and open trial, a
fair and public hearing—*that's* the important thing, not just
tweaking Peter's black beard in public."

Manda turned in her saddle to nod at him. "You're right,
as often I find you are, beloved Librarian! Thank you, but
what can we do about it?"

"Find Freddie," said Tom, glancing back in turn at Clem.
"Once we're clear of this forest, Clem and I will join with
Retruance Constable and search the Sponge out. Give us
a few days. Delay, as I counseled the king. We'll bring
Freddie to Lexor for trial."

Manda made a wry face at the thought of her young
man going off once again without her, but she was her
father's daughter, and deeply aware of the need for her
at court.

"We'll part at Two Mills, then," said Strongoak with a
nod of his head. "Later this afternoon."

"I'll get Retruance to meet us there," decided Tom. "If
he can get away from the court."

"He'll be there!" insisted Manda, dropping back to ride
contentedly beside him.

LOOKING somewhat pale and tired—he had rushed to the
capital the morning after his prisoners had escaped—Peter
of Gantrell made a studied, magnificent picture standing
before the throne, dressed completely in somber black yet
showing his power and riches with diamonds sewn across
his broad chest, forming the Standing Bear blazon.

He was a show in himself and the delegates were eager
for the action to begin.

"My liege!" Lord Peter rumbled. The hall fell absolutely
silent.

"Lord Peter?" responded King Eduard softly.

"I wish to bring before you, Majesty, the matter of certain
accusations made against one of my knights, Sir Fredrick of
Brevory."

The king nodded, leaned back in his great chair, and
steepled his fingers.

"The crown is unaware of any accusations made against
one Fredrick of . . . where did you say?"

"Brevory, Majesty. A small Achievement just to the west of here, perhaps fifteen miles from where we stand."

"Ah, I recall it. Part of your demesne, is it not?"

"Yes, Your Majesty."

"As I said, we have no information and no complaint about this man, Lord Peter. Perhaps you could tell us of what this Brevory is to be accused, and by whom."

"Of course, I cannot speak to that, Lord King, as the accusation is totally false. I do know that my man Brevory was recently imprisoned by Murdan of Overhall, who let it be known he intended to bring Brevory to trial before you at this Session."

"I recall Lord Murdan writing something about it, now that you mention it," conceded the king. "But as Murdan hasn't yet arrived, he couldn't have brought a complaint before Session, could he?"

Peter thought about this for a moment before going on, saying, "My words are more in the manner of an inquiry than a petition, Majesty. I would like to know what Lord Murdan intends in this matter. In order that my legals may prepare a defense in Brevory's behalf."

"Well, Peter, I'm sure I've no idea," claimed Eduard. "Perhaps if you were to find Murdan and ask him? I'm worried about him, to tell you the truth. He's usually quite prompt, and yet both he and my daughter are not yet here, it seems. Can you tell us anything of their tardiness?"

This last was spoken coldly and directly to the nobleman. Gantrell drew back two steps, despite himself.

"I have no . . . word . . . of the Historian nor of the Princess Royal, sire. The last I heard, they were both at Overhall. If it is your wish, I will start inquiries for them."

"I do wish so," said the king, settling back easily into his chair. "Now, if there is nothing more . . . ?"

"I would like to begin general discussion on the royal succession," Gantrell said hastily. Too quickly, many thought.

"This is a new matter before us?" asked the king sternly.

"Yes, it is, Majesty, but one which—"

"Will be brought before Session in due time by myself," Eduard finished for him. "When the time is right we will settle the whole matter to everyone's satisfaction . . . perhaps."

"May one ask, sire, when the time will be right?" asked Gantrell, barely hiding sarcasm.

"As it is undeniably a personal concern of your king," said Eduard, slowly, "you will understand that the timing must be a matter for the king and queen to decide, without undue pressure. Perhaps, as an unmarried man and never a father, you would not understand, but believe me, a father knows when it is time and when it is better to wait for such a public discussion."

The jab at Peter's unwed and unchilded state brought a rustle of comment and some laughter from the delegates, quickly hushed when Peter swung about to stare them down.

"I may at least have the king's assurance, then, that the matters I have mentioned will be taken up in *this* Session?" he inquired smoothly.

"Positively, yes!" said the king. "And on the matter of . . . er . . . Psalter . . ."

"Brevory, Your Majesty," corrected Gantrell, strangling his anger.

"Yes, Brevory. As soon as someone files a complaint about his kidnapping of Lady Rosemary of Ffallmar and her children, we will hear evidence and make fair judgment, you are assured, Lord Peter."

Thus he let everyone know that he knew much more of the matter than he would admit, officially.

"And the matter of the Princess Royal's guardianship . . . ?" asked Peter.

"Will be taken under consideration when I bring it forth, no sooner, Lord of Gantrell. Now, may we pass back to your friend with the fishing rights problem? That kind of fishing I am more familiar with."

Gantrell bowed sardonically to the king and stalked out without asking permission. The murmurs and chuckles in the assemblage were louder than before.

"The king," declared Eduard solemnly, "wishes to remind his loyal delegates that there are rules and procedures that all are expected to follow at Session. Without them there would be utter chaos, I fear. Ah, Sir Triple? May we hear your petition, now? Is the representative of the Fishermen's Guild on hand?"

IN a city overflowing with strangers from all corners of the realm, in all sorts of strange and exotic costumes and uniforms, wearing a half-thousand different house and family badges and blazons, the band of brown-clad foresters riding through the southwest Lexor gate on their sturdy, shaggy forest ponies went unremarked.

"I wish you'd let me send a message ahead," complained Strongoak. "There's no telling what sort of reception will await you if they don't know you're here, Princess."

"Never mind!" said Manda. "I don't need an invitation to enter my father's house. Oh, isn't the city magnificent! Look, Mornie! They've lined the Promenade with the flags from every Achievement! How gorgeous!"

Exclaiming about the gala scenes they came upon and commenting on the personages they saw (but who didn't recognize them in return), Manda and her escorts rode across the city, directly to the royal palace.

A Royal Guard company, splendid in gold-and-red jackets and trousers; black, shiny knee-boots; and gleaming half-armor, blocked the entrance to Queen Alix Amanda Alone Palace, or Manda Palace, as it was commonly called. The officer in charge strode importantly up to turn these dusty brown riders away.

"This is the royal residence," he announced. "All seeking audience with the king must apply in the morning between nine and eleven to the royal secretary, at this door. Until then, I'm very afraid I must ask you to clear the roadway. We are expecting important guests."

Murdan leaned over and flipped his deep hood back.

"Do you recognize me, Colonel?" he asked in a very quiet voice.

"Oh, yes, Historian!"

"Then you will recognize this young person beside me."

The guard captain studied Manda's suntanned face deep inside its hood. Suddenly his face brightened as if someone had uncovered a lamp behind his eyes.

"Oh, yes, indeed I do!" he gulped. He appeared about to bow, but Murdan stopped him with a hand on his shoulder.

"Steady! No names!" he hissed quickly. "We wish to

enter here privately so that this . . . person . . . can talk in peace with her father before our presence is general knowledge. Can you arrange this?"

"Certainly, Lord Murdan! I'll send a most reliable officer to lead you to a postern gateway. No one will suspect you are anything but wandering minstrels or jugglers reporting for work. This is suitable for . . . this person?"

"It'll do," said Manda, waving a brief gesture of thanks. "Strongoak, my father, the king, will offer you shelter, I know."

"It were better if we camp in the open at the Boscery, as we always do," said the Chief Forester. "With your permission I will wait upon you and Their Majesties tomorrow morning at the normal visiting time."

"That suits me," said the Princess Royal, turning her forest pony to follow the young officer waiting to show them the way. Murdan lagged behind a moment.

"Listen, Colonel! If word gets out prematurely, I shall know immediately who leaked it. Do I make myself clear?"

"Most clear, Lord Historian! No one shall learn the news from me."

Murdan nodded in satisfaction, pulled his hood back over his face, waved farewell to the foresters, and followed Manda, Mornie, and the officer around the Palace named for Manda's great grandmother, who had built it.

✷ 27 ✷
Trial and Errors

"THE Royal Historian has at last appeared," sneered Gantrell, standing again before the throne in Session Hall. "I insist, Lord King, that he either bring charges against my man Brevory, or apologize for his slanders!"

"Anger is uncalled for, Lord Peter," warned Eduard, coldly. "You push your prerogatives a bit too far and too fast. There are other concerns the crown has here, not to mention the concerns of our subjects who have petitions to present."

"I happen to know that petitioning will end this afternoon," said Gantrell, switching on a gracious smile. "Will I be unreasonable if I ask that mine be considered tomorrow?"

"Monday, rather," said the king mildly. "As you know, Session Ball is tomorrow night and it's traditional to adjourn for the day of the ball, to allow everyone time to prepare."

"I again respectfully remind Your Majesty," added Peter, now glaring at Murdan, who sat to one side of the dais with Manda, "that I have a personal petition to present. I have waited patiently in line, but I do not intend—"

"Careful!" said the Historian, raising his hand. "You may say something you would not want on record for history to read, m'lord."

"I am in control of my tongue!" snapped Gantrell. He turned to the king, trying to smile smoothly again and almost succeeding.

"I wish to settle the business of Brevory, as a matter of pride and honor, sire, and I insist we shall discuss the succession, a matter of utmost importance to us all, including the abduction of the Princess Royal from my brother's household last spring."

"We shall take up the charges against Sir Fredrick of Brevory on Monday morning," the king decided. "And the rest will be on the agenda at the very end of Session, as it will depend on the outcome of the trial, in some part. As for Manda, I have spoken to her as her father, and she assures me no abduction occurred."

"We shall see about that!" snapped Gantrell, but he resumed his seat in the front row before the throne.

Eduard beckoned to Manda. She rose and bent over her father, the better to hear his whisper.

"This young man of yours, Manda? Do you have any idea how long he intends to be gone? Recapturing Brevory, I mean."

"I'm sorry, Father. All I can tell you is that Tom's fully aware of the need for haste. I trust him, Father!"

"As do I," agreed her father, patting her hand. "Well,

the ball will give us another day of respite, but I can't put Gantrell off past Monday, I'm afraid.

"Tom and Clem and Retruance have four days to find the Sponge, then," said the princess, with more confidence than she felt.

"Sponge?" Eduard chuckled. "Ah! Yes, I've heard that man is entirely too fond of the bottle and cask."

"He is a sniveling, cowardly browbeater, a child stealer, a constant whiner, a foulmouthed drunkard," Manda told him levelly. "And a few other things for which I have no evidence, merely hearsay."

The king threw his head back and laughed aloud. From his seat on the floor, Peter of Gantrell turned from a conversation with three henchmen to scowl at Manda and the Historian.

"Get you to Plaingirt at once," he ordered the tallest of the three bullies. They were dressed for the road, booted and spurred and armed with long sabers. "Brevory is a damned nuisance at all times and now he is liable to be a deadly embarrassment. Kill him and hide his body in the mountains. Cover your tracks well!"

"Aye, m'lord!" said all three, and they paced arrogantly from Session Hall.

RETRUANCE curled himself about the campfire while his companions toasted buns and sausages furnished by the foresters. The night was cold, smelling of autumn and suggesting rain to come.

"I've been racking my so-called brain," said the Dragon, "since we met, but I cannot deduce where Gantrell, blast his liver and lights, would hide anyone, let alone twenty-five soldiers, fifteen courtiers, and a drunkard."

They were camped on a south-facing hillside overlooking the Royal Highway that wound north from the capital to the mountains and the northeast frontier.

"Probably not on his own lands, even scattered as far as they are," mused Clem, popping a hot sausage into his mouth and following it with a last piece of bun.

"As far as Freddie's concerned, certainly not more than a day's ride from the capital," Tom reasoned. "That limits our search a little, anyway."

The other two were silent. They watched the fire burn

down to embers until the Dragon dozed and the young men crawled into their blankets.

"We'll scribe an arc with the capital in the center," decided Tom, "and ask anyone we see if he's seen a large body of men being marched anywhere at all."

"Uuumph," agreed the sleepy Dragon.

WELL after midnight the Librarian suddenly sat erect and exclaimed aloud.

"What is it?" asked Clem, fully awake at once.

The Dragon emitted a puff of steam and smoke to show he was awake, too.

"Listen, fellows! Peter wouldn't put them at one of his own castles or farms. And he probably doesn't trust any of his friends to hide them and keep silent, not even Granger, for all he is a brother."

"Hardly an observation worthy of a rude awakening," grumbled Retruance.

"Who *would* he trust with such a matter? Someone he can control? Someone he could distance himself from, if the Overhallers are discovered?"

"Granted," said Clem. He placed a fresh billet of wood on the embers. The log flared at once and the three realized that it had begun to snow while they slept.

"I can think of only one kind of person he might trust," said Tom. "Someone bought and paid for. A mercenary!"

"The Mercenary Knights? It's worth looking into. You may have guessed aright!" exclaimed Retruance. "But where are they, anyway? I only see them wandering from job to job."

"I *guess* only—that they would return home between commissions. And the Chief of the Mercenary Knights at Overhall—what was his name?"

"Basilicae!" said Retruance Constable.

"Yes! Basilicae said he would return to a place he called Plaingirt. He said it was in the mountains—"

The Dragon interrupted. "Yes, I've heard of it. It's bit more than two days' fast ride on horseback from Lexor."

"More like two days and then some. The town is off the main road, hard to find," said Clem.

"But not for us!" cried the Librarian. "We can fly there in a few hours, can't we?"

"Of course," said Retruance. He heaved his great bulk gracefully to his four feet and stretched his wings, shaking off a blanket of soft snow. "Shall we go now?"

There was nothing left to eat for breakfast, so they carefully drowned the campfire and climbed aboard the Dragon's brow, brushing away an inch-thick crust of wet snow to clear their place.

"It's snowing harder and harder," observed Retruance. He leaped into the air with a rush of cold wind and swirl of ice crystals. "We'll have to fly lower down to make sure we see the road."

"As I recall, this highroad forks not far north of here," said Clem, who had spent a number of afternoons, while Tom attended the king and queen at Sweetwater Tower, poring over the king's collection of charts and maps.

"Maybe we should return to Sweetwater and get some of those maps," Tom suggested.

"No time! No use, either!" exclaimed Retruance. "The way this snow is coming down, we'll have a hard time finding landmarks, anyway."

The Dragon skimmed low over the foothills of the Snow Mountains, between solid screens of hardwood forests. His riders leaned out over the Dragon's eyebrows, as far as it was safe, to scan the highway.

For the most part the road was empty, except for an occasional farmer or wandering craftsman hastening home ahead of the deepening snow. Once they had passed the fork in the highway and taken the north-tending way, they saw no one at all for an hour, until Tom pointed ahead.

Three horsemen rode doggedly against the north wind, heads bowed to the driving snow. The wind whipped the cloak from the foremost rider's back, flipping it high in the air.

"The Standing Bear!" cried both Clem and the Dragon in unison. "They are Gantrell men, for sure!"

Retruance was circling to pounce on the riders when they noticed a fourth horseman, coming from the opposite direction. The wind was at his back. As the Dragon pulled up, the newcomer waved his arm and drew up, waiting for the three Gantrell henchmen to come up to him. They saluted him politely.

Hidden by the heavy fall of snow, Retruance glided

silently behind a stand of fir just out of earshot of the riders.

"By my tail feathers!" whispered Retruance. "That's Plume, Murdan's comptroller. He wasn't with the party that left for Lexor but he wasn't asleep at Overhall, either! What is he doing here?"

"Being a traitor," growled Tom. "There's the culprit who betrayed Manda and Murdan on the road from Lakehead, I am sure of it!"

"He'll know where the Overhall folks and Brevory are held, then," Clem snarled. "Let's take him!"

Said Tom, "Wait until he's alone again."

The Gantrell riders and the traitorous accountant spoke briefly, then parted, going their opposite ways.

"Now!" cried Tom.

The Dragon made a great bound over the firs and landed in the road in front of Plume's startled horse.

"Hold just a minute, Master Comptroller!" yelled the Librarian. "We'd like a word with you!"

Plume tried to rein his mount about to flee, but the horse slipped on the icy surface and fell heavily, screaming with fright and throwing the miserable accountant neatly into a snowdrift.

Tom and Clem leaped from the Dragon's head and fell on Plume as he struggled to rise.

"He made me do it! Gantrell made me do it! He threatened me with prison and torture," wailed Plume, letting his body go limp. "Spare me, dear friends! Don't hurt me. I'm but a pawn in Gantrell's game, please believe me. I dared not say him no."

It took them several minutes to calm the hysterical sneak enough to answer their questions, but when he realized at last that they didn't intend to kill him on the spot, he rattled off his whole sordid tale of deceit and treachery.

"Peter of Gantrell offered you a large sum of silver to report on the doings at Overhall?" Tom recapitulated when the man had finished and fell silent, weeping.

"Yes, yes, noble Librarian!" sobbed the comptroller. "All I was *supposed* to do was write him a letter every week or so and tell him what was done and said at Murdan's hearth."

"So last spring," guessed Retruance, "you told him I was away, Murdan was off to Spring Session, and Princess

Manda was at Overhall, having run away from Granger of Morningside. And you opened the postern to let the Mercenary Knights in."

"I had no choice! No choice at all! It was worth my life to refuse!"

"No doubt of that," said Tom to Clem.

"He could have gone to Murdan and confessed," said Clem sternly. "I don't think the Historian would have had him burned for it."

"And," Retruance went on, "when it came time for Fall Session, Gantrell *forced* you unwillingly to lead his men-at-arms to the North Shore Road to lie in ambush for Murdan and the princess? I imagine Gantrell bought the snowstorm from some magician or other?"

"Yes, wise and wonderful Dragon! He did. There was no chance to it, that snow!"

"Nor this one, either," muttered Clem. "When one begins to mess with climate, there's no telling what'll follow. This snow is even more unusual than the first, for who would expect two such storms in a little over a week at this time of year? It's going to lay down a yard or two before dark, if I know anything at all about weather."

"You have yet to tell us where the Overhall people are being held," Retruance growled menacingly to Plume.

"But Lord Murdan and the Princess Royal are not with them!" cried Plume. "They were taken elsewhere. I don't really know where, believe me."

"We're more interested in someone else," said Tom.

"B-B-Brevory?"

"That you've guessed so quickly shows you are not as ignorant of Gantrell's plans as you pretend," the Dragon charged angrily, snorting a short, hot flame at the groveling villain.

"Oh, mercy, mercy! Lord Dragon! The soldiers and Brevory and the Overhall household are held by the Mercenary Knights in Plaingirt! I swear it! It's but a half day's ride of here. I've just come from there."

Tom was surprised. "Gantrell holds Freddie prisoner?"

"Truly, Lord Librarian! He is held in a cell at Lord Peter's bidding. He weeps and curses all day and half the night."

"He may have good reason," said Clem thoughtfully.

"Who were the three you met on this road a while back?"

The comptroller gulped, "They were sent by Lord Peter to . . . to . . . slay Brevory, they told me. Those three are Gantrell's hired killers! Sirs, may I go before night catches me on this lonely road? I could be of assistance to you, perhaps. I could spy on Gantrell for you, couldn't I?"

"Now doubly a traitor! We should leave you here to freeze, rather," growled Clem. "I recommend it, Tom."

Tom considered what to do while the weak little man howled pitifully, pleading for his life.

"Let him go. Here, Plume, I am going to give you a note to Murdan, telling him you have told us all you know. Take it to the Historian in Lexor and throw yourself on his mercy. We'll leave it to him to decide the fate of a back-stabbing servant!"

"Won't he just go running to Gantrell, though?" wondered Retruance. "Or run away altogether?"

"I doubt it. With Murdan he has a good chance of staying alive. With Peter of Gantrell, Plume is dead meat, even if he tries to run or hide. Gantrell will find him. He knows too much!"

The Dragon caught the accountant's horse. Clem and Tom hoisted the half-fainting Plume into the saddle and tied his feet to the stirrups so he couldn't fall off.

"Get going!" Tom ordered. Clem slapped the horse sharply on the rump. The poor mare shot off down the highway as fast as she could go.

"He'll not make it in this weather," said Clem, with some satisfaction.

"He may have sense enough to stop at a farmhouse or an inn between here and there," Retruance responded.

"This snow is a blessing, at any rate," said Tom. The men remounted the Dragon and hung on while Retruance launched himself into the blizzard.

"Why a blessing?" called the Dragon, steaming north once more.

"We'll reach Plaingirt long before those assassins do," Tom explained. "Take Freddie the Sponge away from the Mercenary Knights, take care of the Overhall bunch, and be back in Lexor in time for the trial."

Retruance devoted all his energy to beating across the wind, and his attention to following the faint trace of highway. In the snow they caught no sight of the three killers, but wasted no time looking for them.

A lone woodcutter on the ragged edge of the forest welcomed them to his hut, although apprehensive about the Dragon, as one might expect. He said the fortified village of Plaingirt was only two miles farther on.

"You can't miss it, even in this mess," he claimed. " 'Tis on the highest hill in front of the Snows and has a wooden tower in the center you can see for miles and miles—even from here, on a clear day."

Even so, the Dragon flew around the area for half an hour before spotting the tower and the palisaded village.

"Direct approach is the best," Tom decided. "Clem and I will go straight through the front gate and demand Basilicae's prisoners. Retruance, circle overhead, just in case he tries something funny."

"Give me a shout," snorted the Dragon, "and I'll knock that rickety tower down about their ears with one swipe!"

MERCENARIES don't stay alive and healthy by acting like fools, especially when it comes to recognizing superior force like a fire-breathing, full-grown Dragon swooping back and forth over their rooftops. Basilicae quickly agreed to cooperate, although his troop outnumbered his enemies, twenty to one.

"Now, as soon as the sun rises, you will escort the Overhallers to Lexor" Tom ordered. "In the meanwhile, you will treat them like long-lost cousins, understand? See them safe at Lexor before you leave them."

"Agreed," replied the Mercenary Knights' captain with alacrity. Retruance dived straight for the tower, swerving just in time to miss it by a hair. The whole structure trembled in the wind of his passing and the lookouts caught on top cried out in fear.

"We'll take your other prisoner with us, bound securely," Clem told the knight.

"No loss there! A damned pain in the posterior," said one of Basilicae's lieutenants.

"One thing else," added Tom. "Tomorrow three Gantrell killers will come straggling in. They've orders to murder Brevory in his cell. Whatever you want to do with them is your business, just keep them from returning to Gantrell."

Basilicae shook his head in doubt.

"Murder is not our style, I swear. But Gantrell is techni-
cally our employer," he argued. "If we hinder his minions,
he has grounds for abrogation."

"That's your problem, Sir Basilicae," said Tom shortly.
"As far as King, Historian, Princess, the Dragon, and I are
concerned, your contract with Peter of Gantrell is already
void anyway."

"I think," said Basilicae, "that it's time to move on to a
milder climate."

"We can use three new recruits," murmured his second-
in-command. "A bit of Knights' discipline should whip
them into shape. They might even find they prefer us to
Gantrell."

"Whatever you wish," sighed Tom. "If you were to ask
me, which you didn't, I'd say vacating Carolna would be
good business policy for your company. Gantrell will no
longer be able to afford a private army. No other noble will
want you."

"You're right on all counts," Basilicae agreed. "Lieuten-
ant, get the drunkard and a length of good hemp rope to
lash him to the Dragon's back."

AFTER the snow had fallen to great depth all of Friday—
Session Ball had been postponed—and all of Saturday,
the weather turned arctic cold and high winds rose, drifting
the snow against walls and between buildings to fifteen
and twenty feet deep, forcing many Lexorans to use their
second-story windows to leave their houses.

By Sunday morning the city was buried. Everyone stayed
snugly indoors, played parlor games, read to each other,
or slept, and therefore didn't see when the hostages from
Plaingirt were dropped at the northeast gate by their escort.
They were sent at once to Murdan's town house behind
Manda Palace.

Dr. Arcolas, Murdan's private magician and physician,
the senior member of the captive Overhall party, came to
report after he'd had a chance to eat and thaw out from
the trek.

"I confirmed early on that this second storm was actually
but the second half of the first, master. Peter of Gantrell
outsmarted himself, I should say."

"It's a good thing you're a passable physician, Arcolas," Murdan grumbled. "As a magician you stink! You should have warned me before we left home!"

"Oh, sir!" The physician assumed a hurt expression. "The snow was the product of strong, very strong, magic. It took me days to discern that it was magical, as it is."

Murdan grudgingly apologized for his sharp words. Magic was neither a certain science nor an easy art. The Historian was restless and anxious, awaiting the resumption of Session, now set for Tuesday. The Session Ball had been moved to Monday night.

Tom and Clem had come early Saturday to place their prisoner in a dry but rather chill dungeon under Manda Palace, his guards sworn to secrecy. Fredrick of Brevory was told of the three assassins sent to silence him. He'd been, ever since, uncharacteristically quiet and sober.

"It's very hard to imagine even Uncle Peter ordering anyone's murder," sighed the princess. "I know he's often wicked and sometimes very cruel . . . but this is plain evil!"

"Take our word on it," Clem insisted. "He intended to wipe all trace of Freddie the Sponge from the world! Those men are professional killers. They'd killed before, for Gantrell's pay and for robbery on their own."

"We're still rather naive," said Tom, taking Manda's hand. They'd hardly been apart since he'd returned. "I'm afraid we've both got to learn to be tougher at times, sweetheart. Speaking of which—sweethearts, that is—how are the twins and the queen?"

"Oh, absolutely splendid!" cried Manda, jumping to her feet. "Come on, let's go see them. My stepmother has been asking for you ever since I arrived alone."

All that remained, Tom said to Clem, was to survive the ball on Monday night, which at least gave them something to do while they waited for Tuesday.

"I don't see why I have to go to the ball," wailed the fur trapper of Broken Land. "I'm a nobody! I never learned manners. Why, I can't even dance!"

"You'll learn," Mornie insisted gleefully. "If you want me to share your life from now on, sir, you must put up with mine at times."

"Wait 'til I get you out to my forest cabin!" Clem threatened. "We'll see how quickly you learn new ways!"

"I've seen you glide like a jungle cat through the very densest woods without making a single sound," his lady scolded good-naturedly. "You can certainly do a few simple dance steps with me as partner."

"The thought of you as partner makes it all possible," moaned her trapper. "Very well! We shall do it until I get it right—or drop!"

The tailor and seamstresses of Overhall were busy with Tom's final fittings. On Monday evening he found himself decked out in emerald green velveteen knee britches, a shimmering silk coat of bright canary yellow and emerald buttons, black slippers of supple kid, snow white hose, and heavily starched shirt that ended everywhere he looked in froths of lace. Even he had to admit that he looked splendid, however.

"You are without a doubt the most handsome man in Carolna," cried Manda when he came to escort her to the ball.

The weather had suddenly turned warm Sunday afternoon. The streets of the city became rivers rushing down to the harbor. Dr. Arcolas predicted that the water would all be drained by Monday's sunset. They rode in carriages the short distance to Session Hall, no longer a solemn meeting place but magically transformed into a ballroom by ten thousand beeswax candles in glittering crystal reflectors, a fifty-piece string orchestra, graceful autumn-toned swags and draperies, and tables laden with the tastiest, fanciest creations of twenty chefs.

"Don't eat the lemon meringues!" hissed Arcolas to Tom and Manda when they danced by. "A Gantrell chef made 'em."

"Too late!" Tom laughed. "I already had two. They are superb!"

To no ill effect, it turned out. Peter's cook's lemon meringues were the crown jewels of the dessert table, but Gantrell himself appeared only long enough to show cold courtesy to the king, queen, and delegates, and then disappeared, a fact commented upon at every hand all evening.

SOMEHOW the Historian's party managed to get a few hours of sleep between the last quadrille and the opening of Session on Tuesday morning. More than a few delegates struggled to hide yawns and winces from aching heads.

Tom and Clem took places beside Ffallmar and Rosemary to one side of the dais. Gantrell and a party of wealthy followers entered in a body and took their places near the front of the hall, looking neither to left nor right, frowning from more than just too much drinking, dining, and dancing.

"He's making a bad show of this," said Clem, with some glee. "You'd think he'd at least pretend to be glad things are coming to a head, for appearance sake."

"Peter is not nearly as sophisticated as he'd like us to believe," commented Ffallmar with a chuckle. "He's the kind who has to be in control—and here, the King is very much in charge."

"Murdan swears Peter had no idea we'd returned, or what we'd done," said Tom. "Thanks to his messing with the weather, communications are not too good . . . unless you have a Dragon to fly you around."

"Where is Retruance Constable?" wondered Rosemary, looking about with curiosity.

"He said he'd be here," Tom told her.

King Eduard and Queen Beatrix arrived at the main entrance and walked slowly down the long aisle to the dais, nodding pleasantly and speaking to delegates as they came, smiling broadly at the applause that erupted, once again, at their appearance.

Eduard seated his queen in her gold chair and picked up the Wand of Justice before he addressed the assembly.

"Good morning! We hope you enjoyed the ball last night. This Session is called to order and I believe the proceedings today will make you forget your aching heads and sleepy eyes."

He allowed the murmurs and groans to die down before going on, a natural master of ceremonies, calm and pleasant yet serious under it all.

"A Court of Royal Justice is now convened to hear the indictment of one Fredrick of Brevory, a liege man of Lord Peter of Gantrell. We call upon the Royal Historian, Murdan of Overhall, to lay his charges before the court."

The Historian stood and walked to the open space between the throne and the audience, looking grave and angry. Without preamble he launched into a vivid description of the events of early summertime, beginning with his return from Spring Session and ending with a description of the pursuit and capture of the kidnappers by his Librarian and the Princess Royal Alix Amanda, accompanied by stout friends and the Dragon Retruance Constable.

"In Wall, a city on your far northwest, beyond Broken Land, Majesty, the rescue party found my daughter and her three youngsters prisoners aboard a ship.

"The ship bore a blazon known on both coasts as the Standing Bear, the blazon of the Gantrell fleet."

Now the crowd roared in surprise, shouting to each other and to Murdan. The king rapped the wand sharply on the dais floor.

"The Librarian and the Broken Land trapper went aboard the flagship of Gantrell's Quietness Ocean flotilla and found my daughter and her children in a cabin, under guard. They rescued the captives and managed to capture, in turn, the Gantrell henchman who had carried them all the way from Summer Pass!"

Peter of Gantrell jumped to his feet, his face purple with rage.

"Base lies! There were no Gantrell ships at Wall at that time. I know nothing of a kidnapping."

"I don't believe," said Eduard, softly, "that anyone has . . . yet . . . accused you of anything, Lord Peter. At any rate, you'll get your chance to reply and explain, shortly."

He turned back to the Historian.

"Go on, Lord Murdan. Who was the kidnapper?"

Murdan identified the culprit by name and Achievement. The delegates insisted on cheering the outcome of the adventure, waving and nodding to Tom and Clem. Manda, from her seat on the dais, smiled dazzlingly, and Lady Rosemary lay her hand on Tom's shoulder, so no one would mistake who had been her rescuer.

"This ends my indictment," said Murdan in a loud voice. "I am at the court's pleasure."

"The court will hear your witnesses, and then hear any rebuttal anyone cares to present," decided the king. "Bring before us the Lady Rosemary of Ffallmar!"

Murdan seated himself and watched proudly as Rosemary left her seat to come to the dais. She was in high color but fully in control of herself. Manda nodded to her in encouragement, and the queen echoed the smile and the nod.

"Lady Rosemary of Ffallmar?" the King asked.

"Yes, Your Majesty. I am she."

"Do you, Rosemary of Ffallmar, swear what you are about to testify to is the truth, and all the truth?" a clerk intoned.

"I do, sire!" said Rosemary, nodding her head emphatically.

"Tell the court, lady, in your own words, what happened last spring," said Eduard. "Get the lady a chair, please. She need not stand to testify."

Rosemary sat down and began.

"I was visiting Overhall, where I had grown up and had many friends, because I had received a message from my father through his trusted comptroller, saying that he wanted me to be there when he returned from Lexor. I took my three small children with me as a holiday."

The Historian's daughter told her story in detail, adding observations that Murdan himself had not mentioned. When she finished, Eduard leaned far forward and smiled kindly at her.

"You are able to confirm that the man known as Fredrick of Brevory was the chief kidnapper? There was no other in charge of the misdeed?"

"Oh, yes, Freddie was in charge. None of the seamen liked or trusted him, but they were obliged to obey him because he had some sort of commission from someone to whom the officers of the ships owed obedience."

"Can you say who that someone was?" asked the king.

"No, I never heard them say nor saw his commission. I assumed, however, that it was Peter of Gantrell. . . ."

"I object most strongly!" cried Peter, jumping to his feet again.

"I assure you, Lord Peter, that I won't overlook the hearsay nature of this part of the lady's testimony," the king said, giving Gantrell a sharp look.

"Lord King!" cried Gantrell, struggling to regain his composure, "I merely object to hearing my name bandied about like this. I know nothing of this lady's capture or treatment. And Fredrick of Brevory, for whom I would normally have furnished legal assistance and support, has not seen fit to be present. His guilt or innocence is not my concern! But my name is!"

"You will have time to rebut, if you please," repeated the king. "Now we must continue hearing the testimony, in order to know what to look for in any testimony that may be offered by Brevory or his representatives. Do you understand, Lord Peter?"

"Perfectly, Your Majesty!" choked Peter, and he sat down, looking rather smug and sure of himself now.

The court called Clem and Tom to testify. Both confirmed the story and answered a few questions about the chase and the rescue. The audience hung on their every word.

"Had you previously ever met or had pointed out to you the man known to you as Fredrick of Brevory?" the king asked Clem.

"No, I never met him or saw him or heard of him before we captured him in Wall, Lord King!"

"So how did you learn who he was?"

"When we captured him he called himself by that name, as well as did those around him who had served him."

"But you have no way of knowing if he actually was Fredrick of Brevory, except that he claimed that was his name?"

"I had no reason to doubt it, Lord King," Clem pointed out. "But no, I cannot swear that he was actually the man he said he was."

"Ha!" snorted Gantrell loud enough for all to hear.

When it was Tom's turn, the king asked much the same questions, including those about the kidnapper's identity. Tom had to admit that he just assumed the culprit had told the truth about his identity.

"For the record, Master Librarian, is it true that you are a human?"

Tom was surprised. The king and he had discussed his humanity at length and he knew it was common knowledge in the court and the city.

"I am a human, born of the world called Earth," he answered slowly. "I am not at all sure what that means here in Carolna. I find very few differences between most natives of this world and natives of my own home world."

"I know no reason myself why a human should be considered more or less than the rest of us," said the king. "I have looked at the laws handed down through fifty-four previous reigns and nowhere does it appear that a human, living in Carolna, gainfully employed, of good reputation and good behavior, should not be considered our subject and a citizen of this kingdom. You have accepted the professional contract from our Historian, Murdan of Overhall, to be his personal Librarian, I understand."

"Yes, Majesty," said Tom.

"And I challenge anyone to say you have not served Murdan well," the king said with satisfaction. "Thank you, Master Librarian. You may sit down."

For a long minute Eduard paused with his hand to his chin, thinking. Whispers and murmurs spread throughout the courtroom.

"This case pivots on the identity of one Fredrick of Brevory, the accused. We will attempt to establish the fact of his identity, first, and mayhap in doing so, clear up the question of his liege lord's responsibility in the matter."

He nodded in a friendly fashion, it seemed, at Gantrell, then said simply: "Bring in the accused!"

The side door swung wide. A very sober, shaken, and frightened Fredrick of Brevory entered and bowed deeply to the king. The whole assembly gasped. Not least in this were many influential men seated about Gantrell.

"You are Fredrick of Brevory, whose Achievement lies just fifteen miles west of here?" asked Eduard when order had been restored.

"Yes, sire, Majesty, I am he!"

"Is there anyone present who gainsays this man's identity?" the king asked. No one spoke. Brevory was well known.

"The court inquires if any disinterested party present can positively confirm this man's claim to be Brevory," said the king, looking out over the assemblage.

Several men raised their hands at once. The king pointed at one.

"You, Fillip Widemead. I believe you to be a man of integrity and honesty. Do you confirm this man's identity?"

"Aye, Your Majesty!" said the man singled out. "I've known Brevory for all his young life. His Achievement is athwart mine. He hunted and schooled with my sons. His mother is a distant cousin of mine. I confirm that he is who he says he is."

"Very good, then, Sir Fillip. Anyone else?"

Several other men present echoed Sir Fillip's words.

Eduard asked, letting his eyes fall upon the glowering countenance of Peter of Gantrell. "You, Lord Peter?"

"He is Fredrick of Brevory, but . . ."

"Lord Peter! I have a question or two for the accused, and then we will hear what you have to say in the matter."

Brevory had stood at attention all this time, with no expression on his face at all. The king gestured to him now.

"Fredrick of Brevory! You have sworn liege to Lord Peter of Gantrell?"

The accused was seen to take a deep breath and let it out slowly.

"I was, Lord King. I am no longer! The bond between us has been severed."

Uproar in the hall. The king allowed it to run its course before continuing.

"Fredrick of Brevory! A bond of loyalty to one's liege lord is not easily broken. Why do you say you no longer owe Gantrell your service?"

"He sent three assassins to kill me, to prevent me from appearing at this trial," said Freddie. "Such an attack severs any bond of fealty ever entered into."

This time the hall was stunned to silence.

"So it does," agreed Eduard Ten with finality. "Will you now tell us your part in the kidnapping of Lady Rosemary of Ffallmar, and especially under whose orders you acted. These events took place while you were still in Lord Peter's service, I take it?"

"Yes, Majesty, they did. I was ordered to waylay Lady Rosemary and her children in Summer Pass and carry them to Wall, where I was to take them aboard the flagship of the Gantrell fleet. I was ordered to do this by the Lord of Gantrell, personally, by word of mouth!" claimed Freddie, pointing at Peter . . . or at where Peter should have been.

"He's gone!" cried Manda.

"By magic!" said Beatrix. "For he was there but a short moment ago!"

✦ 28 ✦
Achievement Awards

"BUT where *is* Peter?" Queen Beatrix asked worriedly.

They were sitting in the queen's music room. The snow was all but gone and the weather cool and crisp. The lindens along the waterfront were antique gold against a background of riffled blue water.

"Are you sure he's left Carolna?" asked the queen.

"Not yet. These things take time, ma'am," said the Historian.

"I'll not rest easy until we know where he is and what he's up to," murmured Beatrix, resuming her needlepoint work. "No, my dear princess, you've dropped a stitch, there."

"How do you see it so well?" cried Manda in exasperation. "You're ten feet away and can see a dropped stitch, and I'm right here and miss it!"

Session had ended with great ceremony and pomp. The king's last act had been to declare perpetual banishment against Peter of Gantrell and the sequestration of his properties, to be held by the crown until his enormous debts had been paid and his legal heir determined.

Tom and Clem left these deliberations to others and were watching Graham drill his men-at-arms in the courtyard of the Historian's town house when a Dragon dropped like a stone from the sky.

"Furbetrance!" Tom shouted. "Old friend! Welcome!"

"Warmest greetings!" cried Retruance's brother, waving a claw at Graham and the soldiers. "Hetabelle and our five kits are an hour behind me. I came ahead to make sure there's room for all these Dragon bodies in Lexor."

"There's always room for more Dragons in Murdan's house," said Tom. "Check with Mistress Grumble. That's her department."

"And my brother? Where is he?"

"Murdan had him watching outside during the trial of Freddie of Brevory," Clem told him. "When Peter whisked himself away by a magic spell of some sort, Retruance followed him. We haven't seen or heard from him for some days."

"The trial is over and Gantrell flown! I need some catching up, friends."

"Let's send for Murdan," suggested Tom, "and sit here in the sun and tell our tales."

And they did.

"I was tiring of stitchery and wedding talk, anyway," said the Historian, arriving somewhat out of breath but beaming to see the younger Constable. "You're just in time to see the procession and awards," he added to Furbetrance. "I hope Retruance will return in time. The parade's at high noon tomorrow."

"What can *we* do? For of course, Hetabelle and the kits will want to help."

"Walk just behind my carriage, one by one, and blow some fire and colored smoke. It'll make a brave show."

"I've got a better idea," suggested Tom. "All the Dragons can fly in formation over the parade. That'll be a splendid sight, especially if they show some fireworks at the same time."

"Marvelous!" exclaimed Murdan, who loved parades and fireworks as much as anyone. "Can you do that, Furbetrance?"

"Not until you bring me up to date on current events," bargained the Dragon.

They sat side by side in the autumn afternoon sun with their backs against a warm brick wall and told the younger Constable everything that had happened since he'd left them at Clem's cabin.

THE Grand Parade had evolved from a simple procession to a grand spectacle, traveling from Manda Palace to Session Hall, officially to close the Session. This one went off wonderfully well by everyone's standards.

Noble houses, wealthy knights, and merchants competed to put the most splendidly accoutred marchers in the line. Craft guilds poured a great deal of time and money into twelve-horse floats bedecked with rich fabrics and semi-precious jewels that told stories from the kingdom's colorful past.

Ladies rode in ornate carriages, dressed in their most sumptuously elaborate gowns—fortunately the weather was cool and clear for them—and children walked the route in vast troops, singing and dancing, clad in brightly colored, homemade costumes.

Everyone agreed that the most spectacular display of all was the flying Constable family.

Retruance, Furbetrance, Hetabelle, and her five lively youngsters—one boy and four girls—began the air show with a flashing flyover, roaring down the length of Grand Avenue at rooftop level at tremendous speed. Spectators craned their necks, and cried aloud in surprise and awe until they recognized the great scaled fliers, then they cheered lustily, for Dragons were very popular now.

When the Dragons returned over the parade route, Retruance led them in a series of breathtaking rolls, dives, inside and outside loops, and upside-down flying patterns in perfect order, releasing great streams of red, yellow, pink, black, and green smoke. The parade came to a halt to watch, and only resumed, amid wild applause, when Retruance led his brother and his family to a perch on the roof of Session Hall to watch the rest of the parade themselves.

THE king addressed the assemblage with the great doors flung wide and the windows all open, so that everyone could hear and see. He was interrupted constantly by thunderous applause from delegates within and spectators without.

He said: "Friends, countrymen, thralls, thanes, and clergy, even Dragons! [Applause.] Despite some very serious problems, this Fall Session has been brought to a successful conclusion.

"The royal succession is settled and agreed upon by all [applause and cheering] . . . I have every expectation of living and ruling yet for many years [wild applause] . . . but when I decide to abdicate, or if I should die [shouts of 'No! No!'] . . . Well, we're all mortal, and these things must be considered, you know! If I leave the Trusslo throne for any reason, the crown will pass to my son, Ednoll. Beyond him, should he die without issue, the crown passes to his half sister, Alix Amanda [cheers, especially from the ladies] and to any issue of her line. If Princess Manda's line fails, the throne and the crown go back to Princess Royal Amelia, Ednoll's twin.

"If, by mischance, Ednoll is still a minor when I depart this life ['No! No!' again, louder] . . . his regent will be his half sister Alix Amanda, assisted by our Royal Historian, Murdan of Overhall [upwelling of applause for Murdan, much admired after the events of the past weeks]. . . .

"The crown declares the question of a regency for Princess Royal Alix Amanda, who is still a minor by but a year, is a dead issue. Manda is her own woman."

Eduard and his queen then brought their twin infants into public view for the very first time. Barely four weeks old, the two slept peacefully in their double cradle despite the uproar of cheers and applause from all sides. If there were some who doubted the fitness of Beatrix to be queen, their doubts were forgotten. Beatrix glowed beautifully with pride and happiness at their acceptance of her babes—and herself.

"One last rite remains," resumed Eduard, holding up the Wand of Justice to still the crowd after the cradle had been carried off, "before we adjourn until spring.

"It is meet and right that the crown recognize, reward, and commend those who have rendered particularly valuable service to us, my family, and the people of Carolna."

The crowd fell silent, for the King's Medal awards were always kept very secret until the king announced them at this final sitting of Session, each fall.

"The honors list is even now being posted on the doors of Alix Amanda Palace," said the king, and sure enough, everyone could hear the distant sound of hammering. "It contains more than fifty names, from all walks of Carolnan life, all recognized for outstanding service.

"One young man on the list deserves special mention, in addition to his medal.

"For his bravery, intelligence, diligence, loyalty, and ready wit. For providing a model for young men everywhere. For his staunch, brave, and timely rescue of Lady Rosemary of Ffallmar, as well as his steady support of and

good counsel to our daughter, Princess Royal Alix Amanda,
I joyfully present the King's Medal and our special gratitude
to Librarian Thomas Whitehead of Iowa and Overhall!"

Tom was pushed forward to stand before the dais, blushing furiously. The applause went on and on, until the king
again raised the slender wand and the accolade at last
subsided.

"In addition, I'm pleased to announce that Thomas of
Iowa and Overhall has won the love of our daughter, Princess Manda. I now publish aloud their betrothal. In celebration of their marriage, I dub him . . . Knight of the Royal
Household!"

The acclaim seemed unending. Tom grinned, bowed, and
waved even though he felt a little foolish for doing so, until
he caught a glimpse of the very dignified Constable family
leaning over the edge of an open skylight in the roof above
the throne, cheering with the best of them.

"And," resumed Eduard, waving the wand back and forth,
"Sir Thomas, having no property other than his good strong
arm and ready mind, and having been chosen consort by a
princess of royal blood, we do hereby invest him with an
Achievement, to be his, and his heirs' and their heirs',
forever!"

This news stunned Tom, who had no idea that the king
planned to make such a gift. Manda left the dais and ran to
his side, hugging him and shedding tears of joy and smiles
of love.

Queen Beatrix came down and led Tom and Manda up
the steps to the throne, where the king embraced them both
and beamed happily as they accepted the continued cheering
and shrill whistles of the multitude.

"I DON'T deserve any of it," Tom protested when Session
had been officially closed. They had retired to Alix Amanda
Palace for tea and cake and friendly conversation where it
was warm and quiet.

"Nonsense!" cried Eduard, who had gratefully shed his
gold-braided, jeweled Robe of State, put aside the Wand of
Justice, and sent the massive crown of the Trussloes back
to the royal treasury. He'd slipped into a plain, comfortable
everyday coat. "You've earned our love and gratitude, as
well as Manda's."

"I've no hesitation about Manda," exclaimed the Librarian, "and I'm overwhelmed with pride to receive the King's Medal. The knighthood, too, is most welcome, although I've been treated like a belted knight ever since I arrived in Carolna."

"I take that as a compliment, then," laughed Murdan, "although I recall almost having you burned at the stake the day we first met."

"Uncle, no!" cried Manda in horror.

"Well, he was rather upset that day," Tom said in the Historian's defense.

"He was a Dragon Companion, already, too. There was no way I would have let Murdan burn him," said Retruance from the window through which he'd pushed his head.

"Well, I was just lucky," said Tom.

"It's much better to be good and lucky than just good," put in Queen Beatrix. "I'd like to add my personal thanks, Sir Thomas . . ."

"Just 'Tom,' between us, please, Your Highness," Tom cried.

"Tom in private, then," agreed the queen. "I was lonely and desperate and very much afraid for myself, my babies, and my husband, also, when you came to Sweetwater Tower. My husband and I were bound and strangling in stifling traditions and foolish restrictions. You set us free! You gave me fresh air, sunshine, and a sense of my true worth once again."

"Just some gardening and some tomatoes," said Tom, and they all laughed heartily at his words.

Tom bowed deeply to the king. "I just don't feel that I've earned an Achievement of my own by what I've done, or just because Manda and I are to marry."

Said Eduard, "Are you claiming you're not capable, or not willing, or not worthy? Why do you object to the gift?"

Manda, close beside Tom, looked at him wonderingly, trying to understand what he was saying.

"No, no! It's . . . I feel . . . well, they're called Achievements, you see. I've achieved so little! I just came along for the adventure and because I liked Murdan from the first, and Retruance. And, of course, Manda!"

The king laughed and the others joined in, except Manda, who took Tom's hands.

"Father, if my young man has a fault, it is overmodesty," she said, not taking her eyes from Tom's. "He forgets that he will have to support a Princess Royal, so he needs the income of a fruitful piece of land. His vote and voice will be needed in future Sessions, too, and for that he'll need an Achievement. Princesses Royal, my dear, do not come cheaply!"

"It's the future that makes me hand out Achievements," the king explained frankly. "I need to keep good men—and women—around me to ensure the future of the kingdom. If I need you, I must provide for you a place to call your home, where you'll be happy and content and at peace. History . . . well, Murdan can lecture us on that. Carolna, although a peaceful nation that minds its own business, has been at war with someone or other for at least two-thirds of its recorded history. Isn't that right, Historian?"

"Correct, Majesty, and the role of Historian is to make sure kings and their followers don't make the same mistakes over and over again."

"I see," said Tom. "I once read that if we don't learn from history, we are condemned to repeat it."

Somehow—Tom never understood quite how—a wedding date was set for the spring to come and at once Manda and Mornie—who would wed Clem of Broken Land—plunged into plans for a royal wedding. They were joined enthusiastically by Beatrix, Rosemary, and Manda's aunt, Lady Phyllis of Morningside, Granger Gantrell's pleasantly plump wife.

Granger, on Manda's recommendation, had been declared his brother's sole heir. The king thus gained a loyal ally—in fact, a large number of allies from among those who had once followed Peter of Gantrell.

"Some of 'em I wouldn't trust with a fishing pole," Eduard confided. "But Granger can keep those in line. Or at least, keep an eye on them for me."

Retruance was busy tracing the disappeared Peter of Gantrell. The Dragon finally managed to track down the wizard who had sold Gantrell the vanishing spell. The mage couldn't say where Peter might have gone.

The king cried in exasperation, "I must know where Gantrell is and what he is about. He's a danger to the tranquility of the realm!"

"We'll keep looking, sire," Retruance promised. "Tomorrow, Tom and Clem and I will fly to the Frontier. We'll make sure the Mercenary Knights have left Carolna as they promised, and give some attention to the garrisons of the border forts. They might get complacent now things are peaceful once more, Lord King!"

Eduard gave his permission readily, as much to give the bridegrooms something useful to do as for any real benefit. Tom said good-bye to Manda late one evening as they walked hand in hand along the seawall below Sweetwater Tower.

"You don't mind my running off like this?" Tom asked anxiously.

"Of course not! You have things to do, and so do I. Not that I won't miss you terribly, my Tom! But I'll console myself with the joy of seeing you again, when you get back. Be careful! I worry a lot."

"I worry about you stabbing yourself with a needle," Tom teased. "I've seen you sew."

"Well, sir! I'm determined to make certain interesting items of clothing all by myself. You and you alone shall judge my skill!"

"You could find a more severe critic," Tom admitted.

"No one else will do!" she giggled, and threw herself into his arms.

WINTER had already gripped the Frontier. The garrison troops were bundled in woolens and furs and their breath made clouds of white steam when they spoke. A major of the Royal Guards greeted the travelers and showed Tom and Clem to warm quarters. The Dragon had a comfortable shelter the size of an airplane hangar awaiting him, with four roaring fires to fend the frost.

"No one's come this way recently, unless you count the weasely little man with a pass signed by Murdan the Historian two weeks ago."

"Weasely little man?" Retruance said, his ears pricking up with interest. "I think I know him. Did he give a name?"

"No, he said his mission for Murdan prevented it. We sent him on with a warm coat, for he wasn't dressed well for our weather, even then."

"Plume, I bet!" cried Clem.

"Nobody else," agreed Tom. "He could forge Murdan's signature and his seal, certainly. Well, good riddance! Although I can't help but feel sorry for Mistress Plume."

He recalled the lady's convenient disappearances when he and Manda needed a moment alone in Middletower.

"If the man is capable of forging a powerful instrument for safe passage," Retruance wondered aloud, "why would he come this way? He could have gone south and been warm as well as safe."

"What do you think?" asked Tom.

"I think he had a destination in mind. Or someone to meet."

"But," objected the major, "there's nothing beyond here save a few scattered Barbarians."

"Quite so," said Retruance. "I recall that Gantrell had contacts among the Rellings, the self-proclaimed lords of the Barbarians. I am considering a flight over their camp, just to check my suspicions."

"Oh no! You mean we missed the first *and* second biggest quarry of the year?" moaned the major, striking his forehead. "How will we explain that to the king!"

"Don't worry, Major. Gantrell used magic to transport himself across the borders. And this Plume is a rascal of the first water. No blame falls to you or your men. You may say I said so, in your report."

The officer thanked the Dragon profusely, but still looked worried and upset when he left them.

"Well, we'll have to keep our eyes on the Barbarians, too," said Clem. "Who appointed me guardian of the kingdom? I was better off as a plain old smelly fur trapper!"

"I have the king's charge to seek out Gantrell," Retruance pointed out. "When I need you and Tom, I will call for help. Agreed?"

"Anytime! Anytime at all!" said the woodsman with a grin.

Epilogue

"WHAT gossip?" called the Dragon into an ice cave in the side of a glacier, fifty miles northeast of the Frontier. From within came a bad-tempered growl and there shortly appeared a big bone-white head, hung with blue icicles and splashed with dirty clumps of snow that looked like some loathsome skin disease—or scale disease, in this case, for the inhabitant of the cave was a Dragon.

"You come calling almighty early!" snarled the Ice Dragon, puffing a cloud of frosted breath at his hot-bodied cousin. "It isn't even November yet, by the gods of sleet and icicles!"

"I was just passing this way, sort of reconnoitering for Eduard Ten," Retruance explained. "Not many people I know in these parts, so I took a chance on you being up."

"October, and he wants to be sociable!" grumped the ice beast. "Argh!"

"I'll leave, then," offered Retruance, and he turned to go. "Good winter, Hoarling!"

"Oh, damn!" swore Hoarling. "Wait. We'll talk awhile! I am a wintry type, as you know, and waken in a foul mood more often than not."

They repaired at the Ice Dragon's suggestion to a frozen inlet covered by foot-thick ice. Hoarling smashed a hole in the ice and fished for his breakfast while they chatted. He didn't offer Retruance any of his catch but gobbled them up as fast as he could snatch silvery cod from the water.

"You've not had time yet to check on your neighbors, then?" Retruance inquired politely.

"I keep an eye on them . . . as they do on me," grunted Hoarling. "We have no love for each other. If they weren't so hot, I'd have eaten them all centuries ago. Yes, I scouted

319

around a few days ago. They were making a hellish great racket for some reason."

"Well, then, did you hear of a Carolnan lordling in the igloos of the Relling? I know he's there, but not exactly where . . . or why."

"Oh, you mean this Gantrell the Exile? Yes, I heard of him from . . . private sources. He's sought sanctuary with the Rellings, I'm told."

"And have they granted it to him?"

"I gather. I also gather that they had a prior agreement, just in case Gantrell fled Carolna, as he did once before."

"What does he ask of the Grand Whatever, the Relling leader?"

"You mean the Grand Blizzardmaker, which is what he calls himself. Ha! Grand Windbag, I call him! These piddling little elflings have grandiose ideas of themselves, hey? How anyone can abide them is beyond me."

Retruance let the observation pass without comment. He watched the Ice Dragon claw-snag and devour six more large codfish in rapid succession before going on.

"The Rellings will suffer Lord Peter to stay among them, you say?"

"They say he's sold the Flatulent Flounder on creating a union with the other tribes. Hell, it's something they do once every seven years. Usually ends in great betrayals, name-callings, and carnages. Barbarians get along least well with other Barbarians, you should know."

"Hmmm," said the hot Dragon, deep in thought. "Tell me, Hoarling . . . what could I pay you to keep watch on Peter of Gantrell for us? He's a thorn in our sides, I must admit."

Hoarling popped two last twelve-pound cod into his rime-rimmed mouth and crunched them thoughtfully while he considered Retruance's offer.

"You think this Gantrell will try to mobilize the Barbarians against Carolna?"

"I certainly think he'd like to"

"Damn all your hot-pots! Barbarians are better left to their own nasty devices."

"I couldn't agree more."

"I'll keep an eye on your Gantrell and the Sacred Sardine for you, cousin, and get word to you if they get snotty.

In exchange, I'll ask a favor of you one day, Retruance Constable."

"A blind favor? You're not that scrupulous, Hoarling, that I would tie myself up with a knot like that."

"Gull droppings! It wouldn't be anything you couldn't in conscience do, my friend. Hey, I'm not a nasty sort. But I have enemies and I may someday need your fire and steam to help me out of a tight spot."

Retruance thought about it for several moments as the fishing hole in the sea inlet quickly refroze.

"Well, will you make a deal, Constable?"

"Yes, I will, but not to do anything that I think immoral or illegal or cruel, you know."

"Understood! Then I shall go back to bed for a couple more weeks, until the weather improves. Gantrell and Rellings won't do a thing but talk before spring, I guess."

The Dragons, fire and ice, touched front claws to seal the bargain, and by sunrise Retruance was sound asleep in the border outpost.